TO STEAL A HEART

K. C. BATEMAN

A thief. With a parasol. On a tightrope.

Even in *his* strange world, it was a first.

Nicolas Valette drew his evening cloak around him, crossed his arms, and smiled into the darkness. Mademoiselle Marianne Bonnard was proving to be everything he'd been promised, and more.

He watched in amusement as she opened the window across from his office, climbed over the balustrade, and settled the tips of her toes on the narrow stone ledge. She turned, extended her arms out to the side, and took a cautious step onto the wire that was suspended across the street. The lamp attached to the cable swayed. Shards of light bounced drunkenly over the cobbles below.

She'd chosen a perfect night for thieving. The Seine rippled a dull, gunmetal gray in the moonlight, and a concealing mist snaked low over the dirty water, blanketing the faint, fetid odor of refuse and rotten fish. Notre Dame lay behind her, Pont Royal to her left, though it was called Pont de L'égalité nowadays. Everything had a different name since the Revolution. Including the woman in front of him.

1

K. C. BATEMAN

Nic shook his head at the incongruous sight she presented, clutching that small black umbrella in one delicate hand—the same parasol she used for her performances at the Cirque Olympique.

She'd just reached the halfway point when a shout broke the silence. Nic held his breath, despite the fact that he'd seen her perform this trick countless times without falling. The parasol dipped but she kept her balance, as sinuous and graceful as a cat.

It was only two late-night revelers staggering home to their beds. They weaved along the street, far too drunk to notice the slim figure wavering above their heads.

Nic's nerve endings hummed with a delicious prickle of anticipation as she closed the gap between them. At the circus she wore a flamboyant pink-frilled corset that made her look like a silk-encased bonbon just waiting to be unwrapped. Tonight she wore black, tight-fitting garments that outlined the contours of her lithe body.

The only inconsistency was her footwear: dainty, pale pink ballet slippers tied at the ankles with silk ribbons. Hardly the usual hallmarks of a hardened criminal. But criminal she undoubtedly was. Nic tilted his head, intrigued by the contradiction she presented, and waited.

When she was within arm's reach of the window, he uncurled himself from the shadows, swung open the glass, and savored her gasp of dismay.

"Good evening, *chérie*." He leaned forward and offered her his hand, enjoying the expression of dawning horror on her piquant little face. "Or should I say good morning?"

CHAPTER 2

Merde!

Marianne's knees buckled, and the wire lurched in response. She seesawed her arms, managed to right herself, and stared at the apparition in front of her with undisguised horror.

Nicolas Valette.

Her quarry. Her target. Her very worst nightmare.

He wasn't supposed to be here.

His reputation among the criminal underworld was legendary, his name breathed in hushed whispers by those who assiduously tried to avoid his notice. One of Fouché's most trusted agents, he was rumored to be as powerful and as omnipotent as his master. And as dangerous when crossed.

Her breath came hard and fast, shallow pants of fright in the chill night air. *Dieu!* He'd send her to prison, or worse, and there'd be no one to take care of Sophie. How could she have been so stupid?

She couldn't turn on the wire without falling. She glanced down at the cobbles twenty feet below. Too high to jump. She'd break her neck. Even if she survived, she couldn't risk an injury.

3

She had her parasol, but with her luck, if she tried to hit him, she'd probably just fall and dash her brains out on the street. The only choice was that outstretched hand.

She didn't want to touch it. It was a beautiful hand—strong and elegant. But it was the hand of the enemy.

Marianne raised her eyes. He was in evening dress: an immaculate black jacket that molded to his broad chest and shoulders like a second skin. He probably needed three valets just to get him into it. Expensive white lace glowed at his throat and wrists, and his midnight-black hair was slicked back to reveal a wicked, clever face with arched black brows and a thin, straight nose. A faint, mocking smile curled the corners of his mouth.

She edged backward.

Valette folded his arms and leaned one shoulder negligently against the window frame. "I can wait here all night. Can you?"

His voice was low and intimate. It brushed against her nerve endings like a silk scarf dragging across her skin. Speech was impossible. Her tongue was stuck to the roof of her mouth. She concentrated on balancing instead.

He tilted his head to one side and studied her. "So, what's one of Duval's little lackeys doing sneaking into my lair?"

That stung. She was nobody's lackey. Well, she was, but she didn't need reminding.

"Did he send you here to steal?"

Marianne shook her head, though the movement made her teeter even more. He raised a brow. His eyes bored into hers, full of wood smoke and shadows, and she had the unnerving thought that he was reading her soul.

"Strangely enough, I believe you," he said finally. "So if you're not here to take anything, you must have been sent here to *leave* something." It was a statement, not a question. He extended his hand again and flicked his fingers imperiously. "Hand it over."

Marianne finally found her voice. "Hand what over?"

"Whatever you've been sent here to plant." He waited, infinitely patient, a spider at the center of his web.

Her face heated with guilt. She pressed her lips together.

Valette sighed at her stubbornness. "What's Duval up to? And why such extraordinary lengths to deliver it to me? Why not a simple foot messenger? Not that I don't appreciate your skills, mademoiselle . . . ?" He let the end of the sentence trail off invitingly.

It was her turn to raise her brows. "You're one of France's greatest spies, monsieur. I'm sure you already know my name."

A smile twitched the corner of his mouth. Marianne wished it wasn't so distracting. It was hard enough to stay upright as it was.

"You're right, of course, Mademoiselle Bonnard. I know far more than just your name."

A chill ran down her back. The wire gave a corresponding wobble, and she had to take a few steps toward the window to avoid falling. Valette's hand was still there. Beckoning. Tempting.

"Come on. Take it. I won't hurt you."

What a lie. Of course he would hurt her. She knew men like him. He'd be as bad as Duval, in his own way. Oh, he might not be so heavy-handed; no doubt he used subtler methods to extract the information he wanted from people. But he would hurt her, all the same. Still, what other choice did she have?

With a sigh of defeat, she took his hand. A jolt rushed through her at the contact, like faint lightning. She gasped, but if he felt it, too, he made no sign. He just hauled her inelegantly over the stone parapet, through the open window, and into the shadowed room beyond.

* * *

IN THE CIRCUS ring she'd been bathed in dramatic candlelight. Here, faint slivers of moonlight crept through the shutters and caught her high cheekbones and startled eyes. She was even prettier close up, Nic realized with a start, despite glaring at him like she was putting a curse on him.

He couldn't resist the temptation. He gave her arm a deliberately hard tug. She fell against his chest with a satisfying little "oomph" and dropped her parasol. He used her momentary imbalance to search her, slipping his fingers under her shirt to brush the warm skin of her lower back. He found a knife in her waistband and tossed it aside, then snatched the sheaf of papers she'd hidden there, too.

She gave a gasp of outrage and tried to grab them, but he held them up, out of reach. He caught a tantalizing whiff of her perfume, the briefest imprint of her body against his, before she pushed herself away and stumbled backward as if burned.

He let her go, regretting the loss of contact. She'd probably slice his hand off if he tried to touch her again. He'd bet she had more than one knife hidden on that delectable body. The top of her head might barely reach his shoulder, but she could take care of herself. He had a file on her an inch thick in his desk to prove it. She was a neat, lethal, little package.

Satisfaction burned through him. Duval's package. And now his.

Keeping her would be like trying to tame a snake: exciting— and potentially deadly. But *hell,* he loved a challenge. Life had lost its luster a long time ago; the promise of danger was all that kept him going. That, and revenge.

CHAPTER 3

He'd taken her blade. With nothing more than sleight of hand and distraction.

Marianne's estimation of her adversary rose, even as she cursed herself for falling for such a basic trick. She felt naked without her knives.

He turned to light a lamp, and she glanced around for something else to use as a weapon. Nothing. He stood between her and the door. Perhaps she could rush past him.

"Don't bother," he said, not looking up. "It's locked."

A taper flared, blinding her, and a warm glow cocooned them as he turned up the flame.

Marianne studied her surroundings. His lair was neat, lavish but not ostentatious. A tortoiseshell-and-brass clock ticked loudly on the mantel. A set of cut-glass tumblers clustered round a bottle of brandy on a side table. Everything looked masculine, comfortable. The place even *smelled* expensive, like leather and tobacco and wood smoke.

A wave of fatigue rolled over her. Tonight's performance had been tiring; the walk above the street had exhausted her. She quelled an insane urge to run her fingers over the soft brown leather of the nearest chair and sink into its welcoming folds.

Concentrate! This was a place of danger, not comfort. It was *designed* to be disarming, to lull the unwary into spilling their secrets and confessing their crimes. She caught back a bitter laugh. They'd be here all night if she started confessing hers.

Valette leaned his hip against the edge of a huge desk. Its dark leather top was piled high with files and papers. Marianne wondered how many of them concerned her.

She crossed her arms across her body, hugging her elbows.

Valette shot her a cool glance. "You're playing a dangerous game, *chérie*. What if the city watch had caught you instead of me?"

She wasn't that lucky.

"The gendarmes are fools. When they study a crime, they look only at their feet. It would never occur to them to look up, at the stars."

"A philosopher as well as an acrobat and spy," he mocked gently. "You're a girl of many talents, Mademoiselle Bonnard."

Marianne flushed.

He unsealed the packet of papers he'd stolen from her breeches, scanned the contents, and glanced up, an amused glint in his eyes. "Do you know what this says?"

She shook her head. It was true. She hadn't wanted to know. Her job had been to plant it in his office and get out.

"Duval sent you to frame me. According to this, I'm a Royalist traitor."

Her stomach dropped, but she kept her face impassive. "That's not my problem. I don't know what's between you and Duval. I'm just the messenger."

"Are you? I wonder." His eyes took on a calculating gleam. She felt like an insect, caught beneath a magnifying glass. He tapped the papers lightly against his thigh, then tilted them toward the lamp and watched impassively as they curled and caught alight. The flames lent a satanic glow to his flawless features, and she shivered against the uncanny notion that she was bartering with Lucifer himself. The smell of charred paper caught her nose, and she suppressed an instinctive shudder. She hated that smell.

He blew it out before it burned his fingers and dropped the blackened remnants into an ashtray on the desk. "Such things are easily disposed of." He tilted his head and studied her. "If only the same could be said of *you*."

The threat hung heavy in the air between them. Her heart pumped uncomfortably. There were any number of ways he could dispose of her. She took a step backward.

"But I don't think this is about the papers at all." He shot her a speculative glance. "I think this is all about you."

Marianne snorted in astonishment. "What?"

"*You're* what Duval was sending to me. A message, of sorts." He pushed away from the desk, graceful as a panther. "Or a challenge."

She couldn't back up any more. She was hemmed in, her thighs pressed up against the window ledge. She tried to slow her breathing. "Stay back! I'm warning you . . ."

He stopped just in front of her. Too close. Marianne tensed, expecting a fight, but he simply reached out and stroked her cheek with his finger. She flinched, but heat flashed all the way to her toes.

"You're very pretty," he said pensively. He brushed the pad of his thumb over her bottom lip, rolling it down slightly. Her stomach lurched as if she'd missed her footing on the wire. She dragged a breath into suddenly tight lungs and gazed up at him in alarm.

"Perhaps Duval intended you as a diversion?" Cool fingers raised her chin, his hand so large he cupped her jaw from ear to ear. She suffered the touch as he turned her face to the moonlight and looked his fill. "You might almost be worth it."

She bit her lip, her pulse hammering in her throat. "You're wrong. I'm the messenger, not the message."

Again that half smile. "Poor little Marianne," he mocked. "You're in way over your head."

Hah. She'd known that for years. Only she couldn't get out, and Duval kept pushing her head under again and again. "Let me go," she croaked.

He shook his head. "I can't."

A shiver of foreboding skittered down her spine. "What do you mean?"

"I've seen you on your wire and with your knives." He paused for a moment to let that sink in.

He'd been watching her? When?

"Why would the secret police bother with an insignificant pawn like me? I'd have thought you'd have more important things to do, with the emperor back in Paris," she challenged.

His lips twitched. "You're too modest, *ma belle*. Rumor has it you're the best thief in Paris."

"You're confusing me with Armin Lafonte." Armin Lafonte had died two years ago. He still made a useful scapegoat. "And I prefer the term 'liberator' to 'thief.'"

His smile widened. "You have some very useful skills."

She shrugged. "So?"

"So, I have a mission that requires those skills."

Her recoil was instinctive. "No! I can't work for you."

"Why not? You work for Duval, and he's a snake. How much does he pay you? Whatever it is, I'll double it."

"I don't want your money."

He raised a dark brow. "Interesting. Duval is such a loathsome creature. I can't imagine there's anything about him to elicit such loyalty. He must have some hold over you." He tilted his head, his eyes intense. "Is it the lovely Sophie?"

Her blood turned to ice. *Merde.* He really *did* know about her.

He gave a triumphant smile. "That's it, isn't it? Your pretty sister."

She glanced away. "I don't know what you mean."

His long fingers turned her face back to his. He looked disappointed. "Don't feign stupidity, *chérie*. It doesn't suit you. He's obviously blackmailing you. What does he do? Threaten you? Threaten her? Tell me."

His voice was cool and compelling, soft like velvet. It made her want to spill every one of her secrets, to confide in the hypnotizing warmth of his eyes. It was deliberate, she was sure, part of his parcel of interrogator's tricks. He was an expert at getting people to reveal their souls. She had to remember that. She had too many secrets. And he was far too skilled.

She settled for a partial truth. "She's his hostage in all but name. If I don't steal for him, he'll make her work in one of his brothels. Please. She's only sixteen."

He dismissed her life's problems with a shrug. "Leave it with me. I'll deal with Duval. We'll leave in one week."

A flush of anger warmed her cheeks. Apparently, her acceptance was a foregone conclusion. "I told you, I won't do it."

The confidence in his smile was maddening. "Let's put it this way, then. If you cooperate, my men will protect your sister from Duval while you're away. If not, well . . ."

"That's blackmail! You're as bad as he is."

"Worse," he said agreeably. "But my agents are far better than his thugs. I employ only the best"—he shot her a challenging glance—"which is why I want *you*. I won't take no for an answer." His voice turned coaxing. "Come, it's just one job. Do it and you'll be free of Duval."

If only it were that simple.

He had no idea how tantalizing his offer was. Or perhaps he did. Perhaps offering his victims the one thing they wanted most was another of his wiles. She was a fool for even hoping. She'd never be free of Duval.

He took her silence as consent. "Now, are the stairs too conventional, or would you prefer to leave the way you came?" He opened the door and gestured for her to precede him into the hallway.

He hadn't used a key.

Marianne shot him an accusing scowl. "You said the door was locked!"

His expression was innocent, but his lips curled up at the edges. "Did I? How odd."

Marianne edged forward, fully expecting a trick. His long evening cloak brushed her shins as she darted past him, but he made no move to grab her. She bolted for the stairs. His footsteps echoed behind her, boot heels clicking steadily on the marble treads. Her feet, in their ballet slippers, were silent. She forced herself to slow down. He didn't need to see her fear.

She crossed a checkerboard-tiled hallway and skidded to a halt in front of the imposing front door, gazing in dismay at the complicated array of locks. She held her breath as he reached around her and unlocked them, painfully aware of his body just inches behind her own.

He caught her hand before she could run. When she turned, he bowed low, mockingly so, as if he were bowing to royalty, and kissed the back of her hand with an exaggerated flourish. Heat rushed up her arm. She snatched it away.

His mouth had that irritating half smile at the corners again. *At least one of them was finding the situation amusing.*

"Mademoiselle Bonnard, it's been a pleasure. I'd offer to escort you home, but I'm sure you're more than capable of making it back on your own. So I'll bid you good night. Or good morning, whichever you prefer. I'll see you in one week's time."

Marianne turned and ran. She was halfway across the Pont Neuf when she remembered he still had her knife. And her parasol.

CHAPTER 4

"*Y*our man in black's here again."

Marianne flinched. The blade whistled from her hand, and she watched in mute horror as it flipped over and over and embedded itself, shivering, into the painted wooden boards a whisker from Laurent Falconi's head.

"*Madre di Dio!* You nearly had my ear off!"

Laurent leaped forward with a scowl, clapping one hand to the side of his handsome face. "What the hell is wrong with you, Marianne? You've been distracted all week." He turned and frowned at the sequined dancer who'd interrupted their last-minute backstage rehearsal. "And you know better than to talk to her when she's aiming a bloody dagger at my head, Françoise!"

Marianne dropped her last three knives and rushed toward her employer. "I'm so sorry! I lost my concentration. It won't happen again, Laurent, I swear."

He gave her hair a brotherly ruffle. "*Eh bien.* No harm done. But I beg you, focus when we're out *there*." He nodded to the red brocade curtains that separated them from the audience. "The audience doesn't pay to see me bleed."

Marianne gave him a cheeky grin. "But just think of all the women who'd rush to your aid . . ."

Laurent harrumphed, but his smile widened. "It might even be worth it, monkey. But Papa won't be pleased if there's bloodshed in his beautiful ring."

"I suppose not." Marianne peered through the gap in the curtains. Fifteen tumblers were forming a human pyramid in the middle of the sawdust circle, a trick known as La Spaniola. She squinted past them to scan the audience in the raked seating beyond.

Light from the candles glinted off opera glasses and pince-nez. The most expensive boxes were high on the right, closest to the ring. Her stomach clenched. Françoise might not know the man in black by name, but she certainly did. She'd done a little digging of her own over the past few days.

Nicolas Valette was the protégé of not one, but two of Napoleon's greatest spymasters, Fouché and Savary. Unlike his masters, however, it seemed he never fell from grace. Savary was currently out of favor, so Fouché was once again in charge, and everyone was scrambling to see which way the cards would fall now that Napoleon was back in Paris after his dramatic escape from exile.

Her breath caught as she located Valette's dark figure. He'd attended the circus three times in as many days, stalking her—no other word for it—since their bizarre rooftop encounter a week ago.

He was wearing black again, as Françoise had said: another impeccably cut jacket with a top hat he'd removed and placed on the edge of the box. The white of his ruffled shirt glowed in stark contrast, and a jeweled pin winked in the folds of his cravat. Light from the huge central chandelier anointed him in a warm glow, like a dark, gilded prince.

Tonight he was sitting with the emperor's son-in-law, Eugène de Beauharnais, and several other dignitaries. He bent toward his female companion—a different woman than last night, although equally stunning—and murmured something in her ear. The woman giggled and flicked her fan as he trailed a casual white-gloved finger over her exposed décolletage.

A slow burn warmed Marianne's stomach. Her own breasts tingled. She was about to turn away in disgust when he raised his head, as if he sensed her gaze. There was no time to draw back. His eyes locked onto hers, even at such a distance, and he sent her a slow, wicked smile, as if he'd known she was watching all along.

She leaped back from the curtain. Nicolas Valette made her break out in a cold sweat. No doubt the ability to reduce people to a quivering mass of nerves with a single glance was another useful skill in his job as an interrogator.

She rubbed her bare arms and bent to collect her knives from the floor, cursing her shaking hands. She was on stage in five minutes. How on earth was she going to perform, knowing *he* was in the audience? Thank the Lord she'd already finished her tightrope act. At least she couldn't fall and break her neck. With the knives, she could only hope she wouldn't slice off Laurent's ears. Or any other body part. She took a deep breath and exhaled slowly, counting to ten, willing herself calm.

She couldn't resist a quick glance up at his box when she stepped into the ring, but his seat was conspicuously empty. Her stomach dropped. With relief, not disappointment. If he wasn't there to distract her, Laurent's ears should be safe.

The knife throwing was her last act. As soon as she could escape the thunderous applause without seeming ungrateful, she bowed out of the ring and pushed through the mass of performers waiting to take part in the finale.

The week Valette had promised her was up, but she wasn't hanging around to see if he was coming for her. Duval had summoned her. Marianne's stomach tightened at the prospect.

She'd rather walk naked through Montmartre than face Duval, but he was an evil she couldn't ignore.

The dressing room was deserted. Not bothering to change, she simply shrugged a hooded cloak over her pink corset and exchanged her ballet slippers for more practical lace-up boots. A shriek from the elaborate cage in the corner interrupted her: Pagnol, the capuchin monkey, wearing his usual outfit of red waistcoat and matching pillbox hat. He tinkled the brass bell suspended in the corner of his cage and sent her a beseeching look with his liquid brown eyes.

Marianne pushed a nut through the bars and he snatched it greedily, sitting back on his hind legs to nibble his prize.

"Say thank you!" she scolded, laughing.

The animal doffed his tiny red felt hat at her and sent her a sarcastic monkey grin.

Henri Falconi, Laurent's younger brother, caught her as she was slipping through the back door. He was still hobbling about on crutches from when he had fallen from the wire and broken his ankle three weeks ago.

"Aren't you staying for the finale?"

"I can't. Something's come up. Sorry."

"Need someone to go with you? You can't be too careful, these days. Pretty *citoyennes* aren't always safe walking alone at night." He shot a droll glance at the blades she'd tucked into her waistband. "Even ones with three knives in their coat."

She leaned up and pressed a kiss to his jaw, grateful for his brotherly concern. The Falconis had saved her life. She owed them so much. "Thanks, but I'll be fine."

He accepted her rebuff with a nod, his attention caught by one of the acrobats lighting a cheroot by the back door. His expression darkened. "René, put that out! You know there's no smoking back here." He gestured at the dressing room behind him. "Use your eyes. What do you see?"

René looked at him blankly. Henri gave him a slap around the ear. "You see sawdust, *imbécile*! You see a dressing room full of clothing. Straw for the animals. Crates of fireworks for the finale."

Still poor René looked confused.

Henri rolled his eyes. "The whole place is a tinderbox." He whipped the cheroot from René's slack lips, threw it down, and ground it out beneath his heel. "Remember what happened at Astley's? It burned to the ground. *Twice.*"

René ducked his head. "Sorry, boss. Won't happen again."

Henri caught Marianne's eye and gave her a despairing see-what-I-have-to-deal-with glance. She smothered a smile as she slipped into the street. Rene's cigar wasn't the only incendiary thing around the circus. Henri's temper had been on a short fuse, too, since his injury. She could only commiserate. She hated inactivity. Not being able to perform must be driving him to distraction.

She half expected Valette to be waiting for her at the stage door, but the street was empty and she set off at a brisk pace. The new gaslights extended only to Rue Lespinasse; after that, Marianne kept to the shadows, her blades, as always, clutched in her hands. The dangers lurking in the alleyways didn't scare her, though. That dubious honor was reserved for Jean-Jacques Duval.

CHAPTER 5

*M*arianne's stomach gave an anxious flip as she neared the Palais Royale.

It had once been the boyhood home of Louis XIV but, as always with the aristos, chronic lack of money had forced the Duc d'Orléans to convert it into a series of shops and cafés and open it up to the rabble. The old king had mocked his cousin's new career as a "shopkeeper," but the transformation had been a huge success. The old money of the ancién régime had been replaced by that of the nouveau riche, even more vulgar and ostentatious.

Some said it was a wicked place, proof that there was nothing in Paris but sin. True, the Camp of the Tartars by the east entrance was a notorious hangout for thieves and low-class tarts. But most people avoided that part.

For drinking, debauchery, gambling, and intrigue, the Palais Royale was *the* place to be. Tonight, as ever, the pavilions, shops, and cafés seethed with life, lit by flaming torches. Rogues and swindlers rubbed shoulders with priests and gentlemen, merchants and activists. Handsome hussars with their bristling mustaches and smart navy uniforms escorted ladies of dubious virtue from one amusement to the next. Street brats darted in and out of the crowd, their nimble fingers finding easy pickings.

Marianne made her way along one of the covered walkways, savoring the warmth of the evening. Posters stuck to the walls advertised the "miraculously preserved 200-year-old corpse of Zulima," and "Monsieur Belon's mechanical model of the solar system." She'd always wanted to see that, but there was no time to indulge her curiosity tonight.

The little shops along the colonnade sold everything. Bear grease for thinning hair, fans, ink, books, telescopes, opera glasses, stolen dogs, fold-up raincoats, lottery tickets. She didn't need such fripperies, but couldn't resist stopping for a moment to watch a shadow show at one of the booths. Tempests, ship-wrecks, even the mythical forges of Vulcan were magically conjured before her eyes.

If only they could spirit her away from Duval.

The scratchy sounds of a violin snaked through the open windows of the Société Philharmonique, and a knot of people gazed upward, spellbound by a galleon-shaped hot-air balloon hanging in the sky above. A few weeks ago it had been a life-size horse, ridden by a chevalier. Pushing past an organ grinder with a dancing monkey that reminded her of Pagnol, Marianne mounted the marble steps of the Théâtre Montausier.

The most expensive brothel in Paris was as elegant as any gentleman's club, and just as exclusive. In a city that prided itself on indulgence, the Montausier catered to every sin, pleasure, and vice one could possibly imagine. And many more besides.

Downstairs, patrons could watch live performances on the stage, anything from a biting satire to a comical musical review. In the side rooms, they could drink, gossip, try a game of hazard, or select a partner for the evening's sport.

Upstairs, the rooms were rented by the hour or the night, depending on the depth of the gentleman's pockets. Anyone with the right money could find a girl to suit his budget and proclivities.

When Duval had first brought her here, she'd been naively shocked to discover the place was a brothel. There was no red lantern above the door, as in Montmartre and Montparnasse. And she'd been surprised at how tasteful it was. A scandalous den of iniquity should have gilt cherubs and garish red wall hangings, surely? The huge beds in each room had conformed to her childish expectations, but the fine paintings on the walls and the exquisite furniture had been unexpected. A brief pain clenched her heart. Odd, but sometimes the place reminded her of home.

She and Sophie had stayed here in one of the back rooms next to Duval's "office" for several weeks, but when Marianne found work with the Falconis, she'd persuaded him to let them rent their own small apartment. Duval hadn't wanted to give them such freedom, but he'd seen the sense in keeping Sophie away from the gentlemen who frequented the club. The conviction that he'd agreed only because he was saving her sister for himself made Marianne's skin crawl.

The doorman, one of Duval's usual thugs, spared her a brief, disparaging glance and opened the door with a sarcastic flourish.

Idiot. Pagnol has more brains than he does.

A huge cut-glass chandelier glittered above the double staircase. Lavishly dressed ladies hovered and flirted in the foyer, drawing prospective partners into convenient alcoves to agree to terms. The low rumble of conversation from the gaming room was interspersed with the occasional chink of glasses and good-natured curses.

Marianne strode forward. She wasn't here for fun and games.

A woman appeared at the top of the stairs, her portly bulk and the alarming puce shade of her gown commanding immediate attention, and Marianne smiled as she recognized the theater's owner.

Sixty, plump, and always jovial, Madame de Montausier was rumored to be worth more than a million francs. Napoleon himself had courted her, but apparently Madame had decided they wouldn't suit. It was the emperor's loss; the woman was wasted as a brothel owner. She would have made an excellent general.

Madame clapped her hands in delight when she saw Marianne, and held out her plump beringed fingers in greeting as she descended the stairs.

"*Chérie!* I swear I haven't seen you in an age! Please tell me you're *finally* coming to work for me, instead of those foolish Italian acrobats?"

Marianne smiled but shook her head. "No, Madame. I'm sorry to disappoint you."

Madame chucked her fondly under the chin. "That face of yours is wasted at the circus. How can men see how pretty you are when you're dangling up there on a wire?"

"I don't *want* men to notice me."

The older woman sighed. "But I take such good care of my girls." She gave Marianne's cloak a dismissive flick and shuddered delicately. "*Must* you wear such hideous things? You're not a stable boy. When I think of how ravishing you'd look in a fine dress and jewels . . ." She studied Marianne with a connoisseur's eye. "With your face, and that husky little aristo's voice, I swear, you could make us both a fortune."

Marianne chuckled. "You already *have* a fortune, Madame."

"That's true. But one can always make more. And all this political turmoil is proving excellent for business." She gave a satisfied smile. "*The Journal* is saying that Britain, Russia, and Austria have all vowed to see the end of the emperor once and for all." She shook her head sagely. "No good will come of it, mark my words. But enough about politics. If you're not here for pleasure, it must be for business, hmm?"

Marianne grimaced. "Duval summoned me."

A frown creased the older woman's forehead. "Tonight? He's been in a foul mood all day."

"He said to come straight after my last performance."

"He's in the back room." Madame touched her arm. "I wish you'd let me help you, *ma chère*. Wouldn't you rather become one of my girls, instead of dancing to his tune?"

Marianne turned away from the sympathy in the older woman's eyes. "I can handle him. But thank you."

Duval was a loathsome slug, but dealing with him was the only way to protect her sister. If she had the courage, she'd kill the fat blackmailing bastard herself, but the idea of dispatching another human, even one as deserving as Duval, was too much. She'd already sunk low enough without adding murder to her litany of crimes.

Marianne's stomach churned as she ascended the rest of the stairs. Her parents would be turning in their graves if they knew what she'd become. Five years ago she'd been Mademoiselle Marianne Elizabeth de Beauvais, a useless, pampered aristo, just like the foolish king and queen who'd lost their heads. If not for the Falconis, she might have lost her own head, too. Madame la Guillotine had been silent for the past few years, but with first another incompetent Bourbon restored to the throne, and now Napoleon back in Paris, who knew what the future would bring?

She was *citoyenne* Marianne Bonnard now. Circus performer. Liar. Thief. At least now she could fend for herself.

She touched the knives at her back as she made her way along the hall; she'd never make the mistake of facing Duval unarmed again. That idiot on the door hadn't even thought of searching her. No surprise. People rarely suspected her until it was too late. By then she'd already disappeared into the night with their jewels, their papers, their secrets. Her innocent face was one of her greatest assets.

Skinny Marie, one of the Montausier's most popular courtesans, was dragging a client along the hallway by his cravat. Her jade-green gown disappeared into a bedroom, and the man followed, unresisting. The sounds of sex emanated from several of the other rooms Marianne passed. Giggles and shrieks, the squeaking of bedsprings. Moans of pleasure. Her heartbeat quickened. How much of it was real and how much feigned? She shuddered.

The last door led to Duval's "office." As a minister for the Department of Morals he had a plush government office in the Quai d'Orsay, but for his less-legal enterprises he used the Montausier.

His official role was regulating Paris's numerous brothels and collecting the revenue due to the state. Marianne shook her head at the irony. Corrupt, paranoid, and vindictive, Duval was the complete antithesis of an upstanding citizen. Her own work for him comprised gathering the leverage he needed to extort and blackmail his underworld contacts and fellow ministers so his numerous scams weren't exposed. Putting a man like him in charge of the city's morals was like trusting a fox to guard the henhouse.

CHAPTER 6

*J*ean-Jacques Duval lounged behind a gaming table and, as ever, he reminded Marianne of a toad. He was bloated and dissipated, with flabby skin, bulging eyes, and a wet, wide mouth that he constantly moistened with his flickering tongue. He was repellent. And also very dangerous. Marianne cursed the day she'd ever met him.

His lackey closed the door with an ominous click and positioned himself just behind her, blocking her escape route. Two more of his seemingly inexhaustible band of thugs skulked behind his chair, one on either side, like twin gargoyles. Remi, the one she recognized, cracked his knuckles and shot her a chilling smile. The other one was equally mountainous. He had a red face and no discernible neck. His head disappeared right into his shoulders, like a prize bull.

A cold shiver snaked along her spine. *Merde.* No chance of fighting her way out. Madame was too far away to be of any help. And the rest of the staff were too well trained to interrupt. Even if they heard her scream.

She treated him to a stony stare. "What do you want, Duval?"

He clucked his tongue at her belligerent tone. "Tsk. Little

Marianne. That's not very welcoming." He tossed a pair of dice idly across the table, and his beady eyes narrowed. "I've another job for you. I want it done tonight."

Marianne frowned. "That's impossible. It's nearly midnight, and I've already done two shows today. Whatever it is, it'll have to wait."

Duval's eyes hardened, but his mouth curved in an unpleasant smile. "You'll do it tonight."

He raked a leering glance down her body. Marianne tightened her cloak around herself and suppressed a shudder as the pink tip of his tongue flicked out over his lips.

"You didn't plant those documents in Valette's office, did you?" he said sweetly.

She bit her lip. She should have known he'd find out. Paris was like that. You went to a salon, there was a spy. You went to a brothel, there was a spy. You went to a restaurant, there was a spy. She shouldn't be surprised. She was one of them.

"Your silence is telling," Duval mocked.

She affected a shrug. "I left the letter just where you said, in his office." *That was technically true, at least.* "He must have found it and destroyed it. What's between you two, anyway?"

Duval's brows lowered, momentarily distracted. "That bastard's been trying to discredit me for years. Him, and Fouché. Always poking their noses in my affairs. Always trying to catch me doing something wrong." He snickered. "I thought I'd return the favor. Unfortunately, *you* failed to complete your mission. Antoine, relieve Miss Bonnard of her cloak."

The mountain behind her moved. She tried to duck past him, but he was surprisingly fast for such a big man. He gripped her arm in a painful squeeze and tugged off her cloak. Her hand tingled unpleasantly.

Merde. Why hadn't she bothered to change? Her peach satin bodice had ridiculous lace ruffles around the neckline and over the shoulders. The short bloomers barely covered the top of her thighs. Rose-colored tights completed the ensemble. It wasn't particularly revealing when she was thirty feet above the audience. Now it seemed ridiculously inadequate, like a tissue paper flower in the rain. She yanked hard against the brute's restraining hand, and he let her go.

Duval raised one eyebrow. "An unusual choice of apparel," he said dryly. "You never fail to surprise, Marianne, I'll give you that. Search her," he ordered coolly.

Marianne feigned indifference as the thug pawed her, his hands lingering on her breasts and thighs. He found the two knives at her back and threw them onto the table with a clatter.

The delicate frame of the armchair creaked in protest as Duval heaved his corpulent form up and stood. His jewels flashed, and Marianne curled her lips at the ostentatious display. For someone who was supposed to support the virtues of *liberté, egalité,* and *fraternité,* his ideas on wealth distribution were hardly egalitarian. Those expensive baubles were paid for by money skimmed from the government-run brothels he was supposed to oversee. Apparently, he didn't see the irony in dressing himself as richly as the aristos he claimed to despise.

Plus ça change, indeed.

He rounded the table and traced a pudgy finger down the side of her cheek. Marianne forced herself not to duck away from his touch.

"Do you remember the deal we made, four years ago?"

As if she could forget.

"You promised to bring in enough income to cover yourself and your sister if I allowed you to work at the circus instead of here," he continued smoothly.

"And I have, haven't I?"

He tapped her chin with a sausagelike finger. "I won't deny that you've been useful until now. But this failure with Valette suggests you've outlived your value as a thief. You have to earn your keep somehow."

Her heart started to hammer in alarm. "I told you, I won't whore for you," she said calmly.

He chuckled. "So proud, my little aristo. There are two thousand prostitutes in Paris. You think you're better than them? Even the great Bonaparte's first time was with a streetwalker." He stretched out his pudgy hand and studied his rings complacently, turning them so the facets caught the light. "Valette came to see me a few days ago, you know."

He paused, like a snake waiting to strike. Marianne kept her face impassive, determined not to give him the satisfaction of a reaction.

"You never said you'd met him, Marianne."

"I haven't," she lied evenly. "I've seen him at the circus a few times, in the audience. He has a box. He must have seen me there."

Duval's eyes glittered. "How delicious. We keep tabs on each other's people. It's a little game we play." He rubbed his hands together. "Well, you seem to have made quite the impression. He made a very tempting offer for your company."

Marianne's heart rate quickened, but Duval waved a dismissive hand.

"I refused, of course. But it got me thinking. If a man like Valette—who scarcely needs to *pay* for female company—would be willing to hand over good money for you, just consider what some of my less-handsome clients might be induced to spend." He gave a lavish sigh. "Genuine virgins are in such short supply. I need a regular batch of virtuous innocents to cater to my most wealthy and discerning clients."

"I won't whore for you," Marianne repeated clearly. "I'll kill myself first."

He smiled, delighted by her resistance. "No, you won't. Because then I'd have to use Sophie instead. Don't forget, she's untouched only because of *my* generosity."

A chill chased over Marianne's skin. "If you touch one hair on her head, I'll kill you." She deliberately flicked her eyes to the scar on his chin. It made her feel better. She'd given him that mark. He'd underestimated her once before.

Duval snorted, his smile reptilian. "Ah, little one. You're like a tigress protecting her cub. Such fierce passion." He stepped closer. His breath stank of wine. She flattened her lips together.

"I wonder what Valette saw in you, my dear? You're not exactly the kind of woman he usually goes for. And by that I mean beautiful and experienced." He sniggered at his own joke. "You *do* have soft skin, I suppose." He brushed her cheek again with his soft hand.

Marianne stood her ground, but her skin shrank from his touch.

"And good lips. Men like nice pouty lips." He snagged a strand of her hair and tested it between his fingers like a cloth merchant testing silk.

Marianne drew her lips back in a snarl as he circled her. "Would you like to inspect my teeth, too? Like a horse?"

He flicked a dismissive glance at her chest. "Your tits are too small, though." He cupped her through the fabric and squeezed painfully. Cruelly.

She forced herself to remain motionless while her fingers itched to rip out his throat.

"Still, some gentlemen prefer not to be smothered. They can pretend you're a boy. Some like that, you know."

She cast a longing glance at the window. Too high. She couldn't let him win. Couldn't risk endangering Sophie. She'd survive, suffer any indignity. Just to thwart him.

He ran a smug gaze from her head to her feet. "You're not as pretty as your sister, of course."

That stung, even though it was the truth. The sky was blue. Spring followed winter. Sophie was beautiful. That irrefutable truth scared Marianne half to death. The past four years had been a hideous balancing act, trying to keep Duval happy and as far away from Sophie as possible.

"I doubt your customers will care when the lights are out," she said coolly.

She still had the knife in her boot. The gargoyle had missed that one. But how to get it out? They'd be on her in a flash.

Duval leaned over her shoulder. His rancid breath tickled her ear. "I'm so glad I left you a virgin, Marianne."

A wave of nausea rolled over her, so strong she almost gagged. She closed her eyes. She didn't *feel* like a virgin.

"I rather envy the first man to have you," he continued silkily. "If you weren't so valuable untouched, I daresay I'd enjoy breaking you in myself." He licked his lips. "Perhaps when your first lover's done with you, I might bestir myself to continue your education."

She wouldn't remember the things he'd made her do. She was ice.

But her mind refused to cooperate. Images seared into her brain, vivid even after four years: Duval pinning her down, rubbing himself against her, so fat and heavy she couldn't push him off. The smell of his hair powder in her throat; his hot, panting breath in her ear. He'd made her kneel between his legs. Made her touch him. She'd made herself sick after he'd left, washed her mouth out with soap. Nothing had been able to wash away the disgust.

She forced the repulsive thoughts away. She'd escaped him then with her virginity intact. She would do the same now. If only she could get to her knife. "If I agree to this, you'll leave Sophie alone?"

Duval nodded. "For now."

"How do I know you won't break your word?"

He tittered. "You don't. You'll just have to trust me."

"I'd sooner trust a rat from the sewers."

He smirked at the insult. "You don't have any choice, my dear. Remember, those who oppose me rarely prosper." His sweet smile was chilling. "Remember what happened to your poor friend Joseph Breton."

His mock-concern turned Marianne's stomach. Joseph had complained about the treatment of his sister in one of Duval's seedier brothels. Duval's thugs had beaten him so badly he'd barely escaped with his life. As it was, he'd been left unable to perform his tumbling act. He'd been reduced to manning the ticket booth at the Cirque Olympique.

Duval's eyes glittered with malice. "So, we understand each other. You can start tonight."

"What? Now?" Horror clenched her stomach. Damn him. The bastard knew better than to give her a chance to run.

"Yes. Now." He cast a final glance at her skimpy outfit and chuckled. "No need to change, my love. You'll be naked soon enough."

CHAPTER 7

*S*he wasn't given time to think. Antoine marched her down the corridor and bundled her into the Montausier's smallest theater, the one used for its most "intimate" performances. Lights blinded her as he dragged her up onto the small raised dais.

Thirty or so men were seated around the stage, grouped at tables. The air smelled exclusive, male; of smuggled brandy and expensive cigars. Her entrance provoked a buzz of conversation. Duval waddled up the steps and stood next to her. Too close, as usual.

"Here she is, gentlemen, as promised," he announced loudly. "Mademoiselle Bonnard. The last virgin left in Paris."

His words produced a roar of appreciation from the audience. His fingers were painful on her jaw as he turned her face this way and that so the perverts could get a good look at her. She was about to snap her head around and bite him, but he wisely dropped his hand.

"I warn you, good sirs, have a care. Only the most vigorous of gentlemen should consider. This is no meek miss who'll bow to your every whim. This one's a fighter. An acrobat, too." He raised one eyebrow meaningfully. "I'm sure many of you've seen her at the Cirque Olympique."

Some of the gentlemen chuckled.

"I guarantee the best night of sport you've had all year." He swept a glance over the audience. "So, how much for the night, eh, gents? What price unsullied innocence? Shall we open the bidding at, say, ten francs? Ten francs for the whole night?"

"Here." A hand shot up, followed by a host more. "I'll pay ten francs."

The first hand belonged to a fat old man, sprawled at one of the front tables. He was dressed like a fop in a pink silk coat edged in lace. Rolls of fat bulged over his too-tight neckcloth. The buttons on his canary-yellow waistcoat looked like they were about to pop with the strain of encasing his protruding stomach. He reminded Marianne of Duval. She shuddered.

"Twenty!" Another hand waved. This time it was one of a pair of uniformed officers who were seated together near the door.

"Thirty." This man was older, with round wire-rimmed spectacles and a thin hook of a nose. He looked like a studious vicar. *Degenerate.*

Fifty francs was bid by a sallow man with eyes too close together. He resembled a weasel. A greasy weasel.

Marianne closed her eyes, swamped by a sense of unreality. This was ridiculous. She was being sold off, her innocence bartered like a slave on the trader's block. She stared straight ahead. None of it mattered. As soon as this sorry farce was done, she would escape. She still had a blade in her boot. Woe betide any man who got in her way.

Of course, she and Sophie would have to leave Paris, go somewhere even Duval's underworld tentacles couldn't find them. She didn't want to leave. The Falconis were the closest thing to a family they had. Where could they go? What would they do? She straightened her shoulders. She'd think about it when the time came. For now she just had to get out of this mess with her virginity intact.

The bidding had reached the incredible price of one hundred francs. Duval was flushed with excitement. Sweat beaded his flabby jowls. Marianne wondered darkly whether she should be honored. Even Odette, the Montausier's most expensive courtesan, couldn't command this kind of money. Still, this *was* a once-in-a-lifetime opportunity. *Her* lifetime, that was. She'd be a virgin only once. And not for much longer, if Duval had his way.

Duval's eyes gleamed with avarice. Even *he* looked surprised at her popularity.

The bidding was slowing. The fat dandy was back in as the highest bidder at a hundred and fifty francs. He leaned forward in anticipation, his buttons straining dangerously. Marianne found herself casting a desperate, pleading glance at the hussars. Either one of them would be better than that pig. At least they were relatively attractive. Then again, the pig would be easier to overpower when the time came. Marianne shot him an encouraging smile.

"One hundred and fifty francs it is, then," she heard Duval saying, delight in his voice. He sounded far away, as if he was underwater. "No one else?" His tone was regretful. "Going once . . ."

The hussar shook his head apologetically and patted his empty pockets, even as his friend encouraged him to bid again.

"Going twice . . ."

"A thousand francs," came a silky voice from the shadows.

A collective gasp went around the room as heads swiveled to identify the madman who'd offer such an outrageous sum. Marianne clamped her jaw shut so it didn't drop open. *Nom de Dieu!*

Nicolas Valette lounged negligently in the shadows, his elegant fingers wrapped around a tumbler of amber liquid. His long legs stretched casually in front of him, but there was a tension about him that suggested he might spring into action at any moment.

Duval paled. "Monsieur Valette, good evening. I didn't see you back there."

"Good evening, Duval."

Duval made an obsequious bow, practically scraping the floor. It was a shame his belly was in the way. He looked like an over-stuffed sausage. "Did I hear you right, monsieur?"

"You heard me," Valette said pleasantly. "I said one thousand francs for the girl. But not just for the night. I want exclusive rights. A permanent arrangement, if you will."

Duval's mouth opened and closed a few times like a landed fish gasping for air. "I don't understand."

Marianne hid a smile at his discomfiture.

"It's quite simple," Valette rose fluidly to his feet. "Even someone with your limited intelligence should be able to grasp the concept." He spoke as if he were schooling a mentally deficient child. A few quickly stifled chuckles sounded through the room. "I'll pay you a thousand francs. But for that, she'll belong to me. Body and soul. Not just for tonight, but forever."

Duval seemed to realize he'd been neatly backed into a corner. He'd never considered relinquishing permanent control over her, but he could hardly refuse so public an offer without damaging the reputation of the brothel. The Montausier, after all, was famed for providing whatever the client required.

"Of course. Whatever you wish," he said weakly. "A thousand francs it is." He placed a sweaty hand between Marianne's shoulder blades and gave her a sharp push. "Come up and claim your prize." He began to clap, slowly at first, then faster as the rest of the audience joined in.

Men swarmed forward to congratulate Valette. He accepted their handshakes with good-natured aplomb, all the while making his way inexorably across the room toward her. A few people raced out of the room, keen to spread this latest, most incredible piece of gossip.

Marianne watched his approach as if in a trance. The room was stifling, closing in. His eyes told her precisely nothing, but the corner of his mouth was curled up in that devilish half smile she was beginning to recognize. Her heart was beating uncomfortably fast. The noise and bustle faded away; it was just the two of them, time balanced on a knife's edge. She parted her lips, unsure of what to say, but he encircled her waist and swirled her down from the stage before she could utter a word.

"Now you're mine," he whispered against her ear.

Her stomach tightened at the fierce possession in his tone. She started to protest, but Duval clapped his hands and once again addressed the audience.

"And now, gentlemen, one final treat for you. I've saved the very best for last, you could say." He caught Marianne's eye, and her stomach turned to lead. His gloating, triumphant face swam in her vision. "The acrobat has a pretty sister!" he crowed. "May I present to you, Miss Sophie Bonnard."

Marianne gasped in outrage as a rousing cheer went up from the boisterous crowd.

That lying swine!

Her younger sister Sophie was ushered into the room and thrust up onto the stage. Marianne lunged forward, ready to claw Duval's eyes out, but Valette's hand clamped around her arm like a vice. He dragged her backward and pushed her, none too gently, into a chair.

"Sit down!" Without releasing her, he sat down next to her, his hard thigh pressing against hers in silent warning.

Sophie's eyes were bright with unshed tears. Her hands were fisted by her sides, but she didn't appear hurt. Even her frightened pallor and the fact that she was dressed as plainly as usual couldn't detract from her luminous beauty. Marianne glanced up at Valette's hard, uncompromising profile, her heart pumping furiously. "If you want any cooperation from me at all, you're going to have to get her out of here," she hissed.

He turned to her, his expression calm. "And what good will that do me? I don't need her. She doesn't have your skills."

"I refuse to let her be bought by some disgusting pervert."

"You're in no position to be issuing ultimatums."

"Please. You have to help her."

Bidding this time was fevered. Hands shot up all around the room. Sophie saw Marianne in the audience and sent her a panicked, pleading glance. Marianne tried to nod reassuringly. The price reached five hundred francs. Marianne jabbed her elbow into Valette's ribs. "I won't leave her behind."

He frowned then sighed. "You'd better be worth it." He raised his voice to be heard above the din. "A thousand francs. Same terms."

A chorus of good-natured groans erupted from the audience.

"Come on, Valette, you've already got a girl!"

"Give another man a chance!"

Duval was pale with anger, but he clearly recognized he couldn't renege on the deal. "Done!" he growled.

Valette shrugged, an elegant lift of his muscled shoulders. "Sorry, gentlemen." He stood and shouldered his way through the crowd, marching Marianne along in his wake. Men slapped him on the back and suggested all manner of obscene things he could do to enjoy the night to the fullest. Marianne ducked her head, her face burning.

Duval forced a smile. "Congratulations, monsieur. I assume you'd like to avail yourself of one of our rooms to confirm that they're both indeed untouched?" He shot a triumphant glance at Marianne. "I don't expect any payment until you've satisfied yourself on that score, of course. The Montausier never cheats its clients. Come, now, I *insist*."

Bastard. He just wanted to make certain she was ruined. He'd probably try to watch, too, the sick monster. Most of the rooms had spy holes in the walls. All the girls knew about them; a few even said they liked having an audience while they "performed."

Valette inclined his head coolly. "Why, thank you, Duval. I'd like to make sure I'm getting my money's worth."

Marianne's stomach lurched. A few of the men chuckled bawdily.

He turned to the crowd. "If you'll excuse us, gentlemen . . ." He pushed Marianne out into the corridor, following Sophie and Duval. His grip on her wrist was inescapable.

"Sophie!" Marianne lunged forward to embrace her sister, but Duval stepped in the way. He gestured to a door a little farther along.

"You can use that room, Valette. I'll look after this one for you." He squeezed Sophie's arm and gave her an oily smile. Sophie cringed away from him. "Unless, of course, you'd like to try them both together?" His porcine eyes gleamed at the prospect.

Valette shot him a cool glance. "No, I prefer to savor my women. One at a time." He marched Marianne toward the door and glanced back over his shoulder. "Oh, and Duval?" he nodded toward Sophie. "See that no harm comes to her. I'll be most displeased if she's mistreated while I'm . . . busy."

Without waiting for Duval's agreement, he tugged Marianne through the door, locked it, and pocketed the key.

CHAPTER 8

*T*he instant Valette dropped her arm, Marianne scowled and rubbed her wrist.

"What have you done? Are you mad? Open this door right now!"

He shrugged out of his jacket, crossed the room, and lowered himself onto the bed as if he hadn't a care in the world. He stretched his long, black-clad legs out in front of him and lounged against the ornate headboard like an eastern potentate surveying his harem.

"Shh, *chérie*." His voice rumbled with sardonic amusement. "Be calm."

"I will not be calm! What's going on?"

"I told you, I don't take no for an answer." His predatory expression made her shiver. The hope that he might somehow—miraculously—be her rescuer died a miserable death.

"Listen, I don't know what's going on between you and Duval, but you can keep me out of it. I don't like being caught in the middle."

"Too late," he said cheerfully. "You're in up to your eyebrows."

She glared at him, unable to refute that dismal truth.

"Tongue-tied by my masculine beauty?" he taunted, stretching like a lazy cat.

Marianne clenched her fingers. His teeth were too straight. And a good punch would certainly improve that perfect nose. "Duval's using you to punish me. He won't let you take me or Sophie out of here, whatever he says."

The confidence in his smile was infuriating. "We'll see."

Marianne took a calming breath. "What do you want from me?"

He raked her with a leisurely head-to-toe inspection that made her body tingle. His gaze lingered on her lips, her breasts, the juncture of her thighs.

"We're in a brothel. I've just paid a thousand francs for the privilege of your company. What do you *think* I want?"

Her heart was racing, but she returned his survey with a scornful inspection of her own. The man was sinfully good-looking. No wonder he had women falling over themselves for the privilege of gracing his bed. The gossips said he favored discreet widows, beautiful opera singers, and the occasional diplomat's wife. Women far more worldly and attractive than herself.

"I'm not a whore," she said with more calm than she felt. "And I doubt you've ever had to pay for sex in your whole, charmed life."

He folded his arms behind his head. The movement made the fabric of his shirt tighten alarmingly around his biceps. The fact that she noticed annoyed her even more.

"There's always a first time," he purred. "Maybe I'm bored of easy conquests? Maybe I fancy a challenge?"

"Duval's made a fool of you. You could've had any other girl here for a hundred francs."

His eyes glittered. "Ah, but I don't want just *any* girl. I want *you.*"

Anger surged through her veins. He was playing with her, and she was tired of being mocked. She feigned a bored sigh and put her hands up behind her, pretending to unlace her bodice. "You want sex? Fine. Let's get this over with."

Just try it, she challenged silently. *Try it and feel the sting of my blade.* She still had that knife in her boot.

Valette rose from the bed, all effortless grace, and she took an involuntary step back. He hadn't looked so tall, lying down. Or so menacing. Her shoulders hit the door. Calling his bluff had been a stupid idea.

He tilted his head as he stepped closer, using his body to trap her against the door, intimidating her with his very size. "What's the matter? It's not as if you're *truly* a virgin. We both know that was Duval's idea of a joke." His lips curled. "I promise I can make you enjoy it."

Marianne gave an unintentional snort. "I doubt it."

He raised his brows. "You doubt I can give a woman pleasure?"

"I doubt you can make me *enjoy* it," she said bluntly. It wasn't *his* talents she questioned, though. It was her ability to respond. Duval had made sure of that. Even a man as undoubtedly proficient as Valette couldn't move her.

His smile just widened. "That sounds like a challenge."

She glanced up in alarm. "It wasn't, believe me."

His eyes were gold, with an outer rim of black. Lion's eyes. Predatory. Terrifying. Her heart pounded uncomfortably against her ribs as she tried to quell the feeling of being trapped with a sleek, dangerous beast that had slipped its cage.

He stepped closer. The lace ruffles of his evening shirt brushed the skin above her corset. She dragged in a breath and pulled back, desperate not to touch any part of him. The scent of his cologne surrounded her—earthy and inviting, overlaid with the subtle, lingering scent of a cheroot. He slid his hand up her bare arm, and her skin prickled with alarm.

"You should be thanking me," he murmured gently. "Would you have preferred one of those other men bidding for you tonight?"

She couldn't prevent a shudder of revulsion at the thought.

He leaned forward. She held herself motionless as his nose brushed her ear, as his breath warm against her skin. He nuzzled the side of her neck.

"Do you know what I think?" he whispered.

Marianne shook her head. Her whole body tingled.

"I think you'd do anything to protect your sister." He dropped a leisurely kiss on her collarbone.

She bit her lip to stifle a gasp and gripped the door handle behind her. She twisted, just to make sure it really was locked. It was.

"I think you'd steal," he murmured, pressing another butter-fly-soft kiss on her skin.

"Yes," she croaked. A strange lassitude was sliding though her limbs.

"Lie."

A bloom of prickly heat blossomed where his warm lips brushed the pulse at the side of her throat. Her knees turned to water. "Yes."

She felt him smile against her skin. "Whore for her?"

A wave of shame rolled over her as she forced herself to admit the unpalatable truth. *To save Sophie? Yes. She'd suffer any indignity.* She closed her eyes in despair. "Yes."

His voice was gentle against her ear, sweet and smooth as poisoned honey. "I think you'd do whatever was necessary, wouldn't you, Marianne?"

He traced the hollow at the base of her throat with his tongue. She wanted to push him away. She wanted to grab his hair and pull him closer, down against her breasts. She tightened her grip on the doorknob instead, locked her arms behind her like Jeanne d'Arc tied to the stake.

As if he'd read her thoughts, he dropped his lips to the top swell of her breast, just above her bodice, soft as a feather, hot as hellfire. Her stomach tightened with a sweet, strange ache. She felt the swirl of his tongue and tilted her head back against the door, dizzy. *What on earth was happening to her?*

She had to concentrate. He'd asked her a question, hadn't he? "Yes," she whispered.

Was she agreeing to the question or encouraging the caress? She hardly knew.

"*That's* what I'm paying for," he murmured approvingly. A sudden rush of air cooled her skin as he lifted his head and pulled back.

"Wait . . . What?!" Marianne blinked as the fog of seduction cleared with unpleasant speed.

He kept his voice to a whisper, watching her out of enigmatic eyes. "I told you, I want you for a job. I need an agent, not a whore."

Marianne tried to jerk away, but his grip tightened on her upper arm.

"Hold still! We're being watched," he hissed against her ear. "Duval, among others. They're expecting a show. Let's not disappoint them."

Marianne sucked in a breath. "That's disgusting! *You're* disgusting."

She released the doorknob and pushed against his chest. It was useless. He just flattened his body against hers, imprinting his heat and hardness along the length of her. He was solid, muscled. Everywhere.

His chuckle was a wicked sound. "Oh, I don't know. Haven't you ever watched another couple make love? It can be quite . . . exhilarating." He seemed to enjoy her shocked expression. "I'm going to kiss you," he whispered, as though confiding a secret. "And you're going to kiss me back. You're going to pretend to enjoy it, too."

"Not for a million fr—"
He dropped his mouth to hers.

CHAPTER 9

*M*arianne clamped her lips closed and pushed against him, but it was like trying to move an elephant. She tried to hit him, but he grabbed her wrists and flattened them back against the door while his mouth pressed onto hers.

She writhed against him and tried to knee him in the groin. He blocked the move with a chuckle.

There was a smile on his lips when he pulled back. "It would help if you kissed me back."

"I don't want to!" she hissed.

"Liar."

Her face heated. How could he possibly know what she wanted? She stilled and he released her carefully, waiting to see if she was going to attack him, then cupped her jaw and pressed a light kiss to the corner of her mouth.

"Open your mouth for me, angel," he whispered. "Duval won't let you leave unless you've been ruined. Now kiss me back."

"I can't," she whispered miserably.

"Of course you can. It's only a kiss."

He didn't understand. It wasn't only a kiss. It would be domination and anger and pain. She opened her mouth to object just as he dipped his head, and she braced herself for the wave of revulsion, for the shame and self-loathing and hurt. They never came.

Nicolas Valette's mouth wasn't wet and demanding; it was warm and inviting. His lips traced hers with tantalizing promise, so sweet that tears pricked her eyes. It wasn't one kiss, it was a hundred—endless, drugging kisses that drained her will and made her senses reel. He took his time, nibbling and licking, as though kissing were an end in itself, not the necessary prelude to something else. Something worse.

Shivers of pleasure spread throughout her body. *How was this possible?* She closed her eyes, amazed, utterly bewildered by her own response.

His tongue swept inside her mouth, a tantalizing advance and retreat. Marianne moaned. Nicolas Valette kissed as if his whole soul depended on it. As if the world would end if he stopped.

He tasted of smoke and expensive brandy. Heady. Addictive. Intoxicating. The brush of his tongue sent heat spiraling through her. It was darkness and sin, a statement of intent. She wanted him to stop. She wanted him to keep kissing her forever.

She was panting when he pulled away.

"That's better," he whispered approvingly.

* * *

HER LIPS WERE LIKE PILLOWS, Nic thought absently. Puffy and bee-stung, just begging to be kissed. He was more than happy to oblige. He kissed her again, hard and deep, not giving her time to think. If he stopped, she'd come to her senses and push him away, and he needed her with him. Lost in him. Only him.

There was a peephole set in the wall, disguised by the flocking of the wallpaper. Nic pulled her away from the door and backed her up against the wall, flattening his body against hers.

He tilted the frame of a picture over the aperture with his elbow and smiled against her mouth as the voyeur—Duval, most likely—gave a hushed oath behind the grille as his view was cut off.

He kept on kissing her, barely coming up for air, even though his head was spinning. Her breasts were squashed up against his chest, nipples pressing through the fabric of her bodice. A flash of heat coursed through his blood. He caught her hips and lifted her up onto the chest of drawers, capturing her gasp of surprise with his mouth.

The move rattled the porcelain jug and bowl on the top. Nic framed her face with his hands and tilted his head to deepen the kiss, using his tongue, his teeth on her lower lip. He pushed her farther back, sliding the basin so it covered the second spy hole. That done, he allowed himself a moment of pure enjoyment.

His body throbbed with urgent demand as he tasted her. She was sweet, delicious, like cinnamon and cream, her mouth more enthusiastic than adept. Despite his earlier teasing, she was obviously a stranger to the pleasures of the flesh. Anyone who shied away from physical contact the way she did was a virgin through and through. Duval hadn't lied about that part. She probably *was* the last nineteen-year-old virgin left in Paris. Nic marveled at the enigma, even as he kissed her. He'd never met anyone more in need of bedding than Mademoiselle Marianne Bonnard. And he'd never experienced anything more erotic than her sweetly inept kisses, either, he realized with a start of surprise. Blood pounded in his ears, desire clouded his vision, and a rush of pure masculine satisfaction ran through him as she moaned.

God, he loved his job.

He dragged their lips apart, surprisingly reluctant to leave the lushness of her mouth. Her eyes were glazed and her lips glistened. His body throbbed in response.

"Enough!" she panted. "What are you *doing?*"

He shot her a cocky grin. "Ruining you, of course."

Before she could say anything else, he dragged her to the edge of the chest and pressed himself between her knees, flush against the heat of her. He was hard as a rock, as aroused as he'd ever been in his life, and she had to be able to feel him even through his breeches and her ridiculous frilly costume. He wrapped her legs around his waist and lifted her off the chest.

She gave a choked cry and grabbed his hair with both hands. She yanked hard, but he ignored her, whirling her around and following her down onto the bed in one seamless move. As soon as he pressed her into the mattress, though, she started to fight like a wildcat. She bucked and kicked. Her elbow caught him in the ribs as she pummeled him with her fists.

"No!" she panted fiercely. "Get off me!"

Nic shifted his weight, amazed at the sudden ferocity of her attack.

She rolled, fell off the edge of the bed with a painful-sounding thump, and scrambled crablike across the floor as if all the devils in hell were after her. She used the wall to push herself upright, protecting her back like a cornered wild animal.

Nic blinked. Her chest was rising and falling in panic. Her shaking hand held a blade.

She raised it level with her ear, threatening to throw. "Touch me like that again, and I'll kill you."

Nic regarded the stormy waif before him. *Bravo, Miss Bonnard.* He was used to being threatened, but damned if he could remember being as aroused by it as he was right now. He rolled onto his side and propped his head on one elbow, trying to appear unthreatening. "See, this is *exactly* what I'm talking about. *This* is the kind of passion I need."

The hoarseness of his own voice amused him. He coughed to clear his throat.

Her eyes were huge, her hair in disarray around her face. She was genuinely frightened, he realized, not just feigning outrage. Interesting. And all from one, innocent little kiss. Well, not so innocent, he amended. God knows how far he'd have gone if she hadn't put a stop to it.

It was quite unlike him to get so caught up. For one brief, glorious moment he'd forgotten all about the mission.

He sat up slowly so as not to startle her and held his hands up in surrender. "I'm at your mercy, mademoiselle. Please say you're going to have your wicked way with me."

She scowled, unimpressed with his attempt at humor.

He sighed. "I suppose we'll have to go with the backup plan then."

CHAPTER 10

$\mathcal{N}$ic bounced up and down on the bed a few times. The bedsprings creaked in protest.

She gave a bemused frown. "What are you—?"

"Shh!" he placed a finger over his lips. "They might still be listening." He gave the headboard a couple of rhythmic bangs against the wall. "I'm living up to my reputation. Can't have our audience thinking I've let you off the hook. Duval won't let you leave unless you're ruined. So ruined you must be."

He smiled at her horrified expression and raised his voice. "Oh, my God, that's good," he moaned hoarsely.

Nic enjoyed the way her mouth dropped open in a perfect little O of surprise. He wanted to kiss her again. "Yes!" he moaned, even louder, "that's it, sweetheart. That's the place. Right there. Oh yes."

She was staring at him as if he was a complete lunatic.

"Yes!" he shouted in his loudest ready-to-climax voice. "God, yes!"

"You could help," he whispered, *sotto voce*. "I don't like to take my pleasure alone. Can't you shout? Moan a little? Whimper?"

She pursed her lips primly. It was all he could do not to burst out laughing.

"Come on," he goaded. "What sound do you normally make?" He joggled the bed a few more times and shot her a searing glance. "Do you scream? I bet you're a screamer."

"I don't know," she said angrily, "I've never—" She stopped herself, and her cheeks turned the most luscious shade of pink. Nic pounced.

"You've never what?" he prompted. "Never had sex? Never come?" He shook his head in mock-amazement. "In this city, that's practically a crime." He pinned her with a wicked stare. "But don't worry. It's something we can remedy right now."

She was still pressed up against the wall, looking adorably confused. Nic couldn't resist teasing her some more. "Here we go. Brace yourself. You're about to have your very first climax."

He banged the headboard against the wall even faster, adding a bit more energetic bouncing to complement the effect. Finally, when the tempo had reached a satisfactory crescendo of furious bumps and squeaks, he let out a long, loud groan of completion and stopped all movement. His laughing eyes met hers. "How was it for you?" he whispered.

She seemed lost for words. He slid to the edge of the bed and got to his feet, watching her the whole time.

She jerked the knife again. "Don't come any closer." Her eyes darted to the door and back to him. "Unlock the door."

"What, no 'thank you, darling'?" he teased. "No 'I love you'?"

He shrugged back into his jacket, located the key in a pocket, and crossed to the door. She followed his every move like a mouse tracking a cat.

He sent her a cynical smile. "I must be losing my touch." Hand on the doorknob, he raised his brows. "Ready?"

She obviously realized her cooperation was necessary, and tucked the blade at her back with a resigned sigh. Eyes narrowed, she closed the distance between them. Nic reached out and slowly took her hand, entwining his fingers through hers. She scowled but suffered the touch.

She was afraid of him; it was there in the tightness of her shoulders and the way she held herself away from him. Someone had treated her badly, to give her such a distrust of men. Nic experienced a hot stab of anger at whoever had frightened her. She was fascinated, too, though. He had enough experience with women to know she was intrigued, drawn to him despite herself. Good. That would be enough for now.

He reached up and ruffled her hair, still annoyingly, inconveniently aroused. She ducked away but he caught her chin in his hand and pinched her cheeks to give them even more color. She swatted his hand. "Ouch!"

"*Now* you look like you've had sex." He smiled. "Do try to look little more satisfied, sweetheart. I've got a reputation to uphold."

He used their joined hands to pull her closer still. She stood rigid as he put his free hand on the small of her back and leaned in to press a light kiss on her softly parted lips.

"Thank you," he murmured wickedly, keeping her attention fixed on him while he pilfered the knife from her waistband.

She blinked slowly, as if coming out of a trance. "For what?"

"For the best night of my life," he chuckled. "Come on."

Duval was waiting outside the door. He looked torn between gloating at her downfall and irritation that he hadn't been able to watch the actual deflowering, Marianne thought bitterly.

"Was she to your satisfaction, monsieur?"

Valette eyed her, his expression deadpan. "Absolutely. A little unadventurous, but what can one expect from a virgin? Still, I'm sure I'll be able to educate her, given time."

Arrogant bastard! Marianne shifted her weight and stepped on his foot. Hard.

He smoothed her hair in a loving caress and gave her a fond smile, but his fingers tightened around hers in silent warning.

"Yes, she was quite enthusiastic once she got into the swing of things. In fact, I'm going to need some time to recuperate before I try out her sister." Seeing Duval's crestfallen expression, Valette added, "Don't worry, I trust she's untouched, too. I'm more than happy to pay for both of them now." He reached into his coat and withdrew a folded piece of paper. "A bank draft will suffice? You can present it at Rothschild's." He gave a slight, crooked smile. "You know my credit's good."

Duval studied the promissory note with narrowed, avaricious eyes, and nodded.

"Where's Sophie?" Marianne growled.

"I'm here."

Marianne exhaled when she saw her sister hurrying back along the corridor, accompanied by the bull-necked giant. She sent her a searching look, silently demanding to know if she'd been mistreated, and her worry retreated a fraction when Sophie gave a small shake of the head.

"I'm fine." Sophie smiled weakly. Her eyes darted from Marianne to Valette and back again, clearly desperate to know what had happened between them. Marianne sent her an I'll-tell-you-later look.

Valette nodded. "Good. My carriage is waiting out front. Ladies, this way."

Marianne glanced at Duval. Was he really going to let them leave? Surely it couldn't be that simple. Then again, he clearly thought he'd won this round.

He stepped out of their way.

Valette, his hand still entwined in hers, swept along the corridor and down the stairs. She had to take two steps for every one of his long, impatient strides. Sophie followed meekly behind. Marianne braced herself, fully expecting the porters at the door to bar their way, but they stepped out into the street unobstructed.

Even at such a late hour the street was crowded. She tried to pull away, but Valette's grip was inescapable. He steered her effortlessly toward a waiting coach. Marianne caught a brief glimpse of a painted crest on the door before Valette shoved her up the steps and settled himself beside her, taking up far too much room on the seat. Sophie scrambled up and sat opposite, her hands resting on her knees.

Valette released Marianne's fingers only after the carriage started to move. She opened and closed her fist a few times to restore the circulation and shot him an annoyed glare. "Where are you taking us?"

He ignored her question. Instead, he leaned forward and addressed Sophie. "My apologies, mademoiselle. Allow me to introduce myself. I am Nicolas Valette." His tone was gentle, but Sophie regarded him with wide-eyed apprehension.

"Monsieur," she murmured politely, shooting Marianne an uncertain glance.

Marianne sighed. "It's all right, Sophie. Monsieur Valette isn't going to ravish you." She speared him with a warning glance, just daring him to refute that statement. "You're perfectly safe. He, ah, works for the government," she said. "He's investigating Duval," she added, seized by sudden inspiration. "He's going to help us. At least, I'm going to help him. To bring Duval to justice."

Sophie gave a skeptical frown, but it was tinged with hope. "Have you really bought us from him? Truly?" She gazed at Valette with something akin to hero worship.

Marianne rolled her eyes. The man was no savior. He was a viper, patiently waiting to strike. She crossed her arms and addressed him. "Duval won't keep his word, you know. He'll try to get us back, I guarantee it."

"I'm sure he will." Valette's lips twitched in the ghost of a smile. "Especially when he discovers the banknote I just gave him is worthless."

Marianne gasped. "You imbecile! Why would you do that? He's a dangerous man. He'll have you killed!"

Valette adjusted the cuffs of his shirt. "He can *try*."

Really, the man's arrogance was astonishing.

He spoke again to Sophie. "I need your sister's help for a short while. I'd like you to stay with a friend of mine, Madame de Sevigny."

"Duval will be furious. He'll try to find us," Marianne interrupted obstinately.

"And that is why you'll be guarded by my men at all times," Valette continued smoothly, still addressing Sophie. "They will protect you from Duval. I give you my word."

Sophie studied his features then nodded obediently. Marianne stifled a snort. Valette made it sound as if she had a choice. Sophie would be no less a hostage there than she'd been at the Montausier, her tenuous position still dependent on Marianne's compliance. She was about to point this out when the carriage lurched to a stop.

"Ah, here we are."

A handsome young man in dark, neat clothing let down the step.

"Good evening, Andrew. I trust everything's in order for Mademoiselle Bonnard's arrival?" Valette said pleasantly.

The young man nodded. "Evening, monsieur. Of course. Madame is inside."

The curved front steps of an elegant townhouse were just visible in the light from the open door. Had they crossed the river? Marianne had been too busy arguing to pay attention, but this was obviously a wealthy area, judging from the fancy street-lamps and flower-filled window boxes. In the poorer parts of town people didn't have the luxury of flowers. They grew only things they could eat.

She frowned. "You had this all arranged. How were you expecting to have Sophie with you tonight? Even I didn't know she'd be there."

Valette glanced at her coolly. "I wasn't expecting anything. I came to the Montausier for you. I'd planned on having Sophie brought here from your apartment because I knew you'd never come with me unless she was beyond Duval's reach. The fact that she was present tonight merely saved me the bother of sending someone to get her."

Marianne quelled a surge of annoyance. He'd let her believe Sophie was in danger of being sold off to a stranger, but he'd been planning to secure her himself all along. *Fiend.*

"Come along, Miss Bonnard."

Sophie seemed to realize she had little choice. With one helpless, searching glance at Marianne, she permitted Valette to help her down the steps. Marianne rose to follow them, but Valette closed the door squarely in her face. She ground her teeth and pulled open the window instead. "Wait, Sophie—"

Sophie turned.

"It will be all right," Marianne said fiercely, praying it was true. "Just . . . stay here until I come for you. All right?"

Sophie nodded as the servant came forward. The man glanced at her and froze, his face assuming the familiar, stunned expression that every man seemed to develop when meeting Sophie for the first time: as if he'd been hit over the head with a frying pan.

Marianne sighed in exasperation. *Dieu!* Always the same. One look and they forgot their own name. Madame was right; she said men had only enough blood to allow *either* their brain to work or their groin, but never both. Here, yet again, was irrefutable proof.

The fact that Sophie herself was utterly unconscious of the effect she had on the male sex, of course, only increased her allure tenfold.

An elderly woman with a shawl around her shoulders appeared in the doorway and Marianne's anxiety retreated a fraction. At least Valette hadn't lied about there being a female on the premises to act as chaperone. Still, if he thought she was going to abandon her sister to a bunch of strangers, he was sadly mistaken.

As Valette stepped aside to converse with his man, Marianne ducked back inside the coach and scrambled across to the opposite door, intending to slip out onto the street while he was distracted. *Merde!* It was locked. She reached for the knife at her back, to force the lock, but her waistband was empty. She narrowed her eyes in fury.

That sneaky, treacherous son of a . . . He'd done it again! Every time that man got *near* her, she lost a blade. And her wits, apparently.

Fuming, she scanned the dark interior for something—anything—to use as a weapon. Providence finally smiled on her. A metal bracket just above her head held a handsome pair of pistols. She grabbed one just as Valette stepped up into the carriage, ducking his head to get through the small doorway. She aimed it directly at his chest.

He straightened, paused almost imperceptibly, then flicked back the tails of his jacket and settled himself on the luxurious velvet squabs opposite her. He rested one arm along the back of the seat and tilted his head quizzically.

Merde.

The pistol was heavy. Her hands were shaking; he must be able to see the muzzle waving about all over the place. And he'd probably guessed she had absolutely no idea how to fire the damn thing.

"First a knife, and now a gun. I do admire your resourcefulness," he murmured. "Are you aiming for my dastardly heart?"

"I doubt you have one," she hissed. "Now let me out!"

"Not a chance. You might as well accept that you're coming with me. Resistance will be tiresome for both of us."

There was no way past him. His body blocked the door very effectively. And then Marianne realized why he was so relaxed.

She lowered the pistol with a growl of irritation. "This isn't loaded, is it?"

His smile managed to be both pitying and patronizing at once. "No. So unless you're going to hit me over the head with it, I suggest you sit back and make yourself comfortable. We've a long way to travel tonight."

She would have taken him up on the suggestion if she thought she could get away with it. Instead, she tossed the weapon onto the seat next to him with a disgusted sigh. Valette leaned forward and replaced it gently in the rack above his head.

She lunged for the door while he was distracted, but he grabbed her wrist almost as an afterthought and hauled her back.

"Don't. I'm stronger and faster than you. You'll only get hurt."

She threw herself back onto the seat with a growl of frustration. "You don't understand. I have to stay with Sophie. I can't let your men look out for her."

"Afraid they'll fall in love with her like everyone else?"

Her head shot up at his perspicacity. How on earth did he know such things? It was uncanny. "You watch," she warned grimly. "I've seen it before. Your Andrew will be no different than the rest of them. Men find her irresistible."

"You think so?" he drawled softly. "She seems a bit timid for my taste. I prefer my women with a little more"—he paused, his gaze flicking to the pistols—"spark." His crooked smile turned her stomach to mush.

Marianne scowled. "My point is, he'll be distracted. Men can't think straight when she's around."

"Andrew's a professional. He doesn't get distracted. He's fully capable of protecting her."

"You're just saying that to make me come with you quietly."

"I could be," he agreed with irritating calm. "But in this case it's true. You're just going to have to trust me."

"Hah! I trust my knives. Unlike people, *they've* never let me down."

"Suspicious little thing, aren't you?"

"Suspicion's kept me alive."

He placed a hand over his chest, above his nonexistent heart, as if she'd truly plunged a knife there. "I'm wounded, *chérie*. Have a little faith." He studied her, as if she were a puzzle he could solve. "What will it take for you to trust me?"

She raised her brows in faint hauteur. "Trust has to be earned. Besides, I've had to fend for myself since I was fourteen years old. I don't need anyone to fight my battles for me."

He rapped the ceiling with his knuckles, signaling the coachman to depart, and Marianne fell back against the seat as the carriage lurched forward. He extended his legs in front of him, brushing hers, and she squashed herself into the opposite corner, unwilling to touch any part of him.

"Speaking of trust, where's my knife?" she demanded sullenly. "I know you have it. And the one from the other night, too."

"All in good time," he said, in a voice that made her want to strangle him.

The cool night air seeping through the window belatedly reminded her of how little she was wearing. She shivered, as much from fear as from the chill. Valette reached under his seat and produced a fur traveling rug.

"Here."

She snatched it from him, glad to hide herself under the silky folds. "If I'd known I was going to be sold at public auction, molested, and kidnapped this evening, I would have worn something more suitable," she snapped.

He ignored her sarcasm and raked her with a thoughtful glance. "Would you call it molested?"

The raw, naked intensity of his look made her skin prickle and her cheeks heat. Her lips throbbed, as if his mouth was on hers again. Marianne bit back a moan of despair. She'd thought herself immune, irrevocably tainted by Duval's abuse. It was highly disconcerting to discover she might have been wrong.

One look from Valette, and her blood heated to a slow boil. It was inexplicable. And truly horrifying, considering she was stuck with the fiend for the foreseeable future.

She ducked her head, grateful for the concealing darkness. "Who *are* you?" she whispered miserably.

He rested his head back against the seat with a sigh, that damnable half smile lurking on his lips.

CHAPTER 11

arianne peered out of the window, waiting for the carriage to slow. Landmark after landmark slipped silently past, absorbed into the murky darkness. When the lights grew more infrequent and then faded altogether, she couldn't keep quiet any longer. "Where are we going?"

"You'll see." His teeth showed white in the darkness when he smiled.

The coach was luxurious, with well-sprung seats and heavy curtains to keep out the drafts. It had been years since she'd been in a carriage like this.

She shifted a little so she could watch him from the corner of her eye. He sat relaxed, apparently unaffected by the jolting of the carriage, his flawless face in profile to her. He took up an inordinate amount of space. In the small confines of the interior she was horribly aware of his big body lounging in the opposite corner, his thighs dangerously close to her own. She drew her legs up, onto the seat.

He frightened her, but not in the same way that Duval frightened her. Duval liked to think of himself as smart, but he was a blunt cudgel in comparison to this man's rapier. Valette was more subtle, more insidious.

"Stop sulking," he said suddenly, his voice rich with amusement.

"I'm not sulking," she growled.

"Yes you are."

She turned to glare at him. "How would *you* feel if you were being forced to do something against your will?"

He pushed a hand through his hair. It fell perfectly back into place. She'd pay good money to see him disheveled.

"I'm going to need your cooperation," he said. "This job won't be easy. We have to be a team. Seamless, working together."

"Choose someone else," she said curtly, averting her gaze again. "I work alone." Her neck prickled. She could practically *feel* his eyes boring into her. "What's the job, anyway? It must be dangerous. Or illegal."

"Both. Don't tell me you've an aversion to breaking the law?" His tone was gently mocking. "I have a file on you in my office that suggests otherwise."

Her face heated. "Laws are often an inconvenience in our line of work, monsieur. Not all of them are just."

He smiled.

She tilted her head, thinking aloud. "It must be a matter of urgency. Something to do with the First Consul's return. Could it get me killed?"

"Quite possibly." He sounded perversely pleased by the prospect. He leaned forward, and she found herself mirroring his action. His cologne enveloped her in its woodsy, enticing scent, and her stomach flipped.

"Know this: if you're caught and suspected of being an enemy spy, you'll be tortured and killed. No questions asked."

"Oh, wonderful!" Marianne clapped her hands in feigned excitement. "I've grown so tired of living."

He smiled at her sarcasm.

"So what's the job?"

"Escorting someone out of the country." He sat back against the seat, and she could breathe again.

"Who?"

"A political prisoner."

"Another spy?"

"No."

"An aristo?"

"Maybe."

Marianne curled her lip in cool distain. "It's bound to be an aristo. They're all useless. Stands to reason one can't even cross the border on his own."

"I had no idea you felt so strongly about the upper classes," he murmured. "What a good little *citoyenne* you are." His tone was ironic. "I'm surprised you don't wear the little gray cap of the Grisettes."

Marianne shrugged. "Why should I care what happens to an aristo? You're asking me to die for a cause I don't believe in."

"No, I'm not. Dying for a cause is easy. Any idiot can do that. It's living for one that's hard. And I'm not *asking* you to do it, I'm telling you. I've paid a total of two thousand francs for the privilege of your charming company."

Ha. He'd "paid" Duval with a worthless banknote, by his own admission, but she still had no choice. She hated feeling trapped. She crossed her arms around her middle. "Fine. I'll do it."

"Wonderful."

She glared at him, sure he was hiding a smile, but his face was perfectly composed. She sniffed. "Aristos are all pampered and soft. The king was a fat wastrel. The country's better off without them."

Fast as lightning, he slapped his hands on either side of her head, imprisoning her within the cage of his arms. Marianne reared back in alarm. He leaned in close, invading her space, his breath fanning her lips. Her heart slammed against her rib cage.

"*I'm* an aristo," he challenged softly. "Do you think *I'm* soft and pampered?"

His strength was a powerful thing in the enclosed space; without even touching her, he made her aware of it, of him, of his absolute domination. She couldn't move an inch unless he willed it. She swallowed the sudden tightness in her throat. Every inch of her hummed as the warmth of his body radiated between them. In a flash she remembered the corded muscle in his arms and back, the strength of his thighs between hers as he pressed against her. Her skin tingled.

She cleared her throat. "No. But you're an exception."

His eyes held hers for a moment longer, then he pushed back abruptly. She dragged in a relieved breath.

"It's better if you don't know his identity." He settled back onto his side of the carriage as if nothing had happened.

"If we're caught, you mean?" she said. "Fine, don't trust me."

His lips twitched. "Trust has to be earned."

She scowled as he tossed her own words back at her. "You're not going to tell me any more?"

* * *

He shot her an enigmatic smile. "Not yet."

She was lying on her side, her head resting on the firm warmth of Papa's coat. She was snug and safe. Maman was stroking her hair. Marianne wriggled closer to the beckoning heat and wrinkled her nose. Papa had changed his cologne. He smelled different, like Maman's special Earl Grey tea . . . smoky, woodsy . . .

Memory returned like a dash of ice water. The weight across her shoulder was Valette's arm. Her cheek was nestled on his muscled thigh. *Good God!* Her head was practically in his lap!

She reared up with a curse and retreated into the corner as

fast as humanly possible. She swiped her hair out of her eyes and heard Valette chuckle in the darkness.

"You fell asleep," he offered calmly.

"*You* were on the other seat."

"You were about to roll off." He shrugged, unrepentant. "Next time, I'll let you fall on the floor."

Marianne retrieved the fur rug that had slipped to the floor and drew it up around her shoulders. She shouldn't have let down her guard. Exhaustion was her only excuse. "Don't touch me again."

She turned to stare out of the window. They were heading south; the rising sun revealed lingering tendrils of mist that snaked low over the fields. They'd left Paris far behind.

The carriage slowed as they turned into the yard of an inn. A creaking, peeling sign above the battered door proclaimed it the Lion D'or. The coach rocked to a halt, and Valette reached up and reclaimed the pair of pistols. He shoved them into the pockets of his coat.

"Don't you need powder and shot for those?" Marianne groused.

He gave an infuriating grin. "Do I strike you as a man who drives around with unloaded pistols?"

"They're loaded?"

"Of course they're loaded."

Merde. Merde. Merde. The man was a walking lie.

He let down the step, got out, and offered her his hand. Marianne ignored it and jumped down on her own, landing in a puddle that had gathered in the worn ruts in the cobbles. *Typique.* Now she had wet feet to add to her woes.

Still, it was a relief to escape the close confines of the carriage. She stretched her cramped limbs and glanced around.

"Citizen Valette." A greasy landlord bustled out into the yard, yawning and rubbing his hands together against the early-morning chill. Chickens scattered, flapping, before him. One glance at him was enough to scotch any idea of escape. The man looked as though he'd kill his own mother for a bottle of gin. Marianne edged slightly closer to Valette.

"It's all ready, as you requested." The man gestured to a hay cart in the corner of the yard where a scruffy groom was backing a brown mare into the traces.

Marianne couldn't hide her dismay. "That's for us?"

Valette looked down at her with a smile at the corners of his mouth. "The carriage has my crest on the sides. From now on we're trying to be inconspicuous. You hungry?"

She was starving. She'd sell her soul for some hot chocolate and a fresh croissant, but the landlord's stained apron was enough to turn her stomach. She shrugged. "A little."

At the landlord's bellow, a skinny pot boy appeared and offered them some stale bread and a hunk of smelly cheese. The accompanying wine had an oily slick and a single hair floating on the surface of the tankard. Marianne put it back down without drinking. The bread was hard as a rock. Perhaps she should save it for a weapon.

The carriage driver transferred a trunk from the carriage into the waiting cart. Valette opened it, rummaged inside, and tossed a bundle of clothing at her.

Marianne caught it reflexively. "What's this?"

"Clothes. Not that you don't look charming . . ."

She'd forgotten she was still in her stupid corset and bloomers. She felt her cheeks heat.

The landlord gave a leering smile. He was missing half his teeth. "You can change inside, mademoiselle." He gestured to the inn.

"I'll use the carriage, thank you." Marianne climbed back in and yanked the curtains closed. The bundle turned out to be a dress, with a long skirt and a ruched peasant top with a tie neck. Valette had guessed her dimensions with uncanny accuracy. The infernal man was clearly well versed in sizing up women.

He eyed her critically as she stepped down from the carriage. Marianne resisted the urge to tug up the low-cut bodice. She raised her chin defiantly. He'd chosen the damn clothes.

"Let's go." He climbed up onto the seat of the hay cart and beckoned her over. Marianne stepped onto the wheel. He grabbed her hand and hauled her up so energetically she practically fell into his lap. Flushing, she scrambled over him and settled on the hard wooden bench at his side. He clicked his tongue, and the horses started forward.

He handled the reins expertly, she noted sourly, flicking the whip with his strong wrists. The man seemed to do everything well.

It was impossible not to touch him. As they swung out of the inn yard he spread his arm along the back of the seat and pulled her into his side. Marianne growled. His broad shoulders took up most of the space. She was squashed against him, his hard thigh constantly banging against hers. Still, she suffered his arm about her. At least it stopped her from falling off.

The roads were appalling, and the farther from Paris they went, the worse they got. Here and there bands of workmen were making halfhearted attempts at repairs, but Marianne was jolted and rattled until her teeth hurt.

The sun rose and the dawn air lost its chill. She drifted into a kind of daze, lulled by the rhythmic *clip-clop* of the horse's hooves and the rocking of the cart. When had she last been outside Paris? It must have been over five years ago. She'd lived the first fourteen years of her life in countryside like this. She hadn't realized how much she missed it. She closed her eyes and absorbed the sounds and smells with the wonder of rediscovery. Snatches of long-forgotten scents brought a strange, yearning ache to her chest.

Paris stank: the stench of the gutters; the great throng of sweaty, unwashed bodies; the stomach-turning reek of the fish-mongers; the piles of rotting fruit in alleyways; the vile smell of the tanneries; the smoke from a million chimneys; the butchers' blocks; the street vendors. Horse piss and manure in the streets. And beneath it all the rich, moldy, damp smell of the Seine.

Here the air smelled sweet. Wood smoke clouded the air as they passed through a sleepy village. An herb garden, fresh with lavender and thyme. A laburnum overhanging the road. All that was missing was freshly brewed coffee and oven-warm bread. Her stomach rumbled loudly in morose agreement.

Finally, a stone marker at the side of the road indicated twenty miles to Fontainebleau, one of the former king's residences.

"Ever been there?" Valette nodded at the signpost.

"No. But I've heard about the stables. The king's horses were housed in pampered luxury while the peasants of Paris starved and prostituted themselves for scraps of bread."

Valette rolled his eyes. "Quite the little revolutionary, aren't we?"

"It's hard not to have sympathy with the cause, monsieur, when horses are treated better than people."

"You're one of those diehards who's got a handkerchief dipped in the king's blood, aren't you?"

Marianne shuddered. Duval *did* have one of those grisly souvenirs. In a show of citizenship, he claimed it was his prize possession. He was always trying to distance himself from his aristocratic background, just like the stupid Duc D'Orléans, who'd restyled himself Philippe Egalité—"citizen equality." The duc had even voted for the execution of his own cousin, the king, but even that hadn't been enough to save him. He'd been guillotined, too, just a few months later.

If only the same thing could have happened to Duval.

"I suppose it's too much to ask where we're going?" Marianne said wearily. Her backside hurt. They'd been in the cart since sunup, and all they'd had to eat was another iron-hard lump of bread provided by the inn and an equally durable piece of dubious-smelling cheese.

Her question was met with silence. She glared at Valette, nursing a seething sense of injustice. He seemed entirely unaffected by either tiredness or discomfort.

The landscape grew hilly, vineyards replacing the fields of crops. Row upon row of neat, tended vines, like wet-combed hair, covered the landscape. Warm, honey-colored stone walls surrounded each *domaine*.

"I saw a signpost back there for Dijon. Is *that* where we're going?" she persisted.

He chuckled and shot her a condescending look. "Try and have a little patience, sweeting. Not long now."

Marianne returned to her new favorite game of imagining slow and painful ways to kill him. He'd already been eaten by wolves and dragged behind a team of wild horses. Even that seemed far too merciful.

CHAPTER 12

*I*t was late afternoon when Valette turned the weary horse through a pair of exquisite wrought-iron gates. One hung askew, dangling loosely off its hinges like a drunkard swinging on a lamppost. Marianne craned her neck, searching for a name etched into the stone, but there was nothing to hint at where they were.

A once-stately avenue of trees flanked the pitted drive, branches sagging heavily. They leaned toward one another like conspirators, whispering and plotting: a guard of leafy sentinels to deter the uninvited. The fields on either side were untended. Row upon row of overgrown vines created a near-impenetrable mass of twisted branches and curling roots.

And then the house came into view, and Marianne caught her breath. It was a fairy-tale castle with soaring white walls; gray, turreted roofs; and a perfect, symmetrical facade.

"Whose house is this?" she breathed in awe.

Valette was regarding it with his usual inscrutable expression. "It belonged to an aristo whose lands were confiscated. The Marquis de la Garde."

"What happened to him?"

"He died," he said curtly.

His tone made her look up. A horrible thought occurred to her. "Did you know him?"

"No."

As they drew nearer, it became clear that the place resembled Sleeping Beauty's neglected castle far more than Rapunzel's fortress. Painted gray wooden shutters hung forlornly from the windows, or were missing altogether to reveal cracked and dirty panes of glass. A climbing plant twined unchecked over one wall as if intent on hiding the building from prying eyes. Even the creaking of the cart seemed to intrude on the peaceful desolation of the house; a raven flew up out of a turret, cawing reproachfully at the interruption.

Valette seemed unaffected by the barrenness. Probably because he didn't fear being alone with her, Marianne thought sourly. Her stomach knotted at the thought.

He seemed to know where he was going, at least. He ignored the grand front entrance, with its double set of sweeping stone steps, and swung the cart around the back of the house, where two wings embraced an overgrown courtyard.

The left and central parts obviously contained living quarters. The right side, once a stable block, showed evidence of a devastating fire.

A familiar churning started in Marianne's stomach as she studied the charred remains. Scorched rafters lay in a spiky black tangle where the roof had collapsed, sticking up like broken ribs. Trails of soot tapered upward from the doorways, soiling the pristine white stone. She shuddered. "What happened there?"

Valette turned from his perusal of the house. "What? The stables?" He shrugged. "The family used to breed horses. After it was confiscated, one of the emperor's cavalry regiments was billeted here. A couple of the officers sneaked out to have a smoke, and one didn't put out his cheroot. They were lucky to save the house. With nowhere to stable their mounts, the cavalry was moved. Now Fouché uses it as a safe house."

Marianne almost snorted. It was hardly safe for her. The greatest threat in the vicinity was sitting right next to her. Still, she was too tired to argue. She watched him secure the horse and locate a key from the trunk on the back of the cart.

The back door gave a creak of protest as he pushed it open with his shoulder, and he stepped back with a flourish. "After you, mademoiselle."

Marianne clambered down stiffly and entered into what appeared to be the kitchen, with a fireplace large enough to roast an ox, and a long, dusty trestle table with wooden benches set on either side. Valette stepped around her and strode forward with the ease of familiarity.

"You've been here before?" she asked.

"A few times. This way." He disappeared through an arched doorway.

Marianne bit her lip, listening to his footfalls fade away. They really were alone, just the two of them, with no help for miles and miles. She glanced wistfully at the door. There was no point trying to run. She couldn't drive the cart alone, and she hadn't ridden a horse bareback for years. He'd catch her before she got half a mile. The thought of what he might do to her then made her shiver.

She glanced around, looking for a poker, a stick, anything. A vase would do. She'd fought off Duval with a broken vase, hadn't she? But Valette was not Duval. He wasn't someone she could catch off guard. His physical superiority was undeniable; he'd proved time and time again that he could overpower her whenever he wished. Her throat tightened, and her heart started to race uncomfortably.

She took a deep, calming breath. It wouldn't come to that. She'd simply to do the job she'd been brought here to do, then return to Sophie and forget Nicolas Valette ever existed.

"Are you coming?" His muffled shout echoed back to her through the hallways. With a sigh of resignation Marianne followed the sound.

She found him in one of the deserted salons, folding back the shutters. The air smelled musty, of dust and mouse droppings, but at least it wasn't damp. In Paris, the moldy odor of the Seine permeated the streets for half a mile on either side. This was infinitely better. Light flooded in, illuminating hand-painted murals decorating every wall, and Marianne's mouth curved up into a reluctant smile.

The artist had depicted a fanciful country idyll; women on swings laughed with carefree abandon, ruffled skirts and ribbon-decked hats fluttering in the breeze. Ardent lovers flirted in flower-filled gardens, while gallants and cavaliers, musicians and dogs all vied for their attention. The effect was both sublime and ridiculous.

She glanced upward. The glass droplets of an enormous chandelier tinkled faintly, like ghostly fairy bells. Even covered in layers of dust, the prisms still caught the light, throwing rainbow shards like daggers across the dusty parquet floor.

A wave of sadness washed over her at the evidence of such faded grandeur. It was so easy to imagine the house in its prime; parties with processions of carriages lining the drive and excited guests tumbling out of each one. The hairs on her arms lifted. She could almost hear the swish of silken skirts, the clink of glasses, the strains of a ghostly quadrille. Almost smell the faint, elusive perfume of powdered wigs and scented fans.

A place like this should be filled with life, with laughter, not with termites and moths. Her skin prickled in awareness, and she glanced over to find Valette watching her, his face half lit by the afternoon sun, half hidden in shadows. As usual, she found it impossible to read his expression. How could she find him both terrifying and fascinating at the same time? She dropped her gaze and turned away.

Some pieces of furniture still remained. A dusty harpsichord stood in solitary splendor in one corner, presumably too heavy to move. Marianne lifted the lid and brushed her fingers over the keys, producing a trill of discordant notes. A few large gilt-framed portraits still hung on the walls, their noble subjects obscured by dust and cobwebs. Elsewhere, paler-colored rectangles and bare hooks hinted at where smaller pictures had once hung.

She jumped as Valette stepped forward. "There's more food in the cart. See what you can rustle up for supper. I'll get us firewood."

Marianne bristled at his tone. She wasn't his servant. Then again, the promise of food and a warm fire was undeniably appealing.

She found a bottle of wine, a hunk of bread, and another dry wedge of cheese in the cart. She set them on the kitchen table, broke off a chunk of cheese, and went in search of Valette. The aroma of a cheroot drifted in through a set of open doors. She followed the smell and found him on a stepped terrace, his broad shoulders resting against the wall, the very image of relaxed indolence.

His flawless face was in profile, and she found herself studying his straight nose, dark brows, and clean-shaven jaw with a kind of morbid fascination. On a purely aesthetic basis, he was perfect. It was no surprise that women were attracted to him. No doubt he could be charming when he chose. He'd probably never treated any of *those* women the way he'd treated her—with bullying, threats, and disdain.

Afraid that he might catch her staring, Marianne followed his gaze out over the fields and vineyards to where the late-afternoon sun gilded the tops of the vines. Golden clouds of insects buzzed around the ripening grapes. Remnants of formal gardens were still visible: brick-lined parterres intersected by low box hedges, overgrown rose arches, and artfully placed statues. The sweet scent of honeysuckle drifted on the warm breeze.

"This is a beautiful place. It must have been amazing when it was furnished and filled with people," she ventured.

He shrugged and exhaled. "I suppose so."

She gave an exaggerated cough and waved her hand in front of her nose to disperse the blue fog he'd blown in her direction. It completely drowned out the honeysuckle, but in truth, she didn't mind the smell. How strange. Since the death of her parents she'd always associated burning with panic and fear. But this wasn't so bad. She'd never smelled anything quite like it.

"What's that you're smoking?"

He glanced down at his fingers. "My own blend. Made by Fribourg and Treyer in London."

Plenty of wealthy gentlemen had their own personalized blend of tobacco. Her own father had done so, she recalled suddenly; Maman had always jokingly complained about the smell. Marianne's chest tightened at the memory. It hurt to remember such ordinary, everyday details.

How had Valette acquired a taste for English tobacco? Had he been across the channel for Fouché? It was more than possible. Or perhaps smoking a foreign blend was a perverse way of teasing those who questioned his allegiances. The man clearly loved being enigmatic.

She forced her expression into one of taunting disdain. "A Frenchman who likes English tobacco. That's rather unpatriotic, considering we're at war. How do you get it? There's an embargo on imported British goods."

He smiled. "Money and contacts can get you just about anything you set your heart on, *chérie*."

She felt her face heat. Was he talking about her again? He'd bought *her*, after all. "A *gentleman* would have asked if I minded," she said haughtily.

He smirked with gentle irony. "Good God. Whatever gave you the idea I was a gentleman?"

She narrowed her eyes at him.

"*Do* you mind?" he asked belatedly.

"Yes."

"Tough." He leaned back and rested his booted foot on the balustrade. "You don't have to stay out here."

"Why do you smoke those awful things?"

He shrugged. "Because it's extremely pleasurable. A habit I picked up in my army days."

Marianne pounced on the snippet of information, adding it to the pitifully few things she knew about the man in front of her. So he'd been in the army. Interesting. She took a nibble of the hard cheese.

"You should be glad of it," he said amiably. "It gives me something to do with my hands. Other than wrapping them around your neck."

She rolled her eyes at the threat, but her heart beat faster at the thought of him touching her again. And then he slanted her a look that was so unashamedly carnal it made her heart stop.

"And because right now it's the most satisfying activity I can think of that doesn't involve two people and a bed," he drawled.

She choked on the cheese.

He shot her a knowing glance and made no attempt to help her. He took one final drag, exhaled a ribbon of smoke, then threw the stub down and ground the cheroot out beneath the heel of his boot. She tensed as he pushed off the wall, but he stalked past without touching her and went back into the house.

"Come on. It's time I told you the plan."

* * *

MARIANNE SAT at one end of the long kitchen table as Valette went out to the cart. He returned with the leather trunk, from which he produced a roll of paper and a leather-bound book. She took a bite of bread while he spread the document out on the table, using the cheese and a wine bottle to hold down the corners.

"You said we're escorting someone across the border," she prompted. "When you say 'escorting,' you mean . . . ?"

"Springing him from prison and helping him over to Holland."

"Of course," she said, taking refuge in sarcasm. "Why did I think it would be something simple? Like recovering the crown jewels, or breaking into the emperor's bedchamber." She narrowed her eyes. "Why does this prisoner need rescuing anyway? If the emperor wants him out, why doesn't he just sign an order to release him?"

"It's not as simple as that. The emperor would gladly leave him to rot."

Marianne raised her brows. "You mean Fouché's acting against Napoleon's orders?"

Valette gave a wry smile. "Fouché serves no one except France. He supports Napoleon when it suits him, just as he supported the Bourbon restoration a few years ago. He's a survivor. He'll back whichever side looks the most likely to win. And in this case, he believes it's more politically expedient for the prisoner to escape and disappear."

"So the man's being *allowed* to escape?" she asked hopefully. "Are the guards going to leave his cell door unlocked and take an extralong lunch break?"

"No. No one at the prison will be aware of our mission. If we're caught, Fouché will deny all knowledge of us and we'll be executed as traitors."

"How reassuring," she said dryly.

"Fouché believes the prisoner's freedom is of national importance and more than worth the risk."

"Ha. Easy for him to dismiss the danger when he's tucked up

safe in his office sipping brandy. He's not the one who could be facing a firing squad. Which prison is it?"

Valette tapped the paper. Her eyes widened as she took in the details. "*This* is the target?" she said in disbelief. "This is the Château de Vincennes."

He nodded, infuriatingly calm. "One of the most fortified prisons in France."

Blood thrummed unpleasantly in her ears. "Why don't we storm the Bastille, too? Or if you want to save time, why not just send me straight to the gallows now?"

He ignored her dramatics. "One man has escaped from both the Bastille and the Château de Vincennes."

She curled her lip. "You, I suppose?"

He raised an eyebrow, apparently amused by her tone. "Not me. A man called Henri Latude. Or Danry, or Masers de La Tude, depending on whom you talk to. He had many names."

"Don't we all?" she muttered. "And is this Monsieur Latude going to help us?"

Valette crossed his arms over his chest and leaned back to study her. "I doubt it. He's dead. He did, however, write a fine account of his escapes." He tapped the small leather-bound book.

"What good is that to us? If this Latude escaped, he must have been *inside* the prison. We'll be *outside*, remember."

"Getting in is easy. We're going to walk in. Then you're going to change places with the prisoner."

She gave a short disbelieving snort. *"What?"*

"You'll stay in the cell while the prisoner escapes, pretending to be you."

She laughed. "That's funny. Because, the way you say it, it sounds like you'll be exchanging me for the prisoner. That you'll be *leaving* me in the cell."

"Exactly."

"No," she said bluntly. "You have to be joking."

"I'm deadly serious. This is where Latude's information comes in. You're going to escape from the cell exactly as he did twenty years ago. Everything's ready."

Marianne frowned. "Why can't the prisoner just escape on his own?"

"He's too weak. He's been confined for years, and his health is poor." Valette's eyes were smoke and shadows. "This needs someone small and agile and fearless. Someone like you."

Marianne's heart gave a pathetic little leap at his compliment, even though it was blatant manipulation. She sighed. "What do I have to do?"

CHAPTER 13

"*I*t's impossible." Marianne tossed Latude's book onto the table.

Valette looked up from his wine. He'd apparently managed to find an unbroken wineglass in one of the cupboards. The man had the luck of the devil.

"Stop whining. Everything's ready for you. Latude even had to make his own rope. It took him months. He and his cellmate unraveled all his linen into individual threads, then reworked it into fourteen hundred feet of cord to make two ladders—one thirty feet long, the other a hundred and eighty feet long.

"He also removed four iron bars that blocked the way up the chimney with only a small piece of metal and his own spit. After making it onto the roof and scaling down the tower, he then bored a hole in the outer wall over the course of nine hours while chest-deep in water, all the while eluding the half-hourly guards who passed by only fifteen feet away."

"I'm not whining," Marianne growled. "I just won't do it. There are too many things that can go wrong."

His challenging look set her hackles up. "Latude did it."

"Latude was lucky. And insane. You know why he was imprisoned in the first place?" She slapped the cover of the book. "I read it in the introduction. He sent a box of poisoned powder to Madame de Pompadour then pretended to discover the 'plot' to assassinate her. Only he was found out." She placed her hands on her hips and glared at him across the table. "It's suicide."

"Don't be silly."

"If it's so simple, why don't *you* do it?"

"I didn't say it was going to be easy. And it's obvious why I need you." He glanced down at his chest and then up at her. "Look at me, *chérie*. And look at you. Do we look the same size and shape?"

An unwelcome heat rose up in her chest. She'd thought of little else all afternoon while she'd been squashed against him in the cart. How different they were, and yet how they fitted together in the most intriguing ways. She was small and supple. He was muscled and hard. Her mouth went dry. What would his skin feel like under her fingertips? Against her tongue? She resisted the urge to bang her forehead onto the table. She was going mad. Just like Latude.

"Which bit is bothering you?" he asked calmly.

His patient tone made her want to strangle him. *Your chest,* she thought angrily. *Your hands, your arms, your whole* body *is bothering me.*

"Oh," she said, practically dripping sarcasm, "what could possibly be bothering me? It's only an impregnable fortress with walls six feet thick and a hundred and eighty feet high. That's not even counting the outer wall and the twenty-foot-wide moat filled with water. Or the guards patrolling the grounds."

He smiled and raised his glass is a silent toast. "You're such a pessimist, *ma chère*. Always a dark cloud to shadow your silver lining." He leaned back in the chair. "Think of your sister, if you need motivation."

Marianne frowned at the subtle threat. "I *am* thinking of her. I'll be no good to her if I'm dead." She narrowed her eyes. Valette had said he couldn't do the job without her. That gave her leverage. She crossed her arms over her chest. "All right then. I'll do it. But I want something in return for risking my life."

He raised his brows in silent question.

"Only this one job. And then Sophie and I will be free, under no further obligation to you. You'll renounce all claim to both of us. Forever."

She held her breath as he studied her, his head tilted, his intense gaze impossible to read.

And then he drained his wine and stood abruptly. "Agreed."

Marianne narrowed her eyes, feeling inexplicably cheated even though she'd got her own way. Was that what he'd intended all along? And could she take his word? It seemed unlikely. The man was as trustworthy as a bag full of snakes.

He strode past her and out into the hall. "Come on. It's time for bed."

Her heart rate doubled. The idea of having to share a roof with him in this isolated spot was disturbing, to say the least.

A huge staircase with wrought-iron supports curved gracefully up to the higher floors. Valette made his way up, his fingers leaving parallel lines in the dust on the wide stone banister. Marianne followed, feet dragging on the stairs, then froze in the doorway of the room he'd entered.

"Oh! I thought it would be empty," she said stupidly.

A huge tester bed stood in solitary splendor in a pillared alcove, a swathe of material falling from a gilt crown above the headboard. Other pieces of furniture were covered in dustcloths; white shrouded shapes in the gloom, like squatting ghosts.

Her heart sank. Bedrooms and Valette were a dangerous combination.

"Spies don't need ballrooms. They do, however, need somewhere to sit and sleep." He whipped back a sheet and sent up a cloud of dust, revealing an elegant gilt wood sofa with pale pink satin cushions, which looked ridiculously feminine next to his tall, masculine frame. Those spindly legs would probably collapse if he sat on it. He pulled off more cloths and, like a magician, uncovered chairs, a washstand, and an inlaid chest of drawers with gilt-metal handles. A satisfied smile curved his mouth. "We'll sleep here tonight."

Marianne sneezed. "We? I'm not sleeping with you! I want my own room."

He bent and evicted a family of mice from the coal scuttle. She watched impassively as they raced along the skirting and found their way out of the door. If he expected her to scream and jump on the furniture, he'd be disappointed. Mice didn't bother her. She'd dealt with far worse rodents in Paris, in both animal and human forms.

He turned away to inspect the chimney. "You seem to be forgetting, I've *bought* you. That means you'll sleep wherever I tell you to." His voice was silky, implacable.

She swallowed her outrage at his high-handed attitude. He'd "bought her" with a fake bank draft for a thousand francs, but it didn't seem wise to point that out now. For the moment, at least, she was completely at his mercy.

"It means," he continued ruthlessly, "that if I tell you to strip naked and get in that bed, you'll do it, no questions asked."

Her heart rate doubled at the determined gleam in his eye. She backed up a pace. "I most certainly will not!"

He shot her a sly, sideways glance. "Come now. Don't pretend you've any maidenly sensibilities left to preserve. Not after your time in the brothel."

"I'll sleep on the floor," she said stubbornly, crossing her arms. "You can have the bed. You'll need something soft for those pampered, aristocratic bones of yours."

"No one's sleeping on the floor."

"Why not? I've done it before." *And worse.* She'd slept underneath a hedge, once, on her way to Paris. A floor was a luxury.

"We're sharing the bed." His tone brooked no arguments. He

stripped off his jacket and laid it over the back of a chair, then tugged the cravat from around his throat. "I need some sleep, and you need to be rested for tomorrow."

"I can rest just fine on the floor," she persisted mulishly.

His eyes narrowed. "What do you think I'm going to do? Rape you?"

The blood drained from her face. He raked her body with a coolly appraising inspection that managed at once to be both insulting and derisive. His gaze flicked dismissively over the swell of her breasts and the juncture of her thighs, his expression making it abundantly clear that he was neither impressed nor tempted by what he was seeing. "I think I can keep my hands off you for one night," he drawled.

Marianne wanted to sink into the floor. He was used to the most glamorous and sophisticated women in Europe. Of course he wasn't going to rape her, despite what he'd done back at the Montausier. He'd been playing a role there, nothing more. He was no more attracted to her than he was to his horse, *thank God.*

Her heart squeezed painfully, but she set her lips and gave a long-suffering sigh, as if being forced to sleep next to danger-ously attractive strangers was a regular, *inconvenient* occurrence in her life. "Fine. But make sure you stay on your own side of the bed."

He disappeared into the adjoining dressing room.

Marianne sank gratefully onto the edge of the bed and began unlacing her boots but glanced up as he reappeared in the doorway.

"Here. You can have this back if it makes you feel any better."

She caught the dagger from the air by reflex, her hand closing around the familiar contours of the grip.

"Feel free to stab me if I breathe in your direction," he said with an ironic smile.

She tightened her fingers, sorely tempted. The arrogant bastard was so sure of himself. She got under the covers fully clothed, slid the dagger beneath her pillow, and rolled over, using her shoulder as a barrier. She heard his muffled snort of amusement and the mysterious swish and rustle of clothing as he undressed.

Marianne squeezed her eyes shut, trying not to imagine him pulling his shirt off. Or unlacing his breeches. *Dieu,* did he sleep in the nude?

The mattress dipped as he slid in next to her. She tensed as every one of the tiny hairs on her body prickled with awareness. When she heard the rustle of fabric and realized he was still wearing his breeches and shirt. She released the breath she'd been holding.

His voice came from behind her, tinged with amusement. "Sleep, Marianne. You're safe tonight, I promise you."

Did that mean she was safe from him completely? Or that she was safe, but only for this one night? She shouldn't believe him, either way. He was a consummate liar. She would wait until he fell asleep, then slip out and make herself a pallet on the floor.

"Don't even think of running," he warned softly, reading her thoughts again with uncanny accuracy. "I'm a very light sleeper. If you try to leave, I'll know. And believe me, you won't like the consequences."

Marianne suppressed a shiver. It was no idle threat.

She tried to hold herself away from him, but it was impossible to stay rigid. The mattress was too soft, her muscles too tired. And the stress of the past twenty-four hours was finally taking its toll. Valette's smell enveloped her, disarmingly clean and pleasant, and she closed her eyes with a resigned sigh. The mattress shifted and she knew without looking that he was lying on his back with his arms tucked beneath his head.

The sheer impossibility of the plan he'd outlined swirled in her brain, potential pitfalls chasing themselves around and around until she thought she'd go mad. She forced her mind to empty, concentrated on nothing but breathing in and out, in and out, just as she did before she stepped out onto the wire. She could get through just one night.

"If you snore, I'll hurt you," she threatened sleepily.

She felt Valette's low chuckle of amusement through the mattress and tightened her grip on the knife. If he touched her, she'd use it. No question.

CHAPTER 14

$\mathcal{T}$he world was on fire.

Marianne was running through the inferno, screaming for her parents, Sophie, anyone, but no one answered. Flames chased her along the walls, licking and clawing like greedy, clutching fingers. Choking black smoke billowed along the ceiling. And the noise: a great sucking *whoosh!* like the roar of a hideous nightmare beast, drowning out her frantic cries.

The cotton of her nightdress burned her skin, her hair stuck to her sweaty cheeks. She raced into her parents' bedroom, came up against a wall of flame, and threw her arms up to shield her face. The paint on the walls was bubbling up, the flame changing color as it blistered and curled, little spurts of green and blue. Even the curtains were burning. They dripped flames like molten liquid—strangely, horribly beautiful.

Her skirts were alight. She beat at the flames, tried to scream, but managed only a broken croak. Terror clutched her chest as she tried to drag air into her burning lungs. Always the same helpless feeling. She was too slow. Too late to save them.

"Wake up."

The voice was gruff and urgent. Marianne fought, limbs

86

flailing even as she opened her eyes and sucked in great gasps of air: sweet and cold and clean. Her heart was racing, and she could hear her own shaky, panting exhalations as she tried to breathe normally. Reality intruded, and with it the leaden certainty that her parents were still dead. Each time she woke it hurt anew, even after all this time.

Strong hands were rubbing her back in a soothing rhythm. Valette. She was in his arms. She dragged in a shuddering, unsteady breath, clutched the front of his shirt to anchor herself to the present, even as the past receded. The scent of him gradually replaced the acrid smell of smoke in her nostrils. He was strong and solid and *real*.

He was crooning nonsense words into her hair, muffled reassurances. "It's all right, *bébé*. Come back to me. That's right."

Full awareness came to her in a flash. His shirt was open; her face was pressed to the hot, sleek muscles of his chest. The heartbeat under her cheek was slow and steady, a humiliating contrast to her own racing pulse. One of his hands stroked her back, and the other cradled her head, fingers tangled in her hair.

He pulled back and lowered his chin to look at her, smoothed the hair from her face. She avoided his gaze, too ashamed to meet his eyes, even in the shadowed room. How humiliating. She hated weakness, vulnerability. Hated showing it to anyone, especially him. At least she wasn't crying. Hers was a dry-eyed terror. Her tears had dried up in the flames.

Without a word he turned her within the shelter of his arms, rolling her over so that her back was to him. She gave a muttered protest, but he just pulled her fully against him, tucking her head under his chin and curving his strong body around hers.

Marianne closed her eyes as confusion and despair churned inside her. It was stupid to allow him to comfort her, wrong in so many ways. He was the architect of her current misery, not the remedy. She hadn't had this particular dream for almost a year. It was the sight of the burned-out stables that had brought it back tonight, she was certain.

She should slide her hand under the pillow and stab him while she had the chance.

But the simple comfort of being held was irresistible. She was so tired of being strong. Sophie always expected her to be the one to soothe her fears, make a decision, come up with a plan. It was strange to have someone comfort her, painfully alluring, even if it was only temporary.

She sighed. Relying on someone else was a weakness, but she was too exhausted, too emotionally drained to care. Tonight could be a truce. She'd go back to fighting him tomorrow.

"Go to sleep," he murmured into her hair. "You won't dream again tonight, I promise."

Marianne snorted softly. What a stupid thing to say. Such things were beyond even *his* legendary control. But what a lovely lie to believe.

* * *

SHE WOKE WITH A START. Remnants of her nightmare came back to her, but what had been so terrifying in the darkness seemed foolish in the clear morning light.

The bed beside her was empty. A pair of riding breeches and a white linen shirt lay on the chair, clearly meant for her. Her knives—all three of them—rested neatly on top. She checked beneath her pillow. Nothing but cool cotton. He must have removed that last one while she slept.

She *hated* that man.

The breeches were small and worn at the knees. She gave them a tentative sniff, remembering the greasy stable boy back at the posting inn, but they seemed clean enough, so she struggled into them and stashed the knives at the waistband, then shrugged on the shirt. It was too big, but she tucked it into the breeches as best she could.

The creak of floorboards in the adjoining dressing room made her freeze. She approached the doorway on silent feet, braced for danger, and stopped dead. Valette was shaving in front of a mirror, shirtless, his long legs clad only in snug brown breeches.

Her mouth went dry. He was long and lean, his hips considerably narrower than his broad, rippling shoulders. She'd accused him of being a pampered aristo, but those ropes of muscle proved he was no stranger to hard work.

He lathered his cheeks. The practiced way he unsnapped the razor—with such lethal economy of movement—was frightening. And mesmerizing. He drew the blade up his throat and over his jaw with a faint, audible scrape, tilting his head back to reach under his jaw. The triangular muscles on his side flexed over his ribs as he leaned forward and swirled the blade in the water.

A heat spread over her cheeks. She'd never seen a man shave before. It seemed strangely intimate. The faint stubble darkening his chin made him seem piratical, more dangerous. She wanted to reach out and touch. To see what those prickles would feel like against her palm.

She made a fist and squeezed her nails into her skin. What was *wrong* with her? She'd seen muscles before. The circus was full of sleek, toned acrobats and bulging strong men. None of *them* had made her fingers itch to . . . explore.

Something on his shoulder caught her eye. He had a drawing there, a design, inked onto his skin. It moved sinuously as he stretched. What was it? A ship? A face? It should have looked wrong—a blemish marring the perfection of his lean back—but somehow it enhanced rather than detracted.

"Seen enough? Or shall I strip off completely?"

His sarcastic comment made her jump. Her startled gaze met his in the mirror, and he leveled her an amused, knowing look.

"I'm sorry. I . . ."

He raised his brows.

"What's that?" She gestured helplessly at his back, abandoning any pretense that she hadn't been looking.

He glanced over his shoulder, as if he'd forgotten what was there. "A tattoo."

"Did it hurt?"

"Can't remember." He gave a shrug that set his muscles rippling again. "I got it in Portugal. Tony—my brother—and I got roaring drunk one night. We both got one." His rueful smile made him look almost boyish. "It seemed like a good idea at the time."

Marianne tried to imagine Valette young, drunk, and carefree. It seemed so unlikely. He had such consummate control. "What were you doing in Portugal?"

His expression clouded. "Fighting."

His curtness suggested she drop the subject, but she refused to take the hint, not when he was finally telling her something about himself. "And where's your brother now?" she asked brightly.

A muscle ticked in his jaw. "He's dead."

She winced. "I'm sorry."

"So am I," he said grimly.

He suddenly seemed to notice what she was wearing. His narrowed gaze slipped from her head to her bare feet and back up again. She smoothed down the front of the shirt, certain he was about to find fault with her appearance. "What?"

He narrowed his eyes accusingly. "You don't look much like a man."

She clasped her hands over her heart, feigning astonishment. "Is that a *compliment*? Be still, my beating heart!"

He frowned. "It's your hair. It's too long. You're never going to pass for a boy looking like that." He gestured with the razor. "Come here. We're going to have to cut it."

Her hands flew up instinctively to protect her head. "No!"

Her hair was one of the few things she actually *liked* about her appearance. She might not have Sophie's rounded, voluptuous figure or Marie's limpid blue eyes, but her hair was long and thick and slightly curly. Laurent was always complimenting her on it. It was the most feminine thing about her.

Valette shot her an impatient glance. "Stop being stupid."

Their eyes met and battled for a long moment.

"You promised me your full cooperation," he reminded her smoothly. "Don't forget whose men are watching your sister. I can have her returned to Duval in a heartbeat."

Bastard.

Marianne crossed her arms with a huff and turned her back to him. "Fine. Get on with it, then."

He stepped behind her, so close she could feel the heat of his bare chest through her shirt, could smell the faint, tangy scent of his shaving soap. Her heart began to pound. She held very still as he gathered her hair at the nape of her neck, his fingers rough and impatient. He twisted it, wrapped it around his fist, and pulled it taut, forcing her head back.

"Ouch!"

A strange, fluttering heat uncurled in her stomach. His touch was primal, animalistic. As if he were about to cut her throat. Or drag her over to the bed and ravish her. She didn't know which would be worse. She shivered as the cold metal touched the nape of her neck. This was how they'd prepared people for the guillotine, hacking off their hair so as not to interfere with the murderous blade. She imagined the hiss and thud of it, like a butcher's block and cleaver, the derisive jeers of the crowd. At least her parents had been spared that final indignity.

Severed strands tickled her shoulders as they fell to the floor, the sound like ripping silk. She squeezed her lids tightly closed, not wanting to see. Tears pricked her eyes. It was only hair. Stupid to get so upset about it. Why should she care about looking feminine anyway? It wasn't as if she *wanted* to encourage his attention. Or that of any man. The worse she looked, the better.

A single, betraying tear splashed onto the dusty wooden floorboards before she could catch it. Her eyes snapped open, and she gazed down at it in mortified horror.

Valette leaned over her shoulder and peered at the tiny black spot then gave an incredulous, unsympathetic snort. "Christ, woman. You're not crying over your *hair?*"

She swiped her eye with the back of her hand. "Of course not. I got some in my eye, that's all."

He caught her chin and forced it upward, then waited, cruelly patient, until she looked at him. His tawny eyes were unreadable. "It will grow back," he growled.

She pulled away. A glance in the mirror confirmed her worst fears: she looked a scrawny boy. *Which was exactly the point.*

"I hate it," she said dully.

"You're not supposed to *like* it."

Unfeeling bastard.

He angled his head, dismissing her. "Go and get some breakfast. I'll meet you on the roof."

CHAPTER 15

*M*arianne watched dolefully as Valette climbed out of the same window she'd used, jumped nimbly onto the stone balustrade, and swung up onto the flat part of the roof. She was grudgingly impressed by his agility. Especially since he was hauling a thick length of rope over his shoulder.

"We always seem to meet on rooftops."

As if she needed reminding.

"I like rooftops," she said coolly, turning back to her contemplation of the landscape. "I'm seldom disturbed."

In Paris, she used to climb up onto the roof of the theater at night and imagine that she was the only one awake. It was silly, of course; Paris was never truly asleep, at any time of night. Especially at the Palais Royale.

Valette smiled at her rudeness. She drew her knees up to her chest and rested her chin on them. "What are we doing up here?"

"You saw the plan. The prisoner's being held in the King's Pavilion at Vincennes. You have to escape from his room, scale down the outer wall, and rope walk across the moat to freedom."

"You make it sound so simple."

He ignored her sarcasm. "I've seen you rope walk. I want to see how you scale down a building." He stepped over to the side, peered over the low parapet, then turned and secured one end of the rope around a chimney. He threw the rest over the side. "Down you go."

Marianne glared at him. She rose and double-checked the security of his knots, pulling them tight and leaning back with her full weight to be certain they would hold.

He leaned back against the wall. "Don't you trust me, my sweet?"

"Let's just say I doubt you have as much interest in keeping me alive as *I* do." Satisfied with the knots, she peered over the side, gauging the distance to the ground. "This is very high."

"The prison walls are high," he reminded her.

"What if I fall?"

He crossed his arms over his chest. "Can you fly?"

"No." *If she were a bird, she'd fly back to Paris.*

"Then don't fall."

"That's your advice? *'Don't fall'?*"

He shot her an irritatingly composed smile. "Not dying is a very good incentive." He flicked a nonexistent speck of dust from his coat sleeve. "If you're caught, the consequences will be extremely unpleasant. There's no room for failure. And I certainly won't be risking my life to come and save you. If you make a mistake, you'll be on your own."

"Wonderful." Marianne slipped off her boots and stepped lightly up onto the balustrade. The warm updraft blew her hair back from her face, and she put her arms out to the sides, enjoying the familiar thrill of being up so high, embracing the feeling of invincibility.

She could see more of the countryside from up here. Undulating fields of vines and lush, wooded parkland stretched as far as the eye could see. Some distance away she could make out the dark wisp of smoke from a chimney. The sight made her feel slightly better. They weren't completely isolated from human habitation, then.

She curled her toes over the edge of the rooftop and balanced on the very edge, testing her nerve.

"I wish you wouldn't do that," Valette said calmly. "It makes me nervous."

"Really?" She laughed and went up on her tiptoes just to tease him. "What if I do this?"

He narrowed his eyes at her, unimpressed.

"Afraid I'll fall?" she taunted.

"No." His expression was deadpan. "Afraid I'll be tempted to push you."

She couldn't tell if he was joking or not. Just to be safe, she stepped back from the edge. "How have you managed to get rope into the prison anyway?"

He smiled, as if pleased by her curiosity. "It's been smuggled in. Every week, the prisoner receives a visit from a priest whose robes are secured by a twisted rope belt. When he arrives, his belt has three strands. When he leaves it only has one. The prisoner's woven the sections together to make one single rope that you will use."

"Any chance the prisoner was a rope maker in his previous life? Or a sailor?"

His lips twitched in amusement. "I'm afraid not. I told you, he's an aristocrat. A Royalist supporter imprisoned for his beliefs."

"So I'll be trusting my life to a rope made by an aristocratic invalid who hasn't done a single day's work in his life," she said sourly. "This just gets better and better."

She reached behind her, pulled the knives from her waistband, and handed them to Valette. He raised a brow and accepted them solemnly, as if the gesture were somehow symbolic. She narrowed her eyes at him in warning. "I'll expect those back when I'm done."

She picked up the rope, straddled it, and turned her back to the picturesque view. The rope pulled taut as she leaned backward over the edge and she eased her weight onto it cautiously, bracing her legs straight against the building. "See you at the bottom."

Despite her outward insouciance, her heart was hammering against her ribs. This was higher than she'd ever attempted before. She walked down the side of the building with her feet, holding the rope with her hands until she was clear of the balustrade, then crossed her ankles around the rope and began to lower herself down, hand over hand, as Laurent had taught her.

As soon as she'd gone a few feet she recognized the flaw in the plan. When Latude had escaped he'd done so with a friend who'd held the bottom of the rope steady while he descended. She didn't have that luxury. The rope started to twist and her shoulder bumped hard against the stonework. She let out a huff of pain. Desperate to get to the ground as quickly as possible, she loosened her grip and started a controlled slide down the rope.

Her palms began to burn with friction, and the insides of her thighs rubbed painfully against the hemp, but she managed to hold on. She landed on the ground with an unladylike thump and gasped out a prayer of relief. A heady sense of achievement filled her as she gazed upward at the distance she'd come.

She'd done it! Ha!

She wiped her shaking hands on her breeches, a smile of pure elation on her lips.

Valette's head and shoulders appeared over the parapet, his dark hair ruffled by the breeze. "Now come up and do it again," he called down.

Marianne gaped up at him in dismay. "*Again?* What was wrong with that time?"

"Nothing. But once isn't enough. You have to be perfect. Come on."

She headed for the open double doors that led back inside, kicking an undeserving flower on the way. *Infuriating man.* She should push *him* off the roof. See how *he* liked it.

CHAPTER 16

*A*fter making her climb down the rope three more times, during which Marianne vowed to stab him in his sleep and stamp on his worthless corpse, Valette allowed her to take a break for lunch.

She found apples, bread, and ham on the table in the kitchen and ate them alone in the sunshine on the steps of the terrace, grateful for the reprieve. She took her time, chewing each bite at least ten times, letting the warmth of the sun soothe her aching body and alternately wincing and cursing at the rope burns on her hands.

"How well can you ride?"

Valette's voice came from so close behind her she jumped. *Dieu!* She was good at sneaking around, but he'd elevated it to a whole new level. She turned from her perusal of the overgrown gardens and glared at him.

"I used to ride a lot when I was younger, but I don't do much at the circus except perform as an extra in some of the big set pieces. I leave the acrobatics to the trick riders."

The Cirque Olympique was famous for its equestrian spectacles, huge reenactments of famous battles, including one called the Courier of Saint Petersburg, in which riders displayed flags from all the countries conquered by the emperor as a tribute to his military victories. They hadn't performed that one for a while. Laurent would probably have to reinstate it now Napoleon was back, she thought bitterly.

A frown marred Valette's brow. "We'll be riding back to Paris after the escape. I'm not having you falling off and getting captured." He strode off, obviously expecting her to follow.

"*Please*, Marianne," she added sarcastically under her breath, "I would consider it the greatest honor if you would accompany me."

Honestly, would it kill the man to ask, *instead of just issuing orders? Autocratic pig.*

She had no choice but to chase him around the back of the house. Stones crunched under her feet as they traipsed between rows of unruly vines. Valette stole a handful of grapes and popped one in his mouth. She watched the way his jaw flexed as he chewed, the dip of his throat as he swallowed, and looked away. The *last* thing she needed was to be attracted to him.

He led her past the burned-out stables to a large building set apart from the main house; it looked like some kind of hothouse. Rows of tall windows ran along one entire wall, and sunlight glinted off the curved glass roof. Instead of flowers, however, the inside contained a huge oval equestrian training ring, similar to the one at the circus.

Marianne stood openmouthed, amazed at such luxury in a private residence. No wonder the emperor's cavalry had commandeered the place.

Bars of light slanted across the floor, and a neat wooden fence separated the arena from a small seating area on one side. Marianne took a deep breath, her fluttering nerves soothed by the familiar scent of warm earth and sawdust. It smelled just like the circus.

Two horses—neither one the ancient nag that had pulled the

cart—were tied to the railing. She glanced around, searching for a servant or a stable boy, but there was no one in sight. Marianne ground her teeth. *Of course he could make two horses materialize out of nowhere.* The man simply snapped his fingers, gave an order, and no matter how outrageous the demand, it was done without question.

"Let's see what you can do," he challenged softly.

She approached the smaller horse warily, careful not to startle it, and offered the flat of her hand. Its velvet muzzle lipped her fingers in welcome, hopeful for a treat. She swung herself up onto its back, wincing a little at the discomfort of the hard saddle on her already-tender inner thighs, and clucked the animal forward tentatively.

An hour later Marianne had reached the conclusion that Nicolas Valette was even more of a slave-driving perfectionist than all the Falconis put together. He treated her like one of Laurent's trick horses, forcing her to repeat maneuvers over and over again until they were flawlessly ingrained: endless mounting, dismounting, turning, stopping, figures-of-eight.

At first she'd wanted to impress him with her tenacity. Now she just wanted to stop. She'd been jolted and thrown about like a sack of flour. Sweat was trickling down her face and between her breasts. She'd fallen off twice. Her backside was going to be black and blue tomorrow.

She bit her lip. This was a battle of wills, and she would not bow down. Duval had tried to crush her spirit and failed. She'd be *damned* if she let Valette beat her.

Just when she thought the humiliating session was coming to an end, Valette removed the saddle from her horse and ordered her to ride bareback, with neither saddle nor stirrups, simply holding on to the horse's mane. The evil creature, sensing sport, cantered forward then stopped abruptly. Marianne slid off and hit the ground. Again.

Her involuntary groan of pain elicited not one ounce of pity from Valette. He made her remount and try again.

High-handed, bossy, insensitive, cruel . . . She contented herself with insulting him in time to the beat of the horse's hooves. After another half hour she'd fallen off twice more and was ready to kill someone. Namely Valette.

"Again!" He stood in the center of the arena, turning occasionally to watch her, and the clap of his hands was like the crack of a whip.

"If you clap your hands again, I swear I'll cut them off," she hissed on her way past him.

"I don't know what I'm more afraid of," he mocked, "your knives or your sharp tongue. Again!"

Marianne imagined one of her knives embedded in his heart. It was a lovely image.

"Again."

She forced herself not to scream. She hated that word. Hated that man. "*Dieu!* What did your last servant die of? Exhaustion?"

His diabolical chuckle followed her around the ring.

Her thigh muscles protested. Her back ached. Her palms were blistered. Her hair was sticking to her forehead in a hot, sweaty mess. He was driving her to the limits of her temper to see how much she could stand.

He clapped his hands. "Do it again," he ordered coolly.

Her control snapped. She yanked the horse's mane and it skidded to a stop, blowing heavily. "Why? I've done it ten times. And each time I've been perfect."

"You need to be able to do it even when you're angry and tired and distracted."

Marianne scowled. "I don't get distracted."

"Really?" he drawled. He strode over to the side and returned with two long, slim fencing blades that had been propped up against the wall. He handed one up to her and mounted the second horse, a glossy brown stallion that had been waiting impatiently while she practiced.

She was used to holding wooden prop swords. The Brave Cossack show ended in a full-scale battle complete with cannon, explosions, and the capture of a scenery château. Her personal favorite was Marzeppa and the Wild Horse of Tartary, a show that included not just choreographed fighting but also a zebra and a mechanical vulture, of all things.

This blade, however was steel, not wood, and so heavy it made her wrist ache just to keep it upright.

Valette rode to the far end of the arena, and she watched him through narrowed eyes. Lord Byron's fictional "Corsair" had been all the rage last year, despite the author's being English. Skinny Marie had been given a leather-bound translation by one of her many admirers, and since neither she nor any of the other girls at the Montausier could actually read, they'd begged Marianne to recite a few cantos whenever she visited. Everyone had declared themselves in love with the dashing pirate captain Conrad, who risked everything to rescue Gulnare, the chief slave in the Turkish pasha's harem.

They'd be in ecstasy over Valette, Marianne thought bitterly. His hair was mussed as though he'd just risen from bed, rumpled and irritatingly attractive; and his shirt molded to the hard planes of his chest. But Valette was no storybook hero. He was an unfeeling, emotionless monster, and she'd give *anything* to see him as ruffled and furious as she was.

He kicked his heels and, to her astonishment, set his horse charging straight at hers, as if they were in a medieval jousting tournament. Sunlight glinted off metal as he raised the sword high above his head and bore down on her like an avenging angel.

Her stomach somersaulted in alarm. She raised her arm to parry his blow, then thought better of it and ducked to the side at the very last moment instead. His blade glanced off hers with a hideous metallic scrape that reverberated down her whole arm.

She yanked her horse around, desperate to escape, but Valette was right alongside her. He steered his mount into hers as they galloped along. His hard thigh jostled hers, and she dropped her sword, almost losing her seat at the impact.

Fils de putain!

Marianne dipped her shoulder and bumped him back with a bone-jarring jolt. She heard him chuckle. He leaned over, grabbed the front of her shirt in his fist, and pulled her toward him so she was leaning precariously off the side of her mount. They were nose to nose.

Marianne shot a petrified glance at the ground, which was thundering past below her in a sickening blur. "You madman! What are you *doing?*"

His grin was diabolical. "Distracting you." His mouth crashed down on hers.

Before she could even think of punching him, he tightened his grip and hefted her clean off her horse. For a split second she marveled at how strong he must be.

And then he opened his fist and let her go.

CHAPTER 17

*M*arianne hit the floor hard.

She rolled instinctively, curling into a protective ball as the horse's thundering hooves missed her by mere inches. She lay stunned and panting in the dirt, her heart racing. Wood shavings stuck to her cheek and tangled in her hair. There were even some in her mouth. She spat them out in disgust and sat up cautiously, checking her body for injury. Finding none, she turned her attention to her persecutor. Fury boiled in her blood.

Of all the stupid, reckless, dangerous stunts!

"*Fils de putain!* I could have broken my neck!"

Valette galloped toward her, utterly unrepentant, and dismounted in one fluid movement. "'I don't get distracted,'" he mocked in a singsong voice.

Humiliated color stained her cheeks. She almost wished she *had* broken a bone, just to spite him. Let him complete his precious rescue mission *then*. "If you don't think I'm good enough, find someone else," she shot back. "Oh no, that's right, you *can't*. You want me here. You need me. So stop being such a bastard."

Valette was impervious to insult. "Get up. You look like a whipped puppy."

Marianne crawled forward and retrieved her sword from the dirt. She'd bitten her tongue; the salty taste of blood filled her mouth. She swiped at it with the back of her hand and pushed herself up, wincing as her bruised body protested. She *would not* plead with him to stop. She was no stranger to pain.

He assumed a readying stance, side-on, sword raised, effortlessly elegant. "Don't be shy. Attack me."

Her knees were buckling, but she stalked toward him, buoyed up by righteous fury. "With pleasure." She slashed at his chest.

He blocked her blade and thrust her away, and they circled warily. She tried again, but he countered with a neat sidestep.

"You're so fucking graceful!" he mocked. "This isn't ballet. You want to kill me, not dance with me." Their blades clashed again. "Show me some anger."

Marianne hit him again, harder. He was trying to rile her, and it was working. "Give me my knives, and I'll show you anger," she hissed. "Right through your miserable heart." She swung at his head, channeling all her pent-up resentment into the blow. Valette deflected it with an effortless flick of the wrist.

"A hundred francs says you can't draw my blood," he challenged.

She slashed again, pressing him back. "I don't have a hundred francs."

"Nor will you." He ducked her blade and stepped in close. That easily, he came under her guard. The tip of his sword settled in the hollow at the base of her throat. Cold steel pressed hot flesh. Marianne froze, tilting her chin up away from the deadly point, her pulse hammering in alarm.

They were so close she could feel the heat rolling off his body, could smell the clean, male scent of him in her nostrils. His gaze dropped to his mouth and then back up to her eyes. She couldn't seem to look away. Something dark and dangerous shimmered in the air between them, a moment of exquisite potential. Marianne stood completely still, certain he was about to lean in and kiss her.

And then he dropped his sword with a sideways swish and stepped back.

He stalked away a few paces, turned, and beckoned her forward again with an imperious flick of his fingers as if the intensity of the previous moment had never occurred.

Marianne released the breath she'd been holding.

"Again. Pretend I have your sister. She's so pretty," he taunted. "I want her. I'll have her, too, unless you can stop me."

He couldn't have calculated anything that would enrage her more.

She ran at him. "You won't touch her!"

He grabbed her arm, twisted, and flipped her onto the sawdust as easily as if she were a child.

Marianne scrambled up, red-hot fury bubbling in her chest. "You leave her alone, you bastard!"

She attacked again, and he knocked her over again, only this time he followed her down, kneeling beside her, imprisoning her wrists on either side of her head, pushing them down into the sawdust with a bruisingly tight grip. Marianne let out a howl of impotent fury.

"Stop letting anger cloud your judgment," he advised coolly. "And stop playing by the rules. There are no rules. The dirtiest fighter wins, every time. Do whatever you can to gain the advantage. Hit me in the balls. Gouge at my eyes. Dislocate my thumbs."

She arched her back, pushed her hips off the floor, but he didn't move an inch. She tried to head butt him, almost blinded by rage. He dodged out of the way with an irritating chuckle. "That's more like it."

When he stood, she lashed out with her legs. Her foot made very gratifying contact with his shin. He yelped and hopped backward, and she gave a satisfied hiss. She rolled and tried to sweep his feet from under him, but he jumped over her, and before she knew it she was facedown, his hand on the back of her head pressing her nose into the sawdust. He was on top of her, his strong thighs straddling her hips, his weight crushing her. He leaned over, his breathing harsh in her ear.

And suddenly it wasn't sawdust against her face. It was the linen of an unmade bed. She could smell sweat and garlic and wine. And it was Duval, not Valette, holding her down. Duval's cloying perfume making her gag.

Her skin felt like it was crawling with maggots. She tried to turn over, to thrust him off her, but he was so much stronger, so much heavier. She couldn't breathe. She heard someone whimpering, sobbing, pleading incoherently. The suffocating darkness rushed up to swallow her.

And then the crushing weight was gone. Strong hands rolled her over onto her back. Marianne dragged in a choking breath as the world came back into focus. Wood shavings on the dirt floor. A horse's hooves. And Valette, kneeling at her side, his face inscrutable.

"Breathe."

She shuddered as the horror receded and humiliation took its place. Ignoring his outstretched hand, she sat up and lowered her forehead to her bent knees. "Go away."

Her voice was shaking, like her hands. She rolled her shoulder to brush him off, and he finally took the hint, rising to his feet and stepping back. She heard the crunch of his boots as he paced away.

Her relief was short-lived. He returned a few minutes later and thrust a glass of water under her nose. *Why couldn't he just leave her alone? Hadn't he tormented her enough?*

"Drink it," he ordered curtly.

She took the glass with trembling hands, took a dutiful sip, then set it down in the sawdust. He lowered himself down next to her.

"Who hurt you, Marianne?"

She shook her head. "No one. I don't want to talk about it."

"Tell me."

Marianne squeezed her eyelids shut. Her temples were throbbing. God, he was like a terrier, never letting go once he had his teeth in something. She supposed she owed him an explanation. After her nightmare last night, and now this, he must think she was a raving lunatic.

Which would be a *good thing,* she reminded herself sternly. Perhaps if he thought she was unhinged, he'd use someone else for his stupid rescue attempt.

She took a shuddering breath. "When our parents died, Sophie and I were sent to our only living relative. A cousin in Paris. One night, soon after we arrived, he came to the bedroom Sophie and I shared. He was drunk. I could smell it on him." Her lips felt numb. "He said our father had been involved in a plot to overthrow Napoleon and if we didn't do as he told us, he'd denounce us as the daughters of a traitor."

"What happened?" Valette asked quietly.

"He said we had to prove how grateful we were."

Marianne opened her eyes and focused on her hands. The pale line of a scar ran over one knuckle where she'd nicked herself during an early knife practice. She didn't want to see Valette's face. Didn't want to see the disgust creep into his expression when he learned of her depravity.

"I agreed. So he'd leave Sophie alone. She was only ten."

"You can't have been much older." Valette's voice was cool, emotionless, as if he knew she couldn't cope with gentleness or pity. She would shatter into a thousand tiny pieces. "How old were you?"

"Fourteen." She stared straight ahead, seeing nothing. "He took me to another room, at least, so Sophie couldn't see. He stripped me." Her voice came out a strangled whisper. A soul-deep shudder ran through her. She yanked a thread from the knee of her breeches and twisted it round and round her finger. "I told myself I wouldn't struggle. I'd just take my mind away somewhere else. He could have my body, but I wouldn't let him touch my soul." She felt her lips twist in bitter recollection. "But he didn't want that. He *wanted* me to fight. He kept goading me, telling me how he was going to have Sophie, too. How he'd have his men hold me down so I'd have to watch."

She dragged in another choppy breath. "I fought him then. He slapped me so hard I fell off the bed and hit my head on the grate. I bit him, but he pinned me down. He—"

"He what . . . ?" Valette prompted harshly. "He raped you." It was a statement, not a question.

Marianne shook her head. "No! He tried, but . . ." She forced the words out in a rush before she could change her mind. "He couldn't get hard."

There, she'd said it. The ultimate humiliation. She dropped her head back onto her knees.

The silence was awful, damning. She wanted to bite off her tongue. Shame crawled through her veins like spiders, then anger welled up, too: a dark, hard knot in her chest. "He blamed me. Said I wasn't woman enough for any man to want to fuck."

When Valette said nothing, she forged on, determined to have it all out now that she'd started. "I grabbed a vase from the nightstand and hit him with it. It cut him, here, on the chin." She indicated the place on her own face. "He still has the scar to remind him." Her eyes narrowed in brief, bitter satisfaction. "It knocked him out. When he came round, I swore that if he ever touched Sophie or me again, I'd cut his throat. He realized I wasn't bluffing."

She hugged her knees. "We came to an arrangement. I'd find a job, do whatever other 'errands' he asked of me, as long as he stayed away from Sophie."

Her stomach churned as she waited for Valette's condemnation. Would he pity her? Blame her? Revile her? She tensed as he shifted his weight. *Why on earth had she told him so much?* She'd never told anyone what had happened, not even Sophie. And now she'd bared her soul, laid herself open to his criticism and his distain. *Idiot.*

She flinched in surprise as he cupped her chin with his fingers and turned her face toward him. His eyes were dark, fathomless. "Who did this to you? Your cousin's name, Marianne."

"Duval."

Valette merely nodded. He stood, brushed off his breeches, and stalked out of the arena without a backward glance.

CHAPTER 18

*M*arianne took herself for a walk in the overgrown gardens. She dreaded having to face Valette, the inevitable censure in his face, but there was no other choice. He was like those exotic spotted cats they kept at the circus; show any fear, and they'd attack. Control was everything. She'd simply pretend her humiliating lapse hadn't happened.

As if she hadn't admitted to him what she'd never told another living soul.

He was pinning playing cards to one of the wooden columns that ringed the arena when she plucked up the courage to return. He'd put his coat back on, she noticed. It made him even more remote and unapproachable than ever.

She quelled her nerves and affected a bored, long-suffering sigh. "*Now* what?"

He offered her throwing knives to her. "Considering your lack of skill with a sword, I thought we'd try a weapon you're supposed to be good at."

She bristled at his insulting tone and snatched up the blades, profoundly grateful that he didn't seem to want to discuss her

earlier confession, either. Irritation was much better than mortification.

The feel of the knives in her hands bolstered her confidence.
She could defend herself, even if she lacked his skills with a
sword. *These* blades she could handle. That night Duval attacked
her, she'd understood how defenseless she really was.

"Your target's the king of spades," Valette said coolly.

Trying to ignore his distracting presence, Marianne took
careful aim and threw. The knives bit into the wood one after
another, the familiar *thunk-thunk* soothing to her ragged nerves.
She marched forward, jerked them out, and took her position
again, farther back.

Valette studied his fingernails. "Again."

She imagined him as the king of spades. *Thwack!* The first tip
pierced his throat. *Thwack.* Right through the heart. *Thwack!* The
last one decapitated him. Let him find fault with *that.* Her aim
was perfect. She suppressed a smile.

"You still haven't told me who I'm risking my life to rescue,"
she said over her shoulder.

"Does it matter? I told you, he's a political prisoner, unjustly
detained."

"Of course it matters!"

He smiled at her evident frustration. "Come now. Surely your
revolutionary little soul believes in '*liberté, egalité,* and *fraternité*'?"

Marianne narrowed her eyes.

"And shouldn't that 'freedom, equality, and brotherhood'
extend to *everyone,* whatever their background?" he continued
smoothly.

She bit her lip. Freedom was a concept she held very dear,
especially considering how little of it she had herself. Who was
she to deny anyone that same basic right?

"The person we're rescuing is citizen Louis-Charles Capet.
Previously known as Louis-Charles de Bourbon, Prince Royal of
France."

Marianne gave a disbelieving snort. The beast clearly wasn't going to tell her. "You've been reading too many fairy tales, monsieur," she said tartly. "He died in prison the year I was born."

"What if he didn't?" Valette said, straight-faced. "What if Napoleon didn't want any stray Bourbons hanging around as a rallying point for Royalist supporters? What if even *he* baulked at killing an innocent child, and had Fouché fake the prince's death and hide him away, first at the Tour in Paris, and later at Vincennes?"

Marianne studied his face. When people lied, they usually had a tell, some minute tic that betrayed them. Henri, for example, always looked down to the left whenever he had a good hand of cards. It was why he'd stopped playing piquet with her. Valette, however, gave nothing away. His face was as serene and unreadable as a mask. The dratted man was so conniving he could probably sell sand to a Bedouin. Marianne made a mental note *never* to play cards with him.

"Fine, don't tell me," she huffed.

He held out his hand for a blade. "May I?"

She raised her brows in surprise.

"Reading my fortune?" he mocked when she didn't immediately comply.

"Yes. I see pain and humiliation in your very near future." She slapped a knife into his palm. "Aim straight, keep your elbow up—"

"Queen of hearts," he interrupted. In one deft movement he flipped the blade end over end and caught it again, testing its weight and balance. Before she could even register surprise at his dexterity, it whistled out of his hand. *Thunk.*

Marianne strode forward to inspect the column, her eyes widening in disbelief. Right in the center of the queen of hearts. *Sang de Dieu.* Was there anything this man did badly?

"Why are we even doing this?" she growled.

"I need to know you can defend yourself if the need arises. Have you ever killed anyone?"

She gave an appalled shudder. "No! Of course not. I couldn't. No matter *how* annoying they might be," she added pointedly.

His jaw hardened. "I have. And you'll learn. Try again. From farther back."

Marianne took five more paces backward and narrowed her eyes in concentration. Valette took up position slightly behind her, hovering near her shoulder. The spicy scent of him tickled her nose, made it hard to concentrate. She was intensely aware of him, so close.

The first two knives hit their mark with satisfying accuracy. But just as she threw the last one he deliberately jolted her elbow. The knife clattered uselessly off the pillar and onto the floor.

Marianne whirled around. "Hey! That's *cheating!*"

His fingers clamped around her upper arms like a vice. "There's no such thing as cheating in war. No honor. No code of conduct. There's only living or dying. It's that simple."

He gave her a shake, as if to underline his words, and she flinched away from the bleak bitterness in his face. "The sooner you learn that, the safer you'll be," he growled. He gave her arms a squeeze as if to impress his point, then released her abruptly and turned away, shaking his head. "Christ. I don't know what the hell I was thinking."

Fury rose up like a scalding ball in her chest. He didn't think she had the guts to hurt someone? Duval had made the same mistake.

He was so dictatorial. So overbearing. So *annoying. He was . . .* almost at the door.

In one swift motion, almost without thought, Marianne bent down, scooped up a knife, and threw. The blade pinned Valette's sleeve to the doorframe with a sickening thud, and she froze in sudden, belated horror.

You stupid, impetuous idiot! What have you done?

A cold trickle of panic slid down her spine. In the hideous silence that followed she could hear the snorting of the horses, the chirping of the birds outside, her own heartbeat thundering in her ears.

He was going to kill her.

Valette bent his head, coolly inspected his sleeve, and glanced at her over his shoulder.

"Better," he said softly.

Marianne could only stare at him in astonishment.

He reached across his body with his free hand and pulled the knife from the wood with a horrible splintering sound. He held the blade out to her, hilt first, like a peace offering. Or a challenge. The corner of his mouth curled upward. "You've ruined my coat. I'll send you a bill."

She swallowed, her eyes drawn to the trickle of red that ran down the back of his hand and dripped onto the sawdust.

She'd only meant to plant the thing in the doorframe as a warning not to underestimate her. A hot wave of shame rolled over her, but she absolutely refused to feel guilty. It served him right. She shouldn't have lost her temper, admittedly, but it was still *his* fault. He'd goaded her into it. Marianne backed away to the opposite door—an unmistakable retreat—even as her stubborn pride demanded she have the last word. She tilted her chin at his hand.

"I drew your blood, Valette. That's a hundred francs you owe me."

And then she turned and ran.

CHAPTER 19

*M*arianne raced back to the house and up the stairs. She heard the kitchen door slam and held her breath, certain Valette would follow her up, but when long minutes passed with no sign of him, she heaved a sigh of relief and collapsed onto the bed.

Her heart was still pounding, and she felt vaguely sick. She couldn't believe she'd lost her temper so completely. She'd never in her life thrown one of her knives in anger. She pressed an arm across her clammy forehead. Valette was the most aggravating man on the planet. And definitely not the sort of man to let an incident like that go unpunished. No doubt he was already devising some hideous retribution.

She washed in the tepid water from the pitcher as the light faded from the sky. Suddenly uneasy in a house so full of shadows and creaking floorboards, and decidedly hungry, she ventured back downstairs. She had to face Valette sometime. And skulking in her room hinted at cowardice.

A welcoming fire crackled in the kitchen's huge hearth, and a candle flickered on the table. Valette was inspecting the padlock on a door set into the far wall. He'd wound a fresh white bandage around his forearm. Marianne glanced up guiltily and caught his sardonic expression.

"Admiring your handiwork?" he asked sweetly.

She bit her lip.

"Bring the candle over here," he ordered. Marianne complied.

He reached into his coat and withdrew a small leather pouch. It unrolled to reveal a set of sleek metal instruments with oddly shaped ends, like the tools of a surgeon. He offered it to her. "Would you like to do the honors?"

When Marianne frowned, he gestured impatiently at the padlock. "Go on. Pick it."

"I don't know how."

"Of course you do. I know all the jobs you've done, remember. Plenty of them required picking a lock."

Marianne raised a haughty brow. "Your information's inaccurate."

"What about the Loyelle job? I *know* that was you."

She couldn't help it; she smiled, even though it was incriminating. Stealing from Monsieur Loyelle had been extremely satisfying. The vicious pimp had lived on the sixth floor, in attic rooms. She'd had to climb up to the rooftop, scale down the outside wall on a rope, open his window, find the safe hidden beneath his bed, then escape the same way, only in reverse.

"How did you get into his safe if you didn't pick it, eh?" Valette persisted. "You didn't force it. I saw the crime scene. There was no sign of foul play."

"Monsieur Loyelle was with Skinny Marie at the Montausier that night. He's one of her regulars. He keeps the key to his safe around his neck. Marie gave him plenty to drink, tired him out with an energetic bout of lovemaking, and took it while he was asleep. She slipped it to me. After the job I returned it to her and she put it back round his neck. He never suspected a thing." She took a perverse pleasure in Valette's obvious dismay.

"Shit. You're not joking, are you?"

She smiled, utterly unapologetic. "Sorry."

He swore again. "You can't ride. You can't fight." He glared at her. "You're not worth even *half* the amount I paid for you."

Her face heated. How dare he insult her lack of skills? "Don't blame me. I didn't ask for this. *You* kidnapped *me*, remember?"

Valette pushed back his hair with an impatient hand and sighed. "For someone who lives in constant threat of being manacled by the gendarmes, I'd have thought you'd know how to pick a lock. Watch and learn, then."

He selected one of the metal tools, placed it between his teeth, and pushed another into the lock. He jiggled his wrist, tilting his head to listen, then took the thin instrument out of his mouth and inserted it into the lock above the first one.

He glanced up at her. "Admit it, you thought I was another useless, talentless aristo, didn't you?"

"No," Marianne lied. "But it's good to see you have some skills besides kidnapping and extortion."

"There's not a lock in Europe I can't open, given the right tools."

"Modest, too," she sneered.

"This is a basic spring and tumbler. Maybe one day I'll round off your criminal education by teaching you how to pick it."

She held the candle farther to the side so he could see more clearly. "There isn't going to be a 'one day,' Valette. As soon as this job's done, I'm going straight back to Sophie. You promised me freedom. If you think I'm going to become one of your agents, you're sadly mistaken."

He dismissed her denial with a shrug and slotted another sliver of metal in the keyhole. "You know, locks are like women. Utterly infuriating. They shut you out. If you try to force them, they resist you with all their might. One has to be gentle, coax them to reveal their secrets." He slanted her a wicked glance.

He wasn't coaxing any more secrets out of her. She'd told him more than enough already.

Marianne rolled her eyes. "Oh, this is priceless. Do tell me more about your women-are-like-locks theory. I can't wait."

He smiled at her sarcasm. "Each lock has its own little quirks. A few yield to brute force, but most are more subtle. You need to apply pressure in just the right places—a touch here, a flick there."

She couldn't help it. She looked at his hands. Such deft, capable hands. His wrist was strong and tanned next to the white of his shirt, and a sprinkling of dark hairs was just visible above the cuffs. Heat rose up her throat. The damned man could even manage to make *housebreaking* sound like flirtation. He was an utter menace.

"Of course," he continued, "the more complex the mechanism, the greater the satisfaction when it finally surrenders." He glanced up, his expression devilish. "It's so nice to come across something hard to crack."

He meant her, she was certain. She put one hand on her hip. "Well, I have a theory about men, too."

He raised a brow.

"They're like the Seine. Full of shit."

He shook his head with a chuckle. "You're far too young to be so cynical. Have a little faith." The lock clicked.

He gave a satisfied grunt, and the door opened with a blast of frigid air. A set of steps descended into a stygian darkness, and Marianne took an involuntary step back as the hairs on her arms lifted.

"What's down there?"

He smiled at her obvious reluctance. "The marquis's wine cellars."

"How do you know?"

His smile was ironic. "Spy, remember? I'm good at ferreting out secrets." He took the candlestick from her hand and started down the stairs. "Come on."

The candle's feeble glow was swallowed by the yawning

blackness, and Marianne hastened after him, careful not to get too close to his broad back. She braced herself for bats to start flitting out from the gloom.

The cellar was a huge underground expanse with an arched and vaulted ceiling, like a cave. The light flickered over row upon row of shelves that seemed to go on forever, stretching back into the darkness on all sides like a regiment of soldiers. Each shelf contained what looked to be hundreds of bottles of wine. Her mouth fell open as she did some swift mental calculation. There must be an absolute *fortune* down here!

Valette went to explore a neatly stacked row of wooden barrels. Each lay on its side, bound with metal hoops and stamped with stenciled letters. He tapped one lightly with his knuckles. "French oak. They toast the inside of the barrel over a flame to lightly char it. It adds a subtle flavor to the wine."

"Fascinating," Marianne drawled. "Next time I'm at a fancy soirée I'll be sure to mention it to my hostess."

He made a face at her sarcasm and crossed to inspect the racks of bottles, stopping every now and then to read a dusty label. The candle's glow threw his features into sharp relief, a sublime juxtaposition of darkness and light, like a Renaissance masterpiece.

No. There was nothing angelic about him. He was a demon from hell, sent to torment her.

He finally selected two bottles, blew on them to dislodge the dust, and returned to the steps. Marianne followed him with a grateful sigh, glad to escape the oppressive darkness.

CHAPTER 20

*T*he comparative warmth of the kitchen was extremely welcome. Valette placed the bottles on the table and ruffled his hair to dislodge a dusting of cobwebs. It fell back, perfectly mussed, as usual.

Marianne almost snarled. How *did* he manage to look so effortlessly elegant? It was beyond irritating. No doubt lesser mortals spent hours with pomade and hair oils to emulate that exact careless style. One lock fell over his brow, giving him the air of a disreputable pirate prince, as gorgeous and corrupt as Lucifer himself.

Her heart gave a funny little lurch. After the things she'd endured with Duval she'd have staked her life on never finding a man attractive, let alone a man as ruthless and demanding as Valette. And yet her insides tingled at the sight of him. It was disturbing, to say the least.

"How do you suppose we open these without a corkscrew?"

"You're the spy," she mocked. "I thought you had all the answers." She offered him one of her knives, hilt first, and he used it to push the corks into the bottles.

"One white and one red. I didn't know which you'd prefer, so I brought one of each."

Marianne narrowed her eyes, instantly suspicious of his affability. Was he trying to charm her into forgetting his perfidy? Or did he plan to humiliate her in some other way?

Indeed, everything around him was conspiring to create an atmosphere conducive to seduction. The candle's glow narrowed the huge, drafty kitchen to an intimate circle enclosing them both. The warm-honey smell of the beeswax was so much more pleasant than the stench of the cheap tallow used all over Paris. Tallow was animal fat and smelled vile, somewhere between roasted meat and refuse. It always made her feel sick.

"I don't know anything about wine," she said flatly, determined not to be drawn in. "I hardly ever drink."

"Well, considering how good these are, that would be an unforgivable sin. The marquis, God rest his soul, had exquisite taste. These are both exceptionally fine years."

He'd found four stemmed glasses in one of the kitchen cupboards. One had a piece missing from the foot, another a chip on the rim, but they were serviceable enough. No doubt he'd be able to produce a tray of bonbons and a pitcher of ice water in the middle of the Sahara desert, if he so desired, she thought waspishly. He could probably click those long fingers of his and a genie would appear, ready to serve his every whim. A genie and a harem.

He poured the red wine into two glasses then reached into his pocket and slapped a hundred franc note down on the table between them. "Never let it be said that I don't honor my debts." He raised his glass in a jaunty toast. "To the Marquis de la Garde."

Marianne raised her own glass and touched it to the rim of his with a little clink. "To the mission," she said pointedly. "May it soon be over."

Valette took a sip and closed his eyes with a heartfelt groan. When she didn't immediately follow suit, he shot her a mocking glance. "Stop looking like I'm about to poison you." He took another swallow. "I wouldn't ruin such good wine with arsenic."

Marianne studied him from across the table, resentment simmering in her blood. He looked sinful and decadent and utterly delectable. Why had he suddenly decided to turn his legendary charm on her? Was he bored? Were two nights without a warm, willing woman in his bed too much for him to endure? Well, it would be a cold day in hell before she offered herself to him in *that* way. It wasn't *her* he wanted. Any willing female would do. The man would probably flirt with a tree stump if there were nothing else around.

"You like wine." She made it a statement, not a question.

"I *love* wine," he amended, leaning back in his chair and crossing his legs in front of him. "If I hadn't been a spy, I'd have been a vintner. Growing my own vines, pressing my own grapes. Imagine the satisfaction of producing something so exquisite."

He shot her that speculative look she now recognized meant he was about to say something outrageous. "Wines are fascinating." He rolled the stem of the glass between his fingers, tilting it so the liquid swirled around, coating the sides of the glass. "Each has its own subtle taste, its own distinctive personality."

She held up a hand. "Wait! I sense another of your priceless 'women are like . . .' theories coming on."

"Not at all." He smiled. "Although, now you mention it, the idea holds definite possibilities. I'll have to give it some thought." He tapped the bottle. "This is a Romanée-Conti, the most noble of Pinot Noirs." He took a sniff. "The domaine belonged to the Prince of Conti before it was seized during the Revolution and sold off. One of Napoleon's generals owns it now." He took a sip. "Mmm. Rich, fruity, almost peppery. Can you taste it?"

Marianne took a large gulp. It burned down the back of the throat. "I suppose so."

He looked aghast. "Not like that! Take a small sip. Hold it in your mouth, on your tongue. Now breathe in. Draw the air over it. Let the vapor fill your mouth."

She tried, but unlike him, made an embarrassing slurping noise. A dribble of wine escaped the corner of her mouth.

He reached across the table and wiped her chin with his thumb then brought it to his own mouth and sucked it clean. Heat curled low in her stomach. The beast was doing it deliberately, of course. Clearly he'd decided she was going to be the entertainment tonight. This must be the punishment he'd concocted. Death by overheating.

"Now swallow," he said gently.

She obeyed. The wine warmed her chest and down into her belly.

He picked up the second bottle and poured them each a fresh glass. "This is a Sauternes. Château D'Yquem." He pronounced it *dee-kem*. "What do you taste?"

She took a reluctant sip. All descriptive ability fled under his expectant gaze. "Um. Flowers?" she said weakly.

He looked disappointed. Pained, even.

She tried again. "It's, uh, sweet . . ." Words failed her. Embarrassed, she stared at the bottle, fixing on the tawny amber-gold color of the wine. It was precisely the same color as his eyes. She'd probably never be able to look at another bottle of the stuff without thinking of him. *Damn him.*

He tilted his head back. "This isn't just wine. It's ambrosia. One of life's sublime experiences." He took a mouthful and sighed appreciatively. "Smooth and subtle. Intense yet fragrant." The look he slanted her from under his lashes made her pulse quicken.

He leaned back in his chair. His evident pleasure was inviting, alluring. She watched the movement of his throat as he swallowed and clamped her lips together against the urge to press them against that tawny skin. He was a fiend. And she was immune.

"Feel the smoothness on your tongue. Can you taste orange marmalade? Caramel? Honeysuckle? They're all there, if you concentrate."

How on earth could simple words be so seductive? It was only a shopping list. He made it sound like poetry. He could probably describe the Parisian sewerage system and turn it into a sonnet. She took another, slower sip, then another. Now he'd pointed them out, she *could* discern the different flavors. Sort of.

He was watching her over the rim of his glass with half-closed eyes, sated and lazy, like a well-fed cat. One that was still contemplating the possibility of dessert. Well, it wasn't going to be *her*. She licked her lips, supremely conscious of his regard. Her skin felt flushed. Could the wine have affected her so quickly?

He studied her in breathless silence. Slowly, so slowly she could have pulled away, he put his wineglass down and leaned across the table. She stilled, her heart beating wickedly fast. Something wild and primitive throbbed in her veins. He was going to kiss her. He would taste of the wine. Powerful and intoxicating.

And far too tempting.

She stood abruptly, her chair grating harshly on the flagstones, and grabbed the hundred franc note from the table. "I'm going to bed."

He accepted her retreat with no more than a cool nod. "I've cleared the chamber next to mine. You can sleep in there. No more sharing beds."

Relief. It was relief she felt, not disappointment. She was here to do a job, and nothing more.

Despite her utter exhaustion, she slept fitfully, alert for every scrape and sigh beyond the interconnecting door. When she finally rose, bleary-eyed, and pushed back the shutters, it was to see Valette already dressed, pacing the dewy grass in the formal gardens below. He had the look of a fighter about him. Still elegant, but impatient, constrained, with an implicit threat of deadliness.

Had he ever fought a duel over some matter of principle? Or over a lady's honor? King Louis had outlawed the practice, but all attempts to eradicate it had failed. One of Skinny Marie's favorite activities was to hire a carriage to the Bois de Boulogne to watch the gentlemen settle their quarrels with pistols or swords. She'd offer to reward the winner or console the loser, whoever was the better-looking. And most alive.

Marianne dressed and went downstairs, cursing the stiffness in her body and the bruises already forming from the previous day. What Machiavellian tortures had Valette devised for her now?

CHAPTER 21

$\mathcal{N}$ic stood at the edge of the arena watching as Marianne cantered one of the horses around the ring. He glanced sideways at the man who'd materialized silently at his side.

"What news from Paris?"

Laurent Falconi frowned. "Not good. The emperor's ordered the army to assemble near the Belgian border. Rumors are, he's planning a big offensive. Fouché's started a huge misinformation campaign, and the National Guard's been sent to Lille to divert attention there. Security's been tightened up everywhere. The borders have been closed, the mail's been stopped, no ships are allowed to leave the ports, and there are roadblocks everywhere."

Nic cursed.

"That's not the worst of it, either. The prisoner's going to be moved."

"Shit. When?"

"A couple of days, at most."

"If they transfer him, he's as good as dead." Nic ran his fingers through his hair. "I thought we'd have more time. Is there any good news?"

"Not really. Duval's looking for you, as expected. And her." Laurent inclined his head at Marianne, still unaware of his presence.

"What about her sister?"

"She's safe enough. Andrew has her in the Montmartre safe house for now."

As if by unspoken agreement both men turned to watch Marianne as she executed a figure-of-eight on horseback.

Laurent gave a soulful sigh. "I love watching her. She has such grace, such balance." He glanced sideways. "Don't be too tough on her, Nic. You always push people too hard. You expect perfection."

Nic frowned. "I have to be cruel to be kind. You know that. On a mission it can mean the difference between life and death."

Laurent chuckled at his brutal lack of remorse. "True. But she doesn't like being ordered about. If you're expecting blind, unquestioning obedience, you've recruited the wrong girl."

"I noticed," Nic said wryly, touching the bandage on his wrist.

Lauren's smile widened. "She's stubborn. And brave. I doubt even *you* can tame her."

"I doubt I'd want to."

It was true, Nic realized with a start of surprise. Marianne drove him to distraction with her constant rebellions, but her single-minded determination had earned his grudging respect. He wanted to master her, certainly, but without breaking that jaunty spirit.

Laurent's eyes narrowed, as if he sensed the direction of his thoughts. "Be nice, Nicolas. She's fragile, despite that tough outer shell. Like an egg." He shook his head, disliking the analogy. "No, not an egg, like . . . crème brulée." He kissed the tips of his fingers in a purely Italian gesture of appreciation. "Yes. Like crème brulée. All sweetness inside."

Nic slanted him a look. "What is she to you, Laurent?"

The edge in his voice surprised him, as did how much he wanted to hear the answer.

Laurent held up his hands defensively. "Hey, I love her, but she's like a little sister, nothing more." He fixed Nic with a level look. "Take care of her. I mean it. Hurt her, and we'll have words."

Nic raised his brows. "You think I'd hurt her?"

Laurent hesitated, clearly choosing his words with care. "Not deliberately. But I think you'd sacrifice anything to achieve your goals. What if you had to choose—Napoleon or her?"

Nic clenched his jaw. "You know it. Napoleon. Every time."

Laurent shrugged, neither condemning nor accusing. "That's what I mean." He turned to watch Marianne again. "The audience loves her—how do you French say?—her élan, no? Her style."

"She's a pain the arse," Nic said succinctly. "But with the right training she could be a brilliant agent." He could hone her into a lethal weapon, but he needed more time. She wasn't ready. Not yet. Anything could go wrong.

The idea of Marianne's bright spark being extinguished wasn't one he wanted to contemplate. He didn't possess anything as inconvenient as a conscience; in his position it was a luxury he couldn't afford. So the twinge in his chest wasn't guilt at forcing her into the mission underprepared. She was resourceful, intelligent, adaptable. She'd be fine.

He turned to watch her again. Her body moved in perfect time with the horse's gait, her slim thighs indecently outlined by her tight breeches. Those breeches had been a stupid idea. And seeing his own white shirt covering her chest made him hard. A surge of hot lust shot through him. He wanted to stride into the ring, pull her down to the floor, and strip it off her. He wanted to—

He actually took a step forward before he stopped himself. He couldn't afford to be distracted. She was a means to an end, an integral part of the mission. Nothing more. Lusting after her could get them both killed.

Laurent glanced sideways at him and chuckled wickedly beneath his breath. "In Italy we have a word for girls like her. 'Belladonna.' Beautiful, but deadly."

Nic sighed. "In French it's 'femme fatale.'"

"She's trouble in any language, my friend. Just think what those knives could do to your manhood." Laurent waggled his brows suggestively. "You have been warned."

Nic slapped him on the shoulder. "Don't worry about me. I can handle one small slip of a girl, Laurent. Come on."

* * *

MARIANNE SQUINTED at the familiar figure walking toward her with Valette. "*Laurent?* Laurent!"

She leaped off the still-moving horse, raced across the practice ground, and threw herself into her friend's arms. Laurent staggered back with the force of the hug then returned it fiercely.

"*Buon giorno, cara.* You look well enough, for all your adventures."

She shot an accusing look at Valette. "Considering I've been kidnapped and tortured, yes."

Laurent stretched out his hands. "I thought you might want these."

Marianne accepted her pink ballet slippers from him automatically, then frowned as the incongruity of his presence hit her. "Thank you. But what are you doing here? How did you find me?"

"I thought Nic could do with a little help."

She wrinkled her nose. "I didn't realize you two knew each other . . ." And then, just like that, it all fell into place like the tumblers of a lock. She drew in a shocked breath and spun to face Valette. "Oh my God! He works for you, doesn't he?" Without waiting for an answer she turned back and poked Laurent in the chest with her finger. "You're a *spy!*"

He backed up. "Now, easy there—"

"I don't believe it!" She scowled as she read the truth in his face.

Valette stepped forward. "Laurent's one of my best agents. The circus is perfect for passing information. Every level of society mingles freely."

Marianne's head reeled. It made sense. The circus was full of eccentric characters, foreigners, risk takers who shared a common disregard for authority. She glared at Valette. "Who *else* works for you?"

"At the circus? Only Laurent and Henri. And Joseph Breton, in the front office. He was a great field agent, until Duval's men broke his legs."

A glimmer of something dark and frightening flashed in his eyes at the mention of Duval, a silent promise of retribution. Marianne gave an inner snort. He'd have to get in line. She had prior claim to Duval.

"You'll be telling me Pagnol the monkey's one of yours, next," she sneered.

Valette smiled sweetly. "He's carried notes, on occasion."

She turned back to Laurent. "And you've known all along that I work for Duval?"

He nodded, and she gave a cracked laugh at the irony. All this time she'd naively thought *herself* the only one at the Cirque Olympique leading a double life.

"I was investigating Duval for Fouché before you even came to Paris," Valette said quietly. "I knew he was your cousin. Just as I know your real name isn't Marianne Bonnard. It's Marianne de Beauvais. Your parents were the Count and Countess of Chanterac."

All the blood drained from her face as the secrets she'd hidden for years were so casually exposed. Valette frowned. "Duval told you the truth. Your father wasn't as innocent as you think. He was an ardent Royalist. He actively supported the *chouans*—the underground Royalist resistance movement—during the Revoluion, although he was careful to keep it a secret. And just before he died he helped Fouché devise a plot to overthrow the emperor."

Marianne shook her head. "That's not true! My father was a scholar. He always hated politics."

"Napoleon was off fighting in Italy. Fouché and some other high-ranking officials considered staging a coup to restore the king while he was out of the country. Your father and uncle were with them. In the end they decided to postpone the plan, but your father held documents that incriminated not only Fouché, but Duval's father as well."

Marianne's head was pounding. She staggered back and felt Laurent catch her arm, steadying and supportive. *Oh, Papa. No.*

Valette kept talking. "The fire that killed your parents was set deliberately."

The room swirled about her. "What? No. It was an accident. A spark from an unbanked fire."

His mouth hardened. "It was Duval. He was desperate to make a name for himself in the glorious new republic. When he discovered his father's involvement in the plot, he became terrified of being tainted by association. To prove his loyalty, he told Fouché's rival, Savary, about the plan. Savary sent him to retrieve the documents from your father, but Duval took matters into his own hands. He set the fire that killed your parents to destroy the evidence."

Marianne covered her mouth with her hand. Her stomach churned.

Nic cleared his throat. "Duval did well out of his betrayal. Thanks to Savary's influence, a suitably grateful Napoleon elevated him to Minister of Morals."

She could barely breathe. Hatred hardened into a black ball in her stomach, a knot of cold, murderous rage. Duval had killed her parents. As if she hadn't enough reason for wanting him dead. He would pay. As soon as she got back to Paris.

"Fouché always suspected Duval was involved, but he couldn't prove anything. He charged me with finding something incriminating we could use to bring him to justice. That's why I've been following *your* movements. Whenever Duval made you steal, or deliver messages, or retrieve information, I've known about it."

"*Following* me?" Marianne repeated in horror.

Valette's mouth gave an amused twitch. "Not me personally. I've been too busy. But my men, yes. Always."

Fury twisted like a knife in her gut. "For how long?" she gritted out.

"Only the past year or so."

She wanted to press her hands to her pounding temples and scream. *A year!* He'd been having her followed for *a whole year?* Was she supposed to be flattered that he thought her worthy of such a dubious honor?

He raised his brows, accurately reading her reaction. "Why are you angry? You should be thanking me. My men have been watching out for you. They've kept the gendarmes off your tail. Kept you safe."

A bitter laugh welled up in her throat. *Safe?* There was no safety. Not from the one person she *needed* protection from: Duval himself.

God, she was so sick of people trying to control her, use her. First Duval, and now Valette. She had no freedom at all. It was an illusion, like those stupid shadow puppet shows at the Palais Royale. She folded her arms across her chest. "I've never seen anyone following me."

Valette's arrogant chuckle raised her blood pressure another notch. "That's because my men are good."

Her fingers twitched. She wanted her blades. Wanted to cut out his black, unfeeling heart.

He smiled, as if he could feel the animosity radiating from her. "Your father would have approved of this job."

Damn him. Every way she turned she became more and more entangled in his web.

CHAPTER 22

*V*alette swept her a mocking bow. "I'll leave you to say your good-byes."

Marianne watched him depart through narrowed eyes, mentally embedding knives between his shoulder blades.

Laurent cleared his throat. "Henri was supposed to do this," he said by way of an apology. "But then he broke his leg. And I'm too big. That leaves you. You can do it, Marianne. Nic wouldn't have chosen you if he didn't think you were capable."

She didn't want to talk about Nicolas Valette. "What about Sophie? Have you seen her? Is she all right?"

Laurent accepted the change of subject with good grace. "I haven't seen her myself, but I've had a message from Andrew Ducrow, her guard. They've moved to another safe house in Paris."

Marianne gasped in dismay. "Together? Alone?"

He shot her a droll glance. "I know Andrew well. He's a professional. And besides, how's that different to your being here with Valette? Together. Alone." He raised his eyebrows suggestively.

"It's *totally* different. Andrew's probably polite. Sophie probably doesn't want to smash her fist into his smug face whenever they're in the same room together."

Laurent chuckled. "They'll be fine."

"If he scares her or hurts her in any way, he's going to feel the sharp end of my blade somewhere vital." Marianne flicked a glance at his crotch to emphasize her point.

"You're a frightening woman, Marianne Bonnard."

"Are you staying here tonight?" she asked hopefully. Laurent would be a welcome buffer between herself and Valette. She wasn't looking forward to another night alone with him. Especially when she had so much else to think about.

"Can't. I have to get back to Paris. I'm still doubling up for Henri in the shows."

"You're abandoning me," she accused. "With him, of all people."

"What's the matter? Don't you trust him?"

"Do *you* trust him?" she shot back.

Laurent kicked a stone with his foot. "I've known Nic for a long time, and I'm proud to call him my friend. I'd trust him with my life. And yours." He slanted her a glance. "But he has only one purpose, and that's Napoleon's destruction. He's waited a long time for his revenge. I won't lie to you, Marianne. He'll put you in harm's way. He'll use you."

She wrinkled her nose. "I know *that*. He's made no secret about it."

Laurent pulled her into his side for a hug. "Be careful, *ma chère*. I don't want to see you hurt."

She kissed his cheek, feeling a warm rush of love for his gruff concern. "I can look after myself."

He gave her a skeptical look. "I don't know . . . he's a hard man. Ruthless. And you women seem to find him dangerously fascinating. Trust him with your life, little one, but don't make the mistake of trusting him with your heart, hmm?"

Marianne snorted inelegantly. "There's no danger of *that*, I promise you."

Laurent chuckled. "I know it's hard to believe, but he's not the enemy. Try to resist the temptation to stab him, eh?"

Her face flushed with guilty heat. *Too late for that.* "I can't help it. He's just so irritating. How can we be a team? I don't even like him," she wailed. "Can't you just take me back to Paris with you?"

Laurent shook his head. "I gave Nic my word. I'm sorry you got dragged into this, but this job really *is* important." He ruffled her hair affectionately. "Good luck, little one."

* * *

Nic stood brooding in the shadows, watching Marianne with Laurent.

She smiled at bloody Laurent. In fact, come to think about it, she smiled at just about everyone, except him. No, for him she reserved all her sulks and scowls. He narrowed his eyes as she threw herself into Laurent's arms with careless abandon, pressing her lithe body up against him. As if they were long-lost lovers, for God's sake. She'd seen the man less than three days ago in Paris.

She kissed him on the cheek. Nic slapped his riding crop against his leg. Laurent was too old for her. And the way he was looking at her . . . was that more than just a brotherly affection, despite his denials? His hands were resting on her shoulders—perfectly respectable—but he was gazing down into her face with that look of mingled exasperation and affection that Nic knew all too well.

He kicked a patch of nettles as he made his way back to the house. He was playing with fire, but he just couldn't help himself.

The cold, logical part of his brain told him it made sense to seduce her. Marianne wanted him. She was fighting it, fighting her own reactions, but he knew women. Despite her evident fear of physical proximity, her body still responded to his touch.

He should use her attraction to bind her to him, to the mission. He'd done it before, with other females: spies, colleagues, enemies. The heightened sense of danger, the thrill of almost being caught, tended to act as an aphrodisiac for both male and female agents alike.

But those women had known the score. They'd used him as much as he'd used them. They weren't wide-eyed little virgins who barely knew how to kiss. Nic shook his head, trying to calm his own heated body.

She was an extraordinary woman, full of contradictions—feisty and innocent, tempting and utterly infuriating. And damned distracting.

He adjusted the uncomfortable bulge in the front of his breeches. He must be losing his mind. Seducing her would be a complication he didn't need. He shouldn't even be considering it. He had no future. Not with her. Not with any woman. He rubbed the back of his neck. Why did life have to be so damned complicated? The lines between right and wrong, ally and enemy, had become fiendishly blurred. This mission was a case in point—a joint operation between Fouché and the British foreign secretary Castlereagh: two ostensible adversaries whose interests had temporarily converged.

But if his cover was blown, he could expect no help from either quarter. Neither nation would claim responsibility for the mission. He'd be entirely on his own. He could only pray that he wouldn't drag Marianne down with him if he fell.

Nic headed for the cellars. She'd taken the news of his intrusion in her life better than he'd expected, but still, he needed a drink.

CHAPTER 23

Marianne found Valette found in the kitchen, an open bottle of wine in front of him. The paper label on the front said Latour, and it had a little crenelated tower on it, just like the walls of Vincennes. She hoped he choked on it, the infuriating ass.

"Why don't you have some lunch?" he suggested mildly, indicating a wicker basket on the floor.

Laurent must have brought fresh provisions as well as information. She busied herself unpacking the food and attacked the contents with ravenous enthusiasm.

Valette watched her with a slight, amused smile as she wolfed down fresh bread and pâté followed by a juicy pear. "Don't eat too much. I don't want you getting stuck."

She frowned at his odd comment. "Stuck where?"

"The chimney." He tilted his head at the enormous fireplace.

The food she'd just eaten swirled unpleasantly in her stomach.

He stood, walked over to the hearth, and kicked the cold ashes aside with his boot. "This is the only part of the escape plan we haven't practiced yet. You have to climb the chimney from the prisoner's cell to gain access to the roof. Come here."

Marianne's backside was glued to the bench. From the first moment she'd read about Latude's escape, *this* had been the part she feared the most. "Surely the chimney can't be the only way out?"

Valette crossed his arms over his chest and sent her a sardonic glance. "Can you pick the lock on the cell door?"

"You know I can't."

"Well, then. Unless you'd like to try single-handedly to slaughter all the guards on your way out, this is your only option."

She shivered. It was humiliating to admit to weakness, especially to a man like Valette, who excelled at everything, but she had to at least try. "I don't think I can do it."

"Of course you can," he said impatiently. "Thousands of chimney sweeps do this every day. Some of them are as young as four or five years old. If they can manage it, so can you. It's not far. Only about twenty feet."

She shuddered at the idea of anyone having to live in such a way, let alone a small, terrified child. "Why don't you just use a chimney sweep, then?"

"Because a chimney sweep doesn't have your rope-walking skills." He waited, hands on his lean hips.

She managed to step closer to the chimney. The stone beneath her palm was still warm from the previous night's fire. She licked her dry lips. "I can't go up there."

"Yes, you can. Don't make me regret paying all that money for you. And for your sister."

His barbed reminder of how much she was indebted to him made her blood boil. "I'm afraid of the dark," she said desperately.

"No, you're not. You were fine in the cellar with me yesterday. And you spend half your life sneaking around at night. Stop stalling."

He bent his head and stepped under the lintel, into the fire-place itself. It was so large only the top part of his head disappeared up into the chimney. "At Vincennes there's a grill inside the chimney to prevent escape, but the prisoner's been working on it for weeks. He's loosened it, so all you'll have to do is lift it up and put it aside."

He caught hold of her arm and tugged her to stand next to him in the restricted space so they were chest to chest. The top of her head came only to his shoulder. Marianne peered up into the darkness, and her heart rate quickened. It looked as welcoming as a crypt. A feeling of utter dread filled her, and she rubbed her hands up and down her arms to ward off a sudden chill.

Valette put his hands on her hips and turned her, pulling her back against him. She tried to concentrate on him rather than the awful black hole looming above her: the warmth and strength of his body pressing into her back, his cheek brushing hers as he leaned forward, the spicy scent of him teasing her nose. If she turned her head, it would bring her mouth up against his jaw. He had a beautiful mouth. She tamped down the tingle in her lips as she thought of it.

"I'll lift you up. You'll need to push against opposite walls. It won't be completely smooth. There will be uneven stones and gaps you can use for hand- and footholds."

She could barely think past the hammering of her pulse. The great weight of the stones above was pressing down on her head, on her chest. The dark tunnel was like the mouth of some hideous beast, opening wide to swallow her whole.

Valette lifted her up with just the strength of his arms, ignoring her whimper of protest.

Marianne wedged herself in the rectangular opening with her back against the wall and her legs, partly bent, braced against the opposite side. Valette loosened his grip, and she glanced down at him in sudden desperation. The palms of her hands were clammy against the rough stone.

"Now bend your knee and put one foot flat on the wall behind you, under your backside. Put your hands on the walls on either side of you, palms flat, thumbs down. Push with your arms and legs until you're fully extended. Then switch feet and do it again. Just inch yourself upward."

Marianne fought a wave of hysterical panic. *Easy for you to say. You're not the one squashed up the chimney.*

He looked up at her expectantly. "Go on, then."

She peered upward again. It was like a tomb. The sooty smell of death filled her nose every time she inhaled, and her panting breaths echoed in the narrow space. She closed her eyes tight. She could feel sweat beading on upper lip.

She managed to scoot upward a few inches. The walls closed in. Her throat was tight, as if she had something stuck in it. There wasn't enough air to fill her lungs. She tried to move her hands, but her muscles wouldn't obey. Her ears started ringing. She could hear Sophie screaming, the windows shattering, the crackle of flames as she raced through the salon at Chanterac. Black smoke billowed overhead. There was no way out. She was going to die.

Valette's impatient voice broke through her panic. "Go on! You have to be faster than that."

She shook her head.

"Stop being such a baby," he growled.

"I can't do it!" Her strangled cry echoed strangely, amplified by the flue. She twisted her body and let herself drop down, falling on top of him in her haste to get out. Her legs were shaking so badly she could barely stand, but she thrust away from him and staggered out of the fireplace.

"What are you doing? Get back up there."

She smothered a sob of distress. "I can't," she gasped. "Please don't make me do it."

Valette's face was implacable, utterly without mercy. "You must."

He made a grab for her arm, but she dodged away and bolted for the kitchen door, desperation lending her strength. His angry curses spilled out behind her as she raced across the courtyard and plunged into the overgrown gardens.

The tangle of plants soon slowed her progress and she doubled over, winded, then sank to the ground. Tears of impotent rage raced down her cheeks, and she swiped at them angrily with the back of her hand.

The man had no compassion, no pity. What right did he have to force her to do such horrible things? She rested her forehead on her bent knees until her heart resumed its natural rhythm. She hated herself almost as much as she detested Valette. Determination balled in her chest as she realized he was right. There was no way to avoid the chimney climb, not if she wanted to get back to Sophie.

She'd run from her fears for long enough.

CHAPTER 24

*I*t was almost dark when Marianne rose from the hard ground and forced herself toward the burned-out stables. Her feet felt like lead. A collapsed beam partially blocked the doorway, and she ducked under it, bracing herself for the memories to come flooding back.

Nothing happened.

She made a slow turn about, inspecting the charred walls and mounds of cracked, blackened timbers, then stepped forward and tentatively sniffed at the charcoal. A faint sooty aroma lingered, but months of wind and rain had diluted its power. It wasn't the same smell of death she remembered.

A splash of color caught her eye. A small plant had pushed through the rubble, its bright green shoots a stark contrast to the bleak decay all around. It looked so out of place. How could something so beautiful emerge from such destruction? But there it was, straining upward, stubbornly clinging to life, hopeful for the heat of the sun. She turned away. Stupid flower. It shouldn't be seeking warmth. Fire had killed its parents. It would only get burned again.

It started to rain, a warm, light patter that misted her hair as it fell through the gap where the roof had once been. This wasn't working. It was too open, not nearly as stifling as the chimney. She turned to leave, and her heart slammed against her ribs as Valette materialized out of the shadows like a phantom. She hadn't heard him approach.

Couldn't he give her a moment's peace?

He stopped a few feet away and leaned negligently against a blackened doorframe. His face was illuminated briefly as he struck a flint and the end of his cheroot glowed red in the twilight. He turned his head to exhale, but the wind still blew a hint of the fragrant cloud back to her. "What happened back there?" he asked quietly.

Marianne looked away. It was easier to talk to him when she wasn't looking at him. Out here in the half-light, she could imagine that he was someone else. That they were friends. She could tell him anything in the darkness.

"You know my parents died in a fire. When I have nightmares, that's where I am, caught in a confined space while everything around me burns." She shot a pointed glance at his cheroot.

His nearness was doing strange things to her. She felt jittery, anxious in a way that had nothing to do with their scorched surroundings. He offered no comment, simply watched her out of those tawny, unreadable eyes.

She tilted her head back, studying the heavens to avoid his penetrating gaze. There was Orion, with his sword belt. There was Perseus. And Hercules. If only she could be as strong as those mythical heroes. Her father used to point out the constellations to her when she couldn't sleep. *Oh, Papa. I miss you so much.* She squeezed her eyes closed against the ache of loss.

"What are you doing out here?"

She rolled her stiff shoulders. "Testing myself, I suppose."

"That's a brave choice. Most people hide from whatever scares them."

She glanced at his profile, etched in moonlight and shadow.

Tiny drops of rain glittered on his dark jacket like sequins. She wanted to brush them away. Wanted to smooth her hands over his shoulders, to absorb the strength of him through the fabric. She could do with some of his invincibility, some of his self-belief.

She looked away, uncomfortable with the strength of the urge. "You're asking me to face my worst fears, and you won't even tell me why. I barely know you."

He leaned back against the wall, lethal and elegant as always. "What do you want to know? Ask me anything you like."

Marianne narrowed her eyes, immediately suspicious of his sudden affability. Was he mocking her again? "You've already admitted you lie."

He exhaled another cloud of smoke. "No lies tonight, I promise."

"All right then. Is Nicolas Valette even your real name?"

"Yes, and no."

"Avoiding the question's as bad as lying," she reminded him sternly.

He sighed. "Yes, it's my real name. One of several I use."

Welcome to the club. Duval had made her change her name to Bonnard. He said it sounded more bourgeois. Of course, everything had had a new name back then, even the months of the year. It hadn't been January, February, March. It had been Brumaire, Ventose, Thermidor.

"Where were you born?"

The end of his cheroot glowed bright in the darkness. She studied his perfect profile, that straight nose, the hard line of his jaw. Her heart gave a funny little ache. He was such an attractive man. On the *outside,* she reminded herself forcefully. Internally, he was still a complete mystery.

"I was born in a little place near Studland, in Dorset."

She couldn't have been more shocked if he'd told her he was the King of France. Her mouth fell open. "You're *English?*"

He gave a crooked smile. "As English as roast beef and York-shire pudding."

She frowned. "I don't know what this pudding is. But you speak French with no accent at all."

"Thank you," he said sardonically. "I'm flattered you think so. As it happens, my father is English. My mother is French. They met in Paris before the Revolution. He helped smuggle her family across the Channel. I suppose all the excitement was inducive to romance. Either way, I learned to speak both languages from the cradle."

"So which do you work for? France? Or England?"

He shrugged. "Neither. Both. I hardly know anymore."

"You mean you're a traitor?"

His smile was twisted. "One man's traitor is another man's hero. It depends on your point of view."

"But I thought you worked for Fouché?"

"I do. Among others."

Marianne hardly knew what to think. "So *this* job. Who is it for?"

"What would you like me to say? For the greater good of France? Would that appeal to your sense of patriotism?"

"I don't have a sense of patriotism," she said. "I'm a criminal. I've stolen property and information. I don't care about France or England. I care about Sophie. I care about putting a roof over my head and shoes on my feet."

He took another slow drag of his cheroot. "We're not so different, then. We both do what we must to protect what we hold dear."

"What's that, then?" she asked again. "If it's not your country. What do you care about? Family? Duty? Honor?"

"You didn't mention love." His lip curled. "Isn't *that* what drives all men?"

It was her turn to scoff. "*Love.* Have you noticed that people 'fall' in love? If it's so wonderful, why don't they 'fly' into it? Why don't they 'float' or 'climb' or 'soar'?" She shook her head. "It's because love *hurts*. The same way falling off my wire hurts."

He turned his head, and his eyes were dark and fathomless. "You're right. It isn't love that drives me. It's revenge."

The bleak determination in his gaze made her shiver. He looked so haunted that she wanted to brush away the pain that furrowed his brow, but she stayed her hand; any sympathy would be countered with scorn, she was sure.

"How did you become a spy?"

"When war broke out my brother Tony and I presented ourselves to Lord Castlereagh, the British foreign secretary, and told him we'd be useful."

Marianne raised her eyebrows, and he smiled in self-directed mockery.

"Presumptuous, eh? I was twenty-four. Tony was eighteen. We thought we'd send Napoleon packing in a matter of weeks." His mouth tightened. "Castlereagh jumped at the chance to use us, fluent French speakers. Our family still owned estates near Paris we could use as a base. We made a great team. We were couriers—spies effectively—running interference back and forth across the Channel. We were having the time of our lives." A muscle ticked in his jaw.

"What happened?"

"We were in northern Spain, crossing the mountains with the aid of some Spanish freedom fighters, and we ran into a French patrol. Our guides were killed, Tony was wounded, and we were both taken prisoner." He smiled bleakly. "They couldn't decide if we were English or French, so we were sent to a detention camp for prisoners of war. Tony urged me to leave him and escape; we still had vital information to relay to Wellington. I didn't want to leave him, but he was in no fit state to travel, and at least he was receiving medical treatment at the camp. So I went, vowing to get back and rescue him as soon as I'd delivered my message."

Marianne's heart clenched at the bleak despair she heard in his tone.

"Back then I still believed there was some kind of justice, some basic human decency in the world. That wars were conducted in accordance with unwritten, but generally accepted, gentlemanly rules. Unarmed citizens would not be harmed. Children and women would be safe. Prisoners of war would be treated fairly." His lips twisted in bitter self-mockery.

"Just after I reached Paris, sickness overran Tony's camp. Napoleon was running out of funds, and sick prisoners are expensive. So instead of caring for them, or offering to exchange them for his own captured men, he ordered for them all to be executed."

CHAPTER 25

$\mathcal{M}$arianne's gasp of outrage echoed in the still night air.

Valette dipped his head. "I suppose I went a little mad. I spent six weeks holed up near Paris deciding what to do. When I finally sent word to Castlereagh—he'd assumed I was dead, too—he ordered me to stay in France. He sent me to Paris and Fouché."

Marianne's eyes widened in disbelief. "And you *went*?"

He shrugged. "I went. What could Fouché do to me? I'd already lost my brother. I didn't care if I lived or died."

She frowned. "But wouldn't Fouché have been suspicious of anyone who was half English? And aristocratic? The man's no fool, from what I hear."

"Of course he was suspicious. And I suppose I had a kind of death wish. He recognized it, calculated I could be of more use to him alive than dead. He saw the same benefits Castlereagh had seen. I still held my English titles and properties, I could move around London society easily. He wanted me to keep tabs on the émigrés who'd fled to England. Wanted to know the plots of the Royalist supporters, those who were trying to reinstate the Bourbon king."

Marianne shook her head.

"You'd be amazed at the amount of information that passes between countries ostensibly at war. Fouché knows he's sharing me with the British. I'm a double agent, in effect. It's all part of the game."

A game. Marianne shivered. *A deadly, frightening game. And she was caught up in the middle of it.*

"So now you know why this mission is so important to me."

Valette took one last drag of his cheroot and threw it away, then pushed off the wall toward her, rolling his shoulders as if to shrug off the black memories. Marianne took an instinctive step back, but her retreat was blocked by a pile of rubble.

"The prisoner is my priority. Understand?"

She nodded.

He stopped barely a foot away and reached up to brush a tendril of hair off her temple. His expression softened. "Your face is all black."

She stood, frozen, as he cupped her jaw with both hands and used his thumbs to wipe her cheeks, almost as if she were a child. His fingers were warm against her skin. His amber eyes flicked to her lips then back to her eyes.

"You know, there's a trick with bad memories."

She swallowed. Her knees felt weak. "A way to get rid of them, you mean?"

He nodded.

"How?"

He brushed her lower lip with his thumb, rolling it down, sweeping across the slick inner. Her stomach flipped. His eyes darkened to the color of old brandy. He curled his palm around the nape of her neck, and she hardly dared to breathe as he drew her closer, closer.

"You replace them with something worth remembering."

He bent and took her mouth.

It wasn't a gentle kiss. It was possession. Marianne opened to him blindly, unconsciously parting her lips as he angled his head. He kissed with an exquisite thoroughness, his tongue invading and retreating, teasing and enticing. She closed her eyes, absorbing his touch, the flavor of his mouth. He tasted of wood smoke and wine. Smoke and shadows, she thought wildly. That summed him up perfectly.

She wanted to fall into the dark spiral of pleasure he was creating and never resurface. She was hot, glowing like newly rekindled embers. She caught his lapels, to drag him closer still, but he stepped back so abruptly she staggered, swallowing a whimper of denial.

He stared down at her, his expression inscrutable, his instant composure like a slap in the face. "Go to bed, Marianne. We leave in the morning."

Her face fell in dismay. "But I need more practice. I haven't even—"

"There's no more time." His gazed dropped to her lips again, and his mouth curled upward. "When you're faced with that chimney at Vincennes, you'll just have to think of something worth living for."

He flicked her cheek in a casual, devastating gesture, then turned and dissolved into the shadows.

Marianne pressed her fingers to her tingling lips. Her breathing was uneven. She felt shaken, shocked, aroused. Why had he kissed her? Was it another ruthless ploy to cajole her into acquiescence? She didn't understand him at all. One minute he was seducing her, the next warning her he'd leave her to die without a qualm.

Her mood sank even lower. Half the time he treated her as an annoying but unavoidable companion. A childish inconvenience. He probably saw kissing her as just one more onerous duty to prepare for the job, like cleaning his guns or sharpening his knives.

An odd kind of elated despair gripped her. She'd spent years building up her emotional defenses, but Valette stripped her of them with nothing more than the touch of his mouth on hers. *Damn him.* She felt raw, off kilter, as if everything solid and dependable had somehow shifted beneath her feet. And for a girl whose life depended on balance, that was the worst feeling in the world.

* * *

VALETTE WASN'T in his room when she crept upstairs, and despite her chaotic thoughts she was so exhausted she fell asleep almost as soon as her head touched her pillow.

Sometime later she opened her eyes to darkness, unsure what had woken her. It wasn't time to rise—the room was dark, save for a sliver of moonlight that slanted in between the shutters. She thumped her pillow and turned over, willing herself back to sleep, when she heard a sound so slight she almost dismissed it, except that it brought with it the conviction that she wasn't alone.

Her heartbeat accelerated, and her stomach knotted with panic. In a casual move, as if she were merely stretching, she slid her hand under the pillow and found the hilt of her knife, reassuringly solid in her palm.

"Valette?" she whispered.

She sensed movement in the far corner and saw him sprawled in the wing chair, shirt ruffled, legs outstretched. The shadows from the window bars fell across his body in thin stripes, like the bars of a cage.

She relaxed her hold on the knife with a sigh of relief. "You frightened me!" she hissed accusingly. "What are you doing? Is something wrong?" She could barely see him, just a dim shadow across the room.

"No, nothing's wrong. I'm just sitting here," he said quietly. "There isn't a chair in my room that I trust not to collapse."

She pulled the neck of her sleeping shirt together with one hand, blinking sleepily. "Aren't you tired?" She sensed, rather than saw him shake his head.

"No. Go back to sleep. I didn't mean to wake you."

She lay back down, turning over so her back was to him, oddly content. It should have been frightening to have him sitting there, watching her. Then again, he'd been watching over her for the past few years without her knowledge. She should resent him for such a violation of her privacy, but for the first time the idea brought comfort rather than anger.

She closed her eyes and listened to the slow, steady cadence of his breathing. He was guarding her, her own dark angel. She'd have no nightmares tonight. Anyone so dangerous would keep them all at bay.

CHAPTER 26

Marianne experienced a pang of regret as she watched the château disappear from view. It was just as well they were leaving. The place reminded her far too much of her childhood home at Chanterac, despite its far greater size. It would have been much too easy to get attached to the place. To imagine another life there.

Their transport was the same trundling hay cart they'd brought from the inn, and she elected to ride in the back to escape Valette's disturbing nearness. She was wearing the colorful peasant's clothes he'd given her. They were loose fitting and comfortable, and she reveled in the freedom of having no corset. Her circus costume had disappeared. Sophie would be cross if she had to sew her another one. All those frills and sequins took *hours*, apparently.

Marianne spread the full skirts and lay on the blanket that smelled of horses and hay. Valette turned his head and she studied his profile through her lashes. His harsh face was arrestingly beautiful, all classical lines and austere perfection in the morning light. An ache of longing, like hunger, warmed the pit of her stomach.

"How did you end up at the Cirque Olympique?" he asked suddenly.

She picked up a blade of straw so she wouldn't have to look at him. "It was an accident, really. My old nurse Jeanne was Antonio Falconi's cousin. She left the circus when she married and settled in our village. She became my mother's maid, then nursemaid and companion for Sophie and me.

"She used to tell us all kinds of outrageous stories about her family; her cousin was a Venetian count, exiled from his home-land after a fatal duel. He was one of the finest riders in Europe. He owned a great circus called the Cirque Olympique in Paris."

Marianne smiled fondly in memory. "Sophie and I would listen, enthralled, sure it was all make believe. One day we begged her to show us some circus tricks, so she set up a tightrope in the garden, only a foot off the ground, and taught us to rope walk. After that we were hooked. She showed us how to throw knives at a target drawn on the trunk of a tree. How to gauge the number of turns the blade would make in the air for it to land point first in the bull's-eye." Her smile faded. "She died the year I turned twelve. I still miss her.

"It wasn't until I had to bargain with Duval that I realized what a gift she'd given me. When I went to the Cirque Olympique and begged for a job, the Falconis welcomed me with open arms."

Valette glanced at her over his shoulder. "So what is it about balancing on a rope that makes you so happy?"

"It's the challenge, I suppose. It's such an improbable thing to do. When I step out on the wire, everything stops. The audience is willing me on, but they're half expecting me to fall, too. Their hopes and fears are in my hands."

"And you like that feeling?"

She shrugged, trying to articulate her thoughts. "It's like . . . I'm giving them a gift. Whatever's happening outside the circus, for those few minutes I can make them forget everything. It's magic. Real magic, not sleight of hand or trickery. Not shadows and mirrors, like the shows at the Palais Royale." She snapped the blade of straw in two. "It gives people hope. After all, if I can do something like that, perhaps other impossible things can happen, too. A husband can come home safe from war. A sick child can get well. A sin can be forgiven."

She could be free of Duval.

She flushed, suddenly embarrassed. He must think her such a fool. She was giving herself away, inch by inch, that private part she'd shielded for so long. She clamped her mouth shut and pretended to go to sleep.

He started to hum.

Do you have to do that?" she asked irritably.

"Do what?"

"Hum. It's not even a tune."

"How do you know what I'm trying to hum?"

"Whatever it is, it can't possibly have been meant to sound like that."

"It's an old English—" He stopped abruptly, whatever he'd been about to say frozen on his lips. Then Marianne heard it, too: the rolling thunder of hooves.

Valette cursed. "Troops. Do you speak Italian?"

"A little. Laurent taught me. Especially swearwords. *"Vaffun-culo,"* she offered sweetly, "means go f— "

"I know what it means," he said with a dark chuckle. "Good. We're Italian. You're my wife, Fatima."

Nerves made her snippy. "My father would be so proud. He always hoped I'd marry a lying turncoat spy."

He grinned. "Quick, shout something. I want them to hear us."

"What do you want me to say?"

"Anything. Use your imagination. Swear at me," he said suddenly, vaulting over the back of the seat to land beside her in the hay. "You caught me ogling another woman's tits."

That was easy enough to imagine. Marianne started

screaming like a fishwife, raining down curses upon him. She told him, in no uncertain terms, what would happen to various parts of his anatomy if he so much as looked at another woman again. How she was going to poison—no—*strangle* him in his sleep. How she was going to skewer him with her knives the first chance she got. How she was going to—

"Perfect, sweetheart. Absolutely shrewish." He slapped a hand over her mouth. "Now we need to kiss and make up."

Before she knew what he intended, he'd grasped the front of her bodice and yanked it down, exposing her breasts to the bright sunlight.

"What in God's name—!"

He ignored her outraged squawk and pushed her back into the straw, pinning her easily when she tried to scramble up. She'd barely registered the shock of his long, lean body pressed full-length against her when he flipped up her skirts and ran his hand up the back of her bare leg.

"No! I—"

"Hush, *cara*! Not so loud. Someone will hear us!"

His deliberately loud "whisper" could have been heard half a mile away. "Kiss me!" he hissed in her ear. "Do it, Marianne. Now."

Oh God. This was just like the Montausier. Only *here* they had to convince what sounded like half the French army instead of a handful of dirty old men. Marianne grabbed the front of his shirt and mashed her lips against his with a desperation born of sheer panic. Their teeth clashed. His fingers tangled in her hair. He repositioned her head and tilted his own, and she gasped at the wicked pleasure of his tongue thrusting into her mouth. The world receded. Darkness and heat filled her brain.

His shirt rubbed against her chest, abrasive yet exciting, and she could feel his arousal in the cradle of her thighs. Her whole body was achy, restless.

"That's good! Keep it up," he whispered against her lips.

It was a game. Only pretend. She had to remember that. But his breathing was ragged, too. He slid his hand down and cupped her naked breast.

Marianne's incoherent yelp was swallowed by his mouth. With a groan, he buried his face in the curve of her neck, raining kisses on her skin while his thumb brushed over her nipple in a maddening caress that had her arching up into him without conscious thought. Something wicked shimmered through her bloodstream, setting her nerves alight. His touch was like a flame. Such sweet, shocking pleasure.

His anguished moan vibrated against her as he kissed his way down, over the swell of her breast. Marianne almost choked at the dark, depraved thrill of it. His tongue swirled. She grabbed his hair to pull him up, utterly mortified, but his mouth was wet, insistent, tugging at her. She was going to die of pleasure, of shame. His hand slid to the top of her thigh. She twisted. She wanted—needed—him to move it inward, upward. Just a fraction. To press against the aching, hot center of her. She arched her hips in a wordless, breathless plea.

More.

"Ahem!"

Someone cleared his throat. Loudly.

Marianne's gasp of shock wasn't feigned.

She snapped open her eyes. At least thirty uniformed soldiers lined the road, all of them peering into the cart with expressions ranging from mild amusement to outright salacious interest.

Sang de Dieu! Her face burned. Valette's mouth was still on her breast. He took his sweet time raising his head, too. A comical look of chagrin washed over his features as he pretended suddenly to notice the squadron surrounding the cart. He flicked the edge of her bodice up with a casual move, wiped the back of his hand over his mouth, and shot the commanding officer a frustrated glare.

"Can I 'elp you, moosoor?" He injected a thick Italian accent into the words.

The officer winced at such butchering of the French language. "You're Italian?"

Valette nodded. "*Sì, Italiano.* Like Napoleon, no?" He tapped his chest proudly.

The officer frowned at the sly reminder that the supreme leader was, in fact, Corsican, not French. Marianne wanted to kick Valette for being so aggravating. It was as if the man was *inviting* trouble. *Idiot.*

"What business have you here?"

Valette frowned. "Business? No business. All pleasure." He winked and gave her thigh an affectionate pat. Even that casual gesture made her blood tingle. The officer frowned, and Valette feigned stupidity. "What I do? My French, he is not so good."

The officer tried again, speaking slowly for the idiot foreigner. "Why are you here? On this road? Where are you going?"

"Where I go? Italy, no? Venezia." Valette kissed the tips of his fingers in one of Laurent's favorite gestures. *"La Serenissima."*

"Papers?"

Valette stared at the man blankly. "No papers." He gave the soldiers a rueful glance, the look of a coconspirator, one man to another. "Me, I say Venezia. Fatima, she say Roma." He shrugged, somehow managing to convey a sense of universal male aggravation. *"Donne. Sono una bella seccatura, no?"*

Marianne scowled. *That* Italian she could translate. He'd just said all women were "a beautiful pain in the arse."

The captain's Italian might not have been so good, but he clearly understood the sentiment. His demeanor softened to rueful sympathy. "I know how it is, my friend." He let his eyes wander over her bare leg. "That's a pretty little thing you have there." He moistened his lip with his tongue. "And these are dangerous times to be traveling. A man needs to be careful, with such a prize . . ."

Marianne's skin prickled with foreboding. He probably thought she was a whore, ripe for plundering. The tension in the clearing rocketed. The troops crowded closer, subtly threatening.

Valette's expression didn't change, but the muscles in his arm tightened under her hand. He shook his head with a smile but his eyes were hard as flint. "My Fatima." His hand caressed her thigh, a light, possessive touch that made her shiver. "My problem."

For one timeless second the captain held his gaze. Marianne slid her hand behind her back and palmed her knife. It would be two against thirty, if they chose to attack.

And then the captain blinked, and the tension dissipated as quickly as it had come. "Well, enjoy your sport, monsieur, madame. *Vive l'Empereur.*" He saluted and turned his horse, urging his men onward. They filed out reluctantly with a few parting jibes and ribald laughs.

"Lucky bastard."

"Service her well."

Marianne held still as the *clip-clop* of hooves faded and the sounds of the countryside returned. Birdsong, the chirp of crickets, the rustle of wind in the trees. She drew a long, unsteady breath and expelled it slowly, letting her head fall back in the hay. Her heart hammered against her ribs. Valette must be able to feel it; he was still on top of her, squashing her. He was hard and muscled and incredibly tempting. Her face flamed again, and she squirmed in mortification.

How could she have forgotten herself so completely? The things he'd done!

It had to be the danger, the chance of being discovered. It heightened normal sensations, just like when she was on the wire. She might have felt this . . . agitated . . . with anyone.

Valette smiled darkly, as if he saw her thoughts all too clearly. She bucked, trying to dislodge him, but it was impossible to gain any purchase in the straw. Her body slid against his.

Their eyes met and held. He reached up and brushed away a

piece of straw that had caught on her cheek, and her stomach clenched at his feather-light touch. She was afraid of him. Of what she felt when she was near him. He made her reckless and stupid. He made her hot enough to burn. Her eyes dropped to his lips. So close. For one insane, terrifying second she actually considered curling up and pressing her mouth to his.

Lunacy.

He rested his forehead against hers with a diabolic chuckle. "Gently, *belle*. Let them leave."

He was dying.

Nic gave an inward groan, closing his eyes against the blissful agony of having Marianne pressed up against him. His brain knew it was all for show. His body, however, wasn't cooperating in the slightest. No, his poor, stupid, confused body was begging him to finish what they'd started. He wriggled to adjust the uncomfortable swelling in his breeches. She felt so damn good against him.

He raised himself onto his elbow and risked a glance down at her. *Hell.*

Her eyes were dazed, her cheeks flushed, her lips red and swollen with his kisses. A tug of satisfaction tightened his gut as he noted the pink scrapes his stubble had left on her skin. It was exactly the image of lush eroticism he'd needed her to project.

"Well done, *chérie*." The roughness of his own voice amused him. He cleared his throat and resisted the urge to kiss the hammering pulse at the base of her throat.

She shot him an uncertain glance. "Was that . . . all right . . . ?"

He managed a wicked smile. "Not bad. But I still suggest more practice. If you want to be truly convincing."

His inner devil gave a sarcastic laugh. *More* convincing? Hell, he couldn't recall a time he'd felt more convinced. He should be ashamed at how much he was enjoying this, but truly, he loved teasing her. It was asking for trouble, but hell, he *lived* for trouble. Trouble made life interesting.

His left hand was still cupping her breast over her bodice. Such a perfect breast. Small, just right for his hand. And the feel of it under his mouth. *God.* He almost groaned again at the memory. He wanted to lick every inch of her.

He gave in to temptation. He bent and pressed his mouth to the upper slope of her breast. She sucked in a scandalized breath, but he didn't give her time to protest. He just pushed down her bodice and took her into his mouth again, sucking that delicious pink bud, flicking his tongue across the pebbled tip.

He closed his eyes, drowning in sensation. God, he loved the taste of her.

She made a breathless little sound. Her hands gripped his hair, but whether she meant to push him away or draw him closer, he didn't know and didn't particularly care. He nosed his way across to the other nipple, lost in the texture of her skin. She tasted so sweet; warm and addictive, like a perfect Sauternes. From faraway he heard himself groan. He was mad. *Fou.* He didn't care. They both deserved a reward for their narrow escape.

How in God's name could she think she wasn't attractive to men? He rocked his hips, forcing her to feel the effect she had on him. She gave a startled gasp.

He'd had numerous lovers, women of infinite skill and unparalleled beauty. He'd never wanted any of them as much as he wanted this brave, innocent girl. The idea was so startling he pulled back and fixed an impersonal smile on his face.

"Good job, sweetheart. Let's go."

"Get off me!" She pushed ineffectively at him, her face flaming.

He laughed at her belated outrage and rolled onto his back. She made a big show of brushing out her skirts and yanking up her bodice as he climbed back onto the driving seat. "Why don't you stay back there for a while, hmm?" he called back.

That would definitely be safest for both of them.

CHAPTER 27

"Shit."

Nic's expletive jolted Marianne from her doze. She shook her head to clear her sleep-fogged brain. It was late afternoon, judging from the sun, and she'd been having an unsettlingly erotic daydream in which Valette had featured far too prominently. And graphically. She blushed just remembering it, her body hot and tingling. Please God, she hoped he'd been too intent on the road to notice.

"What is it?"

"A roadblock. I saw it from the top of the hill. We're hidden right now by the trees, but they've already seen us coming. It will look strange if we don't carry on."

Her heart started to pound, but she tried to match his cool, unaffected tone. He'd paid for an equal, someone to match his icy calm under pressure. Pride demanded that she prove she could be equally professional. "Are we Italian tourists again?"

He shook his head. "French farmers. I have forged papers."

"Of course you do. Who made them?"

"Philippe Lacorte."

She raised a brow, impressed. "Lacorte? Really? I heard his

waiting list was a year long." It had taken *her* six months to get her own forged papers from him. They'd cost a fortune, too, but she firmly believed in getting the best, especially for a fake life. Lacorte was an artist.

Valette shrugged. "He owed me a favor."

Marianne squinted up at him, and her pulse rate increased as she studied his handsome profile. "If you think I'm going to put on another"—she struggled to find the appropriate word—"performance like that last one, you can think again."

"You make it sound like a particularly loathsome task," he drawled. "I thought you were beginning to enjoy yourself. "

His expression was innocent, but the twinkle in his eye was downright wicked. *Beast.* He knew exactly the effect he had on her. How humiliating. Especially since toying with her emotions was nothing more than idle amusement to pass the time. She was an irksome but necessary companion to him, nothing more.

Marianne turned her head to hide her betraying blush. *Anything* would be better than having to kiss him again. She couldn't endure it, having his hands on her skin, his mouth on her . . .

Concentrate, imbecile!

She glanced around at the trees and wildflowers banking the roadside, desperate for an alternative. The serrated leaves of some stinging nettles stirred the memory of a childish trick she and Sophie had once played on their mother. "I have an idea. Let me down."

Valette pulled the horses to a stop, frowning suspiciously. "What are you thinking?"

"We should give them something to look at instead of our papers."

Valette smiled. "That's exactly what we did last time, if you recall . . ."

She shot him a quelling glance and hopped down onto the road, rolling up her sleeves as she did so. Without giving herself time to change her mind, she hiked up her skirts and raced into the nearest patch of nettles.

"What in holy hell are you doing?" Valette's hiss of alarm echoed behind her.

The plants stung ferociously wherever they touched. She bit back a curse and dropped to the ground so the leaves brushed her exposed arms and hands and face.

She stifled a cry. Her skin burned, but she forced herself to roll over and over, letting momentum take her down the slope, crushing the plants under her. Tears pricked her eyes as the pain increased. The devil himself was pricking her with thousands of tiny flaming pokers.

She was a stupid, impetuous idiot! Sang de Dieu! It definitely hadn't hurt this much when she was eight.

She finally stopped rolling and lay still on her back, gasping for breath.

Valette jumped down from the cart and strode toward her, his boots and breeches protecting him from being stung. Marianne forced herself to her feet and trudged back up the slight incline, a wobbly smile pinned on her face. He placed his hands on his hips and looked down at her in horrified amazement. "Jesus, woman, are you mad? Look at you!"

She could quite imagine what she looked like; a glance down confirmed her suspicions. Her arms were a mass of angry red welts, raised and hideous like lumpy rice pudding. She could only assume her face looked equally unappealing. At least now she could stop worrying about Valette wanting to kiss her again.

She climbed gingerly back into the hay and lay down, suppressing a groan as the prickly straw touched her raw skin. "This looks just like the rash from scarlet fever." She pulled the blanket over her and pinched her cheeks. "Add a flushed face and a sore throat, and it's extremely convincing."

"You're insane." Valette was watching her with an expression of mingled bemusement and disbelief. He shook his head, then slapped the reins over the horses' heads. They lumbered forward. "Well, you've done it now. Let me do the talking."

Marianne stared at the sky, feeling the cart slow as they reached the roadblock. She heard sound of booted feet, the metallic clink of swords and muskets. *Calm. She had to be calm.* She'd been in worse scrapes than this and survived.

"Halt. Papers, please."

"Afternoon, Officer. What's all this about?"

Valette had disguised his accent again. Gone was the melodious, aristocratic French he normally used. Instead, he'd added a touch of gutter Parisian mixed with a hint of the Loire. Marianne tamped down a little thrill of admiration for his skills.

He withdrew a packet of travel documents from his coat and passed them down to the guard.

"You alone, Monsieur Guillard?"

"Just me and the wife." Nic flicked his head back at her.

"What's your business?"

"We're on our way to Tours, monsieur."

"Why's she hiding back there?"

Two soldiers came round the side of the cart and peered in at her. Marianne didn't need to try very hard to look miserable. Her whole body was tingling. And not in the good, exciting way in which Valette's gaze had made her tingle, either.

"She's not well," Valette said, a master of understatement. "We'd all but given up hope, until we heard of Monsieur Brettoneau. He runs the hospital at Tours. They say he's cured plenty of people with symptoms like hers."

Marianne watched through half-closed eyes as the soldiers took in the rash on her skin. Their expressions changed from suspicion to horror. They both reared back at the same time.

"Sir! Come and look at this."

The officer looked in at her and frowned. "What's the matter with her?"

Valette shrugged. "I'm no doctor, monsieur. I don't *think* it's contagious but . . ."

Marianne tried to look even more pitiful. "My throat hurts," she rasped weakly. She placed a hand on her forehead, drawing attention to the welts on her arms. She flailed a little and kicked aside the blanket so they'd get a good look at her legs, too. "So hot!" She managed a dry cough.

Valette injected a note of panic into his voice. "Please, sir, let us pass. She grows worse with every hour."

He turned and shot Marianne a quelling glare over his shoulder, and she bit her lip against the mad urge to giggle. Maybe she *was* overdoing it a bit. But the thrill of the subterfuge was like a rush to the head. She was used to working alone, but she had to admit that it was a pleasure to work with such a competent partner. Getting away with it was the best feeling on earth.

It was a surprise to realize that sharing the success with someone else felt even better than when she was by herself.

The commander fumbled in his pocket and pressed his handkerchief over his nose and mouth. "Jesus, get her out of here! And don't stop until you reach the hospital, you hear?"

Nic nodded subserviently and clicked the horses forward. He tugged his forelock. "Thank you, Officer. Good day."

CHAPTER 28

"*I* can't believe they fell for it!" Marianne resisted the urge to scratch her arm again.

Valette shook his head irritably. "If I'd known you were going to take such drastic action, I'd have stopped you."

She started to wrinkle her nose, but even that movement hurt. "I wouldn't have listened. Besides, it worked, didn't it? Admit it, it was a brilliant idea."

"It was a reckless, stupid, idiotic idea. Try something like that again, and I'll wring your neck."

"Yes, monsieur," she said meekly.

He tilted his head, not at all fooled by her sudden show of subservience. "Was the idea of pretending to be my wife again too horrible to contemplate?"

"Absolutely."

His eyes took on that calculating gleam she'd learned to dread. "It does seem odd that you'd go to such lengths to avoid it. Why is that? What is it about kissing me that bothers you so much?"

Her heart hammered against her ribs, but she managed to sound bored. "I don't happen to *like* kissing you."

He snorted. "Liar. One of these days you're going to kiss me back."

She managed a theatrical shudder, even though it hurt. "I'd rather gouge out my own eyes."

His wicked chuckle echoed down the lane.

They traveled for another hour or so, every jolt of the cart agony on her sensitive skin. She supposed they must be skirting the northeastern edge of Paris, but she was too miserable to care. When they finally pulled into an inn, Valette sprang down to hire a room and Marianne looked around tiredly. At least it looked better than the place they'd left the carriage that first night.

It hurt to move. She was still getting down from the cart, wincing with the effort, when Valette returned five minutes later.

"Ow. Ow. Owwww."

He put his hands on his hips, his expression uncompromising. "It's your own fault. You won't get any sympathy from me."

"I saved your rotten hide, Nicolas Valette. You could show some gratitude."

He watched her struggle for perhaps a minute then with a sigh of exasperation simply swung her down into his arms.

"*Owww!* Hey!"

"Shut up. You're in no position to argue."

In truth, she was grateful for the assistance, but she'd die before she told him so. She *was* feeling a little light-headed. He grabbed a cloak and covered her with it to hide her rash as he strode through the open doorway. Marianne laid her head against his chest, feeling his heartbeat beneath her cheek. He said something about his wife being asleep to the hostler and then they were moving again. It was nice to be carried upstairs in his arms, as if she weighed nothing at all.

Valette kicked open a door with his foot and set her down gently in the middle of a huge bed. It was an ancient four-post affair, with curtains to keep out the drafts. Marianne looked up into his face and swallowed nervously. He was regarding her with a strange expression—frowning, yet oddly tender. "Poor little soldier."

He sounded like he was dealing with a naughty child, but there was admiration mixed in with the pity, she was sure. And even—dare she hope—a little bit of pride?

"Those nettles even stung me through my clothes," she muttered plaintively. "I have bumps *everywhere*."

A muscle ticked in his jaw. "I've ordered you a bath. I'll get a drink in the taproom."

Within minutes two servants had placed a huge copper tub in front of the fire and filled it with steaming water. What luxury! She couldn't remember the last time she'd had a real, truly hot bath. She'd barely taken the time to wash at the château, and in Paris she never had the patience to heat the necessary water, so she and Sophie usually took turns in a lukewarm hip bath.

She managed to strip herself of her dress and camisole, cursing as the rough cotton brushed her tender skin. Pale pink blotches still marred her flesh, but it wasn't nearly as bad as it had been. She reached up automatically to twist her hair into a knot before she remembered she had no hair to keep dry. Another crime to lay at Valette's door. She sank into the bath with a sigh. The pain had begun to fade, but now it returned full force, and her eyes stung with tears. Still, it felt heavenly to be clean again.

The low rumble of conversation filtered up from the taproom below, mixing with the crackle and hiss of the fire in the grate and the rhythmic ticking of the clock on the mantel. She leaned her head back, lulled into a sleepy, semi-drifting state by the heat and steam.

The stub of a candle had been pressed into a rectangle of soap and Marianne watched it flicker through half-closed eyes, her body suffused with languid drowsiness. Her limbs felt like lead. She never wanted to move again.

The creak of the floorboards outside in the corridor barely

registered, but when the door latch clicked, she snapped to complete wakefulness. *Merde!* Her blades were across the room. Water sloshed onto the rug as she surged upright in sudden panic, all her dreamy lassitude forgotten. And then she recognized the intruder.

"Valette!" she shrieked, crossing her arms over her chest in outrage. She sank back to her shoulders in the tub. The position brought her knees out of the water, but it was the best she could do. Thank God the soap had made the water murky. "Do you mind?"

He closed the door behind him, his lazy smile in no way contrite. "Not at all."

She glared at him over her shoulder. "Turn around! Or better still, get out."

He ignored her. Instead, he placed the two bottles he was holding on a side table and stepped around the tub. He stood looking down at her, a diabolic smile playing around his lips.

"Stop it," she snapped, sinking farther into the water.

His face was a picture of innocence. "Stop what?"

"Looking at me like I'm a lock you're about to pick," she said tartly.

His grin turned wolfish. "What a graphic image."

"Turn your back so I can get out."

He sat down on the edge of the bed, entirely at ease. *Beast.*

"It's nothing I haven't seen before," he pointed out reasonably. "I'm not a complete stranger to the naked female form."

She suppressed a snort. What a monstrous understatement. He'd probably seen more naked women than she'd had hot dinners. He'd bedded the most beautiful women in Paris. Which meant he'd bedded the most beautiful women in the world, because everyone knew the ladies of Paris were unrivaled.

"I, however, am a stranger to being naked with a man," she countered severely.

"Don't be ridiculous. You used to live in a brothel." He picked up a bath sheet from the bed and held it out toward her. His wicked glance dared her to take it.

This was some kind of test. He thought he had her at a disadvantage, thought she was too much of a coward to take it. Well, he should know better than to issue her a challenge.

Marianne fixed him with her most determined glare, gripped the edge of the bath, and stood.

Rivulets of water slipped down the valley between her breasts and streamed over her belly and thighs. Hot agitation surged through her as she became acutely aware of every sensitive inch of her skin. Her body hummed with mingled terror and excitement. She couldn't believe she was being so brazen.

This was a spectacularly stupid idea.

She quashed the urge to slump back down into the water. Instead, she raised her chin and clenched her fists at her sides, determined not to hide. No man was ever going to make her feel ashamed or vulnerable again.

If she'd managed to surprise him, he didn't show it. His impassive gaze roamed over her, his eyes hooded as he took a brief, devastating inventory. What did he see when he looked at her? He was used to women with perfect skin and perfect breasts and long, shapely legs. Women with gorgeous hair and tiny waists. Next to them she was gauche and plain and unsophisticated. It was ridiculous to think he'd take one look at her bony, boyish body and be overrun by lust. Besides, she was covered head to toe in red welts. He was probably only struggling to hide his distaste.

For a long moment Valette didn't speak. And then he rose up and came toward her, silent as a panther. The air between them thickened. He stopped an arm's length away, and his glittering eyes moved over her with the depth of a caress.

Her stomach flipped, and she felt the blood rise in her cheeks. He wasn't even touching her, but her skin tingled as if it was being brushed by a feather. Her nipples beaded in the cool air, and her heart hammered in her throat. A strange achy sensation curled in the pit of her stomach, half fear, half excitement.

He was mocking and beautiful, flawless and wicked. And she wanted him more than she'd ever wanted anything in her life. The memory of the way he'd kissed her in the cart rose up in her mind. She'd thought of it a hundred times, his hands on her skin, his mouth on hers.

She would not back down. She imagined him a servant and herself a queen. She gave him a haughty, regal lift of the eyebrows and held out her hand for the bath sheet, relieved to see it was steady.

An approving smile curved his lips. "Bravo."

CHAPTER 29

To Marianne's utter amazement, he looked away first.

He crossed to the table under the window, and she released the breath she hadn't realized she'd been holding. She grabbed the sheet and tucked the ends tightly under her armpits, then stepped out of the tub.

He picked up the two bottles from the table; one clearly contained brandy, but the other one was smaller, made of brown glass. "I got chamomile lotion from the innkeeper," he said. "It will help with the rash."

Marianne stood cocooned in the sheet, uncertain what to do next. "Thank you."

He shot her a subtly depraved smile. "You're going to need help applying it."

Her skin prickled anew. "And what's the brandy for?"

He poured two generous glasses, handed one to her, and chinked the rim of his own against it. "The pain. Drink up."

"I don't—"

His fingers closed around hers as he guided the glass to her lips. "Drink it, Marianne."

It was absurdly intimate, to be dressed in only a sheet,

drinking brandy in a bedroom with a man. Marianne felt wicked and sophisticated. And jittery. She took a wary sip, her eyes on his, and felt it burn down her throat and into her stomach. He smiled at her docility, and when he dropped his hand from hers, she felt oddly bereft.

She took another gulp, warmed from the inside out. She should make him leave. It was just asking for trouble, letting him to stay, but she couldn't resist. She finished the brandy.

"Now lie on the bed."

When she hesitated, he stalked forward, put his hands on her shoulders, and turned her to face the bed. It took only the tiniest push for her to fall forward onto the mattress. She gasped as he eased the sheet down. Cool air caressed her back, raising goose bumps on her skin, and she buried her face into the covers, overcome by sudden shyness. What she must look like, sprawled half naked on the covers like some debauched harlot?

Then again, he'd probably seen hundreds of women like this. She'd bet none of *them* had been covered in unattractive red splotches.

The silence stretched her nerves to screaming point. "Is it as bad as that?" she ventured.

"Hmm?" He sounded distracted.

"My skin," she clarified. "What's it like?"

"Cinnamon and cream."

Her mouth fell open against the covers. The mattress dipped as he sat on the edge of the bed, and she jumped as his fingers touched her bare shoulder. "You know, it's all right," she murmured in panic, starting to turn over. "I'm sure I can manage."

He pressed her firmly back down, his hand on her shoulder. "And I'm sure you can't. Lie still." He uncorked the bottle with a pop.

Marianne let out a hiss when he pressed the wet pad of cotton to her skin. The coolness was bliss. A sharp, tangy smell prickled her nose, astringent but strangely pleasant.

"The landlady added lemon juice," he said, as if reading her thoughts.

Pleasure mingled with pain as he stroked the cold compress over her back, alternately stinging and soothing. She shivered as he traced her spine and bit her lip when he nudged the sheet lower to dab at a cluster of stings at the hollow of her back.

This was so wrong. No man had ever seen her like this. Touched her like this.

With one sweep of his hand he both calmed and inflamed. She buried her head deeper into the pillows as a hum of something dark and wicked pooled low in her stomach. Her breasts tingled. Her breath came in shallow pants. What would happen if she turned over and opened her arms to him?

He'd probably laugh, that's what.

"There." His voice sounded rough, as if he needed to clear his throat. He flicked the sheet back over her body, and she suppressed a groan of disappointment.

"Thank you," she croaked.

"My pleasure."

She turned her head to look at him. He gazed down at her for a long moment, and she thought he was about to say more, but he thrust himself off the bed and stood. "You can manage the rest yourself."

"Where are you going?"

"Downstairs."

"Are you sleeping in here?" she asked in a small voice.

"Yes, but in the chair. I'm going to the taproom. Go to sleep."

The door slammed shut behind him. Marianne stared at the wooden planks, fighting an odd combination of disappointment and hurt.

* * *

NIC STOMPED DOWNSTAIRS, desire and frustration boiling in his blood.

He knew precisely what Marianne was thinking—that he'd just rejected her. She already had the ludicrous idea that she wasn't attractive enough to tempt a lover, thanks to Duval's manhandling. In her convoluted female mind, his actions just now would just confirm it.

He bit back a bitter laugh. Nothing could be further from the truth. The fact that he was massive, rock hard for her, barely seemed worth noting. He'd wanted her from the first moment he'd seen her.

She was beautiful. All that warm, rosy flesh beckoning him. He'd wanted to tell her, but for the first time in his life words had failed him.

He'd complimented women by the score, flattered and praised with extravagant, meaningless platitudes. He'd told women he wanted them, adored them, worshipped them. But he'd never once told a woman he needed her.

He needed Marianne. Yearned for her with a soul-deep ache that was disturbing, laughable, inexplicable. Just the thought of touching her made him insane. Everything about her was wrong. He liked order and neatness and efficiency. She was unpredictable, messy, and emotional.

He thumped the wall, welcoming the sting in his knuckles.

Why hadn't he finished it? Any other time, any other woman, and he'd have taken what was being offered without a second thought. She'd been ready, eager. Practically begging him. God, he should turn back round, kick down the door, and just take her. He could be inside her in ten seconds flat. He groaned at the thought. He wanted it so badly he could practically taste it.

And that was precisely why he wasn't going to do anything about it.

Something had changed between them, some indefinable twist to the dynamic that was both unnerving and exciting. He liked her. Respected her. Wanted her. They were no longer master and apprentice; instead of opponents, they were suddenly a team.

Nic forced his feet to continue down the stairs. He *needed* her frustrated. Needed her alert and on edge for the job. But bloody hell, it was torture.

He settled himself in the taproom and was immediately pounced on by two eager serving women. The blond one with dimples bent low over the table under the pretense of wiping up and gave him an eyeful of her ample bosom. She was a ripe, rounded, fleshy handful, but she smelled of stale beer and cloying perfume. The brunette was skinnier, with a thin, pretty face, but Nic felt his desire slipping away.

What the hell was wrong with him? He was thirty-five, not some callow youth of eighteen. He shouldn't be lusting after a prickly little virgin.

But all he could see was the curve of Marianne's back as she rose from the tub. The two indentations at the top of her buttocks as they pooled with droplets of water. The shape of her waist, just crying out for his hands.

Bloody hell.

He stared moodily into his wine. He wanted to trace those droplets with his tongue. Wanted to lap them off her, inch by inch, down between her legs, until she wrapped them around him. He wanted to sink into her sweet, lithe acrobat's body and screw her until they couldn't remember their own names. Maybe then he'd get her out of his system.

The blonde pouted provocatively at him from across the room, batting her lashes. He shook his head, thoroughly annoyed with himself. He should just accept what she was offering and have done with it.

But the last time he'd paid a woman for sex had been the day he'd lost his virginity—his fifteenth birthday. And even then it had been his older brother, Richard, who'd actually hired the girl

—and the room at the Three Bells inn, in Swanage—as a birthday treat for Nic.

In Paris he could snap his fingers and have any number of beautiful, intelligent, accomplished women grace his bed. He always enjoyed their company, but he'd never wanted more from them than a few nights' entertainment. He had absolutely no difficulty keeping his emotions separate from his physical needs.

He gave a frustrated sigh. He didn't want any of those women back in Paris. And he had the awful premonition that even if he sated himself with the buxom barmaid, and her skinny friend, he'd still be plagued with a gnawing sense of dissatisfaction. He kicked the table leg with his boot. When had he started wanting more than just a willing body to service him? He wanted a partner, an equal, someone who understood him, challenged him. Who engaged not merely his body, but his mind and his emotions, too.

He wanted Marianne.

He closed his eyes and thought of her, upstairs in that room. In bed. Probably naked.

He took another long sip of wine.

Merde.

Nic stayed downstairs for a couple of hours, slowly getting drunk. The burgundy was awful, so he switched to brandy instead, but it was only marginally better.

Marianne was asleep, bundled into a tight ball on one side of the huge bed, by the time he slunk back into the room. She'd left a single candle burning by the bed, and he moved so he could study her face, watch the rhythmic rise and fall of her chest under the opaque transparency of his shirt, which she'd obviously stolen to sleep in. He liked her wearing his shirt.

She looked smaller, asleep—younger and more vulnerable. He smiled, remembering the way she'd called his bluff with the bath tonight. Impudent little baggage.

He wanted to lie down next to her, to stretch his long body

onto the narrow bed and hold her close to him. To comfort her, seek comfort himself. He gave a disgusted snort. No, that wasn't true. He wasn't so altruistic. He wanted more than comfort. He wanted her to take him into her mouth. He wanted to push his body into hers. He wanted to have her in all the ways he'd dreamed of having her.

He reached out and brushed a finger across her lips. She made a slight mewling sound and turned her face toward him, seeking him unconsciously in her sleep in a way she never did when she was awake. He stroked her cheek and then bent down and brushed his lips against hers, even as he cursed himself for the weakness.

Her eyelids flickered, and he almost willed her to wake so he could take her into his arms and kiss her again, properly. He wouldn't be able to stop with kisses. Sighing, he stepped back and extinguished the candle with his fingers. He settled into the lumpy armchair.

It was going to be another long, uncomfortable night.

* * *

NIC YAWNED and stretched his stiff shoulders as they pulled out of the inn yard. The chair in the room had been so lumpy he'd barely slept a wink, and he'd left to find some breakfast long before Marianne awoke.

She shot him a poisonous glance from her side of the cart. "Up late, were we?"

He gave her look that mirrored his confusion. "What?"

"With the barmaid." She looked away, clearly annoyed with herself for having brought the subject up. "I saw the way she waved at you. Don't you get tired of women throwing themselves at you?"

Ah. She thought he'd spent the night elsewhere. He shot her a cocky grin. "It hasn't happened yet."

"I thought men liked a challenge?"

"The challenge is seeing how fast you can get 'em into bed." He'd burn in hell for tormenting her, but he just couldn't resist. She rose so wonderfully to the bait. "Jealous?"

Sure enough, her head whipped round, and she raised that pert little nose high into the air.

"Hardly. Your nocturnal activities are no concern of mine. I don't care how many wenches you service between here and Vincennes. If I learned one thing at the Montausier, it's that men have certain . . . ah . . . urges." She flushed.

He didn't bother to conceal his amusement. "You learned that, did you? And what else did the tarts teach you? How to help a man with those . . . urges? Hmm?" He particularly enjoyed the way even her ears turned pink.

She pursed her lips shut. "Nothing. They taught me absolutely nothing at all."

Nic glanced at her stern profile. With her short haircut and slim figure she could easily have passed for a boy, except for those damnably erotic lips and long eyelashes.

One day, Mademoiselle Bonnard, I'm going to fill in the gaps in your education.

She swatted irritably at a fly that dared to hover near her.

That was one thing he loved about her. No, not *loved*, he amended quickly, *liked* about her. Appreciated. For all her vivacity, she was entirely devoid of artifice. She lied to him all the time, of course, but emotionally, at least, she was useless at hiding her feelings. She didn't want to entice or ensnare. And that, ironically, was what he found so attractive. She wasn't immune to his flirtations, but she was doing her very best to ignore them. Unfortunately, her reluctance only fired his blood.

She was so unlike every other woman of his acquaintance. Any other woman would have been using this opportunity to seduce him. Any other woman would have been flirting and simpering, using every feminine wile in her arsenal to engage his attention. Nic gave an ironic smile. He couldn't imagine Marianne flirting. If she wanted something from a man, she'd just threaten him with a knife.

He wanted to kiss the tilt tip of her nose, to cajole her out of her sulks. He wanted to teach her all the astonishing things she could do with that mouth. He shifted uncomfortably on the seat.

"It's going to rain," she said despondently.

Her gloomy prediction broke into his erotic daydreams like an icy sledgehammer. Perhaps that was why she'd done it. Nic glanced at the sky and cursed. She was right. The closer they got to Paris, the darker the clouds became. They swirled ominously overhead, threatening a summer storm of epic proportions, and Nic tamped down a superstitious feeling of unease. Even the weather was going against them.

CHAPTER 30

*M*arianne's stomach writhed with nerves, a hundred times worse than before her opening night at the circus. Why on earth had she ever agreed to do this? Who in their right mind broke *into* a prison? And, *Oh God,* what if something went wrong? Valette said everything was arranged, but people were notoriously unpredictable. Things *always* went wrong.

"Please don't tell me you kidnapped a priest to get this outfit," she murmured as Valette drew the rough hooded cloak over her head. Her teeth were chattering.

He smiled angelically. "Of course not."

She wrinkled her nose and tried to concentrate on the immediate things around her instead of the suicidal task that lay ahead. The cloth smelled of garlic, sweat, and soil. Whomever the previous owner had been, bathing clearly hadn't been high up on his list of priorities. Her stomach pitched, and she scratched herself, horribly suspicious she wasn't the only living creature in the hideous garment.

The long-sleeved robes of a novice were tied at the waist with an unadorned length of twisted rope. The overlong hem dragged on the dusty ground, but at least it disguised the fact that she was wearing thieving clothes underneath: black breeches, black stockings, black shirt. Her ballet slippers, kindly provided by Laurent, were tucked in the back of her breeches.

She suspected the shirt belonged to Valette. It smelled of him. She buried her nose in it, oddly comforted by his scent. Anything was better than garlic.

He drew up her hood and surveyed her with his head on one side.

"What?" she demanded self-consciously.

"There's nothing we can do about your eyes. They should be blue, not green." He sighed, as if it was *her* fault. "Keep them down. And leave the talking to me. I'm Father Beaupré, a Jesuit priest. You're Brother Francis, my apprentice."

She knew the plan. They'd gone over it only a million times.

As they ducked out of the stables she took the opportunity to study Valette in turn. She scowled, thoroughly disgusted. No man should look so enticing while dressed as a monk. He was so handsome. So vitally alive. And that seductive, stomach-melting smile was anything but holy. She fiddled with the sleeve of her shirt, uncomfortably hot.

"I'm sure it's a sin to impersonate a priest," she muttered.

He smiled that wicked half smile. "It's hardly the worst thing I've ever done. Nor you, either, I bet."

His face was alight, his eyes glowing. There was a new intensity about him, an almost tangible aura of excitement. He was enjoying this, she realized with a shock. Here she was, almost sick with terror, and the damn man was actually *enjoying* himself.

But somehow his sense of anticipation transferred itself to her. Just being near him was exhilarating. "You love this, don't you?" she said. "Outsmarting others. Breaking the rules and getting away with it."

He shot her a wicked glance from under his lashes "Don't you think there's something wonderful about the planning of a crime, *chérie*? The buildup of tension, the preparation. That buzz of exhilaration when you succeed." His teeth flashed white as he smiled. "Admit it. You feel it, too, when you're up on that wire. The rush. The anticipation."

His lazy grin was so contagious she had to smile back. "Yes," she admitted. "When I lose my balance—just for a second—it makes me want to laugh, like a mad thing."

"Because you realize how good it is to be alive."

He was right. On solid ground she couldn't fall and break her neck. But then she'd never experience that crazy elation of reaching the end of the wire and taking a bow, either. He understood what it was like to face the danger and enjoy it.

She could do this. It was just another performance, after all.

He leaned closer, and she caught her breath at the warm, masculine scent of him. *His* robes didn't smell.

"We're the same, Marianne. We're both addicted to the thrill." He sent her a sidelong glance. "It's *almost* better than sex."

Her mouth dropped open.

"Time to stop talking." He patted her cheek. "You, I'm sorry to say, Brother Francis, have taken holy vows of silence."

She started to refute him, but he silenced her with a finger across her parted lips. Her stomach fluttered at the light touch.

"Hush now." The twinkle in his eyes betrayed his delight in this mastery over her.

She glared at him from under her hood, silently promising retribution.

"Yes. A vow of silence . . . and chastity," he added, chuckling. "Definitely a vow of chastity. Which, considering how pretty you are, sweet Brother Francis, is a crying shame."

He reached into the back of the cart and handed her a pile of heavy, leather-bound books, then arranged his own hood so that it hid his face and hair.

This was never going to work. His chest was too broad, his body too strong for a benign priest. And then, before her eyes, he seemed to melt into the clothing. He hunched his shoulders and stooped his back, assuming the guise of a much older man. If she didn't know better, she'd swear he had a fat, paunchy belly hidden beneath the folds of his robe, instead of that lean, taut stomach she'd tried so hard to ignore.

As they turned onto the main road of Vincennes, Marianne eyed the ridiculously high walls of the fortress with trepidation. They loomed overhead, gray and imposing, casting long shadows over the embankment and outer moat. Her stomach lurched. Why on earth had she agreed to this? She was going to be sick. It wasn't too late to back out.

She stumbled. Valette caught her elbow and steadied her, then slid his hand down to rest at the bottom of her spine. He rubbed her back, his touch both soothing and propelling her inexorably forward. The wretch.

"Since you can't answer back," he said in a low voice, "I think this is the perfect opportunity to discuss our relationship."

"We don't *have* a relationship," she hissed out of the corner of her mouth. "Unless you count my wanting to kill you a relationship."

"Hush, Brother Francis," he chided gently. "Vow of silence, remember?" He chuckled as she cursed under her breath. "And I beg to disagree. We most definitely *do* have a relationship. An unorthodox one, to be sure, but a relationship nonetheless."

They were getting closer to the gatehouse. *Merde.*

"Shall we talk about how I'd love to get you naked?"

She nearly dropped the books. His pious expression was completely at odds with his wicked words. Prickles flashed over her skin. She seemed to be having trouble breathing.

"Because I do," he continued casually, as if they were discussing nothing more innocuous than the weather. "Quite desperately." He chuckled as he saw her open her mouth to argue. "No talking."

She closed it with a snap.

His eyes crinkled at the corners. "What, nothing to say? I'll take your silence as consent, then. I like to think you keep imagining *me* naked, too."

She couldn't believe he was saying this. It was to distract her, of course, the same way he'd kissed her to take her mind off the chimney, and, dear God, it was working. She bit her lip as his scandalous words burned themselves into her brain.

"Naked together," he mused softly, his voice like a wicked archangel's.

Her heart was going to beat right out of her chest. She felt light-headed. She kept her silence—mainly because she could think of nothing to say.

He chuckled and turned to bless a local passing in the opposite direction with an elegant air-drawn crucifix. The man accepted the benediction with a nod and no hint of suspicion that they weren't exactly as they appeared to be: a priest and his youthful companion. They passed into the cool purple shadow of the château's walls. The sudden drop in temperature raised the hairs on her arms.

"We've sparked off one another from the moment we met," Valette continued silkily. His voice curled around her like the smoke from one of his cheroots. "*Un coup de foudre,* the French call it. A lightning bolt. It's there every time we touch. Every time we get near each other."

"You're deluded," she whispered. "I hate you."

He stopped walking abruptly and faced her. "No, you don't. I've had lots of experience with people who hate me. None of them look at me the way you do."

She stopped, too. "Oh, really? And how do I look at you?"

"Like you want to fuck me," he whispered.

She gasped in outraged shock, as no doubt he'd intended. *Of all the conceited, arrogant . . .*

"Deny it," he challenged softly.

She shook her head. "You're such a bastard."

"That's true. You haven't denied it."

"I don't even *like* you," she hissed.

He chuckled sympathetically. "I know. But you still want me."

He placed his hand palm down on the uppermost book she was holding and Marianne belatedly realized it was a Bible.

"Here's *my* holy vow," he said, holding her gaze. "When this is over, we're going to do something about it. So help me God."

She looked up, fully expecting divine retribution. Surely that amounted to blasphemy? She braced herself for a lightning strike.

"Deep breath, *chérie*," he murmured, turning her back toward the gatehouse. "We're here."

CHAPTER 31

*T*he guard observed them suspiciously. "Where's the usual priest?"

"Father Aretino's ill," Valette said smoothly. He made another airy sign of the cross. "May the Lord bless his speedy recovery. I'm Father Beaupré."

He'd changed his accent again. This was the soft patois of the Vendée.

The guard grunted. "And him?"

Marianne kept her head down, staring at the Bible.

"Brother Francis. He's taken a vow of silence."

Valette sounded so calm. Her own heart was hammering so hard she was amazed the guard couldn't hear it, but he moved aside and waved them in with grunt of assent.

They passed two more sets of guards, and each time they were sent on, deeper into the belly of the beast. Her palms grew sweaty against the leather covers of the books, and she concentrated on keeping her head down and following close on Valette's heels. The last guard left his post to show them up a narrow, winding staircase. Their footsteps echoed off the curving stone. The guard unlocked the door to a cell and ushered them inside.

"Priest's here for confession," he grunted, then nodded to Valette. "You've got one hour."

The door slammed shut behind him, and Marianne finally looked up.

The room was sparsely furnished, devoid of ornamentation, but surprisingly large and not entirely uncomfortable. There was a single wooden table and chair, a small wooden cot, and a few other simple pieces of furniture. A tiny patch of sky was visible through a slit window high up on one wall.

A man was seated at the table, reading. He stood as they entered, and Marianne studied him intently. The first thing she noticed was his hair. It was the same color brown as hers, and shoulder-length. She scowled. Valette needn't have hacked hers off so short, after all.

His eyes were blue, and he had a fine nose and a prominent chin. His lower lip stuck out a little, like that of a pouting child. They were about the same height, and although he looked a few years older than she did, they were of the same slight build. He'd obviously been an invalid, or a prisoner, for some time. His thin shoulders and pale face aroused a twinge of sympathy in her breast. That was the face of someone who hardly ever went outside. How awful. Even on her worst days in Paris, she could still lift her face to the sky and feel the sun on her cheeks.

An odd sense of recognition tugged her. Had they met before? Had he visited the circus? Or the Palais Royale?

Valette removed his hood and sketched a bow. "Monsieur, your servant."

The prisoner acknowledged the greeting with a bow of his own. "Is it time?" His face was composed, but there was a glitter of excitement in his eyes as he stepped forward.

"Yes. May I present to you Mademoiselle Marianne Bonnard?"

Marianne tugged off her hood and the prisoner's eyebrows shot up in surprise. "A *girl*?"

K. C. BATEMAN

She bristled. "What did you expect? A chimney sweep?"

The man appealed to Valette. "But . . . I thought it was to be a man . . . what she must do . . . Are you sure?"

Valette took the books from Marianne and placed them on the table with a thud. "I have the utmost confidence in her, monsieur. In fact, I'd go so far as to say she's the only person in France who *could* do it."

Her heart fluttered at the compliment, even though he was saying it only to bolster her confidence.

"Marianne, may I present to you citizen Louis-Charles Capet. Also called Louis-Charles de Bourbon, Prince Royal of France."

The room swayed, and for a moment Marianne thought she'd heard incorrectly. She could have sworn he said—

She took another close look at the prisoner, trying to deny what her eyes were telling her. Fat King Louis's face was on all the old coins. Napoleon had put himself on the new decimal ones, but gold Louis D'or were still circulated as unofficial currency. Gold was gold, whoever's head was stamped on it. And the man facing her was a thinner version of the one on the coins.

Valette was watching her, patiently waiting for her to arrive at the correct conclusion.

Merde. Merde. Merde.

For once in his life the sneaky bastard had actually told her the *truth*. This pasty-faced man was the rightful King of France.

"Excuse me one moment." Marianne nodded at the prisoner, grabbed Valette's sleeve, and yanked him aside. "Why in God's name didn't you tell me who we were rescuing?"

He raised his brows in that supercilious way that made her itch to stab him. "I did tell you, if you recall."

"You told me he was a Royalist supporter!"

"He is. The *ultimate* Royalist supporter."

"This is not funny," she whispered furiously. "You know I didn't believe you! Did you think I'd refuse?"

The corner of his mouth curled upward. "It had crossed my mind. You're hardly the monarchy's greatest fan."

"It's one thing to rescue a thief or a political refugee. It's another thing entirely to kidnap the *rightful bloody King of France!*" Her voice rose to a shriek, and she made a concerted effort to lower it. "It's treason," she hissed.

"It's mercy."

As if to reinforce his words a fit of coughing racked the prisoner, doubling him over. The man clutched the back of the chair for support. "And as you can see, he's in no fit state to escape on his own," Valette finished.

Marianne's heart softened. If this man really *were* the prince, then he'd spent the past *twenty years* in one prison or another, punished for simply existing. It wasn't right. She shot Valette her best we'll-talk-about-this-later look and turned back to the prisoner with an embarrassed smile. "I'm sorry, monsieur. Forgive me."

The man sketched her a formal bow, and Marianne couldn't resist a smile. She was dressed in stinking monk's robes, with boys' breeches underneath. Should she bow? Curtsy? Offer her hand?

Her mother's voice whispered in her memory. *Remember your manners, Marianne! Skirts out to the side. Chin high. Bend your knees. More! Lowest of all for royalty.*

She bobbed an awkward curtsy. Behind her, Valette snorted.

"My pleasure, mademoiselle." There was a smile twinkling in the prisoner's blue eyes as he straightened, as if he too appreciated the ridiculous nature of the meeting.

Valette pushed past her, all business. "Is everything in place?"

"Yes."

"Then let's go."

The prisoner reached under the table and withdrew a thin piece of metal. It was the hinge that bolted the table leg to the top. He handed the primitive tool to Marianne and tapped his foot over one of the flagstones to the right of the bed. "It's all under here. Be careful, the stone's heavy."

Marianne stripped out of the novice's cloak with a sigh of relief and handed it to him. He put it on, pulled up hood, and picked up the pile of books from the table.

Valette nodded his satisfaction. "Don't say a word. You've taken a vow of silence."

The bed was very hard and uncomfortable. Marianne lay down, pulled the covers up to her ears, and faced the wall. Her heart was thumping against her ribs. *Oh God.* They really were doing this. *What if something went wrong? What if this was the last time she ever saw him?*

The woolen blanket was rough against her cheek as Valette smoothed it over her shoulder. She gazed up at him in sudden panic. She would *not* beg him not to leave her. She still had some dignity left.

He bent over her. "You remember the trick with the chimney?" he murmured. "Think of the thing you want most in the world." His eyes burned into hers. "Think of something worth fighting for. Worth living for." He brushed her lips with his, the very briefest of salutes. "Courage, *chérie*," he whispered. "I'll see you outside." He crossed to the door and rapped on it. "Guard!"

Marianne ducked her head into the blankets as his summons was answered.

"He's too tired for confession today," Valette said. "I will pray he isn't falling victim to the same ailment as Father Aretino."

The guard gave an uncaring grunt.

"Come along Brother Francis," Valette chided, ushering his charge into the corridor. "We'll be late for evening prayers."

The door slammed shut behind them with a clang like a death knell.

CHAPTER 32

*M*arianne strained her ears, waiting for an alarm to be raised, but all remained quiet. As the silence continued she became acutely aware of being alone. Birds swooped and whirled beyond the tiny slit window, mocking her with their freedom. The faint, steady *drip, drip* of water from outside matched her racing pulse, and she realized with dismay that it had started to rain.

Oh, perfect.

Human contact was something she'd always taken for granted. At the circus and the brothel there was always someone interesting to talk to. She frowned. Louis-Charles must have been only eight or nine years old when his parents were executed. And from what she could remember, his only surviving sister, Marie Thérèse, had been sent abroad, married off to some Austrian prince.

What must it have been like to be held here day after day, with no hope of escape, of rescue? To be separated from the life you knew, the people you loved? It didn't bear thinking about. At least she and Sophie had had each other after their parents had died.

Marianne tensed at a sound beyond the door. Valette had told her the guards checked the cells twice a day, morning and evening. If they chose today for one of their extra, random searches, she'd be in deep trouble.

The sky grew darker. It was time to move.

Nervous energy tingled through her limbs. She shook them out and pried up the flagstone Louis-Charles had indicated. The promised rope was underneath, and she looped it around herself on the diagonal, over one shoulder, like a soldier's bandolier, then pulled her ballet shoes from inside her belt and put them on. The familiar feel of them calmed her nerves a fraction. This was just one more performance, after all.

She kicked the cold ashes of the fire out of the hearth, ducked under the mantel, and stood up inside the chimney. It was even smaller than the one at the château, and her stomach clenched in dismay.

The iron bars just above her head came free after a little wiggling. A shower of plaster dust rained down on her, and she blinked hard then squinted up, up. There—high above—was a tiny patch of sky.

Time to get moving.

Marianne braced her legs against the walls and began to climb. It was as tight and dark as a coffin. Soot filled her nostrils; the charred smell of death was binding her like a shroud. Her throat closed. She didn't want to inhale, to soil her lungs with the darkness. If she breathed in, it would hurt her, devour her. Her heart beat out a panicked tattoo against her ribs. Her chest burned.

What had Valette said? *Think of something else.* She squeezed her eyes closed and took a tiny sip of air. *His kiss. Think about that. Sweet, clean air and his kiss.*

Her foot slipped, and she slid down a few feet, scraping her elbows and knees. Her nails broke as she scrabbled for purchase, and she let out a choked sob of pain. She clenched her jaw and wriggled back up. The flue narrowed even farther; she would surely get stuck.

She ducked her chin and buried her face into her shirt, inhaling deeply. Nic's shirt. It smelled of him. Gunpowder and flint, brandy and steel. She concentrated on identifying the individual scents, just as she'd done with the wine. Musky spice. Leather. Something dark and smoky. And a hint of earthiness, like a grassy field on a dry, warm day. She drew him into her lungs and held him there, as if she could draw his strength into herself, too.

He was out there, waiting for her. She could do this.

With an arch of her back she pushed her body upward. The heavy stone pressed in. There was no room to inflate her lungs.

Sophie was out there.

She uncurled her fingers, slid them up the sooty walls.

Nearly there.

She could hear the hiss of rain on the roof. As she neared the top a few drops fell on her upturned face, cold and stinging. She let out a shuddering breath. Nothing had ever felt so good.

Emerging from the chimney was like surfacing from underwater. The night air was so sweet she almost laughed aloud. She took a huge cleansing gulp and wriggled free, hardly caring that she was getting drenched to the skin.

Dieu Merci!

The roof tiles were slick, and she slid the short distance to the narrow parapet on her backside, then leaned over the edge and looked down. Her stomach lurched.

It was almost full dark now, with rain clouds obscuring what little moon there was. Lights were twinkling on all around the keep. On the opposite side Marianne could see a courtyard, then the outer wall, with its canon lined up on a raised platform behind the low crenellations. Below her the water in the moat was a dark, unwelcoming gleam. She squinted into the gloom.

Nothing seemed to be moving. If Valette was out there, he was well hidden.

Fear and exhilaration gripped her at the same time. Everything came sharply into focus: the swallows swooping to their roosts under the battlements, the salty taste of her sweat as she licked her upper lip, the hard patter of rain on her skin.

She unwound the rope and secured it around one of the gargoyle rainspouts that protruded from the edge of the building. It was hard to tell what this one was supposed to be, it was so eroded by rainfall and darkened with soot—some snarling lion or gothic dragon, all teeth and claws. She gave the monster an affectionate pat on the head. It reminded her of Valette.

The rain made the rope slippery and hard to tie. She tugged at it, cursing her scraped fingers, then checked that no guards were patrolling below and threw the coil over the side. It unrolled as it fell with a whirr and a snap.

The damn thing had better hold.

She swung out without giving herself time to think. The wind buffeted her hard against the building, and the rope spun crazily. She held on tightly, praying for it to steady. Worse still, the rainspout was doing its job all too well, sending a freezing cascade of water directly onto her head, blinding her.

When she finally stopped spinning, she began to lower herself, hand over hand, ankles crossed around the rain-slicked rope. It was becoming increasingly hard to grip. A jolt of panic hit her as she missed her hold and she started to slide downward.

The rough hemp cut into her palms, and the friction made them burn. Her arms shook with the effort. The rain splattered her face, but she couldn't spare a hand to wipe her eyes.

Merde.

The rope was too short. It was still fifteen feet to the ground. She dangled for a moment, reluctant to let go, but there was nothing for it. She sent up a silent prayer then dropped. Pain blinded her, and the hard flagstones knocked the breath from her lungs. She rolled instinctively then curled into a fetal position and lay panting until the wave of sickness passed.

Stupid. Stupid!

Her wrist hurt like hell. She pushed herself up, using the wall for support as pain lanced up her shins. She stifled a groan. She felt as though she'd been kicked by a horse.

The thud of booted feet made her freeze. Footsteps were coming closer: two guards, arguing cheerfully over something. Marianne shrank back into the shadows of a doorway and held her breath as they passed by her hiding place.

When they turned the corner, she allowed herself to breathe again and inspected her wrist, terrified it might be broken. She rotated it gingerly. Nothing cracked. It was probably only bruised. She hobbled a few steps forward and cast her eyes over the moat. Valette had said it was at least ten feet deep. The side nearest her was built on an angle, the stones smooth and sloped like the side of a pyramid, impossible to climb. The water at the bottom looked like oil, black and unwelcoming.

The rope was where Valette had said it would be, secured around the trunk of a small tree growing out of the foundations. It hardly looked strong enough to hold her weight, but there was no time to worry about it. It stretched across the moat and disappeared into the trees on the far bank.

A shadow moved in the darkness, and her heart jumped in relief. Valette. He hadn't forsaken her, then. She'd half expected him to follow the prince and leave her to fend for herself.

One last hurdle.

She stepped up onto the rope, using the tree for support, and drew in a deep breath. She knew it was silly—filling her lungs with air couldn't possibly make her lighter—but it was a ritual she couldn't seem to shake. She edged out, feeling with her toes. She missed her parasol.

The rope bounced and swayed. It was thicker than she was

used to. Slacker, too. It wobbled back and forth, and she used her arms to compensate.

Don't look down. You've done this a thousand times.

She was halfway across when she heard a sound like a twanging bow. The rope lurched and she stared in horror at a spot just ahead of her. One of the three strands of the rope had snapped; the broken ends corkscrewed madly around the others. She could actually *hear* them whirring as they unwound. The remaining two strands pulled taut as they took up the strain, and the rope creaked ominously.

Valette must have heard it, too. His low, urgent hiss snaked out of the shadows in front of her. "Come on! Move! Now!"

Marianne started forward as quickly as she dared.

She'd almost reached the center when it snapped.

* * *

SHE HIT the freezing water with a splash and swallowed a mouthful in shock; it tasted disgusting, like rotting vegetation. She surfaced with a gasp and flailed around, utterly disoriented. Her hands tangled in the leaves and slimy stems of water lilies. Something coiled around her waist and she panicked, trying to kick it away, before she realized it was only the loose end of the rope.

Urgent shouts sounded from behind her, and she abandoned any pretense of keeping quiet. She kicked with her legs and clawed for the reeds on the opposite bank, struggling to keep her head above the water.

Something slimy and definitely *alive* brushed her leg. A sense of dread filled her, all those childhood stories of monstrous eels and terrifying sea monsters slithering to hideous life.

Oh God, she was going to drown and get eaten by eels.

The muddy water and pond weeds sucked at her like grasping fingers trying to drag her under. She thrashed about, desperate to escape the nameless horrors of the water. And then she saw Valette, lying on his stomach on the far bank.

"Grab the rope."

She caught the frayed end he threw at her and held on grimly, turning her head to avoid the spray of water as he pulled her toward him. Her feet made contact with the side but the steep, sloping bank was covered in a layer of sludge so thick and slimy it was almost impossible to climb. She tried to grab onto the reeds, the grass, *anything,* swearing under her breath as she struggled. Her ankle twisted awkwardly in the mud, and she slipped backward again with an involuntary yelp of pain and frustration.

And then Valette leaned forward, grabbed her collar, and hauled her up the bank in a wet slither of mud and limbs.

"Oh, thank—"

His palm slapped over her mouth. "For Christ's sake, shut up!" he hissed in her ear. He pulled her back against his chest then half dragged her backward into the cover of the trees. "Shit," he muttered darkly. "Come on!"

And then she heard it, too: the thunder of boots crossing the thin bridge leading out from the gatehouse.

CHAPTER 33

"I can't run," Marianne panted. "My ankle."

Valette cursed again. The patrol was coming closer, crashing through the undergrowth toward them. He draped her arm over his shoulder, and she managed to hobble along but stumbled as her ankle gave way.

"You go!" she hissed, pushing at him. "There's no need for us both to be caught."

He shook his head. "I left Tony behind. I'll be damned if I'll leave you, too." With a growl of impatience he bent down and threw her over his shoulder. Marianne braced her hands on his lower back as he jogged through the trees.

He was barely breathing hard when they slid inside the barn. He put her down and she sagged, boneless, against the wall, scarcely daring to believe that they'd evaded the patrol. Her heart was thundering against her ribs, but a heady sense of elation filled her. She scrambled up into the waiting cart, and he steered it out onto the road, but as they turned the corner her heart sank.

Merde.

"Halt, who goes there?"

Marianne looked up straight into the barrel of a musket. A

group of soldiers blocked the road, their weapons raised to fire. She lifted her hands in surrender. Valette, however, started to laugh as if he'd just heard the world's funniest joke. He bent over, clutching his sides. The guards looked at him in confusion. He straightened, wiping his eye with his finger as his chuckles subsided.

"Evening, Officers." His voice was slightly slurred. "Beg pardon. *Vive l'Empereur!*" He raised a hand and executed an incompetent salute, nearly poking himself in the eye in the process, then slumped against her on the seat. A slow, idiotic grin spread across his face.

Why was he pretending to be drunk?

The guards looked at one another, clearly unsure whether to believe this display of apparent intoxication or not.

Valette began unbuckling his belt. "Got to take a piss," he muttered in a confiding tone. "Shouldn't've had that last beer." He made to get down from the cart.

The guards' muskets tracked his movements.

"Stay where you are. What's your business here?"

He let out an impressively loud belch. "Been at the Red Cat, ain't we, Patrice?" He slapped Marianne on the back so hard she almost retched. She managed to nod.

The nearest guard grabbed Valette's shirt and hauled him down off the cart. He went, stumbling and cursing. The man's suspicious gaze took in Marianne's filthy face, wet hair, and sodden clothing. He frowned. "Why are you wet?"

Valette gave another chuckle. "I bet him ten sous he couldn't catch a frog in the moat." He snorted. "Idiot fell in! It was damned funny."

The officer didn't seem to think so. He motioned his musket at her. "You, get down, too. You're coming with us."

Marianne had no choice but to obey. She tensed, expecting Valette to start fighting his way out, but he just shrugged and went along meekly enough, staggering a little. Perhaps even *he* recognized that eight-to-two odds were not in their favor. Especially since neither of them was armed.

They were escorted back to the guardhouse, Marianne limping along as best she could. The captain of the guard was finishing his dinner; the remnants of a meal and a bottle of wine sat on the table, and he didn't look happy to be interrupted. "What is it now?"

The first guard saluted. "Caught these two out by the moat, sir. This un's all wet."

The officer frowned at Marianne. "What have you been doing?"

Marianne hunched her shoulders and ducked her head, terrified he'd notice that she was a girl. Hopefully she was so plastered in mud that he couldn't see much of her face.

"Could be they're escaped prisoners, sir," one of the guards offered helpfully when she didn't answer.

Valette gave another drunken snort. "Prisoners! Do we look like prisoners?" He wiped his nose on his sleeve.

The captain turned to one of the guards. "I want a head count of inmates right now."

"Yes, sir."

Marianne bit her lip. It was only a matter of time before they found her rope and discovered the prince was missing. Still, the longer they stayed quiet, the more time Louis-Charles had to get away.

The captain gave an irritated shrug. "Inform the commander. And put these two in the holding cells. Perhaps they'll remember more when they sober up." He flicked his wrist, dismissing them, and went back to his supper.

This time they were escorted down a flight of stone stairs, instead of up. The air cooled as they descended below ground and Marianne shivered at the musty, unpleasant odor that pervaded her nostrils. Her ankle was agony. She hobbled along, but the guard cuffed her around the head, impatient with her slow progress.

Valette started to sing a rude song about a buxom barmaid.

They were led to a row of barred cells, like large cages, set together. A guard unlocked the first and gave Marianne a cruel shove. She fell onto the hard flagstone floor with an involuntary cry.

The guard sneered at her. "Shut up. You sound like a sniveling little girl."

Valette was thrown in after her, and the glow from the guards' lanterns faded as they retreated up the stairs.

Marianne looked around in the gloom. The cell was barely ten feet square. The back wall was stone, but the remaining three sides were constructed of stout iron bars, as was the ceiling. The gaps were too small to squeeze through, even for her. A solid wooden pallet with a thin covering of dirty straw lay across the back wall. Other than that there was nothing but an empty bucket and a series of chains and manacles attached to an iron ring, set into the stone floor. Not exactly comforting. She slumped down and rested her head on her bent knees, utterly exhausted.

"It will be all right."

She glanced up. Valette was watching her, his dark eyes steady. It was a little disorienting, to see him suddenly sober and alert.

Marianne screwed up her face. "What do you mean, *all right*? Nothing about this is right!"

"Just think of it as another adventure to tell your grand-children."

She looked at him aghast. "How can you joke?"

His smile was reassuringly wicked. "'Life is a shipwreck, but we must remember to sing in the lifeboats.'" He saw her confused expression. "You never read Voltaire?"

She shook her head.

He sighed. "Philistine. You can either laugh or cry, *chérie.* Panicking won't help."

* * *

AT LEAST THEY'D been thrown in the same cell, Nic thought, grateful for small mercies. The guards hadn't realized Marianne was a girl yet, but it was only a matter of time.

Bloody hell. They should have been miles away by now, on their way back to Paris and her precious Sophie.

Nic looked over at her. She was huddled in the corner, a little ball of misery, her face pale in the darkness despite its covering of soot and mud. She looked haunted, stricken. His heart ached. This was all his fault. She was here only because of him. He'd played down the dangers, counted on her loyalty to him, just as he'd done with Tony. Loyal, sensible Tony, who'd ended up dead.

He'd done everything in his power to bind Marianne to him. Everything except sleep with her. And God knows why he'd restrained himself, when he wanted it more than he could remember wanting anything in a long, long time.

Images of her being raped, humiliated, and tortured crowded his mind. There were myriad horrors a woman could be forced to endure in the power of a bunch of men. And he'd be powerless to help her, just as he'd been powerless to help his brother.

The buzzing started in his ears, and darkness crowded his vision. Nic clenched his teeth as the familiar, heavy bleakness filled his soul. He refused to go back to that horrible place where he was helpless and impotent and afraid. If he allowed himself to think about it, even for a moment, he'd lose his mind. Lose what little control he had.

Jesus, Tony, I'm so sorry. I'm so sorry.

He wasn't used to guilt, and he didn't like the emotion gnawing at his insides now. He'd known the risks involved in this rescue and accepted them as part of the job. And to be honest, he hadn't really cared about living. But Marianne didn't deserve this. She had her whole life ahead of her, a loving sister waiting for her return.

Fouché wouldn't intervene, even if there were a way to get word to him. The political situation was far too volatile. He'd leave them to be executed with only the slightest pang of remorse —convenient, expendable scapegoats to smooth ruffled feathers on both sides.

A week ago Nic wouldn't have cared. Except, now it came right down to it, he wasn't quite ready to die. Somewhere along the way he'd begun to care about life again, as worthless as it was. He glared across the cell at Marianne. It was all *her* fault. She made him vulnerable. Made him care. He remembered her, lying in the hay cart, her face bathed in sunlight, her eyes sparkling with mischief and her cheeks flushed and rosy, as if she'd spent the whole morning making love in the straw.

I give people hope, she'd said.

Damn her. She'd given *him* hope.

What a bloody mess. He closed his eyes, anger and despair a heavy weight on his chest. He was a traitor. He deserved to die, deserved everything they gave to him. It was a miracle he'd survived this long. He'd been courting death for years, ever since Tony had died, beckoning it forward, taunting it to put an end to his miserable bloody existence.

Paradoxically, his lack of interest in living seemed to have amused the Fates. They'd delighted in thwarting his very best efforts to die. The fickle gods had blessed him, even as he willed them to sever the ties of his pointless life. He'd escaped from more life-threatening situations than he cared to remember.

And now, just when it looked as though the humorless bastards might actually be about to *grant* his wish, some sarcastic, cosmic irony had sent him Marianne de Beauvais to fill the aching chasm of his soul. A brave, beautiful, infuriating girl, who'd spilled his blood and stolen his heart.

Nic snapped his head up. There was a disturbance above, shouts and the clatter of hooves. Heavy booted feet pounding down the steps. Voices coming closer along the corridor—two soldiers, plus one other. Nic narrowed his eyes, listening intently. The third step was odd, lopsided, and uneven.

Oh, bloody hell. He knew that gait.

"Scour the countryside. I want that Bourbon bastard found before nightfall, you hear me?"

With an inward groan, Nic recognized that furious bellow, too; Baron Pierre Daumier, governor of Vincennes. The wily old soldier was one of Napoleon's staunchest supporters, a seasoned veteran as tough as nails. The man had lost a leg at some battle or other, and now he wore a wooden replacement, which explained that distinctive walk. Napoleon called him his lucky charm. Unfortunately, he was no friend of either Fouché or Nic.

The door slammed against the wall, and Nic blinked against the sudden flare of light. He cursed under his breath. Four burly men stood in the doorway. And they didn't look like a welcoming committee.

CHAPTER 34

*H*ope rose in Marianne's chest. The commander looked like someone's jovial grandfather, with a ruddy face, protruding belly, and thick bushy mustache. He placed the lantern he was holding on a hook by the door and nodded toward Nic. "Chain them."

Then again, appearances could be deceptive.

Two soldiers dragged Valette backward and attached his wrists and ankles to the manacles fastened to the wall. He barely struggled, accepting the manhandling with a strange passivity, keeping his head down, averting his face.

What was wrong with him? Why wasn't he even trying to fight? Had he given up?

The idea left a dull, hollow void of dread in her stomach.

One of the guards hauled Marianne to her feet and secured her hands in front of her with a set of iron cuffs. She struggled when the cold metal touched her flesh, but the man's hold was inescapable. The hinged loops closed around the bones of her wrist with a horrifying snap and the unnatural position made her shoulders scream in protest. Darkness descended on her vision.

All she could think of was the need to escape. "Get these off me right now! Get. Them. Off."

The commander ignored her protests. He stepped forward, grabbed Valette's hair, and yanked his face up to the light. He studied him for a short, breathless moment, and then his eyes widened. "Jesus!" he said with an incredulous laugh. "Nicolas Valette." He shook his head. "What the fuck are *you* doing here?"

Marianne's stomach lurched sickeningly. *He recognized Valette. Was that good or bad?*

The commander narrowed his eyes. "I should have guessed something like this would be Fouché's work." His disgusted tone made it clear this wasn't a happy reunion. *Bad, then.* "Real soldiers man their guns and hold their position. They don't go sneaking around in the night like rats."

Valette sent him an insolent smile.

The commander gave a signal, and the nearest soldier hauled back his arm and punched Valette square across the jaw. Marianne gave a horrified gasp as his skull smashed against the wall with a sickening crack. When he raised his head, his nose was bleeding; a thin red line dribbled down his chin and dripped onto the front of his shirt. He moved his jaw from side to side, testing it, then wiped the blood on his shoulder.

The captain grabbed his hair again. "Well?"

"I don't know what you're talking about." The corner of Valette's mouth gave a scornful curve as he returned the captain's unblinking stare.

"Again!" the commander ordered.

The next punch caught Nic in the stomach. He folded over with a groan and sagged to the floor. The man punched him again, a brutal hit to kidneys, then a series of kicks to his ribs. With his hands chained Valette had no way to shield himself from the assault except to try to curl into a ball as far as his bonds would allow.

Marianne couldn't take it any longer. She launched herself at the nearest soldier. "Stop!"

She just cannoned off him and fell on her backside on the floor. But she'd got his attention. And then she realized her mistake. Her screech had been unmistakably feminine. She shrank back against the wall, suddenly terrified, but was yanked roughly her to her feet.

"This un's a girl, Commander."

The commander raised his brows. "Well, well, what have we here?" He shot Valette a smug glance. "I didn't think you worked with women, Valette. Perhaps the mademoiselle here can tell us what we need to know?"

Marianne struggled against the grip on her arm as the commander turned to her.

"While it would give me a huge amount of pleasure to have Valette here beaten to a pulp—and rest assured, we'll get to that— I doubt he'll tell me a thing." He shot another glance at Nic's impassive face for confirmation. "But then, I've often found that watching another suffer, a friend, say, or a loved one," he suggested slyly, tilting his head to assess for a reaction, "often does the trick."

Valette pushed himself to a sitting position with a groan. Marianne was glad to see he was still conscious. He shook his head as if to clear it. "You're wasting your time. I don't care for her any more than I cared for any of the other whores I've bedded, Daumier. She's nothing to me."

Marianne flinched. He didn't mean it. Of course he didn't. But he sounded so convincing.

The captain chuckled. "Oh, come now. You don't want her to suffer."

"She doesn't know a thing." Nic's eyes were blank. Cold. He looked like a frightening stranger.

The commander stepped forward, and Marianne pressed back against the wall.

"Who are you working for?" he asked gently.

She shook her head, her heart pumping furiously. Her legs felt like water.

"Where's the prisoner going? Out of the country? Holland? Prussia?"

She bit her lip and said nothing. He grunted, unsurprised by her silence. At his brief nod the soldier nearest her dealt her a casual blow across the cheek. For a split second she saw the closed fist coming toward her and was more astonished than anything else. And then came the ringing agony, a bright pain that sent her reeling against the wall. She crouched down, trying to bury her head in her lap, blinking against the stars behind her eyelids. She heard a gasping, choking sob and realized it was coming from her. Her eyes were stinging. She was damned if she was going to cry. Not in front of them.

She was hauled upright again. The commander pushed his nose into her face, so close she could see the individual pores in his skin and smell the wine on his breath.

"Who's paying you?"

"No one. I don't know anything."

His laugh was chilling. "Oh, I believe you, my dear. Valette never trusts anyone enough to let them in on his plans. I doubt you're any different." He chuckled. "But you might just be the chink in his armor. He always was one for a pretty face." He bent his head and whispered in her ear. "See how he watches you? See how he wants to leap to your defense, even though he's chained to that wall like an animal? He'd like to rip my heart out"—he raised his voice—"wouldn't you Valette?"

Marianne's stomach tightened with dread as the second guard brought in a large metal pail of water and placed it in front of her. It splashed onto the rough dirt floor, wetting her feet. She was still wearing her stupid ballet shoes, she realized numbly. Although they were black now, not pink.

The guard grabbed her hair and she hissed in pain as he

forced her to her knees on the flagstones. A second soldier seized her shoulders and pushed her toward the pail. She tried to resist, but it was no good. The water against her face was a shock, an icy nightmare. She tried to rear back, but those strong hands held her down, impossibly heavy on the back of her neck. She kicked and flailed wildly, wrenching her body, thrashing her head back and forth but they kept her submerged as easily as a kitten.

Horror filled her mind. Her lungs were on fire, her pulse throbbed in her temples.

The pressure eased. She reared back, choking and spluttering, gulping great gasps of air. Water blinded her, her soaked hair flayed her face. She deliberately shook herself like a dog, spraying her captors with water, and experienced a brief moment of satisfaction as they jumped back with howls of annoyance.

"Nothing to say?" the commander asked gently.

As her vision cleared she found Nic's gaze on her. His eyes burned like those of the big cats at the circus, darkness and caged fury, and she knew he was swearing retribution. She found herself shaking her head, silently begging him to stay silent, even thought she knew he had no intention of doing anything else. He hadn't lied to her. He'd watch her die rather than lose the chance to thwart Napoleon. She knew it with a sudden, hideous clarity.

Pressure again on the back of her head. She started to protest and took a lungful of water instead. The cold stung her face, a hundred times worse than nettle stings. The same crushing panic descended. Her throat was burning. A strange muffled silence filled in her ears, as though everything were a hundred miles away. She began to feel light-headed.

She stopped fighting and let her body grow limp. What was the point? She was drowning, and there was nothing she could do to stop it. Nothing Nic could do to save her. Time slowed to the individual heartbeats that pounded in her skull, her throat. A strange calmness stole over her. She was falling, floating, and it wasn't such a bad experience, really. She opened her mouth to pull water into her lungs, to end it.

Sophie would never know what had happened to her. Duval would win.

The thought jolted her out of the peaceful daze. She gave a feeble kick, but all the strength had fled her limbs. A desperate lethargy was tugging on her. *Merde.* She'd waited too long. Darkness came rushing up to claim her, and she gave herself up to it with a sense of angry acceptance.

Someone slapped her face. Once, twice.

She bent over and retched, spewing water onto the floor. Her stomach and lungs were cramping. Agony. The guard stepped back in disgust, dropping her to the floor. Her head hit the flagstones, and she curled into a fetal position, sobbing, even with her arms bound. Her throat was raw. Everything hurt.

She heard the movement of boots, more muffled thuds and groans as Nic was assaulted again. She closed her eyes, willing it all away.

"Think about it," Daumier said, closing the door. "I'll be back soon."

CHAPTER 35

*N*ic's head was ringing.

He ran his tongue over his teeth, checking to see if any were broken, then pushed himself into a sitting position and winced at the stabbing pain in his ribs. He let his head fall back against the wall and tugged again on the chains, brooding and furious, trying to yank them from the walls as if rage alone could lend him the superhuman strength it would take to pull them free from the stone. All he got for his efforts was bloodied wrists.

Marianne was curled up on her side in a miserable ball like a hedgehog, with her back to him. But she was alive, thank God. At least for now.

Shivers racked her slight body. Her wet hair plastered the back of her skull. Nic willed her to move, to look up so he could assess the damage.

"Marianne."

She didn't move.

"Look at me. Are you hurt?" His voice was harsh, accusing almost, and he gentled his tone. "Can you move?"

She shook her head. Her muffled whimper slashed across his heart.

When she finally rolled over, Nic could have howled at the blank look in her eyes. They were dulled with pain, dazed and unfocused. An ugly red mark disfigured her cheekbone and her lower lip was split and already puffed up where she'd been slapped.

Fury boiled like acid in his veins as he added those injuries to the mental list of reasons he was going to kill those bastards. Slowly. One by one. This was how he'd felt when he'd heard Tony had been killed. He could feel his civilized, urbane facade dropping away to reveal the true darkness beneath. He wanted to rip out the throat of every man who'd touched her. Anger was a slow burn in his bloodstream, fortifying and good. He embraced it, let it slide through his veins like expensive, full-bodied brandy.

Marianne managed to haul herself up into a sitting position and scooted across the flagstones on her backside, along the filthy floor. She looked like a chimney sweep, her face still smudged with soot, despite her dunking. Without a word he raised his arm so she could fit underneath it, within his chains, and she huddled up against him without question, as if it were the most natural thing in the world. Her head nestled into the curve of his shoulder.

His sigh came from the very depths of his being. "We're supposed to be safely on our way to Paris by now, you know."

She made an odd sound, somewhere between a sob and a groan, and melted against him even more, burying her face in his shirt. She felt so fragile, so small and delicate. His chest hurt. He wanted his arms free so he could wrap them around her properly.

"You should have left while you had the chance. What's the point in both of us dying in here?" Her gruff little voice was muffled against his shoulder.

"We're not going to die."

"Yes, we are." She raised her head and stared up at him, her eyes luminous in the darkness, her pupils huge. "This is where they executed the Duc D'Enghien, isn't it?"

He couldn't lie to her. All he could give her was the hard, unvarnished truth. "Yes. They shot him out by the walls, next to a ready-dug grave."

"They're going to shoot *us*, aren't they?"

"Probably."

"I don't want to die like that." She bit her lip. "I always thought I was strong. That I could take any amount of pain. But I'm so weak." Her voice cracked.

"You're the bravest person I have ever met," he said, and realized with a jolt that he meant it.

She shook her head. "No, I'm not. Will you do something for me?"

The look in her eyes frightened him. "What?" he asked warily, already dreading her response.

"You've killed people before, haven't you?"

Oh, shit. He knew where she was going with this. "No," he murmured, in denial of what she was asking of him instead of the question itself.

Metal chinked as she took his hand in hers and ran her fingers across the ridges of his knuckles, as if trying to gauge their deadliness. Nic wanted to howl. There was a lump in his throat. She raised his hand to her cheek and rubbed against it like a cat. His fist opened of its own volition so that he cradled her face. There was blood on his knuckles.

"You can spare me that, can't you? You can kill me?" She made it a question, not a statement. "Please. I bet you know a hundred different ways to do it. Without pain."

He closed his eyes against the entreaty in her face.

"I mean," she faltered, "you could break my neck and I'd be dead before I hit the floor." She turned so his hand slipped around her throat.

He imagined cupping the back of her head and her jaw in his hands and twisting, just as she said. He could kill her with a single flick. The thought made him want to retch.

"Or maybe you could just press your fingers to my throat?"

She pressed his hand against her skin, made it into a caress, a gross parody of violence. Her heartbeat fluttered under the pads of his fingers. So warm, so soft. So yielding.

"You'd do that for me, wouldn't you?" she whispered.

"No," he said curtly, glaring down at her. "I wouldn't."

Her eyes widened as if he'd offered her an insult. She pulled back with a scowl. "You won't kill me?"

"Not if you begged for it on your knees."

"You'd rather let me be shot?" Her tone was incredulous.

"Absolutely."

Nic watched the fury gather in her face and felt an almost overwhelming sense of relief. That broken, haunted look she'd had when she'd first turned over had been like a kick in the gut. She'd looked like a whipped puppy. Shattered. Defeated. Anger was far better. He had to taunt her, annoy the hell out of her to keep her alive.

"Is there anything else, madame?" He kept his tone deliberately light. "What service, other than murder, could I possibly provide for you?"

Her gaze was unwaveringly direct. "The soldiers will rape me before they kill me." She said it calmly, without emotion.

"I won't let that happen," he growled.

"You're chained to the wall. You won't be able to stop them." Her eyes held his. She raised her chin. "If I'm going to die, I want a better memory than that to take to my grave."

Anger pulsed through his veins, mingling with a strange, poignant exasperation. He wanted to strangle her and kiss her at the same time. What an absurd, brave, vexing woman.

His heart was pounding in his chest. "Let me get this completely clear in my mind," he said slowly. "You want me to fuck you?" He used the crude word deliberately, just to goad her. She needed the distraction. "Here, now, in this stinking prison cell?"

Her throat worked as she swallowed, and he watched wariness, embarrassment, and defiance flit over her expressive face. "Yes."

Nic suppressed a shout of laughter. God, he loved her strength. He shook his head. She was priceless. Braver than any man he'd ever worked with. His equal in cunning and talent.

"You think I'm so good that I can block out the squalor of our surroundings?" he drawled, in the voice he knew full well reduced even the most sophisticated of society matrons to quivering heaps of desire. "That even *chained to a wall* I could make you forget everything?"

He could do it, he thought, with a touch of arrogance. He could shut out the darkness, the crushing despair. He could make her forget her own bloody name. Christ, he wanted to. He forced a smile he knew would irritate her instead. "I'm good, sweetheart, but not *that* good."

"Nicolas, please."

Nic closed his eyes. She'd never said his name before. Now, hearing it on her lips for the first time, a plea, a promise, almost unmanned him. She was made for silken sheets. For a palace or a château, not dirty straw and a filthy pallet. He wanted to see her where she'd been born to be: in a glittering ballroom, swathed in silk, her graceful body swirling in a waltz. He wanted to see her in diamonds and nothing else. Naked and glowing, just for him.

She leaned forward. Her soaking shirt was practically transparent. He could see her nipples quite clearly through the fabric, dark and beaded from the cold. And it was all he could do not to bury his face against her, to put his mouth over her and warm her with his breath.

His cock throbbed insistently. He deserved a medal for refusing her. There should be an award "For Extraordinary

Restraint Under Extreme Duress and Utmost Provocation." That had a nice ring to it. Suitably heroic. That, or a bloody sainthood.

What if this really *did* end up being their last night on earth? If he died, he'd spend an eternity roasting in hell and cursing the fact that he never took her up on her offer.

No. He refused to accept that outcome. She was going to be his prize for getting them both out of here alive. His groan was heartfelt. "We can't, *chérie*. Not here." His chains clinked as he tucked a strand of dripping hair behind her ear. "Your first time shouldn't be in a stinking prison cell."

"Where *should* it be, then?" she said with a touch of asperity. "Because it doesn't seem like I have many alternatives."

Ah, he could play this game. He'd thought of it only a million times.

Nic closed his eyes and gave himself up to the fantasy. He pictured her in his boyhood bedroom, back in England, the safest place he could imagine. "A country house. A grand château. Somewhere with silk on the walls, satin drapes at the windows. Mirrors and paintings, amber and marble, ormolu and gilt."

"And what would happen, in this room?" Her voice was barely a whisper. "If it were you, in the room with me."

He pressed his face forward so they were nose to nose. "I'd undress you. Slowly. I'd lay you on the covers and fan your hair on the pillow. And then I'd kiss every inch of you." He heard her swift intake of breath and ignored it. The shiver that coursed though her had nothing to do with the drafty cell and everything to do with desire. "I'd use my hands. And my mouth. On you. *In* you. Until you were begging me to finish."

Her lips were parted in shock, and her eyes were wide and dazed.

"And when you couldn't stand it a second longer, I'd cover you with my body and . . ."

Nic shook his head in disbelief. Their lives could probably be measured by an ever-decreasing number of individual breaths, and here he was talking dirty to her. And damned if he wasn't as turned on as she was. At this rate he'd be coming in his breeches like a randy schoolboy without even touching her.

"And . . . ?" she whispered breathlessly.

He banished the erotic images scorching his brain and pasted an innocent smile on his lips. "Unfortunately, my sweet, until we get out of here, we'll have to settle for a kiss."

She blinked slowly, as if coming out of a trance. "A *kiss?*" There was definite disappointment in her tone. He nodded.

She raised her face to his. Her eyelashes fluttered down. Her lips parted expectantly.

He pressed a kiss to the tip of her blackened nose.

Her eyes snapped open, her expression so comical he almost laughed. Her eyes flashed fire. And then she leaned forward, grabbed the front of his shirt, and plastered her mouth to his.

Shit. The first time she'd ever instigated a kiss and he wasn't even free to enjoy it. Her lips pressed his inexpertly, and he suppressed a moan at the sweetness of her, the softness. Nic opened his mouth and deepened the kiss, straining closer, pulling against his chains, heedless of the pain. The momentary sting was lost in the glory of her lips. He wanted to taste her, all of her, craved it like a starving man. She was like a triple shot of brandy direct to the veins. He allowed himself the brief, graphic fantasy of pushing her to the floor, stripping off those stupid breeches, and burying himself inside her.

Oh God, yes.

He pulled away, and her low moan of denial mirrored his own feelings exactly. His breathing was shallow as he leaned his forehead against hers. "Sweeting, this is *not* a refusal," he panted against her mouth. "It's just a delay, I swear. When we get out of here, I'm going to show you how good it can be."

She shuffled back with a reluctant sigh, as if realizing proximity was a bad idea. He noted with satisfaction that her breathing wasn't exactly steady, either.

His words finally seemed to penetrate her fogged mind. "Wait.

We're getting out of here?" Renewed hope flashed in her eyes. "How? Do you have a weapon? Can you pick the locks?"

"No."

"Is someone coming to rescue us?"

"No."

Her expression clouded again. "We'll just ask the guards to let us go, instead of executing us then, shall we?" she said sarcastically. "I'm sure they'll oblige."

Nic suppressed a grin at her acerbic return to form. "Actually, yes. That's exactly what we're going to do. You're going to use your feminine wiles."

"I don't *have* any feminine wiles."

CHAPTER 36

"*Y*ou're a woman and you're breathing. That's pretty much all men ask for."

Marianne winced at Valette's weak attempt at a joke. He didn't understand. She wasn't just being coy. She really *couldn't* do what he wanted.

"You know what Duval did to me," she managed, her voice an agonized whisper. Her face heated. "He couldn't . . . perform because I wasn't attractive enough." She gave a cracked laugh and dropped her face into her drawn-up knees. "I know. I should be thankful he didn't rape me. But a part of me was actually *insulted* that he didn't find me appealing!" She gave a groan of despair. "That doesn't make any sense, does it? I must be insane."

Valette was silent for a horribly long time. She nearly jumped out of her skin as he reached across and tilted her chin up with his finger, forcing her to look at him.

"It's not your fault." His voice was gentle, even slightly amused.

She turned her head away. "I know."

"It's not your fault," he repeated patiently. "Listen to me. I can't believe you've been stupid enough to believe what he told you."

Her stomach fluttered, even though he'd basically insulted her.

"Have you really been thinking you're ugly this whole time, just because some impotent bastard manipulated you?" He shook his head. "Did you learn *nothing* at that brothel? When a man's been drinking, the finest tarts in Christendom could dance naked in front of him, and he still couldn't get it up."

Marianne absorbed his words in hopeful silence.

"What Duval did was nothing to do with lovemaking. It wasn't even sex. It was punishment. He molested you."

Her brain knew he was right. But her soul still felt ashamed. "But I agreed to it. That makes me a whore. In spirit, if not in fact. I was willing to sleep with him."

"To save your sister," he said. "Hell, I'd probably whore myself out, too, if I thought it would spare one of my family." He brushed his thumb across her cheekbone, his touch debilitatingly tender.

She risked a glance up at him. "It wasn't just Duval who didn't find me attractive. No one ever courted me at the circus."

He was eyeing her in astonishment. "Good God, woman, don't you have eyes? Laurent and Henri are like two fire-breathing dragons warning off anyone who comes close!" His smile turned wicked. "I've been in the audience plenty of times while you performed. Believe me, there was no shortage of suggestive comments exchanged between the gentlemen about you."

"Really?" she breathed, scandalously delighted.

"Really," he said solemnly. "Most of it doesn't bear repeating."

She blushed, absurdly pleased.

"And don't you remember that farce of an auction? The bidding was gratifyingly high before I stepped in and put an end to it."

She hadn't considered that. Still, he was probably saying it just to make her feel better. At least he didn't sound like he pitied her. She hated pity even more than she hated weakness. "Not as high as it was for Sophie," she felt compelled to point out.

"Most men don't have my discernment." He tilted her chin up. "Sex shouldn't hurt, you know," he whispered. "It should be . . . extraordinary."

She managed a cynical snort even though her heart was beating uncomfortably fast. "Extraordinary?" she scoffed.

He held her gaze. "Yes."

She grew flustered under his scrutiny. It was as if he could see into every dark corner, as if he was reading her soul. She pulled away with a shaky sigh of resignation. "Fine. What do I have to do?"

He gave her his best leer. "Use your imagination. Flash your tits. Show some leg."

"They won't even take a second look," she said morosely.

He chucked her under the chin. "Have faith, little one. You vastly underestimate your allure." His chains chinked as he placed his hand over his heart. "Fatal. Now, they'll be back to check on us again soon, and you need to be out of those manacles."

She shot him an exasperated glance. "How, exactly? Fairy magic?"

"Relax your hand. No, don't make a fist." He picked up her hand and cradled it in his much larger one. "Now straighten your fingers and bunch them together. See. These are one size fits all. There's no way I can get free, but your hands are so small you can slip out of them if you just wriggle a little."

Marianne did as he said and tugged her hand. It hurt. The tight metal cuff cut into her skin and scraped her knuckles, but he wasn't lying. After a few more tries her hand jerked free.

Pain shot through her shoulders. She let the blood flow back into her hands, flexing her fingers against the prickling, burning sensation, then cradled her hand to her chest, scowling at him, as if it were somehow his fault.

He rattled his chains and shot her a hot look from under his lashes. "You know, some people actually *pay* for this kind of thing."

"What?"

"They ask to be chained. Take pleasure in it."

A hot flush prickled her skin as she caught his meaning. She recalled whispered conversations at the Montausier about clients who liked to be punished, restrained, even whipped. She'd never understood the appeal, but now, with his eyes upon her, all manner of wicked thoughts flashed through her head. The idea of relinquishing control of her body to another person was utterly terrifying. And yet for the first time she could see that trusting someone that much might be strangely . . . liberating, too.

A door banged. Booted feet began to descend the steps. They both froze.

"Quick, onto the bed!" Nic hissed.

Marianne scrambled to the pallet and arranged her hands so it looked as if she were still chained. Nic slumped down against the wall, head lolling, feigning unconsciousness. Her heart began hammering a terrified tattoo.

What on earth was she supposed to do? She didn't have the faintest idea how to entice someone.

She tried to remember all the tricks the girls at the Montausier had tried to teach her. She tugged at the opening of her wet shirt to expose the top swell of her breasts and leaned back against the wall in what she hoped was a seductive pose.

This was ridiculous. She looked like a drowned rat covered in mud.

The sight of her, however, made the single guard pause at the bottom of the steps. Encouraged, she sent him a beseeching glance through the bars. "Please, monsieur. Let me go. I've done nothing wrong." She let her eyes rove over his thin body and linger on the flap of his falls. "I'll do . . . whatever you want."

The man glanced over at Valette, and then behind him, up the stairs, as if afraid to believe his luck. A slow smile creased his angular face. "Is that so?" he leered, stepping closer to the cell. "Whatever I want, eh?"

Marianne nodded. "I'm just his whore. I work at the Montausier. At the Palais Royale."

She could see from his expression that he'd heard of it. Everyone in Paris had heard of it. She pouted her lower lip and worried it with her teeth. "I promise, I can make it worth your while."

With one last glance at the stairs, the soldier put down his lantern and unlocked the cell door. He slipped inside, giving Valette a wide berth, but didn't lock the door behind him, presumably confident that neither she nor Valette posed any danger while they were chained.

Marianne pressed herself back against the wall as he stalked toward her, every instinct screaming at her to run. The man's eyes held a glimmer of sick excitement that reminded her forcefully of Duval.

"Show me how grateful you can be, then," he growled.

He stopped at the edge of the pallet and reached out to fondle her breast. Marianne shuddered at the repulsive touch and gasped when he squeezed hard with his fingers. Bile rose in her throat as she caught his scent, a vile mixture of greasy food and unwashed body. He threaded his fingers through her hair, forcing her head down with one hand while he fumbled with his breeches with the other. Marianne made an involuntary whimper of protest.

"Shut up, you little bitch," he hissed. His breeches and belt fell to the floor with a heavy thud.

Marianne closed her eyes, balled her fist, and punched him as hard as she could between his legs. The soldier let out a muffled groan of agony. He doubled over, tripped on his breeches, and collapsed in a cursing, writhing ball.

Disgusting rutting pig.

Marianne stood and whacked him with the loose end of the manacles. The metal made a horrible thud as it hit his head, but he stilled instantly. She clapped her hand over her mouth, appalled at what she'd just done.

A chuckle sounded from the corner. "Nice work," Valette said. "You're a natural. Now grab the keys and unlock me."

Marianne snatched the keys from the jailer's belt, averting her eyes from the man's naked lower half. *He deserves a sore head.* She knelt in front of Valette and opened his wrist cuffs. He took the key from her and unlocked his own anklets, then caught her hand and released her other wrist. As soon as she was free he drew her into his arms for a crushing hug. She went willingly. He rested his cheek on the top of her head.

"Well done, little one."

"Is he dead?" Marianne whispered, nodding at the soldier on the floor.

Valette bent and pressed two fingers to the side of the man's neck then slipped the knife from his belt. "Don't worry, you haven't killed him." He pressed the blade into her shaking hands and stepped out of the cell. "Here. Take this. Let's go."

CHAPTER 37

*V*alette extinguished the lantern and ushered her back into the shadows at the base of the stairs. "Someone's coming!" he mouthed against her ear.

Marianne could scarcely hear anything over the frantic pounding of her own heart. A second guard stepped into the corridor, and she pressed back against the wall as Valette lunged forward. The man gave a surprised grunt and staggered when Valette punched him, but he didn't go down. The two of them fell to the floor in a blur of punches and kicks.

It was so dark Marianne could barely see, only hear the scuffle of feet, muffled grunts and curses. The guard was a big man, clearly used to fighting, and she raised the knife, desperate to help Valette but too scared of accidentally hurting him to try. Squinting, she saw him straddle his opponent and clip the man a brutal blow across the jaw. The soldier's head cracked back against the stone, but he thrust Valette off him with a growl of fury. He fumbled for the pistol at his hip, but Valette knocked it aside and sent it clattering through the bars of the cell.

The soldier's eyes bulged as Valette threw his arm across his throat from behind. They both fell heavily against the wall. The soldier clawed for air, twisting and struggling. It seemed endless seconds before his big body went limp and he slumped forward. Valette lowered the slack body to the ground and doubled over, his own breathing heavy.

It had all been accomplished in near-silence. Marianne realized she was shaking, her breath coming in frightened pants. Valette's casual brutality was terrifying.

A sound from the cell made her turn. The first guard had regained consciousness. He lunged toward them, blood streaming from his temple, his face murderous. In a hideous moment of clarity Marianne registered the pistol in his hand, heard the hammer click as he cocked it with his thumb and aimed at Valette. She didn't think. She dropped to one knee and threw the dagger before he could fire. The man crumpled and fell.

She stayed frozen in her crouch, her eyes glued to the man on the floor. He didn't move. A deep shaking seemed to have taken hold of her limbs. "Oh, my God. Is he dead?"

Valette pushed off the wall, stepped past her, glanced at the dagger protruding from the man's chest, and prodded him with his foot. "Very," he said dryly. He held out his hand to help her up.

Her stomach heaved. "I killed him."

He slapped her shoulder to force her to take her eyes from the corpse. "It was him or me. You made the right choice."

She'd killed a man. Her breath was coming too fast. She was going to be sick. Her fingers had gone numb. She dropped her head and rested both hands on her knees.

"Breathe, *chérie.*" Valette pulled her to her feet, wrapped his arms around her, and drew her into a tight hug, infusing her with his strength, his warmth. It flowed through her like a wave. "Don't think about it."

His voice sounded as if it was coming from far away. She'd killed a man. Was he someone's husband? Somebody's father? *Oh God.*

"Hey! Look at me." Valette caught her head between his hands, roughly, jolting her out of her misery. He forced her face up to his. "Stop thinking about it. It'll make your head explode. Can you justify killing one man to save another? I don't know. But I can tell you one thing: I'm bloody glad you threw that knife." He softened his voice. "You saved my life, Marianne. I will always be in your debt." He released her and started forward. "Come on."

At the top of the stairs he motioned for her to stay back. He crept forward, and she heard a grunt and a gasp, then an ominous thud, like somebody dropping a heavy sack of flour on the floor. He reappeared and beckoned her on.

Marianne blinked as they stepped out into the courtyard. She'd lost all track of time. It was still dark, but she figured it must be close to dawn. She glanced up at the feeble moon. At least it had stopped raining.

"The stables are over there," Valette whispered. "Stay here. I'll be back."

Her nerves screamed as she waited, fully expecting to hear shouts, but he reappeared leading two saddled horses. She mounted one and he handed her the reins of the second, nodding toward the inner gate that blocked their way.

"I'll deal with that."

He slipped along a wall and disappeared. She didn't want to think that he was doing to silence the guards. She just hoped it wasn't lethal.

As soon as she heard the gate opening she kicked her horse and rode at the gatehouse. Valette appeared in the archway. Marianne barely slowed, trusting him to catch the reins and haul himself onto the horse behind her. He vaulted into the saddle in a single fluid movement and shot her a piratical grin as they clattered beneath the arch. "Laurent taught me a few tricks, over the years. Now stay low and ride!" He spurred his horse straight at the final guardhouse.

The furious tolling of a bell behind them signaled their

escape had been discovered. Shouts rang out. A lone soldier blocked their way, but Nic galloped straight at him, and the man leaped sideways to avoid being run down. He tried to grab Marianne's reins as she thundered past, but she kicked him in the chest and sent him sprawling into the moat. They raced over the bridge and plunged into the shaded cover of the woods.

Marianne's heart was in her mouth, the wild tempo of it matching the frantic pounding of her horse's hooves. She clung to the reins, her knuckles white and the leather digging into her palms. Her mount followed Valette's blindly, crashing through the undergrowth. She could barely see where she was going. Branches loomed up out of nowhere and brambles clawed at her legs. It took all her skill to weave through the trees and keep Valette in sight.

The harsh sound of a horn pierced the air, and he cursed savagely. "That Daumier's a persistent bastard."

Dawn was coming; the sky was getting lighter with every passing minute. Hoofbeats thundered behind them, closer now, as their pursuers pushed through the undergrowth and a shout went up when they were spotted. Her stomach lurched.

Marianne jumped a fallen log, barely keeping her seat. She heard a voice cry out "Stop!" then heard a crack, like a snapping branch. Something whizzed past her head.

Mère de Dieu! They were shooting at her!

Her horse made an odd, wheezing sound. It stumbled, nose pecking the dirt, and she kicked her feet clear of the stirrups and jumped just as the animal collapsed. She rolled as she landed, swearing at the fresh pain in her ankle, then staggered up on shaky legs and bent over, fighting queasiness. A horse loomed out of the bushes on her left and she let out a scream of fright, but it changed to one of relief as she recognized the rider. "Oh, thank God!"

Valette hauled her up behind him with one hand. Marianne

threw her arms around his waist and pressed her cheek to his back as they raced through the trees.

"I thought you'd left me," she panted.

"Never."

"They shot my horse!"

"Better the horse than you," he grunted.

More shots rang out. A tree to their right exploded in a burst of splinters, and something seared her cheek. Valette reached into his waistband and pressed the butt of a pistol into her hand. "Shoot," he demanded.

Another shot rang out. He jerked forward with a muffled curse and bent low over the horse's mane. "Shoot!" he ordered again, more forcefully.

She twisted in the saddle, aimed at the nearest horseman, and pulled the trigger. The gun exploded, and the pursuer crumpled to the ground in a blur of dark clothing.

Oh God!

Nic yanked the horse's head sharply to the side and urged it down a steep embankment. It slid down on its haunches, scattering mud and stones, splashed through the narrow stream at the bottom, then climbed up the opposite bank. The soldiers tried to follow, but howls of frustration and the sound of rolling bodies indicated only a few were successful.

The woods flashed by in a green-brown blur. Valette wove the horse in and out of the trees, stopping occasionally to listen before setting off in a totally different direction. Marianne prayed they weren't going round in circles.

And then the trees parted to reveal a wall and for a horrifying moment she thought they were back at the fortress, but it was only the perimeter wall enclosing the ancient parkland. They followed it for what seemed like miles until they came to a section where the top had collapsed. The remaining part was still over six feet high, and Marianne regarded it in dismay. Surely the horse couldn't jump anything so high with two people on its back? She was about to suggest that they dismount and climb over when Valette spurred the poor animal forward.

Marianne closed her eyes on a whispered prayer. The man was insane. They'd never make it. She felt the horse's hindquarters bunch in readiness to jump, and leaned forward, hugging Valette's back. Her heart stuttered as one of the horse's hooves clipped the topmost stones, and they landed with a bone-jarring jolt on the other side.

Within minutes they found a rough track that led past a small hamlet, then joined the main road toward Paris. The sudden change from verdant woodland to bustling street was jarring. As they merged into the crowd, dodging hay carts and delivery wagons, goose drovers and lace merchants, Marianne finally allowed herself to relax as she realized they'd truly lost their pursuers.

She expected Valette to reenter the city by one of the southern gates, but they crossed the Seine instead and headed west. Marianne said nothing for an hour or so, too dazed to do more than simply hold on to Valette, but when she recognized the ornate entranceway to the Bois de Boulogne, she realized with a start that he'd skirted halfway round Paris.

What were they doing here?

Valette slowed the horse as they entered the park. The poor animal was exhausted, lathered with sweat, its sides heaving from the exertion of carrying two riders instead of one. When they came to a secluded clearing, Valette dismounted and stepped away without offering to help her, so she dropped down unaided. Her legs were so wobbly that she sank to the grass.

Valette still had his back to her, so she leaned back gratefully against a tree and gazed around, savoring the sheer, unlikely joy of being alive and free. The dappled woodland looked so clean and bright after the dungeon, sparkling with the promise of a new day. She closed her eyes and listened to the birdcalls, inhaled the sweet smell of wet grass and moss—all the more precious since she hadn't expected to see another sunrise ever again. She let out a shaky laugh of disbelief.

They'd done it! They'd actually done it!

"Where's the prince?" she asked suddenly. "The king? Whatever you call him?"

Valette looked up from tying the horse to a tree. "I passed him off to another agent while you were scaling the walls. They'll be on their way to Holland by now."

An odd sense of anticlimax filled her. *Was this it? The end of their mad adventure?*

What about all those things he'd said? About sparks? About doing something about them. Had he meant any of it?

She studied him covertly as he checked the horse, deriving malicious pleasure from the fact that his sartorial elegance had been well and truly ruined by their escapade. His black shirt hung open at the neck and his boots were scuffed and covered in dried mud. He looked even more dangerous now, though, like a ruffian, disreputable and deadly. And still criminally gorgeous, despite a cut above his eye, which was already turning purple. Dried blood crusted the corner of his lip.

Her eyes narrowed as she considered something had been nagging at her ever since they'd been captured. "You knew Daumier was the commander at Vincennes."

He glanced up warily. "Yes."

"So you must have known he would recognize you if you were captured. That it would endanger the mission."

"So?"

Marianne's heart started to beat faster. "You told me the prisoner was the priority. That you wouldn't help me if I got into trouble. That I'd be on my own."

His eyes narrowed.

"Why didn't you leave when you had the chance?" she persisted.

His gaze caught hers from across the clearing, and her stomach flipped.

"I changed my mind."

Marianne frowned. *What did* that *mean?* He'd said he wouldn't leave her, as he'd left his brother. He'd risked being recognized, jeopardized the mission for her. He'd done exactly what he said he'd never do: come back and save her. Surely that meant he cared for her a *little?*

Her face heated in sudden recollection at all the other things he'd said. Scandalous, wicked, impossibly tempting things. Oh God, she'd practically *begged* him to make love to her! She forced her tongue to move. "In the dungeon . . . what I said, you know, about not dying a virgin . . ." She gave what she hoped was a dismissive laugh. "I wasn't thinking clearly. I thought we were about to die. Just . . . forget I said anything."

He stalked toward her with his panther's grace, and she shrank back against the tree, unnerved by the intent look on his face. She scrambled up, not wanting to be at a height disadvantage as he stepped in close and glared down at her.

"No," he growled.

"No, what?"

"I won't forget it. Ever."

CHAPTER 38

*T*he air between them thickened.

Marianne gazed up at him as fear and excitement warred in her chest. A hot wave of agitation pooled low in her stomach.

His eyes burned into hers. "I didn't know anything for certain," he said quietly, pressing even closer. She was trapped between the hard tree and his even harder body, and she could feel the strength, the heat of him right through her clothes. He caught her upper arms and gave her a little shake. "We *could* have died in there."

His breath was coming in short pants, as though he'd been running, and the intense expression in his eyes made her shiver. How had she ever thought him emotionless? Gone were his usual cool defenses. In their place was something hot and deep and frightening. Something he felt for her.

"I should have taken you up on your offer," he rasped. "Because if last night *had* been our last night on earth, there's nothing I'd rather have been doing than making love to you."

Marianne's mouth fell open.

He shook his head in exasperation. "Oh, bloody hell," he said, and kissed her.

Everything faded away. The terror of the dungeon, the panic, the pursuit. It was just the two of them, with no barriers between them at all. Marianne gave a muffled sob and threw her arms around his neck. He was real and vital and *alive*. She clung to him, returning his ardor with unashamed eagerness, giving herself up to it with joyful abandon. He kissed her hard and deep, and she lost herself, drowning in the feel of his lips, his tongue. His hands came up to frame her face, and she reached for his shirt, fingers fumbling in haste as she pulled it free of his breeches. She swept her hands over the muscled heat of his abdomen. Her blood sang in her veins.

Oh Dieu! The feel of him.

She wanted to touch him, all of him. Wanted to sink into him and simply dissolve.

"Ask me," he growled against her lips, and she knew what he wanted, what he needed her to say. His hands pushed her shirt up with urgent roughness, and she moaned as he cupped her breasts, pushed them upward, thumbs brushing over her nipples until she was shaking with need.

Yes, yes, please. Now.

He lifted her effortlessly, pulling her legs around his waist as he pushed her back against the tree, his lips never leaving hers. She moaned in delight as his hardness pressed against her core, generating a maddening friction that made her stomach burn. She felt dizzy. She pushed his shirt higher, up to his shoulders, desperate to explore, to learn the planes and hollows of him.

Her fingers slipped in something warm and wet.

Valette took a sharp intake of breath and stepped back with a curse, releasing her so abruptly that she staggered. She stared at him in bewilderment as he paced away, his back to her.

Why had he stopped? Had she done something wrong?

And then she looked down. Her palms were slick with blood.

Her stomach roiled. *His blood.* His black shirt had concealed the fact that he'd been wounded. Desire changed to furious concern in a heartbeat.

"Oh God! You're bleeding! Why didn't you tell me?" She stepped forward and tried to lift his shirt again to see the extent of the damage, but he fended her off with an impatient hand.

"It's nothing," he grunted. "I'll be fine. This isn't the first time I've been shot."

"I'm not surprised," she said tartly. "You're an extremely aggravating man. Let me look."

"No."

She fisted her hands on her hips. *Idiot!* "Well, let's head back into Paris, then. You need to see a doctor."

His level gaze found hers. "We're not going back to Paris."

She narrowed her eyes at the hard set to his jaw. "Don't be stupid. I have to get back to Sophie. We had a deal."

"No one was supposed to know who rescued the prince. Now Daumier's seen my face, the whole mission's been compromised. He'll realize Fouché's behind it. We have to stay away."

"No!" Marianne shouted. "I've kept my side of this stupid bargain." She started toward the horse. "I'm going home, and you can't stop me."

"Yes, I can." He stepped in her way, quiet menace radiating from his tall frame. "Think about it, Marianne. It'll be raining daggers in Paris. If you go back, you'll be in danger, and so will everyone you come into contact with. You'll be putting Sophie at risk."

She bit her lip. *Damn him for knowing exactly what to say to make her feel guilty. Oh God, what had she done?* Perhaps Sophie really would be better off under the protection of his men for the time being.

Valette's fingers encircled her wrist. She tried to pull away, but he held fast and threaded his fingers through hers. They were sticky with blood. He lowered his head. "I swear to you, she'll be safe. Andrew will protect her with his life."

A bittersweet ache of longing pierced her as she studied their joined hands. She'd been alone for so long. The idea of relying on another person, of trusting another person, was utterly terrifying. But he'd put himself in danger, allowed himself to be beaten and chained. To save her. She owed him this much, at least.

She exhaled in temporary defeat. "A few days. That's all."

And then she'd leave him, whether he agreed to it or not.

Daumier might have recognized him, but he didn't know *her*. There was no way he could trace her. So her only real problem was Duval. Her heart hardened. She'd killed a man last night, maybe two. If she had to kill Duval be free of him, then she would. After what she'd learned about his role in her parents' deaths, he deserved it. And if she was caught and brought to justice, so be it. As long as Sophie was safe, she'd accept her fate gladly.

Valette glanced up, wary of her sudden acquiescence. "You'll come with me?"

She nodded, but he narrowed his eyes, studying her face as if he could read her mind. "Promise me you won't do anything stupid. Like go back to Paris on your own and try to confront Duval. I'll help you deal with him. Just give me a few days to get over this." He nodded at his shoulder.

Marianne avoided his eyes, uncomfortable at how well he knew her. She disentangled herself from his grip. Tears stung her eyes, but she kept them downcast so he wouldn't see. He had his own ghosts to battle, his own promises to keep. She couldn't ask him to take on her problems, too.

"Promise me?" he repeated urgently.

"Yes," she lied. She took a deep breath and turned away. "So, which way? We can't go far. You're in no fit state to ride."

"It's just a scratch."

She gave an exasperated sniff. "Fine, what do I care if you're determined to bleed to death? Just let me know where you'd like to be buried. I'm sure I can arrange it."

He chuckled at her morbid humor. "That's what I love about you, *chérie*. Always so optimistic."

CHAPTER 39

$\mathcal{H}$e stole two fresh horses from a group of distracted picnickers, and they set out across country, through fields and narrow lanes, heading west. Road markers flashed by; signs for Ivry, Bicetre, Rouen. Marianne protested loudly and often, but he simply ignored her and kept on riding. She was half tempted to turn her horse around and leave him, but what he'd said about endangering Sophie made sense, and besides, she didn't trust him to get his wound seen to.

Around midday they pulled into a tiny inn, and she prayed they'd reached their destination, but the innkeeper merely exchanged their two stolen horses for a single, magnificent bay stallion, and Marianne was forced to sit behind Valette once again.

Her thighs bracketed his, her breasts rubbed against his back, and her arms wrapped around his waist as if they belonged there. To distract herself, she demanded to know why the innkeeper hadn't wanted payment. Valette muttered something about *chouans,* and she realized that the secretive, underground resistance movement of Royalist sympathizers her father had apparently supported was still extremely active. Valette lapsed into an uncommunicative silence after that, and Marianne drifted in and out of a dazed reverie, too tired to question him further.

She must have dozed off because when she opened her eyes again she saw to her amazement that the sun was setting. *Why in God's name hadn't they stopped?*

She opened her mouth to insist they rest at the next village and felt Valette sag against her in the saddle. She nudged him. Had he fallen asleep, too?

His head lolled to the side.

She peered around him. "Valette?"

No answer.

She poked him in the ribs. Nothing.

With a gasp of dismay she realized he'd actually lost consciousness.

Merde. Merde. Merde.

Stupid, stubborn imbecile of a man! Why hadn't he stopped to take care of his wound? She shook him roughly by the sleeve. "Don't you dare die!" she hissed savagely. She took the reins from his slack fingers. "Nicolas! Stay with me."

He jerked awake again with a groan.

"Where are we going?" she demanded urgently. "I'll handle the horse."

His voice was slurred. "Can't stop. Have to get there tonight. Got to get to Raven," he muttered.

"Where?"

He shook his head with a weak chuckle, as if she'd made a joke. "Not a where. A who." He sat up slightly and peered around. "We're nearly there. Just over this hill. Give me the back the reins."

With a jolt of amazement Marianne realized they were at the coast. The air bore the faint tang of salt and brine, like oysters, and she could hear the constant suck and crash of surf.

A stand of tall pines gave way to dunes covered with tussocks of grass, and they finally came to the sea itself, leaden and gray in the moonlight. The sand muffled the sound of the horse's hooves. Her hair whipped across her face as Valette looked up and down the beach as if searching for something. To her right she could see a cluster of lights, a port, presumably, although whether it was Le Havre or Saint-Malo or somewhere else she had no idea.

Valette turned the horse away from the lights and headed for a cove at the far end of the beach. The tide was in high, narrowing the sand until the horse was finally hock-deep in the surf and Marianne gasped as cold water splashed her legs. They rounded the rocky headland just as a rowboat was pulling into the cove, the unmistakable dark uniform of a French officer crouched at its front.

Her heart contracted in fright. *Merde!* They were caught.

But Valette relaxed against her. "Raven," he sighed. "Right on time."

A small group of men jumped ashore, led by a tall, dark man who ushered the uniformed man onto the beach, pointed at the dunes, and watched him scamper off into the darkness. The rest of the men busied themselves with unloading several wooden kegs from the rowboat and piling them out of sight among the dunes.

Valette let out a low whistle, like the call of a bird, and the man turned in surprise, then hurried toward them.

Understanding dawned: these men were smugglers. Official trade between England and France had been banned for years, but the black market for stolen goods still flourished, especially in Paris. Tea and brandy were always in demand, but also salt, leather, soap, chocolate, and cigars. And of course, France made things craved by the British upper classes, like silk from Lyons and lace from Arras, Dieppe, and Le Puy.

A movement in the rocks to their left caught her attention. Marianne tensed, anticipating an attack, then gasped as she recognized the bedraggled figure that huddled beneath a monk's cloak.

Louis-Charles. He was supposed to be on his way to Holland.

The prince looked thoroughly cold and miserable, and she felt a pang of pity for him. After twenty years in the tranquility and endless monotony of prison, he'd been thrust into the middle of this frenetic, mad escapade. He rushed forward.

"You, mademoiselle! I never thought to see you again . . . I must thank you . . ." He dropped to one knee on the wet sand and bowed his head. "I owe you a debt I can never repay," he said gruffly. "You saved my life."

Marianne kicked a foot out of the stirrup and slid to the ground, her thighs weak and shaky. "Thank me when you're safe, monsieur. We're not there yet." She turned to glare up at Valette. "And *you* lied to me! You said he was going to Holland!"

The corner of Valette's lips curled upward. "Did I?" he murmured. "How odd." He slumped and slid sideways off the horse.

Marianne only just managed to break his fall. "Help!"

The dark-haired man reached them and together they laid Nic on the sand. His face was pale, his brows drawn together in a thin line. Marianne felt sick as she pressed her hands to his chest. Blood. There was so much blood.

"Are you the Raven?" she asked. "Nic said to find you. He said you'd help us."

The man called the Raven smiled. "Listen, love, I'll help anyone, if the price is right. Hell, I'd even smuggle out the King of France if you paid me enough." His eyes twinkled mischievously, and he flicked a sly glance at Louis-Charles. He slapped Nic on the cheek, hard.

Marianne scowled at him. "He's been shot. Left shoulder."

"I can see that," the Raven said snippily. "Got eyes, ain't I? Nic, mate. Can you hear me?"

Valette groaned, which the Raven apparently took for assent. "Didn't think you was comin' this way," he muttered. "What do you want to do about the girl?"

Marianne frowned. "Don't talk about me as if I'm not here!"

Nic muttered something unintelligible. Then he opened his eyes and grabbed the Raven's coat. "Keep her." His eyelids fluttered. "Stays with me."

"What? Are you mad?" Marianne hissed. "I can't come with you to England! We had a deal." She turned to the smuggler. "Get him on the boat. He's your problem now. I'm going back to Paris."

Nic's hand dropped to the sand. "Not Paris. With me," he panted through his teeth. He raised his hand to her cheek, and Marianne hissed in a breath at the intense, burning look in his eyes. His fingers were cold, but they warmed her all the way to her bones, turned her insides to jelly. "Marianne, *ma mie.* I need you," he rasped.

"I can't," she wailed. "I have to go. You'll be fine. These men are your friends. They'll take care of you. You don't need me anymore." The look he gave her was reproachful. She hardened her heart. "No. I can't come. I have to go back."

The Raven shook his head. "Paris? Now? Bad idea."

"My sister needs me," she said stubbornly.

The Raven nodded at Nic. "Looks like 'e needs you more right now, wouldn't you say?"

Nic half laughed, half sighed. "Knew she'd refuse." A look passed between the two men, one of devilish understanding.

Marianne leapt backward just as the Raven's hand shot out and grasped her wrist. She twisted and turned, but his grip was inescapable.

"Stop wriggling. Shh!" he laughed, pinning her arms to her sides.

"Oh no! I'm not getting on that boat. Not even to save *your* sorry hide, Nicolas Valette."

Every head shot up at the sound of hoofbeats coming from higher up the beach.

"Shit!" the Raven muttered. "Customs. Time to go."

Two burly sailors grabbed Nic by the ankles and under the arms and dumped him unceremoniously into the rowboat. The Raven dragged Marianne, and when she dug her heels into the sand, he gave a chuckle, dipped his head, and shouldered her in the stomach. She folded with a winded "oof," and he hoisted her over his shoulder then deposited her on the wet planks of the boat, in between the rows of wooden seats. Louis-Charles clambered in and huddled down at the far end.

The shouts from down the beach were getting louder. Marianne tried to stand up, but the men pushed the boat into the waves and she toppled over backward, right on top of Nic. He grunted in agony.

"Time to go, lads!" the Raven shouted above the roar of the surf. The muzzle of a gun flashed on the beach and a bullet whistled past his head. His teeth flashed white in the moonlight as he laughed. "Get moving!"

No wonder he was friends with Valette, Marianne thought dazedly. They were both completely mad.

A group of mounted soldiers raced down the beach. The boat bucked against the waves as the men pulled hard on the oars, and Marianne didn't stop to think. She threw herself over the side.

CHAPTER 40

*T*he freezing water went straight over her head.

She kicked her legs and managed to gasp a lungful of air, only to be pushed back down by a huge crash of surf. Water rushed up her nose. She bobbed up again and a bullet hit the water with a splash and a whine, just inches from her head.

Merde.

She struck out toward the beach, toward Sophie and France and home. Away from the boatload of pirates. Away from England and Nicolas Valette. Another wave crashed over her head, pushing her under again, and she felt the helplessness of trying to fight such immense power. It buffeted her, the fierce undertow sucking at her clothes, wrapping around her like a shroud. She was back in the cell at Vincennes, her head in that pail of water. She was sick of bloody water.

She surfaced again and gasped a breath, blinded, disoriented.

A strong hand grabbed the back of her collar and hauled her up. "Up you come, little miss mermaid," the Raven chuckled, not unkindly. "No time for swimming tonight."

Marianne slid into the bottom of the boat and coughed up a stomach full of water. She curled into a ball, feeling utterly wretched. When she finally opened her eyes, she found both Nic and the Raven watching her with identical bemused expressions.

"You must be losing your touch with the ladies, Nic." The Raven pulled hard on an oar. "Ain't never seen one so desperate to *leave* your company before."

The smuggler's galley was almost invisible in the darkness; painted black with black sails. Numbly, Marianne followed Louis-Charles up a swaying rope ladder and over a carved wooden rail. Then it was through a hatchway, down another ladder, and along a swaying passage. The men half carrying Valette laid him down on a surprisingly large bed, and Marianne blinked at the luxuriousness of the cabin. She'd always assumed sailors slept in hammocks.

The Raven turned to her. "He's all yours. I gotta sail us home. Patch him up, would you? There's bandages in there." He nodded at a trunk along one wall. "And try not to ruin my room, all right?" He winked, then closed the door.

Her teeth were chattering. She should probably change into something dry. She found a length of bandage in the trunk the smuggler had indicated and glanced over at Valette. He was lying on the bed, one arm flung across his face. His eye was blackened and swollen, his lip puffy, his cheekbone scraped and raw. Bruises circled his wrists from the manacles.

She crossed the cabin soundlessly and gazed down at him, then jumped guiltily when she realized he was watching her from under his arm. A smile curled the corner of his wicked mouth.

"Are you going to stand there all night admiring my manly form, or are you going to make yourself useful?"

She fisted her hands on her hips, relieved to see he was at least conscious. "I think what you mean to say is, 'Thank you, Marianne, for saving my worthless hide. Again.'"

He sat up with a groan and tried to peel off his shirt. "I need you to dress my shoulder." He gave a glimmer of a smile. "Think of it as a last request."

"You're not dying," she said with more confidence than she felt. He looked like hell.

"Bloody feels like it," he grumbled.

The wet shirt stuck to his chest, defining the broad muscula-ture beneath with clinging clarity. She peeled it off him, taking care to avoid his injury, but he hissed in pain anyway. She winced at the ugly red bullet wound.

"You know, this is not how I imagined things going when I finally got you to undress me." His amber eyes glowed with a wicked sparkle.

Her face heated. She looked away, trying to sound reassuring and brusque, like a physician. "The bullet's gone straight through. It's not even touched the bone."

"Had lots of experience with bullet wounds at the circus, have we?" he mocked.

She narrowed her eyes. "Maybe not bullet wounds, but injuries aplenty. Definitely knife wounds."

She bit her lip as she wound the bandage around his ribs and over his shoulder, trying to ignore the expanse of smooth, tanned skin beneath her fingers. His shoulders were so different from her own. Bonier. Harder. Definitely more muscled. His damp hair curled slightly behind his ear, and she resisted the urge to brush it with her fingers. He smelled of sea salt and gunpowder.

She tied the end of the bandage with a knot and stepped back, away from temptation. "Sorry. I've not done a very good job."

He glanced down at her handiwork. "It's fine. I need a drink."

"There's water there." She indicated a jug on the side.

"Not water. A real drink. Look around, there'll be brandy somewhere. Trust me, smugglers always have spirits. Raven especially."

Sure enough, she found a decanter and glass in a cupboard. She poured it out and handed a glass to him. He took a healthy gulp and sighed in pleasure. "Thank God. Armagnac."

She sank down onto the captain's chair in front of the huge

mahogany desk, recalling the last time they'd drunk brandy together, back at the inn. When he'd seen her naked. It seemed a lifetime had passed since then. She shivered again then jumped up, belatedly realizing she was soaking the leather seat with her clothing.

Valette's gaze lingered slightly too long on her shirt. "Get changed. There'll be clothes in that trunk."

"Close your eyes," she chided sternly.

He gave an exaggerated sigh. "Looking's all I can manage. Even Don Juan himself couldn't do anything else in this state." He closed his eyes and sank deeper into the bedclothes.

She found a voluminous white shirt in the trunk. It smelled of camphor and some exotic spices she couldn't name. She had no choice but to remove her sopping breeches, exposing her legs. The skin on her bare back prickled when she stripped off her shirt, but when she turned around, Valette's eyes were closed and he wore a beatifically innocent expression on his face.

Perhaps he'd fallen asleep.

She padded across the boards of the cabin and stopped at the side of the bed, grateful that the dry shirt came down past her knees.

Pain and longing spiraled through her, tugged at her chest as she gazed down at him. She'd built him up in her mind into something inhuman, invincible. But he was just a man. Begrimed and bruised and beaten. At the château he'd seemed so far above her touch, so much more worldly and sophisticated. But now, suddenly, he was within arm's reach. And she'd never wanted anything so much. Without thinking, she extended one hand and traced the outline of his lips with the tip of her finger, very softly, a caress. His amber eyes cracked open, and she froze.

"I'm cold," he murmured plaintively. "Come here."

Blood rushed to her cheeks. "I don't think—"

"Get on the bed, Marianne," he said wearily. "I need to get warm. And so do you." His hand snaked out and grabbed her wrist, surprisingly strong. He pulled her down next to him and she went, unresisting.

He lay on his uninjured side and drew the covers over them both, and she shivered, trying to concentrate on anything other than the nearness of his body behind her. She held herself rigid, but the warmth of him along the length of her back was melting her resistance. "How long will it take to cross to England?" she asked desperately.

"Depends on the wind. A few hours."

"I'm getting right on the next ship back again, you know."

He chuckled. "You can try. Sleep now."

He threw an arm over her waist and hauled her back against him, molding his body to hers, like nestled spoons. Marianne released the tension in her limbs and melted into his embrace. What was the point in fighting? It felt so good.

He tucked her head into the hollow of his uninjured shoulder and rested his chin on her damp hair.

"This is only to raise your body temperature," she muttered.

His chuckle rumbled in his chest. "Oh, believe me, you're certainly doing that."

She closed her eyes. "This still doesn't mean I like you."

She felt his smile against her hair. "Of course not."

Her heart was battering her ribs. "It's pity, nothing more. I'd do the same for a three-legged dog." She didn't need to see his face to know that he was looking insufferably smug. Perhaps she could smother him with a pillow while he slept. "What do you want me to say?" she scowled. "That I *love* you?"

God, she hoped that sounded scornful, not desperate.

The muscles in his arm tightened under her ear. "Do you?" he asked, very softly.

"Not even a little bit," she retorted.

"You're right. You don't love me," he said, suddenly harsh. "Loving me would be a very bad idea."

CHAPTER 41

*M*arianne was floating in a sea of sensation. The blood in her veins was sluggish and molten. She arched her back in a languid stretch, like a cat, and encountered warm, hard skin. Her eyes popped open.

A very masculine leg was draped over hers. A very masculine body was pressed against her back. Her heart stuttered, then began thudding painfully. Her borrowed shirt lay open in a deep V at the front where the neck tie had come undone. And Valette's large warm hand was inside, curled possessively over one breast.

She stopped breathing. It was so sinful, so decadent, the feel of skin on skin. She moved, just a tiny bit, and her nipple beaded against his palm. She bit her lip to stifle a moan of pleasure.

Was he awake? His breathing was rhythmic, unhurried. She feigned another stretch and rubbed her bare leg up the front of his shin, then wriggled her bottom experimentally. Her eyes widened farther as the rock-hard evidence of his arousal pressed hard against her buttocks. Her stomach fluttered, and lower still, between her legs, a strange, warm, aching tension throbbed.

Oh God.

"Keep moving like that, and I'm going to forget all about the hole in my shoulder." Valette's murmur was half chuckle, half groan.

Her face flamed. She tried to scoot across the bed, but his arm tightened around her like a steel band. He buried his face into the back of her neck and inhaled deeply, drawing her scent into his lungs. All the hairs on her body stood up on end.

"You smell like sea salt and soot," he said huskily.

She turned over to face him, which dislodged his hand from her breast, but put her into dangerous proximity to the rest of his body.

He smiled down at her, sexy and sleepy and rumpled. "Good morning. Or good evening." He squinted toward the window. "What time is it?"

Her heart thumped wildly as she studied him. The slight stubble on his jaw only made him more attractive. "Morning, I think," she managed breathlessly.

It was impossible to ignore the huge bulge in the front of his breeches. His eyes crinkled at the corners as he deliberately rocked his hips and pressed himself against the V of her closed thighs. Only his breeches and the smuggler's shirt separated them. Her whole body burned. She glared at him.

"What?" He shrugged defensively. "I can't help it. It's a totally natural result of a man waking up with a beautiful woman draped all over him."

Her heart beat dizzily. Did he think she was beautiful? She edged away. He followed her, trapping her against the side of the bed.

"How about a good-morning kiss?"

She hadn't cleaned her teeth in days. Her breath was probably revolting. She shook her head and sat up and he rolled onto his back with a sigh.

"Oh, well. It was worth a try."

Her clothes were dry but stiff as a board. The breeches crackled when she pulled them on. And then she realized that the boat wasn't moving. She raced to the window and studied the rocky coastline in the pale dawn light.

England looked a lot like France.

She opened the door of the cabin and came face-to-face with the Raven, his hand raised to knock. He shot her a piratical grin. She'd barely noticed last night, but the man was ridiculously handsome. His flashing green eyes, tanned skin, and long black hair were exactly right for a dashing smuggler. He needed only a gold tooth. Or perhaps an earring.

He peered over her shoulder at Valette. "Time to go."

Nic grunted and sat up, dragging his shirt on over his bandaged shoulder. If he was pleased to be back in his homeland, he didn't show it.

Louis-Charles was already on deck when they emerged. They clattered down the gangplank onto a narrow beach surrounded by rocky cliffs. For the first few moments the ground seemed to be in the wrong place, going up instead of down, but the unpleasant sensation soon passed.

Valette started up a set of steps cut into the side of the cliff, followed by the Raven and Louis-Charles. Marianne had no choice but to follow along in their wake. They trudged uphill for some time, then passed through a tunnel of towering rhododendrons and emerged at one end of a lush valley. Acres of rolling, tended parkland spread out before them like a glossy green counterpane.

The Raven slapped Valette on the back. "Welcome home."

Marianne stopped dead on the path. Louis-Charles cannoned into her back with a muffled cry of surprise.

The house that lay across the valley was quite clearly the home of one of England's most noble families. She gazed in dismay at the acres of rich, mellow stone, the endless glinting windows, the pillared porticos. She started to count the number of chimneys and gave up at seventeen.

Home? This *was Valette's home? This* palace? *And he'd mocked* her *for being an aristo. She was going to kill him. Actually kill him dead.*

She plotted his demise while they trudged downhill, past a Grecian-inspired temple and a stepped cascade of water, past a folly and a boathouse and a Palladian-style bridge perfectly reflected in the ornamental lake below. With every step her heart shriveled a little more.

Up close the house was even more imposing than it had appeared from the hill. The entire Palais Royale could have fitted in the circular driveway with room to spare. Marianne took another despairing look and added hanging, drawing, and quartering to her list.

The enormous front door was opened by a tall, thin gentleman dressed in a smart black uniform that made his white hair appear even lighter. He noticed the Raven first, and a disapproving frown crossed his patrician features. He raised a supercilious brow.

"Ravenwood," he intoned, in a voice that suggested he'd just been presented with the corpse of a dead mouse.

The Raven grinned mischievously. "Got a delivery for 'is lordship."

The elderly majordomo looked aggrieved. He pursed his lips as he glanced first at Marianne, then at Louis-Charles, clearly dismissing them as disreputable acquaintances of the smuggler.

She couldn't blame him. She looked like a scruffy cabin boy. With a bad haircut.

"Then I'm sure it's something better dealt with at the kitchen door . . ." The servant's mouth dropped open as he finally spied Valette, leaning heavily against one of the pillars.

"Hello, Hodges," Valette said calmly. "Not dead yet, then?"

"Master *Nicolas?*" the servant whispered hoarsely, blinking his eyes as if afraid to believe what he was seeing. His expression turned to one of astonished delight. "It *is* you!" He threw the door wide open. "Oh, saints be praised! Your mother will be overjoyed.

Come in, my boy, come in!" He suddenly seemed to notice the bandage on Valette's shoulder, and his brow creased in alarm. "But you're hurt! What on earth have you been doing to yourself? Mrs. Belford!"

A rotund housekeeper bustled forward in response to his shout. "What's all the fuss, Mr. Hodges?" She stopped at the sight of Valette, her double chins wobbling alarmingly. "Good God!" she exclaimed.

Valette gave a wry smile. "No, Mrs. Belford, just me. Please inform my father that I'm here. Hodges?"

The elderly majordomo snapped to attention. "Yes, sir?"

"I take it my rooms are still my rooms?"

"Of course, my lord. No one's touched them, save for cleaning, since you left."

"Excellent. In that case I'll take a bath and some food as soon as you're ready. I trust you can make my guests equally welcome?"

The servant bowed. "Of course, sir." He beckoned to a footman and turned to Marianne and Louis-Charles. "If you'll just follow Ned, here."

"Not me," the Raven said cheerfully. "I got stuff to do. I'll see you later, Nic." He doffed an imaginary top hat and sauntered away across the manicured lawns. "Have fun, *mes enfants.*"

Marianne found herself following the servant as if in a daze, through an enormous marbled entrance hall and up a flight of stairs. Their footsteps echoed as they crossed another huge room and ascended one side of an elaborate double staircase.

A thousand different impressions jostled for attention: the shine of marble beneath her feet; the dazzling height of the ceiling; the graceful pillars; the murals decorating the entire stairway, celestial visions of heaven and hell. It was all so incredible, so much like a dream that her brain refused to process it.

Before she could summon a protest, both Nic and Louis-Charles disappeared into other rooms. She was ushered into a sumptuous bedroom and left alone, with promises of food and a hot bath to arrive imminently. All Marianne saw was the waiting bed. It was high and inviting, the pillows and coverlet rose-colored velvet. It looked so soft.

The room smelled of lavender and beeswax. Solid, comforting smells, so different from the scents of France. The Montausier always smelled of perfume, but it was the mix of a hundred different scents rolled into one, cloying and overpowering. This was different, a lighter fragrance, like lily of the valley and roses.

She was so exhausted that she lay down fully clothed, stopping only to remove her ruined ballet slippers. There wasn't even a trace of pink on them now. She would rest for a moment. Only a moment, to gather her wits. And then she was going to have serious words with that lying, scheming, worthless Nicolas Valette. The first thing she was going to demand was his name. His real name.

Every single one of them.

CHAPTER 42

*T*he rustle of skirts and a cool hand brushing her forehead roused her.

"Maman! She's waking up!" said a soft voice.

Marianne frowned, utterly disoriented. Perfume? Women? Was she back at the Montausier?

A beautiful girl was leaning over her, sitting by the bed. Marianne gazed up at her. The girl's features were exquisite, her eyes an unusual lavender color, but it was impossible not to notice the pale scar that ran down her forehead. It bisected the edge of one eyebrow before it disappeared into her hairline at the temple. Marianne was about to ask about it when an older woman joined them, and they both gazed down at her with the same, faintly worried expression.

Where on earth was she? And then she remembered. *England. The Raven. Valette.*

The older lady was unmistakably Nic's mother. There was definitely a family resemblance, despite her softer, more feminine features. It was easy to see how she'd had such handsome children. Easy, too, to see where Nic had inherited his amber eyes.

"I'm so sorry you were left alone, *ma chère.*" the lady said gently.

She had the faintest French accent. Marianne had forgotten she was French. She struggled to sit up.

"Here, we've brought you some food. I'm Heloise, by the way," the pretty girl said. Marianne nearly moaned in ecstasy at the pot of hot chocolate and fresh bread roll that were waiting on the tray. Her stomach grumbled in approval, and she flushed. "Marianne Bonnard."

"*Enchanté.* And please, call me Thérèse." The older lady sat on the bed. "My son told us you saved his life, mademoiselle." Her smooth forehead wrinkled in perplexity. "Please excuse my rudeness, but I do not fully understand. When I first saw you, I assumed you were a servant." She looked more intrigued than outraged. "But now I think you are not a servant at all. Tell me, what are you to my son?"

Marianne felt her face heat at such direct questioning. She wasn't sure how to answer, how much Nic's family knew of his life in Paris and his involvement with Fouché. She swallowed a mouthful of chocolate. "A colleague, madame. Nothing more."

His mother seemed relieved, and Marianne winced inwardly. Of course she would be. She must look like some ragamuffin beggar girl. Hardly the sort of company a mother would want consorting with her son.

Heloise grinned playfully. "Well, I'm sure you're more to Nic than that. He nearly bit my head off when I told him you were sleeping and weren't to be disturbed."

Her mother frowned. "We've missed him so much. Thank you for bringing him back to us, mademoiselle. How can we ever repay you?"

Don't offer to pay me, please, Marianne thought desperately. *It would be vulgar and insulting.* And she'd be far too tempted to take it. "How long have I been asleep?" she asked instead.

Heloise smiled. "Hours. Nic's been asking about you. Well,

more like *demanding* to see you, all day. But Maman told him you needed to rest."

"Where is he? Can I see him? Has he seen a doctor?"

His mother patted her hand. "He's fine, he just needs to rest. The doctor says he should be fully recovered in a week or two, provided he does nothing too strenuous."

Marianne shifted on the bed and flushed when she realized she was still wearing her smuggler's clothes.

Thérèse sucked in a breath at the rumpled shirt and stained breeches. "Oh, goodness. We must get you something more suitable to wear," she said faintly.

Marianne gave a wry smile. "Madame, your son won't care, believe me."

Thérèse gave her an odd, assessing look. "Nonsense. Besides, I'm certain Heloise has something that would suit. Come, Heloise." She stood and started for the door.

"Oh no, I'm perfectly fine, madame . . ." Marianne protested. "That is, I won't be staying . . ."

Heloise rose, too, her eyes twinkling. "It's no use arguing. Maman always gets her way. Ask anyone."

"Heloise!" her mother scolded with a fond smile. "That's not true!"

Heloise winked. "Well, everyone but Nicolas does what she wants, anyway. Even Papa and Dickie." She waved a hand toward an interconnecting door and lowered her voice so her mother wouldn't hear. "He's right through there." She shot Marianne a conspiratorial grin.

Marianne stared at the door in shock. She'd been put in the suite of rooms next to Nicolas? Surely it wasn't the done thing for a woman to be placed in the room next to—? Her face heated as the implications of it sank in. They thought she was his . . . paramour. His whore.

She found she couldn't look at either Thérèse or her daughter. "Thank you," she whispered, mortified.

Thérèse nodded briskly. "It is almost time for dinner. Do you feel well enough to come downstairs? I know the family is extremely keen to meet you."

"Yes, madame," Marianne said politely, knowing she couldn't refuse. "Of course."

* * *

HER HAND WAS TREMBLING as she turned the handle to Valette's room. She half hoped it would be locked, but it turned easily enough. She had to stop being so stupid. It was a sickroom. He was an invalid. To be worried about proprieties, after everything they had been through together, was absurd.

He was sitting up in bed, bare-chested, propped against a mountain of white pillows. A copy of the *London Times* balanced on his knees.

"Welcome to my humble abode."

He looked well enough, despite the new bandage on his shoulder.

Words failed her. They'd shared so much. Done so much. He'd saved her life, seen her in her darkest moment, kissed her soul right out of her. Yet here, in this austere, elegant room, he seemed further from her than he'd ever been. So far removed from the daredevil pirate she'd come to know.

His scrutiny was making her nervous. Marianne glanced desperately through the tall windows at the blue sky beyond. "I thought it always rained in England."

Idiot! A comment on the weather? Was that honestly the best thing she could think of to say? She wanted to dash her brains out on the mantelpiece.

Valette's mocking smile told her exactly what he thought of her pathetic conversational gambit. She forced herself to walk forward and take a seat in the chair on one side of the ornate bed.

"Are my family being nice to you?" he asked.

"Of course." She bit her lip. "They've been exceedingly kind. But I can't help but wonder what they'd say if they knew what I was?"

"And what are you?" he asked with dangerous calm. "Apart from the girl who saved my life?"

I don't know, she thought desperately. *I don't know what I am to you. Your means of revenge against Duval? A potential conquest? Your protégé? Your equal? Your friend?*

"A circus thief," she said. "And a traitor."

"They would think you were extraordinary," he said. "As I do."

She looked away, embarrassed by the sincerity in his voice. She indicated a nearby tray. "There's food here. You should try to eat it."

He caught her wrist. "Only if you stay with me."

Her heart warmed at his obvious bribery. "All right." She lifted the domed metal covers and eyed the contents with undisguised revulsion. "What *is* that?"

He leaned over to take a look. "Looks like roast beef followed by spotted dick. Good, hearty English grub."

She shook her head in disgust. "Laurent always said the English did barbaric things to meat. It is true. That's burned like Jeanne d'Arc." She turned her attention to the dessert and pushed a spoonful around scornfully. "And what is this 'spotted dick'?"

He chuckled. "I've a strange fondness for it. I used to have it at boarding school."

"It looks like it's made with dead flies."

"I believe they're raisins," he said, straight-faced.

"Only an Englishman could conceive of such a pudding. How can you prefer this to crème brûlée?" She glanced up and frowned at his amused expression.

"Only the English part of me likes it. Believe me, the French half has an overriding passion for crème brûlée." His lips quirked as if at some private joke.

The sudden heat in his eyes made her flush. He reached across the coverlet and took the spoon from her nerveless fingers.

"You should rest," she scolded, trying unsuccessfully to pull her hand from his.

He rubbed the inside of her wrist with his thumb and adopted the look of a sulky schoolboy. "I'm not tired. I'm going out of my mind with boredom." He shot her a wicked, sinful glance from beneath his lashes while his fingers traced a scalding path up the inside of her bare arm, from wrist to elbow and back again. Her stomach fluttered.

"Do you like this room?" There was a suspicious gleam in his eye, one she instantly mistrusted. She looked around. Chinese silk papered the walls. Satin drapes hung at the windows and around the bed. There were mirrors and paintings, ormolu and tortoiseshell, amber and marble. Her breath caught in her throat. It was the room he'd described in the darkness—the fantasy room from the dungeon. The image of it was seared into her heart.

Her eyes shot to his. *All those wicked things he'd said, back at the prison.*

She didn't know how to ask. She wanted to, so badly, but her lips couldn't frame the words.

An awkward, pregnant silence fell between them, full of things unspoken. He raised his eyebrows at her, waiting . . .

"Well, I have to go," she said, flustered. She pulled her hand from his. "Your mother wants me to go down for dinner. Will you come?"

He gave her a reproachful look that said he knew she'd dodged a bullet. "I look forward to it."

CHAPTER 43

*N*ic lay back on the pillows with a sigh as the door closed behind Marianne. It was strange, seeing her here, in his childhood home. In his bedroom. He gave a wry chuckle. This was the room he'd described in his fantasy back at Vincennes. Had she realized it?

He'd heard her sudden intake of breath, savored the pink tinge that crept into her cheeks as she recalled all the scandalous things he'd promised to do to her. Oh yes, she recognized it.

It was harder than he'd thought, being home again. He'd barely set foot in the place over the past ten years. Now memories assailed him at every turn, mental vignettes of a happy, carefree childhood. Messing about with his brothers in the rock pools and caves along the shore. Climbing trees, skinning their knees, playing pirates and smugglers and highwaymen. Anthony stuck up a tree. Richard dunked in the stream by his ill-tempered horse.

Nic swallowed a knot of nostalgia. He'd missed being part of a family. He realized how much only now that he was back in their midst. His life in Paris was glittering and glamorous, full of intrigue and excitement. But it was a lonely existence. He could count the number of people he trusted on the fingers of one hand. It was better that way, in the game, where he sent good men to risk their lives every day. He'd deliberately kept people at arm's length, even the Falconis and Andrew Ducrow, men he loved like brothers. He'd thought that to be friendless was to be free.

Marianne had somehow made that seem nonsensical. His happiest memories were the times he'd spent at the Cirque Olympique, watching her from the shadows. The time he'd spent with her.

Nic frowned at the ornate ceiling. He'd spent years building up an impenetrable wall around his heart, around his emotions. Defenses as thick as the walls of the Bastille. Marianne had broken them down. Not with a direct attack, but slowly, insidiously, trickling through the gaps like the water through sand: undetectable, unstoppable, and utterly destructive.

He'd already made the very great mistake of allowing himself to care for her. In his line of work that was unforgivable. Loving was not just dangerous, it was impossible. He closed his eyes. If only they'd met before the war. Before Tony had died. Before he'd become traitor and a liar and a killer and a thief.

He shook his head. It was stupid to think of impossible scenarios. He didn't have a heart to give to her. He'd dedicated himself to seeing the murderer Napoleon defeated, and he wouldn't waver from his course.

He scowled down at the newspaper he'd been reading. The emperor was heading north from Paris. The showdown everyone had anticipated was about to come to a head. Nic stared at the newsprint blankly. He'd made a promise, wouldn't rest until it was completed. Love was a binding thing, and he wasn't ready to be bound. He didn't want roots holding him on one place. He still had too much to do.

* * *

A DRESS WAS LAID out on her bed when Marianne returned, along with stockings and garters, a sheer cotton nightdress, and a dressing robe. A hot bath was waiting in front of the fire.

She took her first real look at her surroundings. A huge silk canopy draped above the bed, matching the pink silk–papered walls and gilt scrollwork of the furniture. Toile-de-Jouy shepherdesses and lovers on swings frolicked over every surface. A gilt clock with a sunburst pendulum ticked quietly on the mantel between porcelain figurines of monkeys with musical instruments. The one playing the flute wore a little red hat and waistcoat. He looked just like Pagnol.

The whole effect was dainty and elegant. It was an unmistakably feminine room, the architectural counterpoint to the blue-silk room next door. It reminded her, suddenly, of her childhood bedroom at Chanterac, before the fire. No wonder it felt so achingly familiar.

Marianne stroked her fingers over the dress, assailed by a brief memory of her mother, dressed for a grand ball. Of herself and Sophie peering through the banisters from the landing, watching their glamorous parents meet in the hallway to be ushered out into the waiting carriage.

Mother had looked so beautiful, like an enchanted princess, exactly what the Comtesse de Chanterac should look like. Diamonds glittered at her ears and throat, nestled in her hair like tiny raindrops, sparkled on the sticks of her fan. Father had been tall and handsome in his finery, a silk sash across his chest, a pale blue evening coat edged in silver lace, white knee-high stockings, and diamonds shining on the buckles of his shoes.

The memory faded. She stripped off her rough breeches and borrowed shirt and bathed, scrubbing her skin until it was pink and glowing, erasing every last trace of Vincennes.

But when it came time to dress, her heart constricted. Of all the hardships she'd endured over the past six years, she'd never cried, not once. Not when her parents had died. Not when she'd been pawed by Duval. And yet the softness of the material was her undoing. The lace was so fine, like baby's breath, countless hours of work. It made her want to weep.

She might have been born to this life, but the last five years in Paris had erased the girl she'd once been. This luxury was as alien to her as this foreign country. She felt a stab of anger. Such a life had been stolen from her by Duval. If her parents had lived, she'd have been accustomed to this level of luxury. She was the finest thief in Paris, but she could never steal back what he'd taken from her.

Marianne touched the pair of stockings lovingly. It felt like a betrayal of her new life to wish for such things, but they were so beautiful. If only Sophie could see them. She'd look astonishing in such finery.

A callus on her palm snagged the thin silk, and she snatched her hand back with a cry of dismay. She'd ruined it. She wasn't fit to touch it. She should put her boy's clothes back on, but they were rumpled and filthy. Tears stung her eyes. *Idiot.*

The dress was silk, the same amber color as Nic's eyes. Beautiful, with a pleated bodice and a full skirt that fell in soft folds around her legs and swished when she moved. It had a ruffle of fichu netting at the bodice. She was aware of every caress of the fabric on her skin.

A maid came in to fix her hair. She exclaimed at the short style, declaring it quite à la mode, and began pinning and curling with tongs and combs. Marianne didn't have the heart to explain that necessity, not fashion, had dictated the style.

When the girl left, Marianne stared at the stranger gazing back at her from the mirror. It was only a veneer. A borrowed dress, a temporary dream. Where was the girl who could dance on a wire? Where was the thief, the housebreaker? Where was the girl who'd thrown a knife at Valette? Killed a man? They were all there, and yet they weren't. She was pale and slim and elegant. A stranger to herself.

The color of the dress made her green eyes glow in her pale face. She pinched her cheeks and bit her lips to try to add some color, then turned away from the mirror.

It would be impossible to run in a dress like this. And she desperately wanted to run.

She was a coward. She'd faced torture and death and rape. And yet here she was, petrified of descending the stairs and meeting Valette's family in the drawing room. Her legs trembled as she started downstairs.

It was worse than she'd imagined. She paused in the doorway to the salon, desperately uncertain. There was no sign of Nicolas at all. His family was gathered round. One by one they turned and stared at her, as if she were one of the performers in the gardens of the Palais Royale. What they would do if she suddenly did a somersault, right there, in the middle of the parlor? If it weren't for her cumbersome skirts, she would do it.

And then the awkward moment was broken as Thérèse came toward her and drew her gently into the conversation.

CHAPTER 44

*M*arianne gave a grateful sigh as Louis-Charles crossed the room and bowed low to her. He appeared much improved—still frail, but his skin had lost the deathly pallor of imprisonment, and his clean hair shone golden in the light from the candles.

He looked elegant, in what must have been borrowed clothes. Buff knee breeches, tall leather boots, and a navy superfine jacket.

"You look beautiful, mademoiselle," he said with quiet sincerity as he bent and kissed her hand.

She blushed. "You're only saying that because you've been stuck in a prison with ugly old men for so long," she joked.

He chuckled wryly.

"So what will you do, now that you finally have your freedom?"

He sighed. "I've imagined this day for so long, it seems impossible to believe that it has actually come to pass." He considered her question. "I do not wish to become a part of fashionable society – to be amongst so many people after such a long a time alone does not appeal. I thought perhaps I might become a parish priest, somewhere here in England."

"You don't want to return to France?" she asked, surprised. "But you're the rightful heir to the throne."

The prince shook his head, his eyes wise beyond his years. "The situation is too volatile. There's been enough bloodshed, without adding myself to the mix. Riches and power would not, I think, make me happy. Freedom will suffice. And companionship and love, if I am fortunate enough to be granted them." His gaze flicked past her, to something over her shoulder.

Marianne turned, and her heart stopped in her chest.

Valette was framed in the doorway. He looked utterly beautiful, leaning against the doorjamb, supremely relaxed and indolent. His dark blue coat was cut to perfection; his breeches were molded to his long, muscled legs. His hair was swept back in perfect waves, and his snowy-white neckcloth was practically blinding.

No, it was the diamond pin securing it that dazzled, she amended. The single stone was as big as a pea. A jewel like that could feed a family for a year in the backstreets of Montmartre.

She turned away, suddenly flustered.

Nic lounged in the doorway, surveying the room for Marianne, but there was no sign of her. His arm ached, but he'd been shot before. And stabbed. It was nothing.

Louis-Charles was standing by the fireplace, in animated conversation with a young woman in a gold-colored dress. Must be one of his sister's friends. Nic gave an inward sigh. His mother was clearly wasting no time in matchmaking. She did it every time he came home. It was one of the reasons he came back so infrequently.

He watched as Dickie joined them. Judging from the stupid smile on his elder brother's face, he was clearly enchanted with the creature, too. Nic took a moment to study her from the back. She had a trim figure, he supposed. Her dress had a ribbon at the waist and a row of tiny buttons running up the back. The skin above the scooped back was pale and smooth. She had a pretty neck, too, with little wisps of hair curling at her nape, shown to perfect advantage by her fashionably short coiffure.

Dickie laughed at something the young woman said. He raised his head, caught Nic watching, and beckoned him over.

The young woman in gold turned, and all the breath left Nic's lungs. *Christ.*

His chest hurt, as if someone had punched him square on the solar plexus. He'd seen her filthy and beaten. He'd seen her in circus clothes, and dressed as a boy. Hell, he'd seen her naked and rosy and dripping from her bath. He'd never seen her like this.

This was how he'd imagined her, back in that god-awful dungeon. Her short hair was arranged in artless curls around her head, leaving her smooth shoulders and the alabaster skin of her neck bare. The color of the dress brought out the astonishing green of her eyes and the soft, rosy pink of her lips.

Nic scowled, feeling oddly ill-used, as if she'd somehow misled him. She wasn't just pretty. She was breathtaking. Elegant and poised and incredibly alluring.

What the hell was wrong with him? He'd known she'd look good when she was finally cleaned up. He'd slept with some of the most beautiful women in Europe. Flirted and seduced and abandoned with consummate ease. Next to her, they were pale, tawdry imitations. Like paste stones next to a glimmering diamond. *Bloody hell.*

He managed to recover just enough to raise his brows haughtily as she glanced up at him. "Nowhere to stash your knives in that outfit," he murmured.

* * *

MARIANNE TENSED, acutely aware of his height, the heat of his long fingers as he took her hand. At least for the first time she felt his sartorial equal. His eyes roved over her body, an appreciative glow in their tawny depths that made her blood thrum. Louis-Charles chuckled, and Marianne felt her skin heat even more.

Valette bowed low over her hand, as if they were in a Parisian ballroom. "You look radiant tonight, mademoiselle."

The prince nodded his agreement. "Yes. How is it you English say? A diamond of the first water?"

Marianne scowled at him.

Louis-Charles's blue eyes twinkled. "Of course, I haven't been out much in society. But even *I* know how rare it is to find a woman who possesses not only beauty, but courage and talent and wit."

Marianne gave an unladylike snort even as she blushed at the compliment. "Monsieur, you are being ridiculous! Go and practice your flattery on someone else."

He gave her an exaggerated bow before crossing the room to talk to Heloise. Richard, too, made his excuses, leaving her alone with Valette.

She stared at his chest. His shirt studs were mother-of-pearl; they shimmered slightly as he breathed, ripples of rainbow color.

"You're very dismissive of royalty," he murmured indulgently.

"The prince doesn't want me. He's been watching your sister for the past half hour." She suppressed a smile at the way his jaw clenched predictably at that.

"I thought he was going to become a priest?" he growled.

"The poor man's been incarcerated for twenty years. I expect he's just happy to see a pretty face, instead of his grim-faced jailers every day. And Heloise is so lovely she'd tempt a saint." Marianne nudged him gently. "Stop glowering! Your sister isn't interested in him." She paused dramatically, just to savor the moment. "*She* only has eyes for your smuggler."

His expression of astonishment was downright comical. "*Raven*? How do you know that?"

Marianne smiled. "I saw them in the hallway just now. Your sister was spying on him from the top of the stairs, lurking about on the landing. But he must have known she was there, because when he'd finished talking to your brother, he looked up and caught her watching. I swear, the look that passed between them could have melted rock. Heloise blushed bright pink and fled down the corridor. And the Raven laughed."

Valette scowled. "Never spy on a spy."

She glanced at him under her lashes. "He *is* rather wicked. And terribly attractive. Women find debonair pirate charm fatally attractive."

"Well, he can bloody well keep his 'debonair pirate' hands off my little sister." Nic frowned. "She's not for the likes of him."

"*Now* who's being an aristo snob?" she taunted smugly.

"It's not his background," he said. "Raven's pedigree's as good as mine. But that man's done things that would make your hair curl. Heloise is a complete innocent. She's got no reason to get infatuated with a scamp like him."

"That scamp saved both our lives," Marianne reminded him gently.

"Yes, well, it's not up to her to show him how grateful the bloody family is."

"Speaking of pedigrees," she said carefully, "care to tell me yours? You said your real name was Nicolas Valette. I'm assuming you have some others." She raised her brows and waited for him to explain.

He gave a long suffering-sigh. "Yes. My full name is Nicolas Sheridan Guy Valette Hampden. My father, whom you've met, is Sir William Hampden, also known by his honorary titles of

Viscount Lovell and Baron Trevor. My mother, before her marriage, was Thérèse Valette. Dickie, over there, is the heir. My younger brother, Tony, was killed in Spain, and Heloise is the youngest. If you want any more information, you'll have to consult *Burke's Peerage*," he finished grumpily.

CHAPTER 45

"*H*ave you heard the news from France?" he asked, clearly keen to change the subject.

Marianne's stomach dropped. "What is it?"

"The emperor's heading north toward Belgium. He's left General Davout to hold Paris. The Austrian and Russian armies are on their way to meet up with the British, under Wellington. Napoleon means to engage them just across the border."

Her heart started beating too fast. "You want to go, too, don't you?"

The grim expression on his face frightened her. "He has to be stopped."

She hit his arm, and he winced. "You are an idiot, Nicolas Valette."

He raised his brows. "How so?"

"You have a family who loves you. A life of privilege and luxury."

"Life here's not half as exciting as scaling castle walls and swimming moats with you, my sweet," he joked.

"You've just been shot. You're not fit enough to go and face Napoleon."

"It's not about holding a weapon. There are other things I can do. Information wins more battles than muskets and sabers."

A flash of anger warmed her as she realized the utter futility of arguing with him. "What is it with you men? I'm sure you manufacture wars just to have an outlet for your aggression. Otherwise, you'd all be wandering around, getting in the way and fighting nonsensical duels." Marianne knew she was ranting but was past caring. "When a *woman* gets angry, she eats chocolate or goes shopping. You *men* have to invade another country. It's ridiculous!"

Valette was unmoved by her tirade. "I have to do this, Marianne. I have to see him beaten once and for all."

Fury pounded in her temples. "And then what? You think you'll be able to rest easy? Another tyrant will just take his place. Someone equally bad. Will you fight them all?" Her anger suddenly blew over, leaving her exhausted. She gazed up into his set face. "It will consume you, this revenge. When will it end? When will it be enough?"

His gaze was haunted. "I don't know."

She tried one last time to convince him. "Your family needs you as much as your country does. *More*. You still have both your parents, a brother and sister who love you. You've given France and England so much of your life already. Let that be enough. It's time to do something for yourself."

She knew she'd lost him, even before he answered.

"I can't."

Marianne closed her eyes in defeat. She understood his compulsion, even if she couldn't condone it. His revenge had prior claim. She was almost jealous of the intensity of his hatred, the depth of his animosity toward Napoleon. Except she felt the same way toward Duval.

"Why? Why must you stop him?"

"He killed my brother. My little brother. Who should have been at home, messing about with girls and fishing and drinking and playing stupid pranks with his friends. Instead, he died at that bastard's orders, miles away from home." He took a deep breath, striving for calm. "The worst thing is, I used to admire Napoleon's ideas. I still do. Half of his reforms are excellent. But that was the ideas, not the man. Before his egomaniac nature became more and more apparent. It's all about making himself immortal. He wants to burn the brightest star in the night sky of history. And in trying to do that, he's taken the lives of thousands upon thousands of people. *That's* the cost of his glory."

His face was fierce. "It's not just his enemies. Every one of those soldiers on a battlefield is someone's brother or father or son. Boys just like Tony. Silly, idealistic boys who leave aching holes in the families they leave behind." His eyes burned with a feverish intensity. "That's why. To stop him from doing it again. To stop him from ripping families apart for nothing more than hubris and personal vanity. If I can prevent just one more family having to go through what mine had to face, stop one more man losing his brother, then it's worth it."

Hopelessness and grief rose up together in her chest at the awful, heartbreaking irony of the situation. The very qualities that made her respect him were the qualities she so desperately wanted him to abandon. His honor, his stubborn principles. His desire to be a part of something greater than himself. He put the well-being of an entire nation above his own personal desires. How could she ask him to give up his essence, his deeply ingrained responsibility?

Marianne squeezed her eyes shut. *She couldn't.*

Her chest hurt. All the things she admired about him were conspiring to break her heart. He had to go. And he could so easily die. He'd made his peace with it, but she couldn't. She wanted to rage and scream.

She blinked back tears as dinner was announced. Laurent had warned her not to let herself care for him, but she'd been too stupid to listen, too caught up in her own fears to take note. And now it was too late.

* * *

Marianne barely recalled dinner. Valette's family kept the conversation light, despite the fact that they must have been dying to know what was going on. She excused herself as soon as she could, claiming exhaustion.

She stood in her room with her back to the door, clutching the handle for support. Indecision churned in her gut. She had to leave. She had to see Valette. There was still too much left unsettled between them.

It seemed hours before she heard his footsteps in the hallway and the soft click of his door. She strode across the room and opened the connecting door before she lost her nerve. He glanced up, paused in the process of pouring himself a brandy. He'd removed his jacket, cravat, and boots, and his white shirt now lay open at his throat. He set the decanter down very gently on the tray, watching her with those inscrutable amber eyes. He waited for her to speak.

"At Vincennes," she blurted out, stumbling over her words in her haste to get them out. "You said . . ." She stopped, suddenly tongue-tied. *What on earth was she doing?* Back in her room she'd been so certain this was a good idea. She swallowed and tried again. "This room has silk on the walls . . . and amber and marble and . . ." Again she came to a stop.

The pause before he answered was so profound she could hear the ticking of the clock on the mantel, the thrum of her own blood in her ears. She thought she might pass out.

"So it does," he said carefully.

He must know what she was asking.

"You promised," she said breathlessly. "You said we'd finish what we started."

He took a slow sip of brandy and simply stared at her from across the room.

A knot of misery lodged in her chest, and she closed her eyes in silent despair. *Was he going to her refuse her, now, after all?*

She jumped when his fingers stroked her chin. Her eyes shot open. Damn the man! He'd crossed the room as silently as a cat.

"Are you saying you want me to make love to you, Marianne?"

She managed to nod.

"And you trust me? To show you how it should be?" He sounded skeptical.

"I *want* to . . . so much . . . but . . ."

He sighed. "Making love's not some sordid power game. It's not hurt and humiliation. It's giving and taking. Playing and pleasure." He gave a crooked half smile that made her insides somersault. "So much pleasure you think you might die from it."

"I don't think that's possible," she said, determined to be honest. "Not for me anyway. What if I'm broken? Beyond mending."

He rested his forehead against hers and brushed his thumbs over her jaw. "I don't believe it. Think about it. Think of all the times you've let me touch you without flinching." He let that sink in while his fingers continued caressing her cheek, a butterfly touch. Her stomach fluttered. "When you lay with me in the bed at the château. In the cart when the soldiers came." His eyes were wicked with memory, his tone teasing. "Did you hate my touch then?"

Marianne's heart was beating wildly in her throat. "No. But I can't bear to have a man's weight on me. It makes me feel . . . helpless, angry."

He shook his head. "Oh, sweeting. For someone who lived as long as you did in a brothel, you are woefully uneducated." His tone was grave, but his eyes were laughing.

It jolted her out of her self-pity. "Are you *mocking* me?"

His smile was infinitely tender. "Only a little. The man doesn't have to go on top."

She frowned.

He chuckled. "The woman can ride him like a horse. Or he can take her from the side, lying down. Or from behind. Or standing up." His thumb slid over her lower lip, rolling it down. Heat spread and curled like wood smoke through her veins.

It was such an enormous thing. To put her body, her soul into his keeping.

"We can go as slowly as you want. Any time you want to stop, I'll stop."

His touch was turning her inside out. "You lie all the time," she said weakly.

His eyes locked on hers, burning in their intensity. "Never in this. I swear to you."

"Then, yes."

A deep tremor ran through him, and she realized he'd been holding himself taut, drawn tight as a bowstring, waiting for her decision. She swallowed, suddenly terrified of the momentous step she was about to take. *Oh God, she was actually going to do this.*

His hands cupped her face gently, reverently, as if she were made of the finest Sèvres porcelain. He bent and kissed each eyelid in turn, then the tip of her nose, the very corner of her mouth. She trembled, weakening, melting with his touch like ice thawing in the spring.

He pulled away, and she suppressed a sigh. She could keep on kissing him forever.

"So now what should we do?" she asked breathlessly.

CHAPTER 46

*V*alette crossed to the edge of the bed, sat down, and leaned back on his arms. "What do you want to do?"

Her heart was beating in terror at the strength of her desire. "I want to touch you," she whispered, feeling her face heat.

"Then do it."

She moved forward to stand between his legs and reached for the hem of his shirt, astonished at her own daring. She tugged it from his breeches. He raised his arms over his head to help her, and she pulled it up and sent it sailing to the floor.

For a breathless moment she just studied him, the lean perfection of his body. Each muscle and sinew flowed in perfect symmetry, his skin smooth and tawny in the flickering candlelight. Only the white bandage on his shoulder interrupted the sleek fluidity of line.

Tentatively, she touched her hand to his chest, over his heart. His skin felt hot, his heartbeat strong and steady beneath her palm. She splayed her fingers and ran them lightly down over his chest, enjoying the way his sculpted muscles leaped under the caress. His stomach was all ripples and hollows, dips and troughs, like the pattern left on sand at low tide.

She traced her finger down his flat stomach, following the intriguing line of hair that disappeared into the waistband of his breeches.

How many times had she dreamed of doing this?

Valette sucked in his breath. He caught her wrist, stopping her downward progress with a gentle tug. His mouth curved in a faint, rueful smile. "Enough of that for now. Turn around."

Marianne did as she was told.

He began to unbutton the row of tiny buttons down her back. The gentle pop of one after another was deafening in the sudden silence. The dress gave way, loosening inch by inch with a slow whisper of silk. It dropped from her shoulders, but she held it to her chest, suddenly shy.

She shivered as his fingers brushed her skin, unlacing the strings of her corset. When he turned her to face him again, her heart was pounding against her ribs. Warmth heated her face. He was devouring her with his eyes, and she realized that the color on *his* cheeks was the flush of arousal, too.

"Drop the dress," he commanded softly, sitting back again on the bed.

She unclenched her hands. The fabric collapsed at her feet in a graceful amber puddle. His eyes never left her face.

"Now the corset."

She bit her bottom lip, and his eyes followed the move hungrily. The loosened corset joined the dress on the floor, and she stepped out of them both, left in only her thin cotton chemise. She should have been cold, but his smoldering gaze heated her blood and she could think of nothing else.

"Now that," he whispered, nodding at the shift.

Hands shaking, she complied.

There was nothing except her stockings underneath. She bent to untie the ribbon that held them up, more to cover herself than anything else, but his quiet command stopped her.

"No. Leave them on. Come here."

She took a tiny step closer, and he pulled her between his knees. He placed his hands on her hips and splayed his fingers, then leaned forward and rested his head just below her breasts.

Marianne drew in an astonished breath. She tangled her hands in his hair, holding him against her. His breath on her skin was like thin fire, icy flames.

It wasn't enough. Not nearly enough.

And then he turned his head and closed his mouth over her nipple. Marianne gasped. He nipped her with his teeth, a slight pain immediately soothed with his tongue. And then he sucked, hard, and her whole body shook. A jolt of sensation shot down to her stomach, between her legs. Her knees turned to jelly. His tongue traced the crescent below one breast, and the slight rasp of his unshaved cheek made her quiver.

"Mmm," he murmured dreamily. "Cinnamon and cream."

Marianne was on fire, and for once she welcomed the flames. She wanted to burn up, wanted the bright, cleansing power to purify her body and leave her clean and whole and new. She didn't resist when he drew her down onto the bed beside him and pressed a gentle kiss against her mouth, sweet and questioning.

Tears pricked behind her eyes at the exquisite care he was taking with her. He made her feel beautiful, precious, cherished. She kissed him back tentatively, loving the feel of him, and when she moaned, he tightened his arms around her and captured her mouth with fierce possessiveness. Her head whirled.

* * *

NIC WANTED to weep at the tiny perfection of her body. He pulled back, bracing his weight on his forearms, wanting, no, *needing* to look at her.

The unexpected beauty of her still took his breath away: that dark hair splayed out around her head; her small, perfect breasts;

her tiny waist and shapely legs. She was covered in scrapes and bruises, injuries that were all because of him. A constricting ball of guilt and tenderness tightened his throat. He bent and kissed each abrasion in silent apology, soothing the sting with his lips, his tongue.

He kissed the slope of her neck where it met her shoulder, and she arched into him, sweet and trusting, and all the jaded cynicism of his past began to crumble.

He could taste the pleasure on her, smell the arousal rising from her skin, and it made him harder than ever. He used every one of his considerable skills to rouse her, skills honed by women more beautiful, more knowledgeable. He regretted those women, but he was glad of the expertise they'd given him. As if every faceless encounter had just been a prelude to this—this room, this moment, *this* woman. He wanted to give her everything. Give her the best of himself.

He slid his hand down over the smooth, taut muscles of her belly and skimmed the triangle of soft curls below, then followed the path with his mouth, kissing a line down her stomach. She whimpered, but he stroked her until she relaxed beneath his touch once more.

"Relax, little one. I won't hurt you. I promise."

Marianne tried to squirm away when he pushed her thighs apart. She was open to him, completely exposed, vulnerable. She caught his wrists, halting his progress, but the look he shot her was so full of challenge, as if he fully expected her to balk, that she released him and sank back against the bed, determined to prove him wrong.

His warm breath tickled the inside of her thigh, and then he put his mouth between her legs. She nearly shot off the bed. "What are you—? Oh, my God."

285

And then he was stroking and lapping at her with his tongue, nipping with his teeth, circling gently. He found that secret, silky place and pushed deep inside to taste.

Oh merde.

She jerked in astonishment but his chuckled "Shhh" vibrating against her made her writhe even more. Heat, singing and vibrant, crackled through her veins. Blinded, driven by pure instinct, she arched her hips to meet his mouth. The things he was doing! It was a sin, a terrible, wonderful perversion. It felt so good.

He took his time, kissing, stroking, caressing, whispering soft words of encouragement against her, pleas and demands in both English and French, driving her mad with want so she clutched at the covers with her fists.

She begged him to stop, to keep going, *anything*. He pulled back, rising up over her, and this time it was his hand that found the hot center of her. There was no respite. He stroked her with his fingers, round and round in maddening circles until Marianne writhed against the sheets and sensation built and eddied like the waters of a river. "Valette!" she panted, breathless. "Have mercy."

He chuckled. "Never."

And then his finger was pushing inside her, and she cried out in astonishment. His touch wound her even tighter, like a spring. She dug her heels into the bed and arched her hips up to him. She was burning up, and something was building—a tightness, a confusion. She wanted to hit him, to scream at him to stop. And never stop. Never stop.

And then a surge of blinding pleasure burst over her body, a sudden shimmering cloudburst, and she cried out at the piercing intensity of it, convulsing around him as it surged through her, wave after wave of darkness and delight.

All the tension melted right out of her. She couldn't breathe, couldn't see. Didn't care. No wonder it was called *la petite mort.*

The little death. When she floated back down to earth, surfacing slowly from the hot, sweet oblivion, he was leaning on one elbow, watching her with a smugly satisfied expression on his face.

"Nice?"

Marianne gazed at him, incredulous. Nice was such a ludicrously inadequate word for such a blinding, heady rush of pleasure. She nodded dazedly.

CHAPTER 47

*M*arianne watched as Nic's hands went to his breeches. Her heart was still hammering from the astonishing things he'd just done. She'd forgotten he still had clothes on.

She swallowed a gasp as he stripped them off. He was huge, fully aroused. Entirely out of her sphere of admittedly limited experience.

As if he could read her mind he glanced down and smiled wickedly. "See, *nothing* like Duval."

Fear trickled in, muting her excitement. He was such a daunting, virile, *experienced* man. What if she couldn't do this? What if he didn't have the patience to deal with her? What if she was a huge disappointment?

Nothing separated them, not even a sheet, and she sucked in a breath at the feel of his hot, male skin against her. He burned for her, too. She must be doing something right.

"I promised you naked together," he murmured.

He moved over her, covering her body with his, favoring his uninjured shoulder as he supported his weight on his elbows. He gazed down at her. She blushed as she felt him move between her legs, sliding against her damp curls like smooth, hot silk. He held her gaze as he pushed against her, rocking slowly, insidiously, the faintest pressure where his fingers had been before.

"Nicolas," she whispered.

He stilled. "Look at me." He was breathing heavily, his chest rising and falling. A pulse beat in his jaw. "Please tell me this is what you want. Because I really want to be inside you." His voice was a hoarse croak. He rested his forehead against hers with a despairing laugh. "Oh God. I want you so much. But I don't want to hurt you."

All her fears evaporated. She placed her palm against his cheek. "I'm sure."

It was as if her words finally broke down some invisible dam of resistance. He dropped his head to her shoulder with a relieved sigh. "Thank God."

He moved his hips, and she felt a strange, stretching sensation between her legs. She tensed in anticipation of pain, but he bent his head, caught her nipple in his mouth, and sucked, hard. Marianne wrapped her arms around him and arched upward just as he gave one smooth thrust and sheathed himself inside her. Her eyes opened wide at the sensation. *So this is what it feels like.* An exquisite, hot, wet burn. A feeling of fullness and completion.

Nic groaned, a deep sound of satisfaction, and kissed her, his tongue invading even as he held the rest of his body still inside hers. And then he drew back, slowly, and pushed again and Marianne gave a gasp of surprise as the initial discomfort was replaced by that same tension she'd felt before. She moved her body tentatively in awkward counterpoint, trying to recapture the elusive rhythm, and suddenly, they were moving together, settling into perfect synchronicity.

She held back a bubble of laughter, of delight. This was so easy, so right. Just like riding a horse. He pushed deep again, and she experienced a sharp rush of pleasure. Each thrust brought a new height of exquisite heat.

The skin of his back was taut and sleek under her hands. Sweat-slicked for her. He was panting now, shaking with the effort of controlling himself. And suddenly, that wasn't what she wanted. She wanted the full fire of his passion, with nothing held back. He was so strong. He could easily overpower her. But she was safe with him.

"More," she panted, raking her hands over his back. She grabbed his hair and pulled his head up from her breast. "All of you," she managed, between breaths. "I want all of you."

He shook his head, but she kissed him, hard, and he groaned into her mouth. "Yes," she demanded fiercely.

A look of exquisite pleasure crossed his face. "Yes," he breathed in assent.

And then, finally, he let himself go. He wasn't gentle. He was blessedly, thrillingly rough, and she reveled in it, gloried in the fierce possession of his touch, lost in a tumble of heat and limbs and passion. She let go of her body, willingly relinquishing control. And in doing so she was the one who received the gift.

He arched his back and drove into her, an aggressive thrust that should have frightened her but instead made her feel invincible. His hands framed her hips and pinned her down as he surged upward, gasping. He swore, incomprehensible pleas and promises, his breath hissing at her ear as he drove into her again and again. "Come for me now, angel, please. God, I can't wait. Come now."

She burned up in that moment, clenching and releasing around his shaft. The world spiraled away, and it was like being on the trapeze, flying and falling all at once, splintering apart and reforming, while all around the fireworks were exploding like some glorious circus finale.

She almost forgot to breathe.

Nic gave one last thrust, then his whole body went rigid, racked with rhythmic shudders as he spilled himself into her. He collapsed on her with a wordless groan of completion.

Marianne wrapped her arms around him, drained and exhausted, and savored the weight of him pressing her down. It was something she never thought she could enjoy: this utter weakness, this total, unguarded lethargy. Her heart was racing, and she couldn't stop the tears that slid from the corner of her eyes, wet on her temples and in her hair.

He noticed, of course. He wiped them away, his expression tender, amused.

"Tears, little one? Was it so bad?"

She sniffed, embarrassed. "I never cry. I'm just tired. And overwrought. It's been an extremely trying week. And that was"—she struggled for some adequate word to describe what they'd just shared, and settled on—"extraordinary."

He gave a very self-satisfied chuckle. "I'll take that as a compliment."

"Is it always like that?"

He stroked her hair and turned them both to one side, cradling her in the shelter of his arms. "No," he said quietly. "It's not."

* * *

MARIANNE WOKE TO DARKNESS, with Nic's body still wrapped around hers. She was facing him, his arm slung heavily over her waist.

She couldn't believe she'd finally done it. And it had been everything the girls at the Montausier had described and more. Her chest tightened as she blinked back tears. She had to say good-bye. Her brain acknowledged it, even as her heart ached with a poignant sense of loss. There were no happily-ever-afters for people like them. She and Nic were from different worlds. Their paths had always been destined to part. It had been foolish to yearn for more, even for a moment.

But she would have this one perfect night, to remember forever.

She loved him. It was neither pure nor simple, but it was definitely love.

She couldn't say it, not aloud. To say it would harden it into something concrete and frightening and requiring a response. She was too much of a coward. Instead, she pressed her lips to his chest and breathed them against his heart, a secret of the flesh.

His eyes opened, and she froze. *Oh God, had he heard?* Her heart pounded as he stared at her, and then his features softened and she blushed at the knowing look that kindled in his eyes. A faint, satisfied smile played at the corner of his mouth as he leaned down to brush a kiss against her lips.

"Hello," he said huskily.

She felt his body stir against her and raised one eyebrow, opening her eyes wide. *"Again?"*

"Again."

"I thought I *hated* that word coming from your lips, Valette," she sighed.

CHAPTER 48

*M*arianne sat up and drank in the sight of him: gloriously naked, unashamed, spread out on the bed. It amazed her that she could make his body react like this. That he wanted her.

Nic's mouth curved in a wicked smile. "I think we should pretend we're back in that prison cell. Only this time, I'm *your* prisoner."

Marianne felt a flutter of something wicked and forbidden spring to life deep in her stomach.

"I'm your prisoner," he repeated slowly. "So you're in control. I'll do whatever you want me to do." He paused, let that sink in. "And you can do whatever you want to me."

She let her gaze move over him, taking her time, remembering every whispered trick the ladies of the theater had taught her.

Let him anticipate the pleasure to come. Don't rush. Tease him.

Her body throbbed with a sudden, urgent hunger. Her hands were shaking.

"You don't have to . . ." he murmured, starting to sit up.

She shook her head. "Let me."

He dropped back to the pillows and folded his hands behind his head, seeming to understand how important it was for her to set the pace. A jolt of joy pierced her. She *wanted* to do this for him, to give him pleasure. It was a privilege, not a punishment, so different from what Duval had made her do. Duval had left her feeling defenseless. Nic made her feel invincible.

She trailed her fingers down his chest, over his hard stomach.

He watched her with those sleepy tiger eyes. Hungry. Burning. Her blood thrummed with anticipation, a delicious sizzle she felt right down to her toes. She brushed against him with the back of her hand.

He sucked in a breath.

She encircled the base of him with her fingers. He was hot and hard, an intriguing combination of baby-soft skin over tight, rigid muscle. She moved her hand experimentally and he arched off the bed.

"Christ!"

Encouraged by this gratifying response, she moved between his legs. He curled up and caught her shoulders with a murmur of protest, but she slanted a wicked look up at him from under her lashes. "Please. I want to."

She leaned down and put her tongue to the sensitive tip.

With a heartfelt groan he threaded his fingers through her hair. Marianne smiled as he began to move against her, guiding her gently.

He tasted salty and clean and utterly delectable. A wave of raw feminine power surged through her at the fact that such a strong, virile man could be mastered with nothing but her hands and her mouth. In that moment she ruled him utterly. The pleasure of it made her tremble. His chest was rising and falling rapidly, and a sheen of sweat had broken out on his skin.

"You don't know what you do to me," he growled.

*   *   *

NIC WAS GOING to die of pleasure.

Marianne's lips teased him with butterfly kisses and licks. And when she took him completely into her mouth, he jack-knifed up off the bed. The feel of her around him was so erotic, so incredible, he could barely contain himself.

He gazed down at her with something akin to awe. Her simple trust shattered him. She'd been abused and bullied, had more reason to fear him than anyone. But instead of the fear he'd expected, she welcomed him with selfless, uninhibited giving.

He knew how much her surrender cost her, how foreign it was to her nature to offer her body and her emotions to another so freely. She'd been taught to hate this intimate act, and her desire to give *him* pleasure was profoundly touching. He felt both proud and oddly humbled by her gift. He wasn't worthy of it. But he'd take it all the same, black-hearted scoundrel that he was.

With a groan he pulled her back up.

* * *

MARIANNE STRADDLED NIC'S LAP, on her knees. He ran his hands up the front of her thighs then slid them back down, raising the hairs as he went.

His touch set her nerve endings alight. Her stomach clenched, and the secret place between her legs throbbed. She brought her hands up to rest on his shoulders then swept them down over the sculpted planes of his arms, then over his flat male nipples, enjoying the way he sucked in his breath again. With a devilish impulse, she leaned forward and flicked his chest with her tongue, as he'd done to her.

"Vixen," he breathed. He fisted his hands in her hair, pulled her up, and slanted his mouth fiercely over hers. She answered the thrust of his tongue with her own. Passion exploded between them, hot and bright, an instant flame. This was no sweet exploration, no gentle seduction. It was fierce and demanding, rough and elemental, exactly as she wanted it.

His hand tightened possessively on her nape and she felt a wild thrill of desire snake through her. She raised herself up on her knees without breaking the kiss as he slid his hands to her buttocks. The head of him slipped against her core, teasing and tormenting with promise and anticipation.

"Think you can take me?" he whispered wickedly.

"Anytime, Valette." Marianne leaned forward and kissed him, sinking down, down, claiming him fully. She swallowed a moan.

He rested his forehead against hers. "You're going to kill me, you know that?"

"It's no worse than you deserve."

He started to say something else, but she cut off the words with her lips. She didn't want to talk. This was going to be the last time. The knowledge made her want to weep. She put everything into the kiss: all her yearning, all her sorrow, all her regrets. She buried her hands in his hair and pulled him close, as if she could keep him with her forever, could pull him even deeper into herself than even this physical coupling.

He growled when she bit his shoulder with her teeth. In a quicksilver move he pulled out of her and flipped her over onto her stomach. His teeth grazed the nape of her neck, and she cried out as a primitive thrill of arousal ran through her.

"I knew it would be like this," he panted. "So good."

Marianne arched her back, urging him on. He slid into her again, and she gasped at his intrusion, poised on the edge of both pleasure and pain. But there was no fear, only the joy of discovery. Everything felt so right, as if they were two halves fitting back together.

He rained fevered kisses over her shoulders. His fingers found her mouth, and she sucked them in, taking him that way, too. Need spiraled out of control. She was sweating, shaking, her whole body convulsing as she slipped away, down into the hot, wicked darkness. He climaxed as she did, spilling inside her with a guttural cry that seemed to vibrate throughout her entire body. She threw her head back, gasping for air, then collapsed under him, boneless and panting.

Nic nestled them together like spoons as her heart tried to resume its normal rhythm. Maybe it never would. She had the awful feeling it would never be the same again.

He yawned into her hair. "You've worn me out, woman. Sleep now."

Within moments he was asleep, his arm once again thrown possessively over her waist.

Marianne waited for as long as she dared, until she was certain that he slept. Careful not to wake him, she turned over in his embrace. He looked more boyish, asleep. More innocent, somehow. She stroked the hair back from his forehead. Her stupid hands were shaking.

She'd told him her philosophy on love, on falling. And she'd been right. It hurt. Just like every other fall she'd ever experienced. Only this fall hadn't broken her leg or her head. *This* fall had broken her heart.

She had to leave him. Sophie needed her more. Nic might want her on a physical level, but he'd survive without her. He didn't really need anyone.

He didn't love her. Perhaps he held her in affection. He seemed to have a certain reluctant admiration for the way she fought him and argued with him and defied him. But love? No. Not the way she loved him. Not this all-encompassing yearning.

Her heart breaking, she wriggled out of his embrace.

His diamond stickpin glittered invitingly on the table next to the bed, just begging to be taken. For once in her life Marianne wished she could ignore the temptation, but she slipped it into her palm. It felt so wrong, another betrayal, but her need was greater than his. It had to be this way. She was a thief.

She glanced back at his sleeping form. His hair was mussed,

his cheek already showing the faintest hint of beard. She wanted to slide back into his arms. Wanted to let him hold her and protect her from the world. Impossible. He had to save the world from the butcher Napoleon. She had to go back to Paris and face Duval.

Unable to help herself, she leaned forward and pressed her lips to his. Even in his sleep his lips clung to hers, and it took all the strength she possessed to draw back.

Tears stung her eyes. This was *adieu,* not *au revoir.* The English didn't make the distinction—the one word "good-bye" sufficed for both a temporary parting and a permanent one. There should be a differentiation. The possibility of seeing him tomorrow was a far cry from the stomach-wrenching misery of knowing they'd never meet again.

CHAPTER 49

It was easy enough to slip away; Marianne was adept at becoming invisible. Compared to some of her other jobs, it was ludicrously easy—no scaling walls or balancing on ropes. Avoiding a sleeping hound in the kitchens and an equally dozy night porter in the front hall was no challenge at all.

The shirt and breeches she'd worn at Vincennes had mysteriously disappeared, presumably disposed of by Nic's horrified mother, so she had to make do with the plainest dress Heloise had left for her to choose from—a simple cotton day dress in a deep indigo blue. It wasn't rough or abrasive, as the coarse woolen breeches had been, but her body seemed strangely sensitive. Every movement of the cloth against her skin made her recall what she'd been doing. Muscles she hadn't known she had now ached.

She didn't want to think of the astonishing things Nic had done to her. His claiming had been so absolute she had the depressing conviction that he'd managed what Duval had tried and failed to do: to spoil her for anyone else, ever.

She retraced the path across the valley and down the cliff and breathed a sigh of relief when she saw the black ship still moored in the bay, bobbing and creaking on the tide.

The Raven seemed neither surprised nor pleased to see her when she walked up the gangplank. "What do you want?"

"Safe passage back to France."

His handsome face remained impassive. "And what makes you think I won't just haul that pretty arse of yours back to my friend Nic?"

She'd spent enough time in the Parisian underworld to answer that. He might be Nic's friend, but he was also a business-man. She held out the diamond pin.

The Raven's eyes narrowed. "Valette give you that, did he?"

She met his gaze levelly. "Yes."

He swept her with a leisurely glance that was both intimate and insulting. "You must have been good."

Her body burned in mortification. Could he guess what she'd been doing? Did she look different, now she wasn't a virgin anymore? She raised her chin. "It was my fee for the job."

The Raven eyed her curiously. "You know, British goods have been blockaded for ten years. But the quality can't do without their brandy and their silk shawls anymore than the frogs can do without their English guineas, newspapers, and prisoners of war. It's a win-win situation for me. Letters. Secrets. Hostages. Spies. Days where we smuggled aristos out from under the guillotine. Less of that now, of course," he shrugged eloquently. "Anyway, a man's got to make a living as best he can." He plucked the diamond from her hand and pocketed it. "We're for Gravelines, just north of Calais. You'll have to make your own way back to Paris."

Marianne let out a relieved breath. "Thank you."

She couldn't face the thought of going back down into the cabin again. Too many memories. Instead, she spent the crossing huddled beneath a damp woolen blanket that smelled of fish, staring out into the darkness.

She should have been feeling happier. She was going home, to Paris, to Sophie. But her stomach felt like lead, as if some vital part of her had been ripped out and left behind. She shivered and wrapped her arms around herself, suddenly cold.

The Raven came and stood next to her at the rail. He indicated a thin strand of lights, like a twinkling string of pearls, bobbing on the horizon. "Gravelines. The smuggler's city."

Marianne studied him in the moonlight. He really was astonishingly handsome. It was easy to see why Heloise had been so fascinated by him. The wind whipped strands of long black hair across his cheekbones. He had the same wicked smile, that same reckless, uncompromising beauty as Nic. And yet he left her supremely unmoved. She could appreciate his features without feeling like she'd been kicked in the gut.

Why couldn't she have fallen in love with *him*?

She glanced away and noticed a man leaning precariously over the rail. He appeared to be affixing a wooden plank to the side of the ship. "What's he doing?"

The Raven followed the direction of her gaze. "Replacing the nameplate." He scratched the faint dark stubble on his chin. "'Funny thing, it is. *Hero* left Kent, but *Hope* will arrive in Gravelines." His smile was wicked. "It plays havoc with the customs boys. Hard to keep track of dark ships with dark sails on dark nights. Especially when the names don't tally."

He reached into his jacket and withdrew a folded piece of paper. "Here. Take it," he said gruffly.

Marianne stared down at the bank draft without understanding. A cold slick of foreboding prickled along her spine as she read the obscene amount. "You're giving me ten thousand francs?"

"No. *Nic's* giving you ten thousand francs," he said softly.

She gripped the rail, knuckles turning white. "He told you to give me this?"

The Raven's silence was all the confirmation she needed.

Oh God! She'd been such an idiot. "He asked you to take me back. *Didn't* he?" Her temples were pounding. She turned away in disgust. "No wonder you agreed so readily."

"You think I'd take you away without his permission?"

Of course not. Merde, she'd been so stupid. Valette had always known what she was thinking. He'd been one step ahead of her the entire time. He'd known she'd run for Paris at the first opportunity. He'd known she was lying when she promised to wait for him before dealing with Duval.

And he'd done nothing to stop her.

Nothing except make love to her. Nothing except bind her heart and make it even harder for her to leave.

She rounded on the Raven, even though he wasn't the cause of her simmering anger. "I'm not his property! He has no say over what I do or where I go!"

The smuggler merely shrugged. "If you don't want it, I'll just give it back . . ." He took the bank draft from her nerveless fingers.

Her stomach heaved. Valette had orchestrated it all, as usual. And she'd gone right along with his plans. He must have given this money to Raven before she went to his rooms last night. Must have known it would be the last, the *only* night they'd ever spend together. *Bastard.*

Marianne snatched the paper back, sorely tempted to hurl it over the side, but practicality won out over fury. Instead, she folded it neatly and stuffed it into her bodice, then stared out at the tops of the waves.

Hope was a stupid name for a ship. She should be named *Betrayal.* Or better yet, *Revenge.*

Her heart was cold, shriveled in her chest like a stone, as bleak and gray as the waves beneath them. The English called this thin stretch of disputed water the English Channel. The French called it La Manche. Yet another thing with two names. Like her, like

Valette. Why was nothing simple anymore? Was everyone hiding something?

She couldn't wait to be back in Paris with Sophie.

CHAPTER 50

*N*ic stared at his brother blankly.

"Gone? Are you sure?"

"On her way to France as we speak, I expect." Richard's smile faded as he noted Nic's expression. He set down his knife and fork, with which he'd been attacking a hearty breakfast.

"Bloody hell!" Nic slapped his hand on the table.

Richard raised his brows. "What's the matter? I thought you *expected* her to go. Last night you told Raven to take her back if she asked."

Nic scowled. Of course he had. He'd known she'd try to leave, as surely as he'd known that he couldn't go with her. When he'd met with Raven after dinner, he'd done the only two things he could think of to make her life easier. He'd written her a bank draft for ten thousand francs and ordered Raven to kill Duval.

But that had been before he'd made love to her.

When he'd woken up alone this morning, he'd assumed that she'd had been overcome by shyness. Or that she was afraid of being discovered in his bedroom by his family. Now, it seemed, she was already halfway across the Channel.

He shook his head in self-disgust. What had he expected?

That their lovemaking would miraculously affect her decision to stay? That she'd wait for him meekly while he went off to challenge Napoleon? He had nothing to offer her except the likelihood of a broken heart. It was for the best. Still, it chafed that she'd left without even saying good-bye. Left him while he was weak and defenseless. Left after giving him the best sex he'd ever had in his life.

The dull ache in his chest felt a lot like disappointment.

He glowered down at his coffee. She'd think the worst of the money, of course, after what they'd done last night. The timing couldn't have been worse. He had no doubt she'd see it as a payoff, relegate herself to nothing better than a whore accepting coin for services rendered. He didn't care what she thought of it, so long as she took it. She'd earned every sous. Come to think of it, ten thousand francs seemed a paltry amount for saving his undeserving life.

Dickie stalked over to the side table and poured two healthy shots of brandy into the waiting glasses. "Bit early for spirits, but this'll do you the world of good. Doctor's orders. Now, why don't you explain to me what's going on? What is she to you, Nic?" His brother regarded him closely. "I assumed she was one of your Parisian street urchins. Or some tart you'd paid as part of your escape."

Nic raked his fingers through his hair. "My what? Hell, no. She's . . . she's my . . . God, I don't know *what* she is." He realized he was acting like a madman and forced himself to sit down at the table. "Jesus, Dickie, she's not a tart."

"Didn't really think she was," Richard said placidly, taking another mouthful of bacon and eggs. "Not after talking to her last night. Anyone could tell she's gently born."

Nic snorted. "She's got more blue blood in her veins than all of us put together, except maybe Louis-Charles. She's Marianne de Beauvais, daughter of the dead Count and Countess of Chanterac. She's also the best thief in Paris."

Richard had just taken a sip of brandy. He inhaled sharply and was seized by a paroxysm of coughing. Nic whacked him helpfully on the back. Hard. When he stopped spluttering, Dickie rubbed his hand over his chest and Nic gazed absently into his glass.

"They tortured her, you know. At Vincennes. And she didn't say a thing. Even though telling on me would have spared her a great deal of pain."

"Christ. I had no idea." Richard looked appalled. "She never said anything. Just told us she helped you leave Paris and come here."

A reluctant half smile curled Nic's mouth as he gazed at the amber liquid. "She wouldn't. She's too stubborn. Too proud."

The brandy felt good burning a path down his throat, setting his nerve endings on fire, streaking through his blood. It was like her. Dangerous. Intoxicating.

Richard regarded him solemnly. "God, Nic. A blind man could see she's in love with you."

Nic sighed. "I know. But I *made* her love me. I used every trick I knew to gain her cooperation. She was such an innocent. She didn't stand a chance."

"And you love her!" Dickie said with quiet amazement.

Nic scowled. "Of course I bloody love her. How could I not? I swear, Richard, if you'd seen her in that prison, you'd love her, too. Anyone else would have rolled up into a ball and cried. She saved my life. More than once. Shit, she's braver than fifty men I know."

"And extremely beautiful," Dickie felt compelled to add, raising his glass in a jaunty toast.

"And beautiful," Nic agreed quietly.

"So what will you do now?"

"Honestly? I don't know."

Richard sat back. "I never thought I'd ever say this, Nic. But maybe you should let it go. Tony's dead. Killing Napoleon won't bring him back. And that girl's alive. Hell, she's more alive than anyone I've ever met. She practically glows, dammit."

"I know." Nic knocked back the last of his brandy and poured himself another.

"So what do you want?"

What *did* he want? He was thirty-five years old. Old enough to stop playing war games. But he was fifteen years and a lifetime of bitter experience older than Marianne.

He'd deliberately avoided emotional entanglements since Tony's death. The idea of staying in one place and starting a family scared the hell out of him, but it also filled him with a profound sense of yearning. He wanted to plant vines and tend them through the changing seasons. He wanted to make wine, sit on the warm flagstone terrace of a château, and watch his children play. Children who looked like her.

He'd been running. Not just from Tony's death, but from his own family, from life, from settling down, consumed by a guilty need to be doing something concrete to atone for his own survival when the brother he'd loved had been lost.

Marianne had seen him so clearly. She went straight to the heart of the matter, like one of her knives. She looked into his eyes and didn't flinch at the darkness she found.

"It's not all that complicated, Nic," Richard said gently. "It's about choosing a living, breathing woman who loves you over a dead brother who'd want to see you at peace."

What Richard was suggesting sounded so simple. Going after Napoleon meant losing Marianne. And quite without his realizing it she'd become a necessary part of his soul, like breathing.

"Fuck," Nic said succinctly.

"Will you go after her?"

"No."

"Why not? Don't you care?" Dickie asked, bewildered.

Nic closed his eyes in quiet desperation. "I care too much to ruin her life by tying her to someone like me. I've nothing to offer her. She has her own life back in Paris."

It wasn't bloody fair. The two halves of his life were utterly irreconcilable. He'd sworn himself to Tony before he'd ever met Marianne; duty and honor bound him to keep his promise to see Napoleon dead. He wouldn't feel complete unless he followed through on his vow. And yet Marianne needed him, too. Christ, he wanted to slay dragons for her. He wanted to storm castle walls.

He'd got Duval off her back, at least. Before he'd even left Paris he'd ordered Laurent to deliver proof of Duval's corruption to Fouché. The bastard would be ruined by now. But simply ruining him wasn't enough. Duval deserved to die for the things he'd done to Marianne. Nic only wished he could do the honors himself, but for once he'd have to trust others to do it for him. He'd ordered Raven to make it as slow and painful as he could.

He was going to Belgium. And maybe, once the emperor was as dead as Duval, when his revenge was finally complete, he'd find the peace he'd been craving for six long years.

CHAPTER 51

*I*t seemed to take no time at all to return to Paris by coach instead of by horse. When Marianne slipped ashore at Gravelines, she'd thought Raven would insist on accompanying her, but the smuggler had simply wrapped a cloak around her shoulders and hired her a carriage.

She discovered Valette's diamond stickpin hidden in the pocket of the cloak an hour into the journey and stared down at it with alternating annoyance and gratitude. She must seem truly pathetic if even the *smuggler* took pity on her.

She arrived at the Cirque Olympique just after the final evening performance. Laurent was ushering the last stragglers out of the door. He greeted her with his usual ebullient hug.

"*Dio!* Little one! It's good to see you. We were getting worried. The mission was a success?"

She grimaced. "It didn't quite go according to plan, but I'm here now, and that's all that matters."

He peered over her shoulder with a frown. "Where's Valette?"

"In England, I expect." She tried to keep all inflection out of her voice. "Or on his way to face Napoleon. We parted ways once the mission was done."

Laurent shot her an odd, surprised look, as if he sensed there was far more to the story than she was telling him, but he let the subject drop. "Well, I have some good news. Duval's disappeared. No one's seen him for at least a week."

Marianne eyed his smiling face with suspicion. This was Valette's doing, she was sure. Although how he could have accomplished such a thing when he hadn't been anywhere near Paris was a mystery. "I don't suppose *you* had anything to do with that, did you, Laurent?"

He shrugged innocently. "Me? Why would you say that? All *I* did was deliver a package of documents to Fouché. Seems Duval's been implicated in the murder of a prostitute, as well as in skimming profits from most of the brothels he was overseeing. The emperor's not happy, from what I hear. Duval's been stripped of his offices, and a warrant's been issued for his arrest."

But Marianne no longer wanted to hear about Duval. "Where's Sophie?"

Laurent nodded in understanding. "Avenue Junot, in Montmartre. Number 23. Used to be the Hotel de Berty. Do you want me to come with you?"

"No, you close up here. Just let me get some things from the dressing room."

Laurent ambled away as Marianne hastened to the rooms behind the stage. Pagnol the monkey chattered his usual greeting as she crossed to his cage. She fed him a nut then slipped open the catch and unhooked the little bell suspended from the roof of the cage. Valette's diamond fitted nicely inside, secured to the brass clapper with a twist of wire. She ruffled the little monkey's fur. "Take care of that for me," she admonished him sternly. "I'll be back for it soon."

She found her spare set of throwing knives in a trunk. Just having them back in her hands made her feel better, more in control. For a brief moment she wondered what had become of her other knives, the ones she'd used at the château, and then she shook it off. It didn't matter. They were gone. She'd never see them again.

She swapped the silk slippers Heloise had given her for her lace-up ankle boots and slipped one of her daggers inside.

She could have walked to Montmartre, but she hired another carriage for speed, desperate to make sure her sister was well. Despite Laurent's assurances, she wouldn't rest until she saw Sophie with her own eyes.

Valette's young agent, Andrew, answered her knock on the door, and Marianne recalled the last time she'd seen him, his handsome face disappearing from view as she'd driven off into the night with Valette. It seemed a lifetime ago.

He greeted her politely and showed her into an elegant parlor, where her sister was reading a book by the fire. Marianne's heart contracted with relief.

"Sophie! Thank God you're all right."

Her sister looked up in surprised delight. The book fell unheeded to the floor as she rushed forward to embrace her. "Oh, Marianne! Where have you been? What have you been doing?" She pulled back, and her eyes roved over Marianne's face, scrutinizing every detail. She let out a shriek of dismay. "What on *earth* happened to your hair?!"

Marianne put her hand up to her shorn locks. She'd forgotten it was short. "I had to cut it. For the job. I had to pretend to be a boy."

Sophie's eyes were as round as saucers. She looked like she was about to cry. "But your hair was so lovely," she wailed.

"It'll grow." Marianne's smile froze on her lips as she realized that had been Valette's original response. She swallowed the sudden lump in her throat. "I'm used to it now."

"I'll leave you two ladies alone for a moment, shall I?" Andrew interrupted with a smile. "I'm sure you have a lot of catching up to do."

Sophie turned and bestowed him with a radiant smile. "Thank you."

He nodded and bowed his way out of the door. Marianne heard his footsteps retreating along the corridor. She hugged Sophie again. "I'm so sorry I left Paris without you. You know I had no choice."

Sophie smiled. "It's all right. Andrew's taken very good care of me."

Marianne didn't miss the pink tinge that flushed her sister's cheeks. "Andrew?" she teased, picking up on her sister's familiar use of the man's name.

Sophie blushed even more and drew her down on the sofa. "Monsieur Ducrow," she amended. She glanced up, her eyes wide, her expression somber. "I've been so scared and worried. About you. About Duval. It must have driven Andrew mad, but he's been so patient and understanding." She glanced down shyly. "He's the finest man I've ever met."

Marianne's stomach tightened as she saw the expression in her sister's eyes. She'd never looked like that for any of her other innumerable suitors. A jolt of shock slammed though her. Her quiet, studious sister was in love! Marianne's broken laugh was terribly close to a sob.

"But enough about *me*," Sophie said. "Tell me all about you. What happened with Monsieur Valette? Is he as bad as they say? Where on earth have you been?"

"My, my, what a charming family reunion. Welcome back, sweet cousin."

Marianne's blood turned to ice. She turned slowly to see Duval framed in the doorway, a pistol leveled at her head.

"Thank you for leading me here," he smirked. "I've been hoping you'd show up at the circus for some time."

He was barely recognizable. His face was drawn, pale and saggy like a deflated balloon, and his clothes were stained and rumpled. "Stand up," he said with a wave of the gun. "Now take off your cloak, put your arms out, and turn around. Slowly."

Marianne complied, her eyes never leaving the pistol. *Where the hell was Andrew?*

"I'm not armed," she lied coolly. "What do you want, Duval? You need to leave, now. From what I hear, you're a wanted man."

His expression darkened at the reminder, his face flushing pink. "Valette's ruined me. I know it was him. Even that bloody banknote he gave to me in payment for *you* was a useless forgery, the bastard."

Marianne shrugged. "So? It's your own fault. What's it got to do with me?"

Perhaps if she could keep him talking, Andrew could overpower him.

"You're the only thing that can hurt him." Duval narrowed his eyes at her surprise. "Oh yes. I've spent enough time in brothels to know when a man watches a woman and mentally undresses her. He couldn't resist you, could he?"

"I don't know what you're talking about."

Duval's face grew mottled. "Of course you do, you little whore. I know what you've been doing with him. I can practically smell it on you. He's had you every way he can think of, hasn't he?" His eyes flicked over her contemptuously.

"Yes," she said, very deliberately. "He has. And it was astonishing."

She heard Sophie gasp but kept her eyes glued on Duval. Unfortunately, he didn't rise to her baiting. *Something must have happened to Andrew. Had Duval's men killed him already? Merde.*

Marianne's heart thumped in her chest as she realized she and Sophie were on their own. Time for a different tack. "I have money," she said calmly. "Ten thousand francs from Valette. You can have it all, if you promise to leave Paris and never come near us again. Do we have a deal?"

Duval's eyes narrowed as he searched for a catch. Reluctantly, he nodded. "Fine. Yes. Give it to me."

K. C. BATEMAN

"It's not here." The banknote was pressed snugly against her skin, and Marianne suppressed a bizarre surge of inappropriate amusement. She was getting as adept at lying as Valette. Almost. "I left it at the circus."

He waved the gun. "Let's go then. My carriage is outside. And don't try anything stupid. One word from me, and Remi will snap your neck."

Marianne had no choice. With a sigh, she took a shaking Sophie's hand and allowed Duval to usher them into the nondescript hack that was waiting outside. The hunched form of Remi crouched in the driver's seat, huddled beneath a cloak, his ugly face hidden by a large hat.

The carriage smelled of mildew and wet dog. Marianne thrust Sophie into the corner and squashed her body up against her, protecting her as best she could. The coach groaned and rocked as Duval hauled his ungainly bulk in after them.

She had the knife in her boot, but Duval still had the gun, and she didn't fancy her chances in such close quarters. She'd wait until they reached the circus, where there was less chance of Sophie's being hurt.

CHAPTER 52

The distant peals of midnight floated across from Notre Dame as Marianne slipped through the side door of the circus followed by Sophie and Duval. The backstage area was dark but Pagnol gave an excited whimper from his cage as he sensed their presence.

"This way," Marianne said curtly.

"Light a candle," Duval ordered. "It's as dark as the grave."

Marianne crossed to a dressing table and lit a trio of candles. Duval gestured at Sophie with the gun. "Sit down." Sophie sank obediently onto a dressing stool, her blue eyes wide and frightened.

"Now where's the money?" Duval demanded.

A flicker of movement in the doorway caught Marianne's attention, and her heart leapt as Andrew stepped into the room, his own pistol leveled at Duval.

"Put your gun down, Duval," he warned softly.

Duval reacted with surprising speed. He grabbed Sophie and pulled her in front of him, using her body as a shield. She let out a terrified whimper as the muzzle of his pistol pressed against her temple. "I don't think so," he rasped. "You wouldn't want me to hurt her, would you?"

Andrew looked torn. His face registered fury, but he seemed to realize he had no choice. He uncocked his weapon and lowered it to the side.

"That's better," Duval crowed. He took his gun from Sophie's head and shot Andrew in the stomach.

Sophie screamed and jerked away from Duval's hold. She threw herself onto the floor next to Andrew, who was writhing in pain. "No!" she sobbed hysterically, trying to stem the blood pumping out of the wound. "You bastard!" she shrieked at Duval.

Duval watched the scene impassively then turned to Marianne. "I want you to get me that money now, Marianne." He pulled a second pistol from his coat and leveled it at Sophie. "Quickly now, or she's next."

Marianne's heart was racing. "It's in the monkey's cage." She crossed to the cage, opened the catch, and tilted the brass bell so Duval could see the diamond fastened inside.

His face darkened in rage. "That's no good! If it came from Valette, it's probably paste. You said he gave you money."

He hit her, hard across the face. The butt of the pistol caught her cheek, and she let out an involuntary cry as she stumbled away from him. Stars winked in front of her eyes as he grabbed her hair and yanked her back against him. His foul breath hissed in her ear, and Marianne tried to block out all the hideous recollections the sensation dredged up. She concentrated on how she'd felt with Nic instead. Pretended it was *his* body, *his* breath. A measure of calm returned to her limbs.

"You killed my parents, didn't you?" she gritted out between her teeth.

Duval stilled. And then he smiled. "I didn't mean to. I simply wanted to destroy your father's study and the papers it contained. But the fire spread so much more quickly than I ever imagined. How was I to know your parents wouldn't escape?"

Something shifted inside her at hearing him actually admit it. It was one thing to have been told he was responsible, quite another hearing him confirm it.

"So yes, I killed your parents," he continued smoothly. "Just as I'm going to kill you."

The cold steel of the pistol kissed her temple. The hammer drew back with a click.

Do whatever you can to gain the advantage. Valette's voice echoed in her brain. *Hit me in the balls. Gouge my eyes. Dislocate my thumbs.*

Marianne moved without thought, arching backward. The back of her head smashed into Duval's nose with a sickening crunch. The pistol discharged by her ear, deafening her, and he threw it aside, howling in fury. His hands flew to his nose as blood sprayed out from between his fingers.

"Little whore! You'll pay for that!"

Marianne sidestepped, but a trunk of clothes stopped her retreat.

Duval spat, dripping blood as he advanced. "I was going to make it quick, but not after that little trick."

Marianne threw herself to the side, shielding her face, but he backhanded her and she tumbled backward over the trunk. Before she could scramble to her feet, she felt his hamlike fists close around her throat and squeeze. His face was only inches from hers, red with fury, bloody spittle dripping from his mouth. Marianne punched at him, but he pushed her down beneath him, crushing her with his weight. She clawed at his wrists, scratched with her nails. His fetid breath washed over her, and it was the night he tried to rape her, all over again. Lights were swirling in front of her eyes. Her blows fell weaker, her fingers tingled. All the strength was draining out of her.

"No!"

The scream came from Sophie. Marianne saw a blur of movement just as her meek little sister brought a brass candlestick down on the back of Duval's head. He fell to the side, and Marianne gasped as the constriction on her throat eased.

Duval shook his head with a roar and staggered to his feet. Ignoring Marianne on the ground, he lunged at Sophie and caught her across the cheek with a blow that threw her sprawling against a dressing table and sent the contents flying. He advanced on her like an enraged bull.

Marianne rolled to her side, blinking rapidly, fighting nausea. She pulled the knife from her boot and staggered to her feet. Duval was kicking Sophie now, panting obscenities between blows. "Hit me, will you? Little bitch!"

"Stop!"

Duval turned, his eyes wild, and Marianne didn't hesitate. She threw the knife straight at his heart. He jerked and gasped, a surprised expression on his face as he looked down at the blade protruding from his chest. Marianne watched in horror as he staggered toward her. She braced herself to fight him again, but he dropped to his knees in a sick parody of a suitor proposing, or a vassal kneeling obeisance. And then he slumped to the ground and lay still.

For a few seconds she just gazed at him in frozen amazement, expecting him to get up, to start crawling forward like some obese caterpillar. Then realization came. He was dead. A thin line of blood trickled from his nose onto the rug.

She was going to be sick. Marianne bent over and braced her hands on her knees, her head pounding, her stomach churning.

Oh God.

Sophie struggled to her feet and gazed down at Duval's prone figure in disgust. Her right eye was already bruised and swelling. "He shot Andrew," she said simply. "He was a wicked man." She stepped over the body, dismissing it, and rushed back to Andrew's side. "Andrew, please God, wake up!"

Andrew let out a weak groan. A dark red puddle had formed

beneath him on the floor. Marianne started toward him, but a flash of orange behind her caught her eye. She turned and stilled in horror.

One of the candles had fallen under a rail of clothing. Flames licked up the clothes, feeding hungrily on the netting, lace, and feathers of the gaudy costumes. For an endless moment Marianne simply stood and stared, strangely transfixed. Every one of her countless nightmares sprang to life. She was back at Chanterac, the same coppery smell of blood and smoke in the air. She started to shake, gazing immobile as death crackled and curled its way toward her.

"Marianne! Help me!"

Sophie's sharp cry jolted her back to the present. She looked around for water to douse the flames, but there was nothing to hand. She grabbed a cloak and tried to beat at the fire, but if anything, it seemed to fan it. She couldn't believe how quickly it was spreading; now it was clawing up the fabric-lined walls like a caged beast.

They had to get out.

She raced over to Andrew and helped sit him up, heedless of his wound. He groaned faintly in protest, but there was no time to be gentle. He might well be dying, but she wouldn't leave him to burn. She slung one of his arms over her shoulder, and Sophie followed suit. Together, they raised him up, grunting under the weight of his body.

The whole room was aflame now. Great rolling black clouds billowed up toward the ceiling, making it almost impossible to see. It was all so horribly familiar. Hot air singed her lungs with every breath. Heat seared her cheeks as they stumbled forward.

Andrew was too heavy. His legs dragged uselessly behind him, hampering their movements. Sophie tripped, and all three of them fell to the floor.

It was marginally cooler down here. Marianne rolled Andrew

onto his back and grabbed his collar. Sophie did the same, and between them they dragged him along. Bent double, they staggered out onto the stage.

A sudden shriek pierced the room behind them, and for a horrifying moment Marianne thought it was Duval, risen from the dead, but then she realized it was Pagnol, the monkey. The poor creature was leaping back and forth in his cage, screeching in terror.

"Stay here! I'll be right back." She shot Sophie a reassuring look and raced back into the searing room, throwing her arms up to shield her face from the heat.

The thin wire latch of the cage was already hot to the touch, and she burned her fingers as she fumbled with the hook. The door swung open, and the terrified monkey bolted, leaping up onto her head, its sharp nails leaving painful scratches in her scalp. He jumped down, and she watched his long curly tail disappear into the auditorium. No doubt he could find his own way out.

Almost as an afterthought she grabbed the little brass bell swinging above his perch and shoved it into her bodice. Ignoring Duval's prone body, she rushed back to Sophie, and together they pulled Andrew down the ramp for the horses and into the ring itself. He mumbled something incoherent, but his eyes remained closed.

"Hold on, Andrew!" Sophie croaked, her voice raw. "We're nearly there. Stay with me! Please."

Marianne's eyes were streaming. The deep red velvet curtains framing the proscenium arch were alight now, a frame of orange and white, more dramatic than any spectacle the Falconis had ever conceived. The heat was intense, smoke billowing, filling the auditorium, obscuring her tightropes suspended high above.

She glanced up, barely able to comprehend what she was seeing. Great swathes of silk hung from the ceiling like the inside of an enormous tent. The flames raced up them, devouring the fabric in seconds, sending burning sections fluttering onto the red velvet seats below. The pungent smell of burning horsehair only added to the nightmare.

A series of explosions came from the back room; the blaze must have reached the fireworks. The shrieks of rockets, Roman candles, and Catherine wheels were hideous, deafening. Marianne wanted to clap her hands over her ears and scream.

This is what war must sound like.

Andrew's body left a dark path in the sawdust as they dragged him toward the set of double doors at the far end of the ring. From outside Marianne could hear shouts of *"Fire!"* as people on the street saw the smoke.

The timbers above them creaked as if they were alive. A huge piece of scenery collapsed onto the stage, and the blast of heat knocked them backward, showering them in a hail of sparks.

The door was barred. It took endless seconds to struggle with the thick wooden slat rammed through the handles. Marianne's hands were slick with Andrew's blood. Splinters pierced her palms as she shoved at it, swearing and pleading. When it finally gave, she grabbed Sophie's arm and shoved her forward, out into the cold black night.

The ceiling gave a sudden, ominous crack. Marianne glanced up just as a huge rafter came down with a great hot *whoomf* of air. She threw herself over Andrew's body and instinctively shielded her head with her hands against the blinding sheet of flame.

Something struck her shoulder, and she cried out. More rubble fell from above and pinned her to the floor. Pain shot up her leg. She rolled to her side and grabbed hold of her knee, but it was like a dead weight. She kicked the rafter with her free foot and dragged her injured leg out from underneath. Her own choking gasps were all she could hear as she crawled forward on her elbows. And then she heard Sophie screaming her name.

A figure loomed through the smoke, and for a brief, hallucinating moment she thought it was Valette, but it was Laurent's voice that spoke. "Thank God. Come on."

Strong hands pulled her up. Marianne cried out in agony as she tried to put weight on her leg, and he swept her up and carried her through the smoke. They spewed out into the street, gasping and stumbling into the rain.

CHAPTER 53

*M*arianne turned her face up to the sky. The cool kiss of the rain was heaven, a blessing, washing away the pain. Laurent released her and plunged back through the doorway, reappearing seconds later with Andrew slung over his shoulder.

Dark shapes rushed forward to help. Marianne let them guide her farther away from the building, across the cobbled street to safety. She sat, legs shaking, on the high stone curb at the edge of the pavement, her feet in the rivulets of water that streamed toward the gutter.

Her leg was agony. Her throat hurt. Her eyes were stinging and raw. *But she was alive, and Sophie was, too.*

Her brain seemed disjointed, fuzzy. She'd killed Duval. Andrew had been shot. Pagnol had escaped. The circus was burning down before her eyes. It was a fireball now, beyond all hope of rescue. Flames were shooting out of the roof, reaching up into the sky.

The clanging of bells and clattering of horse-drawn carriages heralded the arrival of one of the new city fire engines. The brigade that manned it joined the crowd of locals in throwing buckets of water, but it was a futile effort. The fire was a living thing, a monster unwilling to give up its prey.

Marianne felt a strange detachment from it all. Someone draped a coat over her hunched shoulders, and she huddled beneath it. Her teeth started chattering.

She caught sight of Sophie through a gap in the crowd. Andrew had been lifted onto the back of a cart. Someone—a physician of some sort, she assumed—was applying a bandage to his wound.

Sophie was next to him, her face blackened with soot and stained with tears. She should have looked ugly for once, with her eyes red and puffy from crying, but as Marianne watched, Andrew lifted his hand and gently stroked the side of her face.

Sophie burst into tears. And then she lowered her head and kissed him. Right there, in the middle of the street, with the fire behind them and the clamor of the crowd and the rain beating down on their heads. Oblivious to it all.

Marianne closed her eyes, feeling guilty for watching, as if she were intruding on their private moment. It was so obvious they were perfect for each other. She prayed Andrew would have the strength to live.

She dropped her head to her knees, suddenly empty, drained of everything. Laurent squatted down in front of her. His dark hair was gray with ash, his handsome face full of concern. He took her shoulders and enfolded her in a hug.

She buried her nose in his chest. "Oh God, the circus. I'm so sorry."

"It's nothing. So long as you're safe. Duval?"

Marianne shuddered. "Dead."

"Good," he said grimly. He carried her to the carriage with Sophie and Andrew.

Marianne could hardly keep her eyes open. It was as if her body was shutting down without her permission. Everything seemed very far away. "Where are we going?" she murmured.

"To Madame," Laurent slapped the side of the carriage. "You can't go back to your own apartment like this. The girls at the Montausier will take care of you."

Marianne nodded, too exhausted to argue.

A flash of brown caught her attention. It was Pagnol, on the balustrade by the river across the street. As she watched he did a little dance then stood up on his hind legs and gave a salute, like a miniature soldier, before he scampered off. *How bizarre. She must be hallucinating.*

The coach was spinning, faces blurring.

Marianne closed her eyes and embraced the beckoning blackness.

SHE AWOKE TO PAIN. Her left leg throbbed, her entire body ached. She felt as though a horse had fallen on her. A wave of competing perfumes assaulted her nose, and she opened her eyes to the lavish interior of one of the Montausier's best rooms. She squinted at the scantily clad nymphs and underdressed dryads cavorting in an improbable landscape on the ceiling. The mermaid room.

A crowd of women clustered around the bed.

"She's awake!" Skinny Marie patted her hand in delight.

"I'll go tell Madame." That was Odile.

Panic gripped her. "Sophie?" she croaked. Her throat was raw.

"She's fine. She's with Andrew, next door."

"My leg?"

"Not broken," Madame said, bustling into the room like one of the emperor's flagships in full sail. "Just bruised," she said briskly. "Nothing serious."

Marianne looked down at her hands. They were smothered in bandages, too. Then she remembered. She'd burned them when she'd saved Pagnol. "The bell! Where is it?"

"What, this?" Skinny Marie frowned, picking it up from a side table and tinkling it. "It's right here."

"Oh, good," Marianne mumbled, subsiding on the pillows.

"Drink this, it will help you sleep," Madame ordered.

She was too tired to argue. She simply drank the bitter concoction and wrinkled her nose at the taste. "Ugh. What *is* that?"

"Laudanum."

As she rested her head back on the pillows, Marianne realized why the room seemed so familiar. It was the one into which Nic had pulled her, that first night he'd bought her from Duval. An ache pierced her chest. This was where he'd first kissed her. Had it really been just over a week ago? The girl who'd left with him that night was an entirely different creature to the woman she was now.

Oh God, Valette. She closed her eyes in abject misery. *Where are you?*

* * *

WHEN SHE WOKE AGAIN, her head was much clearer. Sophie was sitting in a chair by the bed, calmly sewing sequins onto a corset. Marianne tried to push herself up, then yelped as pain shot through her palms.

"Here, let me." Sophie plumped the pillows behind her and helped her to sit up.

"How long have I slept?"

"Just over two days." Sophie's cheeks were pink, her eyes sparkling. She had a slight bruise over her eye where Duval had struck her, but she looked surprisingly well, considering their ordeal. Marianne could tell from her expression that she was just bursting with news. "Oh, Marianne, you've missed so much. Napoleon's been defeated!"

Marianne closed her eyes against a wave of dizziness. "What?"

"There's been a huge battle, just over the border in Belgium, near a little place called Waterloo. Everyone says the emperor's in retreat and the allied armies are advancing here. They'll be in Paris any moment."

Marianne couldn't frame a response.

"The world's going mad. No one knows what's happening. People are crowding the streets. Skinny Marie says we're going to be invaded by the Prussians. Odile predicts we'll all be slaughtered in our beds!" Sophie didn't seem too worried by either prospect.

"Oh God." With a sudden, horrible clarity Marianne knew that Valette would have been there, right in the thick of it. A huge aching black chasm opened up inside her. Was he dead? Injured? Surely she'd know if he was dead? Her heart would know.

Seeing her stricken expression, Sophie took her bandaged hand. "Are you all right?"

Her face was as fierce as Marianne had ever seen it. Her clear blue eyes turned hard, and her lips firmed into a tight line. "I hope you're not upset over killing Duval," she said sternly. "I'm sorry, Marianne, but I *refuse* to feel guilty about him, and neither should you. He was a horrible person, and he deserved to die. There was no excuse for the things he did to us. To you."

A wave of shame heated her cheeks. She'd always prayed Sophie had never truly understood what she'd done to protect her. Apparently, she had.

"I think everyone has a choice in how they live their life," Sophie continued quietly. "Duval *chose* to be like that. He was unhappy, and he tried to extend that unhappiness to everyone else around him."

Marianne shook her head in wonder. When had her little sister grown so wise? "How is Andrew?" she asked.

Sophie blushed prettily. "Recovering, slowly. The doctor managed to remove the bullet, and he hasn't developed a fever, so we're optimistic. He's in a room just down the hall. The red one with all the awful gilt cherubs." A giggle escaped her lips. "He said when he first woke up he thought he'd died and gone to heaven!"

Marianne's smiled, recalling the room. "I sincerely hope the *real* heaven isn't nearly so gaudy!"

"Or with quite so many naked putti!" Sophie joked. "If you don't mind, I'll go and see him now. I promised to read the newspapers to him."

Marianne forced a smile. "Of course, you go. I'll be fine."

Sophie pleated the sheet nervously. "Seeing him get shot . . . nearly losing him . . . it made me see things so clearly." She glanced up. "I love him."

Marianne sighed. "I know."

Sophie's eyes grew wide. "You don't mind?"

Marianne swallowed the constriction in her throat and pinned a bright smile on her face. "Of course not. I'm glad. I only ever wanted you to be happy, Sophie."

Sophie have her a gentle hug, careful of her injuries, and slipped out the door.

The brass bell from Pagnol's cage rested on the bedside table. Marianne reached for it and turned it over. Valette's diamond was still there. She wiped a black smudge from its surface and gazed into the icy facets. Fiery shards of red and orange glinted in the light, as if the stone had somehow sucked the inferno at the circus into its heart and trapped it there.

She knew what she had to do.

CHAPTER 54

More details of the battle emerged over the
following days. Since Marianne was one of the
few at the Montausier who could read, the girls brought her the
newspapers and sat around the room like brightly colored birds
of paradise while she read aloud.

The allies—Prussians led by Field Marshal Blucher and the
English led by Arthur Wellesley, Duke of Wellington—had
defeated the emperor's troops. Napoleon had surrendered to the
English forces and was returned to Paris, where he duly
abdicated.

As soon as Marianne could get out of bed, she borrowed the
most modest dress she could from Odile and set off across the
river. Her leg burned and chafed under the bandages, but it felt
good to be outside again, with the warm sun on her face.

Chaumet, one of Paris's most respected jewelers, had made
the Empress Josephine's tiara for her wedding. The shop, in the
austere elegance of the Place Vendôme, was just across the bridge
from the Palais Royale—only a few steps, yet a million miles
away in terms of taste and refinement.

A bell rang discreetly as Marianne stepped through the shop

door and crossed to the gentleman behind the counter. His eyes flicked over her, expertly appraising her net worth in one brief, disparaging glance.

"Can I help you, mademoiselle?"

"I hope so." She placed Valette's diamond on the glass-topped counter.

The jeweler was presumably accustomed to seeing extraordinary things on a daily basis, so his initial, unguarded reaction was extremely gratifying. His eyes grew wide. Marianne hid a smile. She had him. He was practically salivating.

"Might I be so bold as to inquire how you came to be in possession of such a fine piece?" His tone was politely interrogating. "The provenance?"

She was so tempted to give him the truth. *Oui, monsieur. I stole it. From one of France's greatest spies. As payment for saving the king.*

"Of course. I am Marianne de Beauvais, daughter of the Comte and Comtesse de Chanterac." Her real name came naturally to her lips without hesitation. It felt right. She lifted her chin and met his eye, daring him to dispute her claim. "This belonged to my family. It grieves me that I must sell it, but the situation being what it is . . ." she trailed off delicately, looking stricken.

Monsieur murmured apologetically. "May I?"

She nodded, and he picked up the stone, placing a magnifier in his eye. The tick of the ormolu clock behind him was deafening as he examined it carefully.

"*Magnifique.* And such a clear color. Such fire."

She gave him her brightest, sweetest smile. "That's just what my mother said when my father gave it to her. Alas, they're both lost to me now."

Monsieur bowed his head. "My condolences. The past years have scarred us all." He shot her an assessing glance. The old buzzard was sharp. He might not entirely believe her story, but he was also quite willing to turn a blind eye to the gray area of legality when such a fine piece was involved. Marianne suppressed a cynical snort. Everyone had their price. Hers, apparently, was ten thousand francs. She pushed the thought away. She would *not* think of him.

"You will find us extremely discreet, mademoiselle," the jeweler murmured, and Marianne suppressed a triumphant smile. They understood each other perfectly.

Now for the negotiations.

Monsieur made the opening gambit. He gave an exaggerated sigh of regret. "Of course, you must know that the price of gemstones is still scandalously low, mademoiselle. After the Revolution there was a glut of émigrés desperate to escape the terror. They sold their jewels to finance it. Nowadays there aren't many buyers for diamond tiaras and fancy necklaces." He shrugged. "Do you have any idea of the price you are looking for?"

The diamond was easily worth five thousand francs, but she wasn't greedy. They settled on four.

"I'm sorry I cannot offer you more," the jeweler said, trying to hide his delight. Marianne smiled graciously, equally satisfied with the outcome.

As she walked away with the jeweler's bank draft in her pocket, she felt as if she might blow away. It was as if a great burden had been lifted from her shoulders. She was freer than she'd ever been in her life. Duval was dead. She had money enough to make her financially secure for the rest of her days. A host of endless futures stretched out before her.

Selling the diamond had been harder than she'd imagined, though. She tamped down a faint pang of regret. It was just an unusual piece of rock.

Marianne crossed the river, jostled on all sides by the crowds. She had a fortune in her hands, but she couldn't shake the feeling of loss, of defeat. *She could go back to England now.* She shut off the thought ruthlessly. Back to what? If Valette had wanted her, he would have followed her back to Paris. He'd made his choice: revenge over her. She'd never see him again.

And yet she yearned.

Instead of returning to the Montausier, she walked the few extra streets to the circus. She found Laurent sifting through the charred, wet ruins. There was hardly anything left. The roof had collapsed, and only a few of the interior walls remained. A small section of the raked seating was recognizable, but little else. A few ragged children were poking around, searching for anything salvageable, and Laurent himself was overseeing a team of laborers trying to clear the site.

Marianne found herself scanning the rubble for Duval's body, but the intense fire had destroyed any trace of her cousin. She refused to mourn him. It was justice.

Laurent waved and came forward, wiping his filthy hands on his clothes. He looked like a chimney sweep. She reached into her reticule and handed him the bank draft Valette had given her. "I want you to have this."

He gasped as he read the amount. "What? No! Where did you get this from?"

She smiled roguishly. "Don't ask, Laurent. Just accept it."

"I can't. That's for you and Sophie."

She scowled and thrust it at him. "Yes, you can. You must. Your family took us in and treated us like your own. You gave us skills and love and a sense of worth. I can never repay that. Not with all the money in the world." Her voice was husky with emotion.

"Do you think we need payment, little one?" Laurent asked gently, wrapping her in a hug. "*Dio*, we did it for love."

Marianne sniffed. "I know. That's why I have to give this to you. Don't you see? With this, you can rebuild the circus. It can rise from the ashes, even better than before, then provide a future for everyone. Not just Sophie and me." She took his hand and closed his fingers around the banknote. "Take it. Don't argue. I'm sure."

Laurent looked dazed, like a child on Christmas morning. Then his eyes came alive with excitement. He threw back his head and laughed.

"My God! I have so many ideas for improvements. The boxes were getting shabby anyway. And we can build new stables out in back. And I have a plan for an additional ring with ramps leading from one to the other. This is going to blow Astley's out of the water . . . !"

With a smile, Marianne left him to his plotting.

* * *

IN THE DAYS THAT FOLLOWED, the defeated emperor was escorted to the coast and handed over to the British. King Louis XVIII, Louis-Charles's uncle, returned from exile to a boisterous reception. The Tuileries Palace gardens had been so thronged with bystanders shouting and rejoicing that, according to the Duke of Wellington, he could not hear to converse with the king.

Marianne wondered what Louis-Charles would have had to say about it all.

Now the Congress of Vienna was arguing about where France's new borders should be set.

There was still no news of Valette.

At first Marianne scoured the newspapers, feverishly scanning the lists of the dead, until she realized he'd probably never use his real name. He didn't exist. At least, not officially. It wrenched something deep inside her to think of him.

At night she had nightmares of him dead or dying, calling out her name. Even worse, she dreamed of him alive and happy, flirting and dancing. She could just imagine the gossip sheets.

". . . the latest newcomer to London . . . hero of Waterloo, handsome Nicolas Hampden and his elder brother, Sir Richard. Sons of Sir

William Hampden, Viscount Lovell and Baron Trevor. These two eligible bachelors have been seen dancing with a string of beautiful young ladies . . . setting hearts aflutter in ballrooms across the capital."

He'd scandalize the stupid English *ton,* with his wicked looks and mysterious, half-French past. The less he spoke about himself, the more intrigued everyone would become. He'd be fêted and adored, welcomed with open arms to the festivities celebrating the emperor's defeat. He was probably cutting a swathe through the merry widows and courtesans alike, sending foolish debutantes into heart palpitations.

Her heart burned with acid jealousy.

She told herself it would be enough to hear that he was alive, that she wished him well, but it wasn't true. She'd like to shoot him through his black heart, share the pain of living without him. She was surprised at how vindictive she could be.

* * *

IN ADDITION to the new circus, Valette's money paid for Sophie's wedding dress.

She looked utterly beautiful, as Marianne had always known she would. The pale cream silk of her dress had been hand-embroidered with thousands of tiny seed pearls and silver sequins by the circus seamstresses. Sophie complained that it was so heavy she could hardly walk, but Marianne told her it was a small price to pay to look like a princess.

Certainly Andrew looked at her as if she were enchanted as he watched her walk toward him on the arm of the elder Signor Falconi, and his eyes glowed with a fierce pride. He stood, waiting, under the Montausier's enormous glittering chandelier.

Sophie had initially wanted to get married in the center ring of the circus, but it would still be under construction for several more months, and she and Andrew hadn't wanted to wait. The Montausier was an elegant alternative. The curving arms of the staircase had been decorated to look like a bower, with garlands of real flowers cascading down toward an arch of roses. Madame had spared no expense.

As with any wedding, Marianne was amused to note the various factions dividing the guests. All the circus performers were there, but the haughty equestrians sat apart from the lowly tumblers, while the animal trainers deigned to fraternize with the chorus girls.

Everyone had donned their most extravagant outfits. The rows of seats were a riot of sequins and feathers, ruffles and flounces. Peacock green and daring scarlet clashed with canary yellow and midnight blue. Laurent was murmuring sweet nothings in Françoise's ear. Henri, finally freed from his crutches, was trying to catch the attention of a statuesque blonde in the front row.

All the girls from the Montausier were there, too, of course, along with Madame, resplendent in a gown of emerald green that barely contained her quivering bosom as she dabbed at her eyes with a lace-edged handkerchief. Skinny Marie was flirting with one of the stagehands, and Odile was busy fending off the advances of one of the acrobats. She wasn't trying very hard.

Even Pagnol had returned, although he refused to go anywhere near a cage. Instead, he sat balanced on the banister, chattering incessantly and dropping nut shells on everyone below.

What a strange mix of people, Marianne thought fondly. And yet it worked, because they were all bound together by common love for the bride. Tears stung her eyes, and she blinked them back as Andrew took Sophie's hand in his. Sophie's life was just beginning. So why did it feel like yet another ending?

She would not cry.

If only her parents could have been here. They would have been so proud. *She* was proud. She'd done her job; Sophie was happy and healthy and safe from Duval. That was all she'd ever wanted.

Well, almost all.

Marianne swallowed a lump in her throat. She'd always known she and Sophie would be separated eventually, but it had been in some far-off, nebulous future.

She mustn't be selfish. She was happy for Sophie.

Her ankle ached from standing for so long. The sprain was slowly mending, the bruises all but faded away, and she forced herself to do a little more each day. She hadn't dared go anywhere near a tightrope, though.

There was still no word of Valette. She'd been both relieved and strangely disappointed when her monthly courses had arrived. There was no baby as a result of her time with him. Her heart sank as she realized she'd been clinging to that last shred of hope, that last possibility of keeping something of him with her.

It was hard to smile as Sophie and Andrew said their vows and walked back up the aisle, husband and wife, their happiness a palpable force. Marianne hugged Sophie and scowled playfully at Andrew over her shoulder. "Take care of her," she warned direfully, "or you'll feel the kiss of my knives."

Andrew laughed. "Of course. With my life."

Everyone crowded out the door and waved them off in the carriage. Marianne wanted to call them back. She tried not to feel melancholy, but an intense wave of loneliness gripped her, the kind that can only be felt in the midst of a huge crowd of people.

She had to get away from Paris, from the stink and the bustle, from the memories. She knew exactly where she could go without fear of being disturbed.

CHAPTER 55

*T*here had been only one place to lick her wounds: the abandoned château at Auxerre where she'd trained for the mission.

Marianne spent a few days pottering around in the gardens, sweeping dust from the empty rooms, trying not to think of Valette every minute of the day. She'd go back to Paris soon and put her life back together. She just needed time to think.

What she was going to do with herself? The threat of Duval that had been hanging over her like a fog for the past four years had been lifted, but she couldn't see her way forward at all.

Madame had offered her a share in the theater. Marianne had told her she needed time to think about it, but she knew she couldn't do it. However content the women seemed, however well they were treated, she didn't want anything to do with running a brothel.

She could return to the circus, of course. Her leg had healed, and she wasn't a cripple, but she'd lost her nerve. It would come back, of course, with practice, but emotionally she still hadn't regained her balance. Nic was her balance. She felt bereft without him, as unsteady as a ship cut adrift from its moorings.

She couldn't sleep. The dawn was still a faint gray sheen in the sky when she wandered down to pace the overgrown gardens. Beads of dew showered the grass like thousands of tiny tears. They wet her satin slippers as she turned into what had once been the orchard. The trees stooped like old beggars in the pale half-light, hunched over under the weight of their drooping boughs. A few apples had already fallen to the ground, their sweet alcoholic decay attracting wasps.

Her skirts brushed the raised beds, sending up the scents of lavender, mint, and thyme.

She shouldn't have come here. Everything reminded her of him.

A footfall crunched on the gravel.

Marianne froze, then scrabbled for the knife she always had in her pocket, her heart racing.

The approaching footsteps were measured, assured. Terrifying.

Merde. Had that horrible Daumier tracked her down? Or Fouché himself? Her hands were shaking as she brought the blade up to shoulder height.

The tall figure that ducked through the gate was so familiar she caught her breath. "Nicolas?"

Valette's amused glance took in her fighting stance and the weapon aimed directly at his heart. He inclined his head in casual greeting. As if they'd seen each other merely hours ago, instead of a lifetime.

Marianne was breathing so fast she thought she might pass out. He was here. Alive. Unhurt. Her eyes drank in every aspect of his appearance. He looked different—gaunt, tired, unshaven. His hessian boots were spotted with mud, the capes of his great-coat thick with dust.

"Good morning, *chérie*. Or good night. Whichever you prefer."

She narrowed her eyes. He'd said that the very first night they'd met. She tightened her grip on the handle of the knife. She wanted to throw herself into his arms and demand to know where he'd been. She wanted to tell him everything that had happened since she'd left England. About the fire, and Duval, Sophie's wedding, and the new improved circus.

She did none of those things.

What had he been doing these past weeks? Had he even spared her a thought?

"It's morning," she said briskly, relieved that her voice came out at all.

Why not just mention the weather, while you're at it, imbecile?

He didn't even glance at the sky. "So it is."

"How did you find me?"

The corner of his mouth gave that familiar quirk that made her heart contract sharply. "Spy, remember?"

She crossed her arms. "What are you doing here?"

"Isn't a man allowed to visit his own property?"

A horrible trickle of premonition ran through her. "What do you mean 'your property'?"

He sketched an ironic bow. "You see before you the newly reinstated Marquis de la Garde."

She was going to kill him.

"This has been my family's estate for hundreds of years," he continued. "On my mother's side. Her father was the previous marquis. It was seized by the state when they fled to England during the Revolution, but King Louis has seen fit to restore it to the family. In gratitude for services to the crown."

Marianne closed her eyes. No wonder he knew where the wine cellar was. He *owned* the damn place. She remembered gazing around like some lovestruck idiot. *"Whose house is this?"* she'd breathed, weaving fairy tales, utterly besotted. How he must have laughed at her. "You lied to me!"

"Many times." His light tone made her want to throttle him.

"You said the man who owned this place was dead."

"He was. But now he's very much alive. I thought I'd try to restore the place to its former glory. What do you think?"

"If it's a reward for rescuing Louis-Charles," she snapped testily, "I think half of it should belong to me."

His slow smile was infuriating. "That's not how it works, *chérie*."

No, of course it wasn't. Life was never fair.

She wanted to curl up and die. They'd always been from different spheres, she'd known that, but he was even more above her touch now. She'd finally gone to see Monsieur Belon's model of the solar system back at the Palais Royale. She was like one of those little moons, dragged into orbit by a mightier planet then hurled away into space when the fickle pull of attraction waned.

She had to go before she humiliated herself completely. She tucked the knife in the waistband of her skirts. "Give me an hour to pack my things. I have to get back to Paris, anyway."

"You lied to me, too," he said softly.

She paused, midturn.

"You promised you wouldn't do anything stupid. We agreed to deal with Duval together. I thought we were a team."

She swallowed a ball of guilt at his gentle reproof. "Only for the mission. Duval was my problem. You had your own things to do. Congratulations on Napoleon's glorious defeat, by the way."

"I didn't do it single-handedly," he said dryly. "And it was horrible, not glorious. The worst thing I've ever seen in my life."

The raw pain in his voice, the shadows that clouded his face, made her heart ache for him. He'd given so much for his country, for his friends, his family. For her.

"I hear Napoleon's on his way to Saint Helena now," she said stiffly. "A tiny island a thousand miles from nowhere. I looked it up on a map."

She couldn't bear to look at him. His image hurt her eyes. She stared down instead, at the herringbone pattern made by the broken red bricks in the path. Bits were flaking off. Moss was pushing through the cracks. She scuffed it with the toe of her shoe. "What will you do now your quest for revenge is finally over?"

"It's not over. There's still work to be done."

A bitter laugh welled up in her throat. Of course it wasn't over. It would *never* be over. Napoleon had escaped an island prison once before. He could do the same again. Spying never took a rest.

"I thought you might be ready for a new assignment."

Disbelief was swiftly overshadowed by rage. Blood thrummed in her ears. *Another job?* Was that all she was to him? A useful ally? A colleague? Someone to call on for the next great adventure?

"I'm not interested."

He took a step closer. "You should be. I told Fouché you'd be perfect. The only one I'd recommend, in fact."

Marianne clenched her fists against the overwhelming urge to punch him. *Infuriating ass.* "What is it this time?"

His lips quirked. "Another impossible task."

There was a smile in his voice, and despite her fury, his palpable excitement, his boyish enthusiasm, piqued her interest. She *hated* that he could still draw her in.

He reached into his coat and withdrew a flat leather case. She narrowed her eyes as she recognized the maker. Chaumet. The same place she'd sold his diamond stickpin. A shiver of foreboding skittered down her spine.

He flicked open the lid with the ease of long practice, and she sucked in her breath at the exquisite necklace that nestled inside. A graduated fall of diamonds glittered against the velvet like an elegant shower of rain. He nudged the central stone with his thumb.

"Recognise this one, my little thief? It's the one you stole from me."

Her cheeks heated with guilt even as her heart plummeted. *Dieu! He wasn't here to demand she pay him back, was he?*

He took a step closer, studying the flawless stones with lazy complacency. "Chaumet sold it to a diplomat attending the Congress of Vienna, who gave it to his mistress. It cost me a fortune to buy it back."

Marianne frowned. "Why bother? It's not as though you can't afford a hundred others like it," she added bitterly.

His smile was infuriatingly enigmatic. "That's true. But I wanted *this* one. It has a certain . . . sentimental value."

She didn't trust the calculating look on his face. "You mentioned a job. What exactly does it entail?"

The corner of his mouth curled, the way it did when he was about to say something outrageous or throw a challenge in her face. "You'd have to be the Marquise de la Garde."

Pain lanced through her, sharp as a knife. *Of all the cruel tricks.* She'd already posed as his Italian wife, his invalid lover, his lowly apprentice. *Of course* he'd assume she'd play this role, too. But she couldn't do it. Not even for him.

"Pretend to be your marquise?" she repeated dully. Her heart ached.

He took another step toward her, and she retreated instinctively. Her backside hit the wall. His final step brought them nose to nose, but he didn't touch her. He just gazed down at her, blocking her escape. There was nowhere left to run.

"No," he said softly. "Not pretend."

Marianne couldn't breathe.

He shook his head with a rueful sigh. "I've been in love with you since you pinned me to that damned wall with your knife."

Her heart was beating uncomfortably fast, but she narrowed her eyes, waiting for the catch. With Valette there was *always* a catch. "You love me?" Cynical disbelief laced her tone.

His gaze held hers, open, unwavering. Honest. "Yes."

"More than defeating Napoleon? More than spying? More than France or England or anything else?"

"Yes," he said simply. "More than anything else."

He was so close. She could feel the heat of him, feel herself swaying toward him.

"I want to say good morning to you *every* morning." His voice was rough, aching. "I want to go to sleep with you and wake up next to you. Every day for the rest of my life."

All the emotions she'd ever wanted to see were burning in his eyes.

"You asked me once, in England, what I would do if I got my wish. If Napoleon was defeated. I didn't have an answer for you then. But I have one now. I want to live. To live in the world with *you*."

Marianne shivered, appalled. This was falling. This was the ground rushing up to meet her, everything she'd trained to avoid. He held up the necklace. The sparkling prisms blurred with the tears pooling in her eyes.

"In the prison, at Vincennes, I imagined you wearing something like this," he murmured. "Diamonds and nothing else."

The longing in his voice cut through her like an exquisite blade. Words caught in her throat. She stood stock-still as he reached up and fastened the clasp at her nape, fingers brushing gently. She shivered as the cool stones warmed to the heat of her skin.

She should tell him to stop. Tell him to take it off. Such things weren't meant for her, a circus thief.

He traced the line of it with his fingers, smoothing it down against her collarbone. Her blood heated at his touch.

"Marry me."

It wasn't so much as question as a demand. Typical Valette.

Marianne closed her eyes against the piercing joy that flooded her. And then she threw herself into his arms, almost knocking him over. The sun broke over the wall.

He pressed his face into her hair with a sound that was half sigh, half groan. He framed her face and kissed her closed eyelids, her jaw, the corner of her mouth with fierce, urgent desperation.

Pleasure poured through her like rays of sunlight as his lips found hers—warmth and redemption, forgiveness and happiness.

Home.

When he pulled back, breathless minutes later, he raised an incredulous eyebrow. "What, no fight? No argument?" He narrowed his eyes in suspicion. "Are you *truly* Marianne Bonnard?"

She shook her head, barely able to speak. "No. I'm Marianne de Beauvais. But I'd like to be Marianne Valette. If you really want me."

He kissed her again. "I want you. God help me."

"Our children will speak French and drink coffee," she said, trying to sound stern, and failing.

"English and tea," he countered. He palmed the knife at her back and pitched it headlong into the shrubbery, then placed another leisurely kiss on her lips to silence her gasp of protest. "And wine, of course. Most definitely wine."

Marianne smiled against his mouth. "Oh, all right then. Yes."

THE END.

ABOUT THE AUTHOR

Kate Bateman, also writing as K. C. Bateman, is the #1 Amazon bestselling author of Regency and Renaissance historical romances, including *To Steal a Heart, A Raven's Heart and A Counterfeit Heart*. Her Renaissance romp, *The Devil To Pay* was a 2019 RITA award nominee.

She's also an auctioneer and fine art appraiser, the co-founder and director of Bateman's Auctioneers, a fine art and antiques auction house in the UK. She currently lives in Illinois with her husband and three inexhaustible children, but returns to England regularly to appear as an antiques expert on several popular BBC television shows, each of which reach up to 2.5 million viewers.

Kate loves to hear from readers. Contact her via her website: www.kcbateman.com and sign up for her newsletter to receive regular updates on new releases, giveaways and exclusive excerpts.

MORE BY K. C. BATEMAN / KATE BATEMAN

Secrets & Spies Series:
To Steal a Heart
A Raven's Heart
A Counterfeit Heart

The Devil To Pay

Bow Street Bachelors Series:
This Earl Of Mine
To Catch An Earl
The Princess & The Rogue (Coming Winter 2020)

Novellas:
The Promise of A Kiss
A Midnight Clear

FOLLOW

Follow Kate online for the latest new releases, giveaways, exclusive sneak peeks, and more! You can find her at:

Amazon
Barnes & Noble
Apple Ibooks
Kobo
Google Play

Join Kate's FB group: Badasses in Bodices

Sign ip for Kate's monthly-ish newsletter via her website for news, exclusive excerpts and giveaways.

Follow both K.C. Bateman and Kate Bateman on Bookbub for new releases and sales.

Add Kate's books to your Goodreads lists, or leave a review!

SNEAK PEEK

Read on for a sneak peek of the next exhilarating historical
romance in K. C. Bateman's Secrets and Spies series
A Raven's Heart . . .

A RAVEN'S HEART

ENGLAND, JUNE 1816

"*I*'m a spy, not a bloody nursemaid!"

William de l'Isle, Viscount Ravenwood, glared across the desk at his mentor, Lord Castlereagh.

The older man shook his head, supremely unmoved by his outburst. "Miss Hampden needs immediate protection. Someone's targeting my code breakers and whoever killed Edward could also have discovered her identity. I can't afford to lose her, too."

Raven narrowed his eyes. "Use another agent."

Castlereagh gave him one of those level, penetrating looks he so excelled at. "Who? Neither of her brothers are here; Nic's in Paris, and Richard's following a lead on that French forger he's been after for months. Who else is left?" He pinched the bridge of his nose. "We've lost too many good men. First Tony got himself killed in France, then Kit disappeared. There's been no news of him for months."

Raven frowned. He refused to consider the distasteful probability that his friend was dead. Kit was like him, a master of survival. He could be deep undercover. But with every week that went by with no word it became harder and harder to stay positive.

"And now another good man, Edward Lamb, had been murdered," Castlereagh sighed. "I don't want Miss Hampden to be next."

The older man was a master of applying just the right amount of pressure and guilt. He hadn't made it to head of the Foreign Office without knowing how to manipulate people.

"You think I should entrust her to a less competent operative?" Castlereagh mused softly. "You're not burdened by false modesty, Ravenwood. You know you're the best I have. I was hoping you'd use your exceptional talent for survival to keep Miss Hampden alive, too."

Raven sighed, well aware he was being backed into a corner. If it had been anyone else he wouldn't have hesitated. But Heloise Hampden was the fly in his ointment. The spoke in his wheel.

A total bloody menace.

Hellcat Hampden had been the subject of his guilty daydreams for years. What had started out as adolescent musings had matured into fevered erotic fantasies that showed absolutely no sign of abating. He'd told himself the attraction was because she was forbidden, tried to lose himself in other, far more available women. Nothing had worked. And while he'd rarely paid much attention to the monotonous sermons preached by the clergy, he was fairly sure there was something in the bible that said "thou shalt not covet thy best friend's little sister." Or words to that effect.

He was the *last* person she should be entrusted to. He'd sworn to stay away from her. Had avoided her quite successfully—give or take a few blessedly brief skirmishes—for the past six years. Hell, he'd traveled to the far corners of war torn Europe to try to forget her.

And now here he was, drawn back to her by some malevolent twist of fate.

As if his life wasn't cursed enough already.

Over the past few years they'd settled into an uneasy, albeit barbed, truce; it was a sad reflection on his twisted nature that he preferred sparring with her to holding a reasonable conversation with anyone else.

His blood thrummed at the prospect of seeing her again and he smiled in self-directed mockery. Few things increased his heartbeat anymore. In combat he was a master of his emotions, sleek and deadly and efficient. Fighting barely elevated his pulse. He could kill a man without breaking a sweat. But put him ten paces away from that slip of a girl and a furious drummer took up residence in his chest, battering away against his ribs.

He shook his head. Being near her was a torture he both craved and abhorred, but he had a duty to keep her safe. A duty to her family, to Castlereagh, to the whole damn country. Much as he'd like someone else to deal with her, he didn't *trust* anyone else. She was *his* to torment.

Castlereagh, the old devil, smiled, as if he already sensed Raven's grudging acceptance. "That's settled, then. She's safe at home right now. You can go over and get her in the morning."

He rose and strode to the door of the study, then flashed an amused glance at Raven's immaculate evening attire and the mask resting on the desk. "I apologize for interrupting your evening, Ravenwood. I'll leave you to your entertainments."

* * *

SHE WAS IN.

Heloise smiled in triumph as she trailed a group of masked revelers toward Lord Ravenwood's infamous ballroom.

She'd never been invited to one of these masquerades. Raven and her brothers had always excluded her from anything remotely interesting as a child, and the situation hadn't improved now she was twenty-two and perfectly capable of looking after herself. Tonight, however, she had a perfectly valid reason for sneaking in; the crumpled translation she'd stuffed down the front of her bodice. Raven would forgive her when he heard what she'd discovered.

The extravagant debauchery of his annual gathering was the stuff of legend. Even the most sophisticated members of the *ton* discussed it in scandalized whispers, behind twitching fans. She was finally going to discover whether its reputation was justified.

Heloise reached the entrance to the ballroom, glanced up, and stopped dead. Her lips formed a soundless O of astonishment. The gilt-edged invitation she'd "borrowed" from Richard's study had promised "An Evening of Heaven and Hell." The rumors had *not* been exaggerated.

She blinked. The guests had embraced the suggestion of depraved licentiousness with enthusiasm. Scantily-clad gods and goddesses mingled with angels and devils in a dizzying sea of color. Grotesque masks, all curved beaks and twisting horns, swirled above acres of exposed flesh. A hundred perfumes entwined with the smell of warm bodies, hair powder, and wine, while the string quartet in the corner was almost inaudible over the boisterous hum of conversation.

Heloise glanced down at her own comparatively simple costume. She'd pilfered an authentic second-dynasty Egyptian beadwork collar from her father's collection of Ancient jewelry and improved a black silk half-mask with whiskers and a pair of papier mâché ears. There: Bastet, the Ancient Egyptian cat goddess. Not that anyone here would have any idea who she was supposed to be.

Her stomach gave an excited flip. She didn't need to find Raven *immediately*. A few extra minutes wouldn't make any difference. There was such a delicious freedom in being masked and anonymous. No one was who they appeared. That gilded lady over there could be a duchess or courtesan, actress or spy. That silver-masked satyr could be a diplomat or a prince.

Heloise shivered, despite the stifling heat. The possibilities of the evening shimmered in the air like a summer haze, magical and dangerous. She could be anyone she wanted. Not someone's unmarriageable little sister. Not the bookish code breaker. She could be flighty and irresponsible, the secret, daring girl she'd been before her face was scarred. The beautiful one, for once, instead of the clever one. Anticipation tingled through her body as if she were poised at the top of a steep, smooth slope. Just one small nudge would send her hurtling down, toward adventure.

She grabbed a glass of champagne from a passing servant and took a few fortifying sips as her skin prickled with the unpleasant conviction that she was being watched. That was foolish. Neither of her brothers was here to curtail her enjoyment and the only other person who could potentially unmask her—tonight's host, their neighbor and most irritating man on the planet, William Ravenwood—wouldn't be expecting to see her. She was going to have the devil of a time finding him in this crowd.

As if the very thought had summoned him, all the fine hairs on her arms lifted in warning and Heloise glanced around with a sense of impending doom. The crowd parted obligingly, and there he was. The god of the Underworld, staring at her.

Oh, hell and damnation.

He stood motionless, a pillar of darkness amid the colored gaiety, his tall frame somehow managing to radiate a barely leashed tension, as if he was poised to attack. Heloise repressed the instinct to cross herself.

His mask was black like hers, only far more elaborate. The long muzzle of a jackal, ears pricked and alert, eyes rimmed with thick lines of gold, covered the top half of his face. Only his jaw was visible; hard and male, with unfashionably tanned skin shadowed by the hint of a beard. Dark hair curled out from beneath the mask to brush his snowy cravat and pitch-black evening jacket.

The tiny part of her brain not frozen into immobility—and inexplicably concerned with historical accuracy—whispered that to be *totally authentic,* Anubis should be bare-chested. Her mouth went dry as she imagined the broad shoulders and well-defined chest concealed beneath all that black silk.

The role of Anubis fitted him to perfection. The jackal guardian of the Underworld, a creature of the night, perfectly at home in darkness and shadows. She shivered as he turned and looked directly at her. He tilted his head to one side, the mannerism exactly like that of a dog—a hint of interest, a silent question.

Her first instinct was to run, but her feet seemed glued to the floor. She took another gulp of champagne and when she looked up again he'd disappeared, swallowed up by the swirling mass of dancers. Her heart hammered unpleasantly against her rib cage. Surely he hadn't recognized her from all the way across the room?

You recognized him.

She shook herself. It didn't matter. She'd run from William Ravenwood far too often. Tonight she would stand her ground.

SPEAK OF THE DEVIL.

Raven narrowed his eyes at the slim, white-clad figure slinking around his ballroom, and cursed. She was supposed to be tucked up safe in bed. What the hell was she doing here? The debauched, cynical world he inhabited was no place for someone like her.

His heart pounded in anticipation as he weaved through the excited throng, keeping to the shadows out of habit. There. Black mask near the door. It was definitely her. He'd know her from half the world away, in a crowd of a hundred thousand. It was a simple enough matter to spot her in a room of two hundred. She alone made his blood sing in his veins, made his body vibrate with awareness, as if he were a tuning fork that responded only to her pitch.

Bloody woman.

She was dressed as a cat. He almost laughed at the irony. And here he was, a dog. How utterly appropriate. Bastet and Anubis. Both Egyptian gods of the Underworld. Both black as midnight. As different as night from day. Opposite, and yet at the same time oddly connected. It had been like this between them since they were children. It was a bloody curse.

At this distance the tilted cutout eyes of her mask hid her face but he already knew the astonishing color of her eyes; lavender-gray, the exact hue of a thunderstorm-ready sky.

He circled the room and approached her from the back. She turned, an elegant sweep of shoulder and throat, and he clenched his fists against the insanely erotic urge to press his mouth to her nape and bite her. He shook his head. Such a perverse attraction. She was light. He was darkness. Not for him. Never for him.

She'd tried to tame her dark blond hair into some kind of elaborate twist, but stray tendrils curled down the graceful line of her neck, refusing to conform. He leaned one shoulder against a marble pillar. To all outward appearances the creature in front of him was a respectable member of the ton; cool and poised and infinitely alluring. It was a lie. The rebellious nature she tried so hard to suppress was like those little wisps of hair — always trying to escape.

It amazed him that no one else could see it, even her own brothers. They thought she'd outgrown her childish yearnings for adventure and equality, but he knew better. No doubt that was why she'd come here tonight; she simply could not resist an adventure.

The devil in him relished the idea of coaxing all that repressed mayhem into breaking free. Heloise Hampden needed to let her hair down, both literally *and* figuratively. Except God only knew what would happen if she did.

She placed her empty glass on the tray offered by a passing servant. She was so small he could tuck the top of her head under his chin and pull her into his side. His hip would fit neatly into the curve of her waist. Her breasts would press perfectly into his chest. His mouth would fit precisely—

Raven banged his head against the pillar. Insane. Which was ironic, really. He'd managed to remain *compos mentis* despite spending eight weeks of his life locked up in a cell expecting to be executed. He'd witnessed some of the worst sights a decade of warfare could inflict upon a man and stayed sane. Yet Hellcat Hampden made him crazy. And, idiot that he was, he *enjoyed* it.

He stepped up behind her and caught a hint of her midnight-and-roses scent. It tightened his gut and turned his knees to water, but he composed his features into their usual expression of cynical boredom. The day she discovered the effect she had on him was the day he'd cut his own wrists. Not. For. Him.

"All alone, mademoiselle?" he murmured dryly. "Who are you waiting for?"

Want to read more? Check out A Raven's Heart on Amazon, Barnes & Noble, Kobo, Apple iBooks.

Made in the USA
Columbia, SC
17 December 2022

74379890R00217